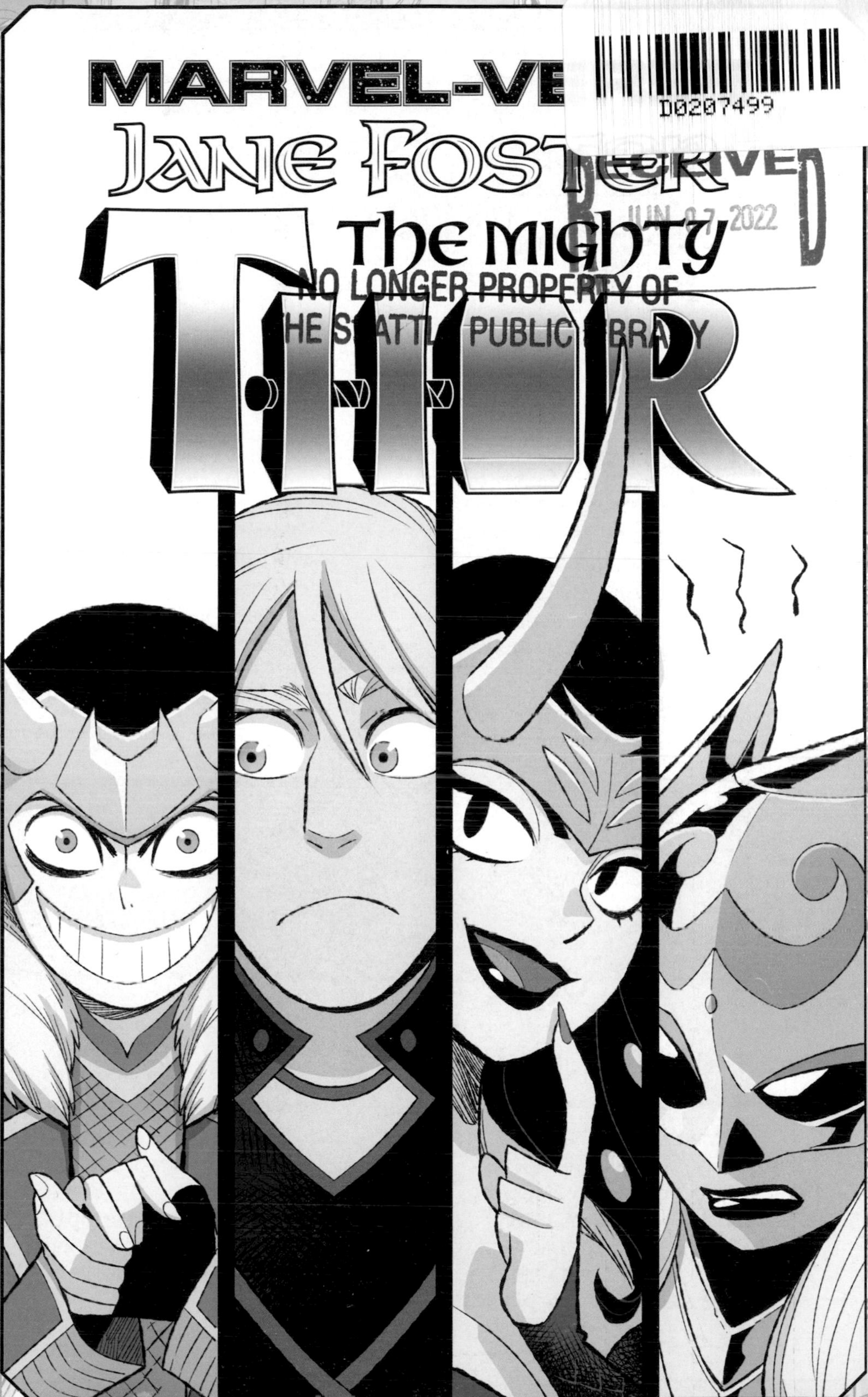
MARVEL-VE
JANE FOS
THE MIGHTY
THOR

MARVEL-VERSE
JANE FOSTER
THE MIGHTY THOR

THE MIGHTY THOR: MARVEL LEGACY PRIMER

WRITER: **ROBBIE THOMPSON**
ARTIST: **VALERIO SCHITI**
COLORIST: **RAIN BEREDO**
LETTERER: **VC's JOE SABINO**
ASSISTANT EDITOR: **KATHLEEN WISNESKI**
EDITOR: **DARREN SHAN**

THOR #2

WRITER: **JASON AARON**
ARTIST: **RUSSELL DAUTERMAN**
COLORIST: **MATTHEW WILSON**
LETTERER: **VC's JOE SABINO**
COVER ART: **RUSSELL DAUTERMAN
& MATTHEW WILSON**
ASSISTANT EDITOR: **JON MOISAN**
EDITOR: **WIL MOSS**

ALL-NEW, ALL-DIFFERENT AVENGERS #4

WRITER: **MARK WAID**
ARTIST: **MAHMUD ASRAR**
COLORIST: **DAVE McCAIG**
LETTERER: **VC's CORY PETIT**
COVER ART: **ALEX ROSS**
ASSISTANT EDITOR: **ALANNA SMITH**
EDITORS: **TOM BREVOORT** with **WIL MOSS**

THOR ANNUAL #1

WRITER: **ND STEVENSON**
ARTIST & COLORIST: **MARGUERITE SAUVAGE**
LETTERER: **VC's JOE SABINO**
COVER ART: **RAFAEL ALBUQUERQUE**
ASSISTANT EDITOR: **JON MOISAN**
EDITOR: **WIL MOSS**

THOR & LOKI: DOUBLE TROUBLE #3-4

WRITER: **MARIKO TAMAKI**
ARTISTS & COLORISTS: **GURIHIRU**
LETTERER: VC's **ARIANA MAHER**
COVER ART: **GURIHIRU**
ASSISTANT EDITOR: **MARTIN BIRO**
EDITORS: **ALANNA SMITH**

WAR OF THE REALMS OMEGA

WRITERS: **AL EWING** & **JASON AARON**
ARTIST: **CAFU**
LETTERER: VC's **JOE SABINO**
COVER ART: **PHIL NOTO**
ASSOCIATE EDITOR: **SARAH BRUNSTAD**
EDITOR: **WIL MOSS**
EXECUTIVE EDITOR: **TOM BREVOORT**

JOURNEY INTO MYSTERY #100

WRITER & EDITOR: **STAN LEE**
ARTIST: **DON HECK**
LETTERER: **SAM ROSEN**
COVER ART: **JACK KIRBY**

THOR CREATED BY STAN LEE, LARRY LIEBER & JACK KIRBY

COLLECTION EDITOR: **JENNIFER GRÜNWALD** ASSISTANT EDITOR: **DANIEL KIRCHHOFFER**
ASSISTANT MANAGING EDITOR: **MAIA LOY** ASSOCIATE MANAGER, TALENT RELATIONS: **LISA MONTALBANO**
ASSOCIATE MANAGER, DIGITAL ASSETS: **JOE HOCHSTEIN** MASTERWORKS EDITOR: **CORY SEDLMEIER**
VP PRODUCTION & SPECIAL PROJECTS: **JEFF YOUNGQUIST** RESEARCH: **JESS HARROLD**
PRODUCTION: **JOE FRONTIRRE** BOOK DESIGNERS: **SARAH SPADACCINI** with **JAY BOWEN**
SVP PRINT, SALES & MARKETING: **DAVID GABRIEL** EDITOR IN CHIEF: **C.B. CEBULSKI**

MARVEL-VERSE: JANE FOSTER, THE MIGHTY THOR. Contains material originally published in magazine form as THOR (2014) #2; ALL-NEW, ALL-DIFFERENT AVENGERS (2015) #4; THOR & LOKI: DOUBLE TROUBLE (2021) #3-4; THOR ANNUAL (2015) #1; WAR OF THE REALMS OMEGA (2019) #1; and JOURNEY INTO MYSTERY (1952) #100. First printing 2022. ISBN 978-1-302-93403-3. Published by MARVEL WORLDWIDE, INC., a subsidiary of MARVEL ENTERTAINMENT, LLC. OFFICE OF PUBLICATION: 1290 Avenue of the Americas, New York, NY 10104. © 2022 MARVEL No similarity between any of the names, characters, persons, and/or institutions in this book with those of any living or dead person or institution is intended, and any such similarity which may exist is purely coincidental. **Printed in Canada.** KEVIN FEIGE, Chief Creative Officer; DAN BUCKLEY, President, Marvel Entertainment; JOE QUESADA, EVP & Creative Director; DAVID BOGART, Associate Publisher & SVP of Talent Affairs; TOM BREVOORT, VP, Executive Editor; NICK LOWE, Executive Editor, VP of Content, Digital Publishing; DAVID GABRIEL, VP of Print & Digital Publishing; MARK ANNUNZIATO, VP of Planning & Forecasting; JEFF YOUNGQUIST, VP of Production & Special Projects; ALEX MORALES, Director of Publishing Operations; DAN EDINGTON, Director of Editorial Operations; RICKEY PURDIN, Director of Talent Relations; JENNIFER GRÜNWALD, Director of Production & Special Projects; SUSAN CRESPI, Production Manager; STAN LEE, Chairman Emeritus. For information regarding advertising in Marvel Comics or on Marvel.com, please contact Vit DeBellis, Custom Solutions & Integrated Advertising Manager, at vdebellis@marvel.com. For Marvel subscription inquiries, please call 888-511-5480. **Manufactured between 2/25/2022 and 3/29/2022 by SOLISCO PRINTERS, SCOTT, QC, CANADA.**

0987654321

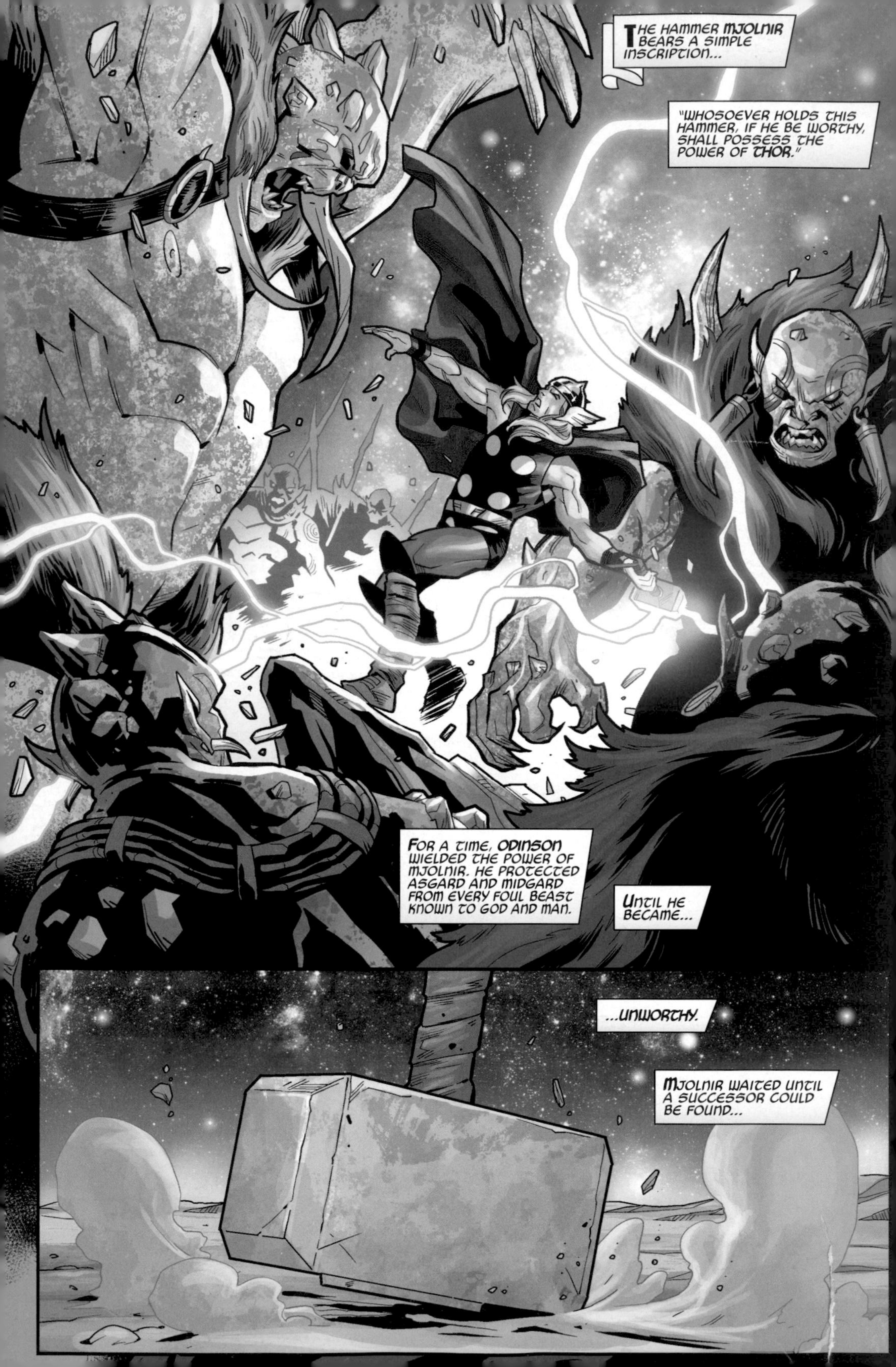
THE HAMMER MJOLNIR BEARS A SIMPLE INSCRIPTION...
"WHOSOEVER HOLDS THIS HAMMER, IF HE BE WORTHY, SHALL POSSESS THE POWER OF THOR."
FOR A TIME, ODINSON WIELDED THE POWER OF MJOLNIR. HE PROTECTED ASGARD AND MIDGARD FROM EVERY FOUL BEAST KNOWN TO GOD AND MAN.
UNTIL HE BECAME...
...UNWORTHY.
MJOLNIR WAITED UNTIL A SUCCESSOR COULD BE FOUND...

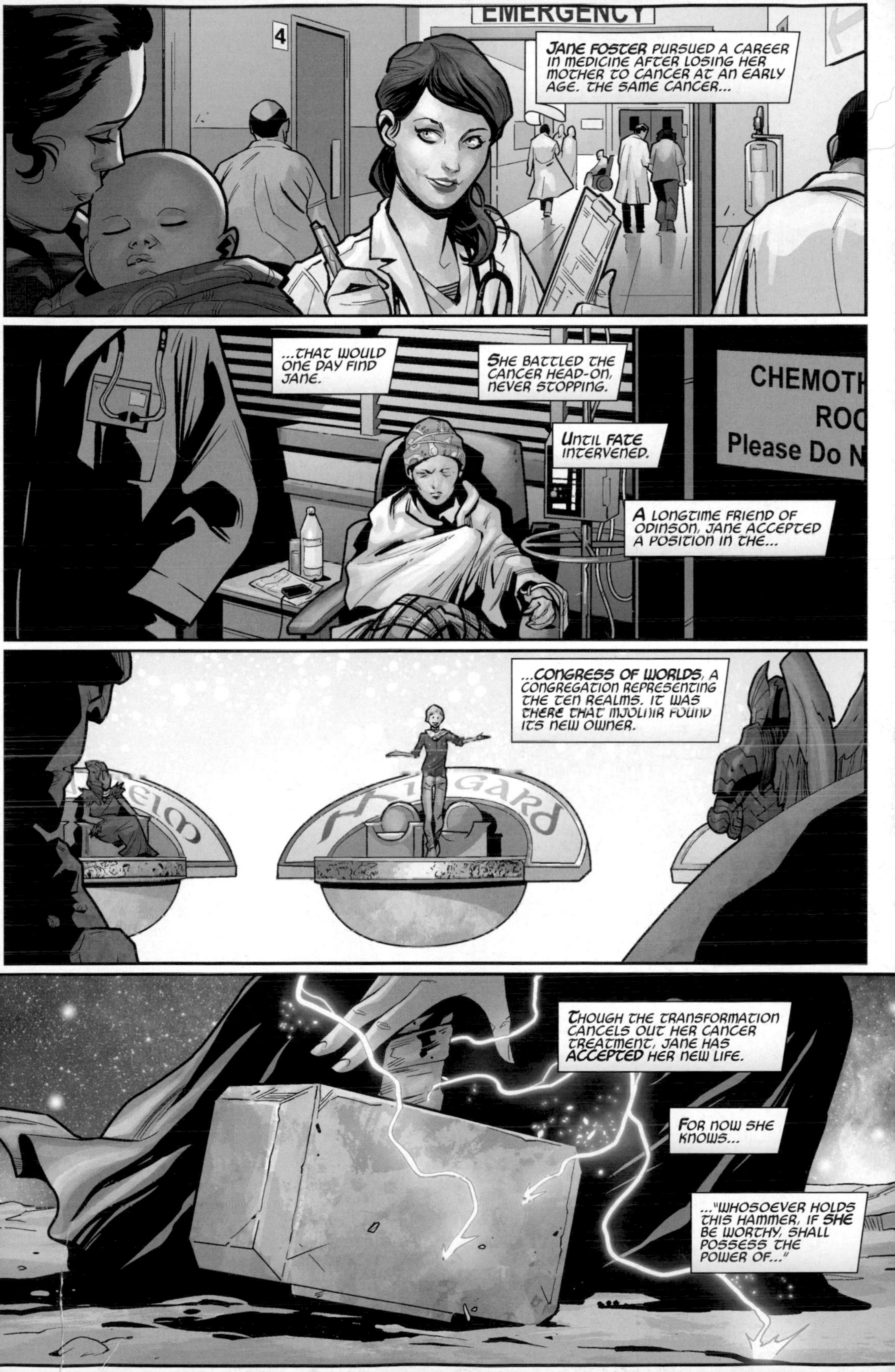
EMERGENCY
4
JANE FOSTER PURSUED A CAREER IN MEDICINE AFTER LOSING HER MOTHER TO CANCER AT AN EARLY AGE. THE SAME CANCER...
...THAT WOULD ONE DAY FIND JANE.
SHE BATTLED THE CANCER HEAD-ON, NEVER STOPPING.
CHEMOTH
ROO
Please Do N
UNTIL FATE INTERVENED.
A LONGTIME FRIEND OF ODINSON, JANE ACCEPTED A POSITION IN THE...
...CONGRESS OF WORLDS, A CONGREGATION REPRESENTING THE TEN REALMS. IT WAS THERE THAT MJOLNIR FOUND ITS NEW OWNER.
THOUGH THE TRANSFORMATION CANCELS OUT HER CANCER TREATMENT, JANE HAS ACCEPTED HER NEW LIFE.
FOR NOW SHE KNOWS...
..."WHOSOEVER HOLDS THIS HAMMER, IF SHE BE WORTHY, SHALL POSSESS THE POWER OF..."

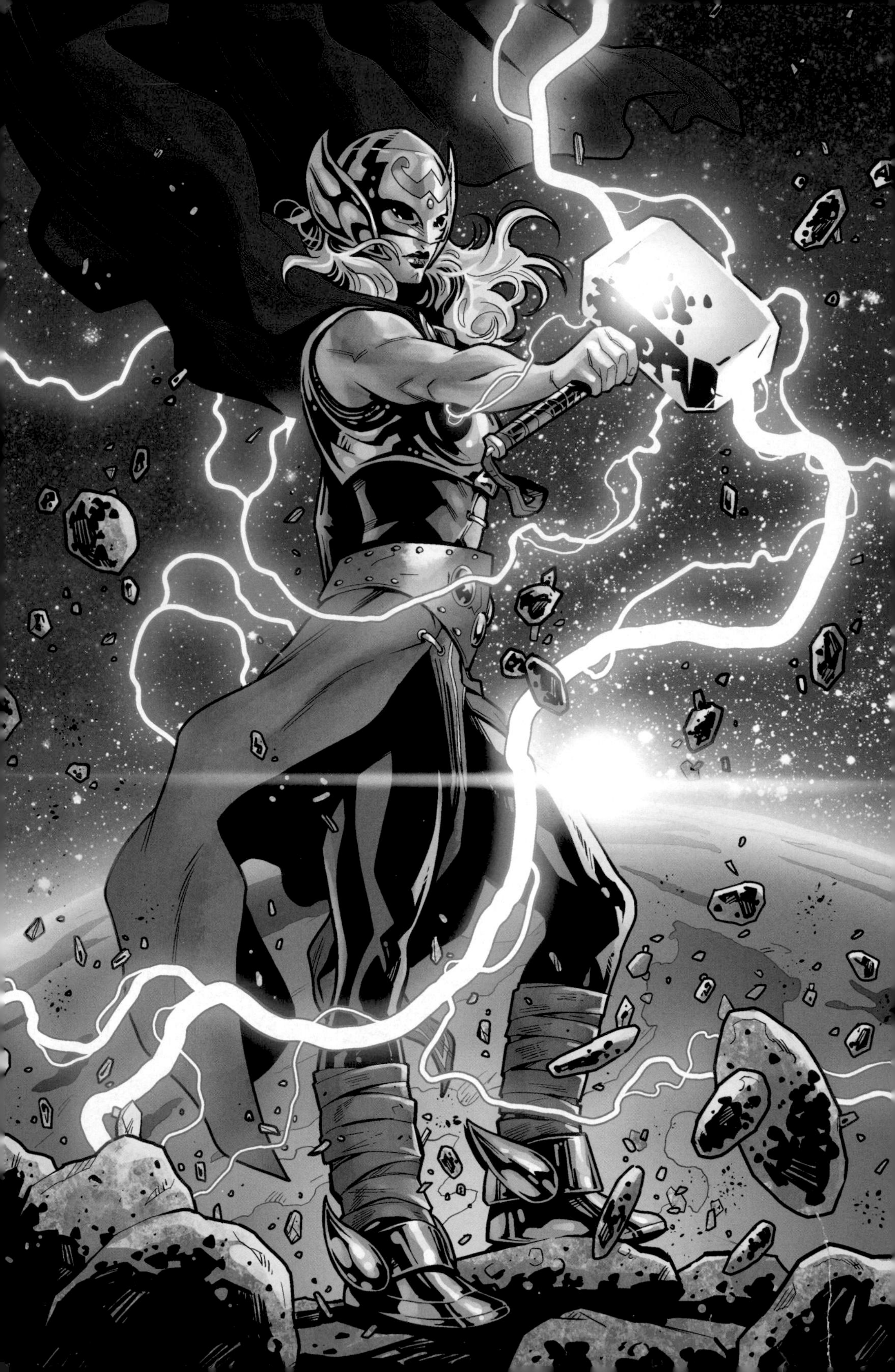

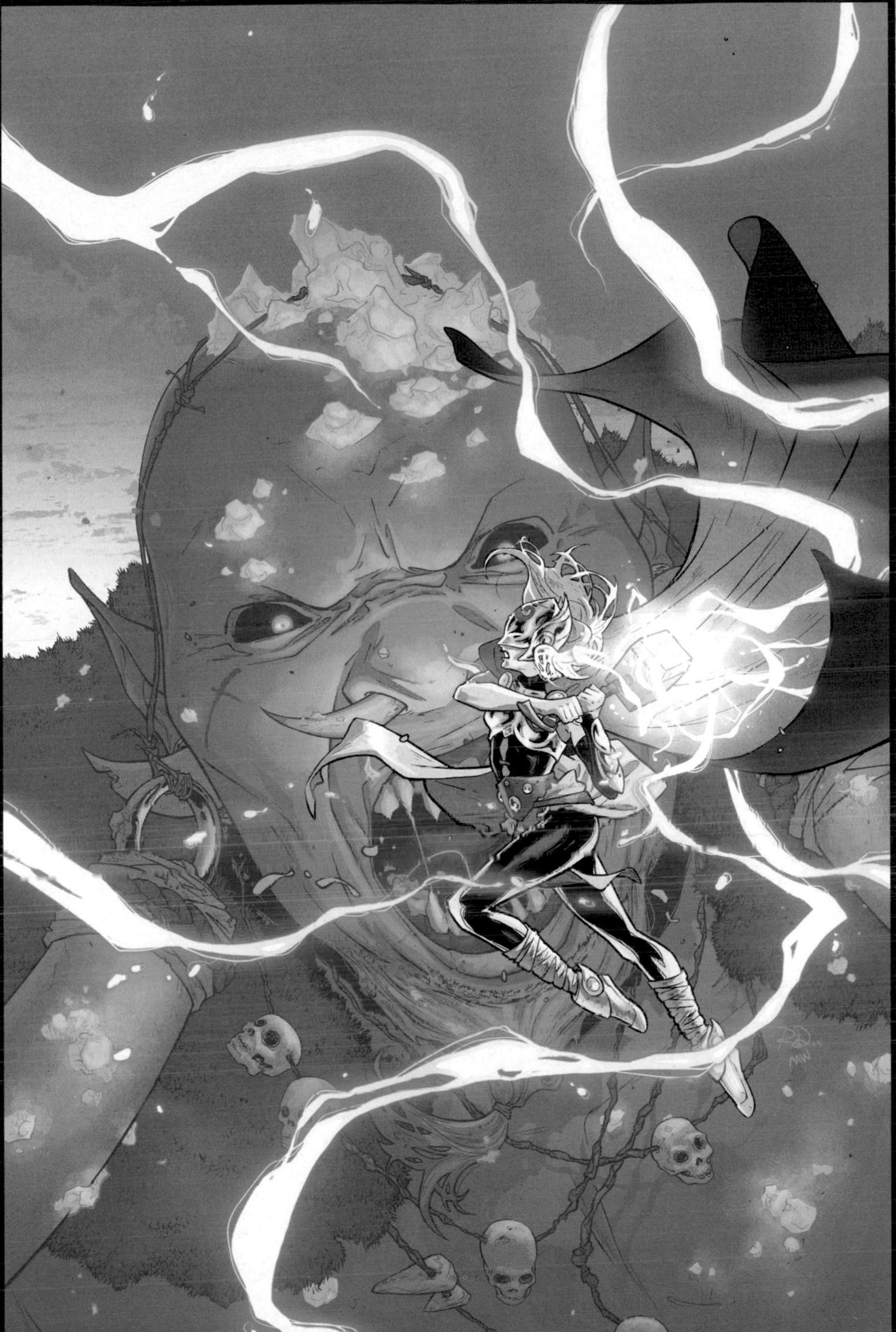

THOR #2

JANE FOSTER IS A THOR LIKE YOU'VE NEVER SEEN BEFORE — AND WITH AN ARMY OF FROST GIANTS INVADING, SHE MAY BE EARTH'S ONLY HOPE!

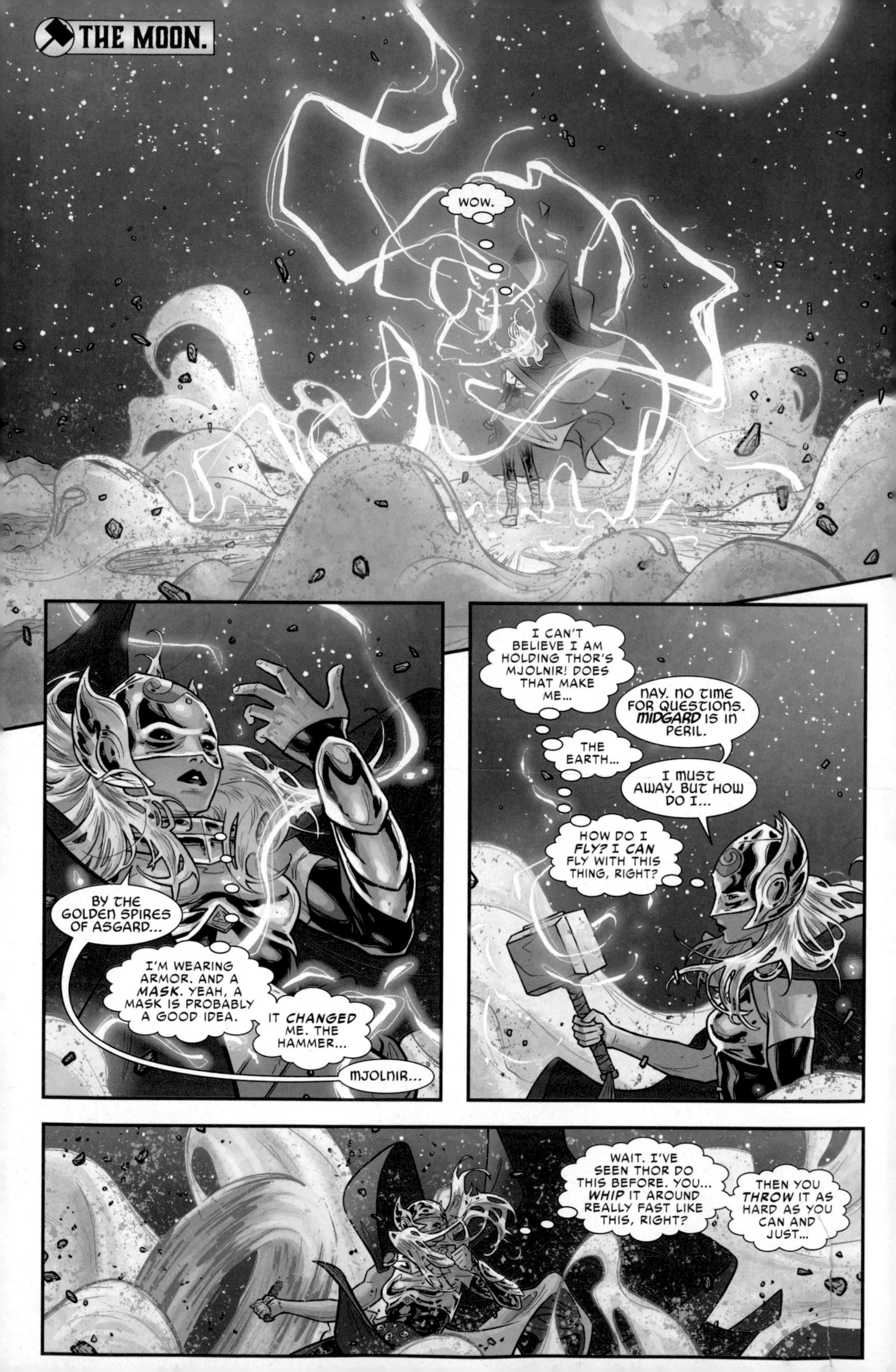
THE MOON.
WOW.
BY THE GOLDEN SPIRES OF ASGARD...
I'M WEARING ARMOR. AND A MASK. YEAH, A MASK IS PROBABLY A GOOD IDEA.
IT CHANGED ME. THE HAMMER...
MJOLNIR...
I CAN'T BELIEVE I AM HOLDING THOR'S MJOLNIR! DOES THAT MAKE ME...
THE EARTH...
NAY. NO TIME FOR QUESTIONS. MIDGARD IS IN PERIL.
I MUST AWAY. BUT HOW DO I...
HOW DO I FLY? I CAN FLY WITH THIS THING, RIGHT?
WAIT. I'VE SEEN THOR DO THIS BEFORE. YOU... WHIP IT AROUND REALLY FAST LIKE THIS, RIGHT?
THEN YOU THROW IT AS HARD AS YOU CAN AND JUST...

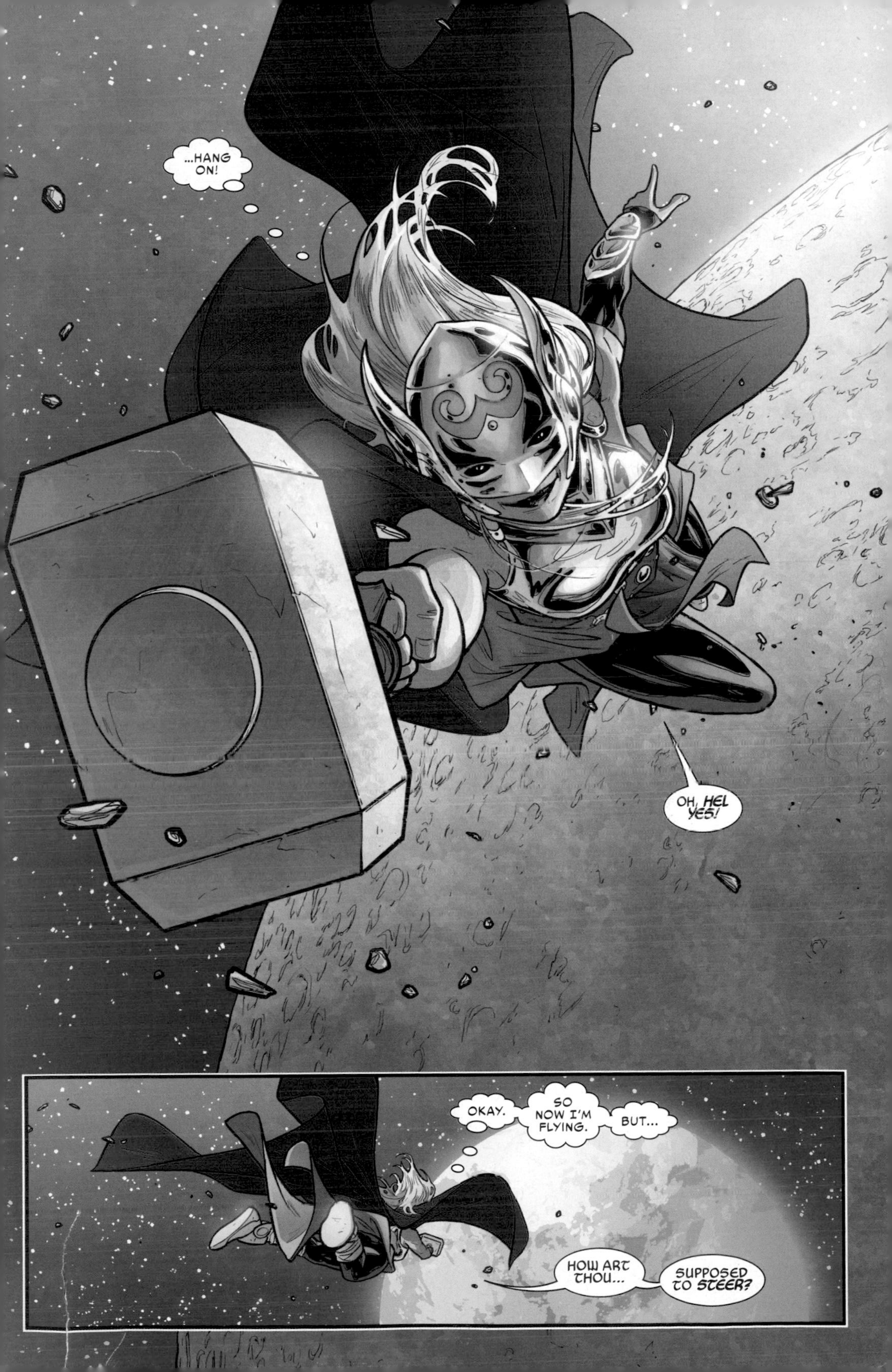
...HANG ON!
OH, HEL YES!
OKAY.
SO NOW I'M FLYING.
BUT...
HOW ART THOU...
SUPPOSED TO STEER?

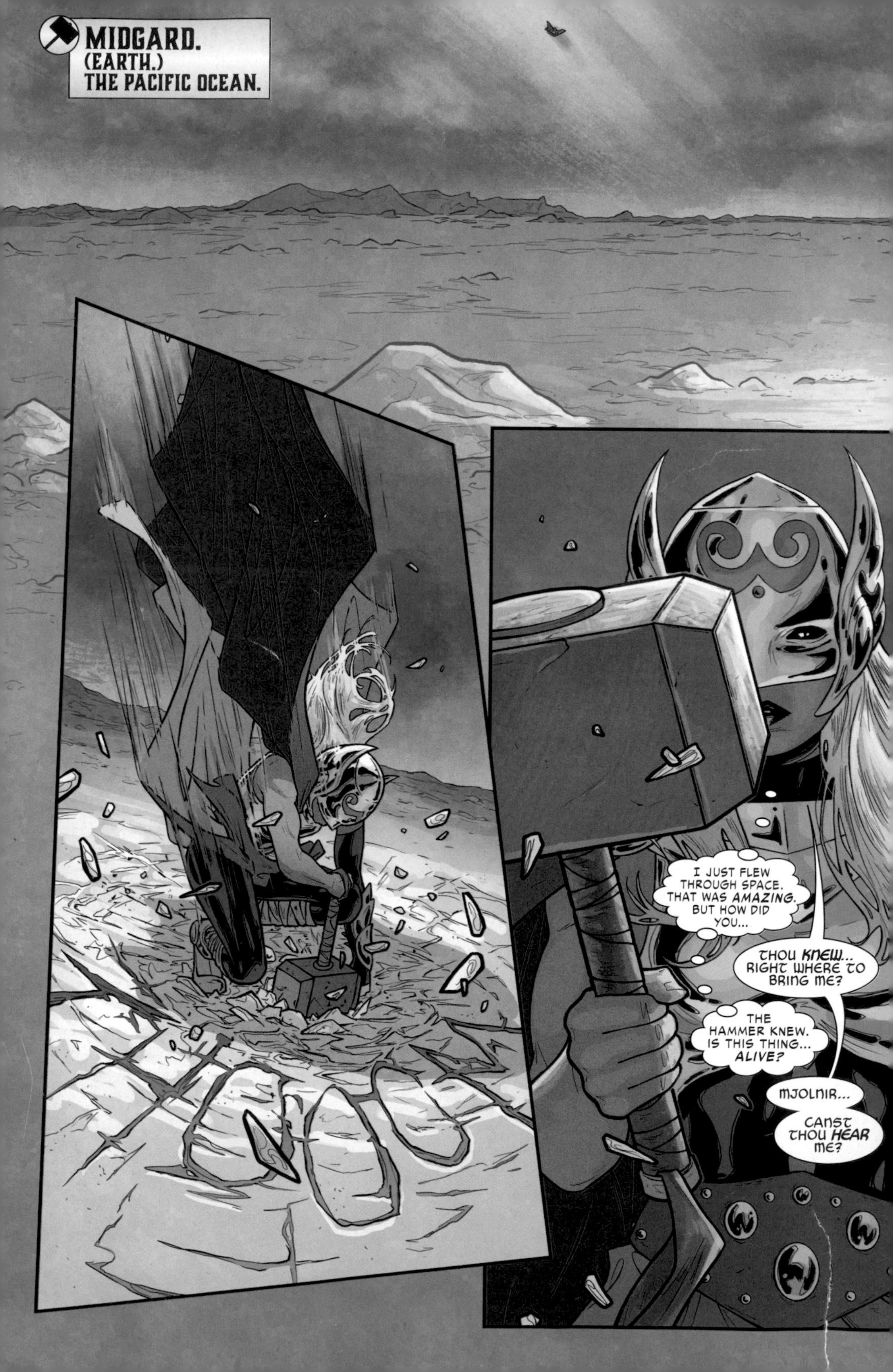
MIDGARD.
(EARTH.)
THE PACIFIC OCEAN.
I JUST FLEW THROUGH SPACE. THAT WAS AMAZING. BUT HOW DID YOU...
THOU KNEW... RIGHT WHERE TO BRING ME?
THE HAMMER KNEW. IS THIS THING... ALIVE?
MJOLNIR...
CANST THOU HEAR ME?

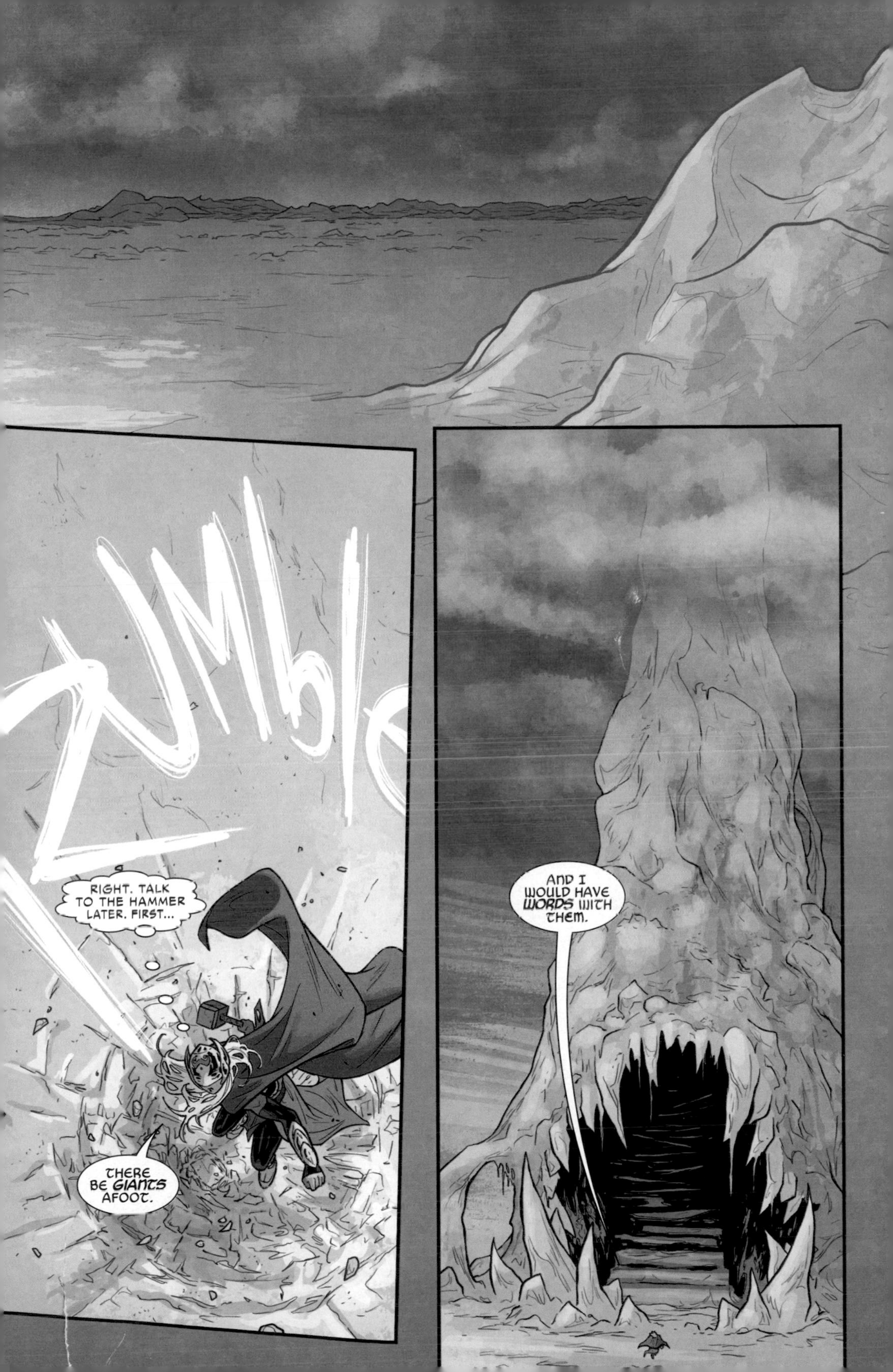
RUMBLE
RIGHT. TALK TO THE HAMMER LATER. FIRST...
THERE BE GIANTS AFOOT.
AND I WOULD HAVE WORDS WITH THEM.

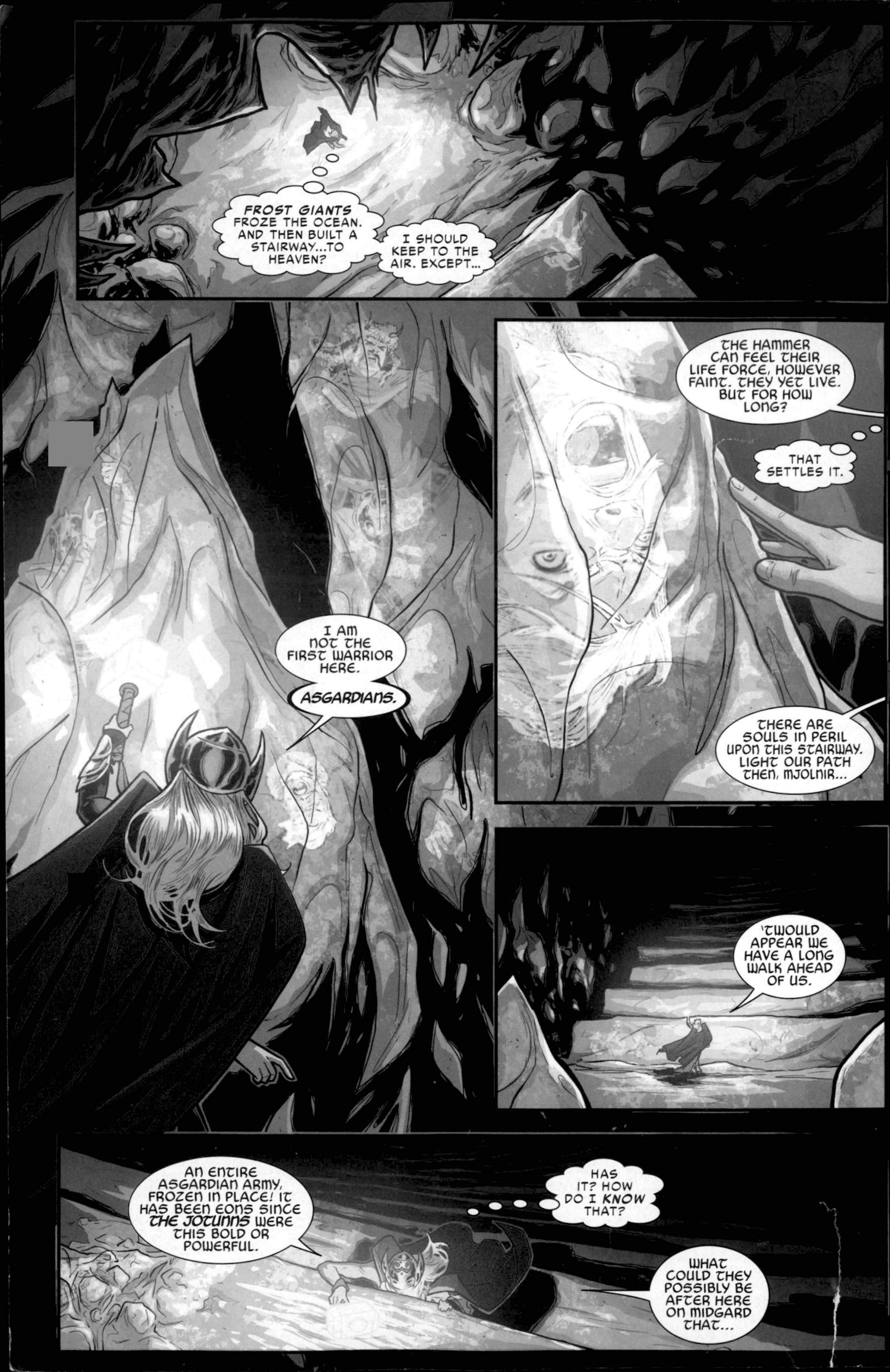
FROST GIANTS FROZE THE OCEAN. AND THEN BUILT A STAIRWAY...TO HEAVEN?
I SHOULD KEEP TO THE AIR. EXCEPT...
I AM NOT THE FIRST WARRIOR HERE.
ASGARDIANS.
THE HAMMER CAN FEEL THEIR LIFE FORCE, HOWEVER FAINT. THEY YET LIVE. BUT FOR HOW LONG?
THAT SETTLES IT.
THERE ARE SOULS IN PERIL UPON THIS STAIRWAY. LIGHT OUR PATH THEN, MJOLNIR...
'TWOULD APPEAR WE HAVE A LONG WALK AHEAD OF US.
AN ENTIRE ASGARDIAN ARMY, FROZEN IN PLACE! IT HAS BEEN EONS SINCE THE JOTUNNS WERE THIS BOLD OR POWERFUL.
HAS IT? HOW DO I KNOW THAT?
WHAT COULD THEY POSSIBLY BE AFTER HERE ON MIDGARD THAT...

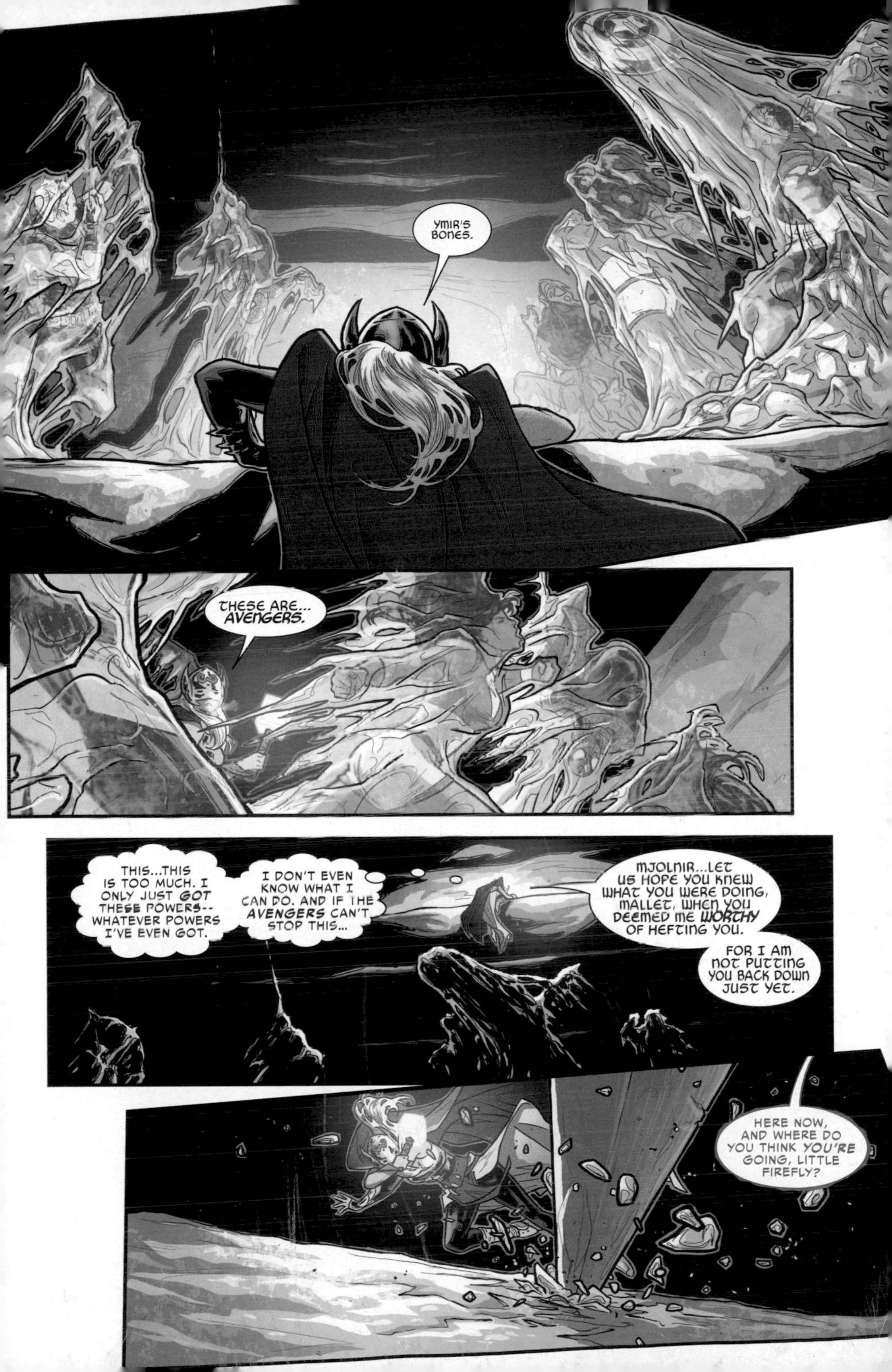
YMIR'S BONES.
THESE ARE... AVENGERS.
THIS...THIS IS TOO MUCH. I ONLY JUST GOT THESE POWERS-- WHATEVER POWERS I'VE EVEN GOT.
I DON'T EVEN KNOW WHAT I CAN DO. AND IF THE AVENGERS CAN'T STOP THIS...
MJOLNIR...LET US HOPE YOU KNEW WHAT YOU WERE DOING, MALLET, WHEN YOU DEEMED ME WORTHY OF HEFTING YOU.
FOR I AM NOT PUTTING YOU BACK DOWN JUST YET.
HERE NOW, AND WHERE DO YOU THINK YOU'RE GOING, LITTLE FIREFLY?

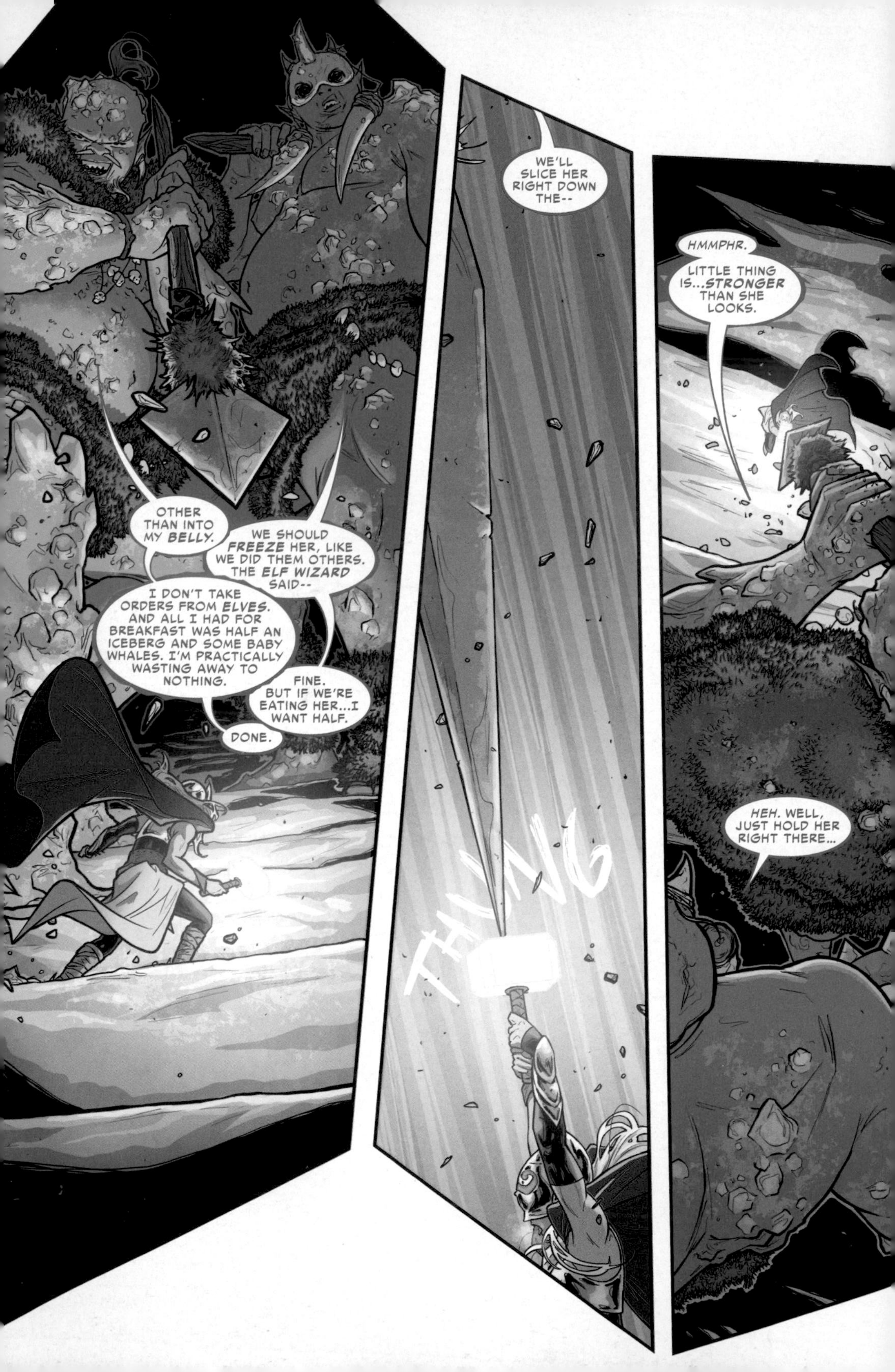
OTHER THAN INTO MY BELLY.
WE SHOULD FREEZE HER, LIKE WE DID THEM OTHERS. THE ELF WIZARD SAID--
I DON'T TAKE ORDERS FROM ELVES. AND ALL I HAD FOR BREAKFAST WAS HALF AN ICEBERG AND SOME BABY WHALES. I'M PRACTICALLY WASTING AWAY TO NOTHING.
FINE. BUT IF WE'RE EATING HER...I WANT HALF.
DONE.
WE'LL SLICE HER RIGHT DOWN THE--
THUNG
HMMPHR.
LITTLE THING IS...STRONGER THAN SHE LOOKS.
HEH. WELL, JUST HOLD HER RIGHT THERE...

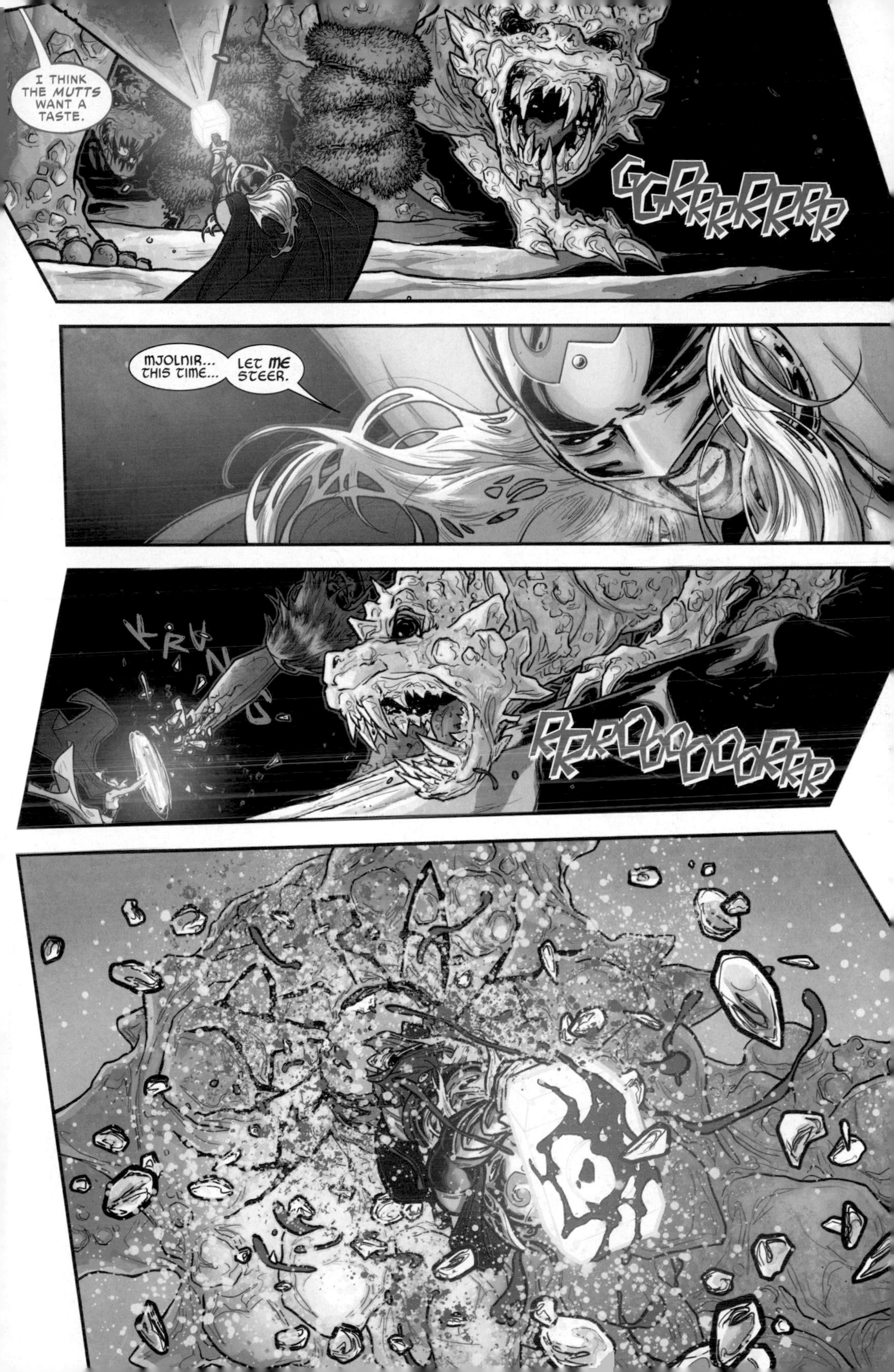
I THINK THE *MUTTS* WANT A TASTE.
GGRRRRRRRRR
MJOLNIR... THIS TIME...
LET *ME* STEER.
RRROOOOOOORRR

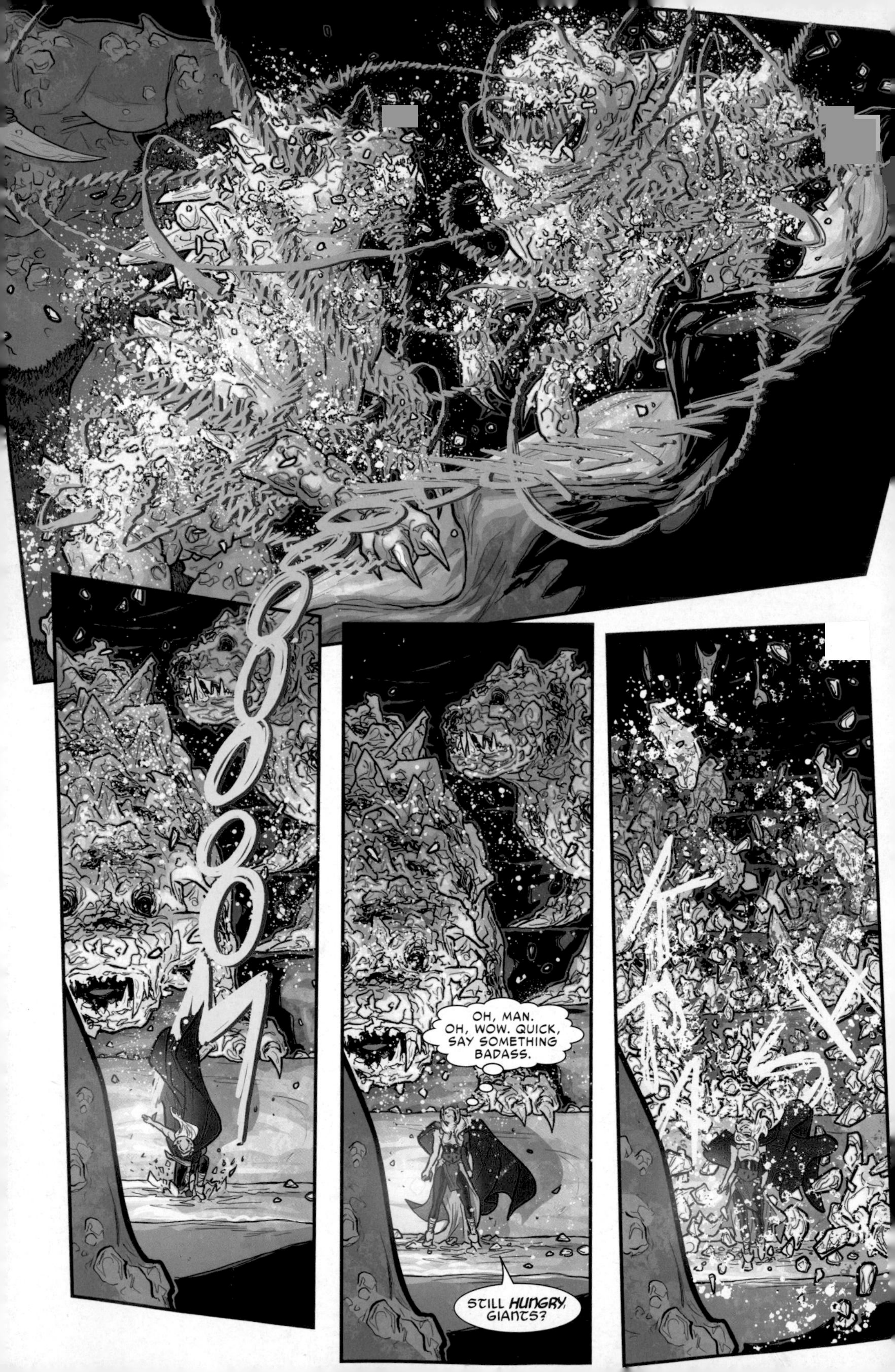
KRACKK
BOOOOOOM
OH, MAN. OH, WOW. QUICK, SAY SOMETHING BADASS.
STILL HUNGRY, GIANTS?

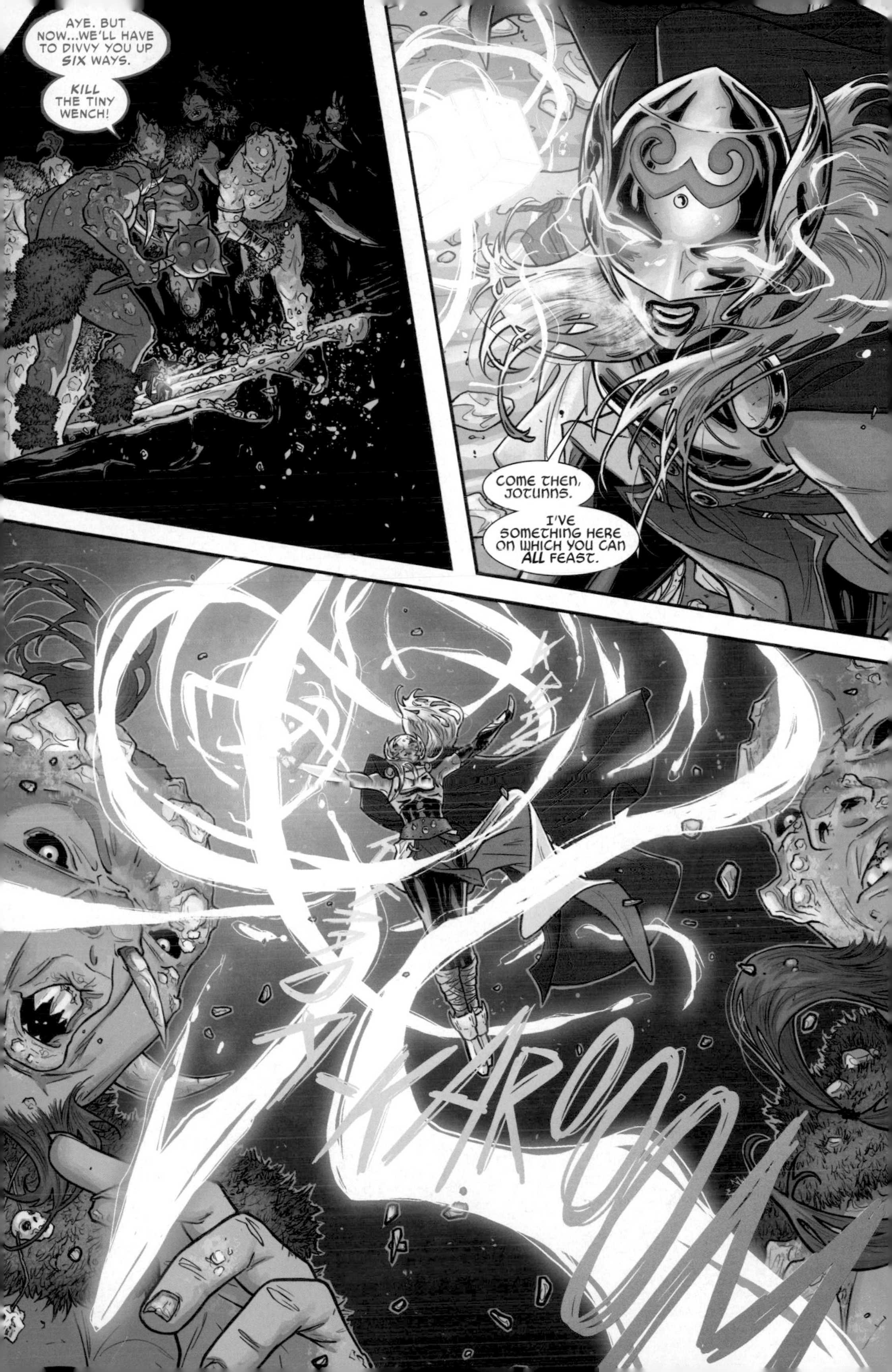
AYE. BUT NOW...WE'LL HAVE TO DIVVY YOU UP SIX WAYS.
KILL THE TINY WENCH!
COME THEN, JOTUNNS.
I'VE SOMETHING HERE ON WHICH YOU CAN ALL FEAST.

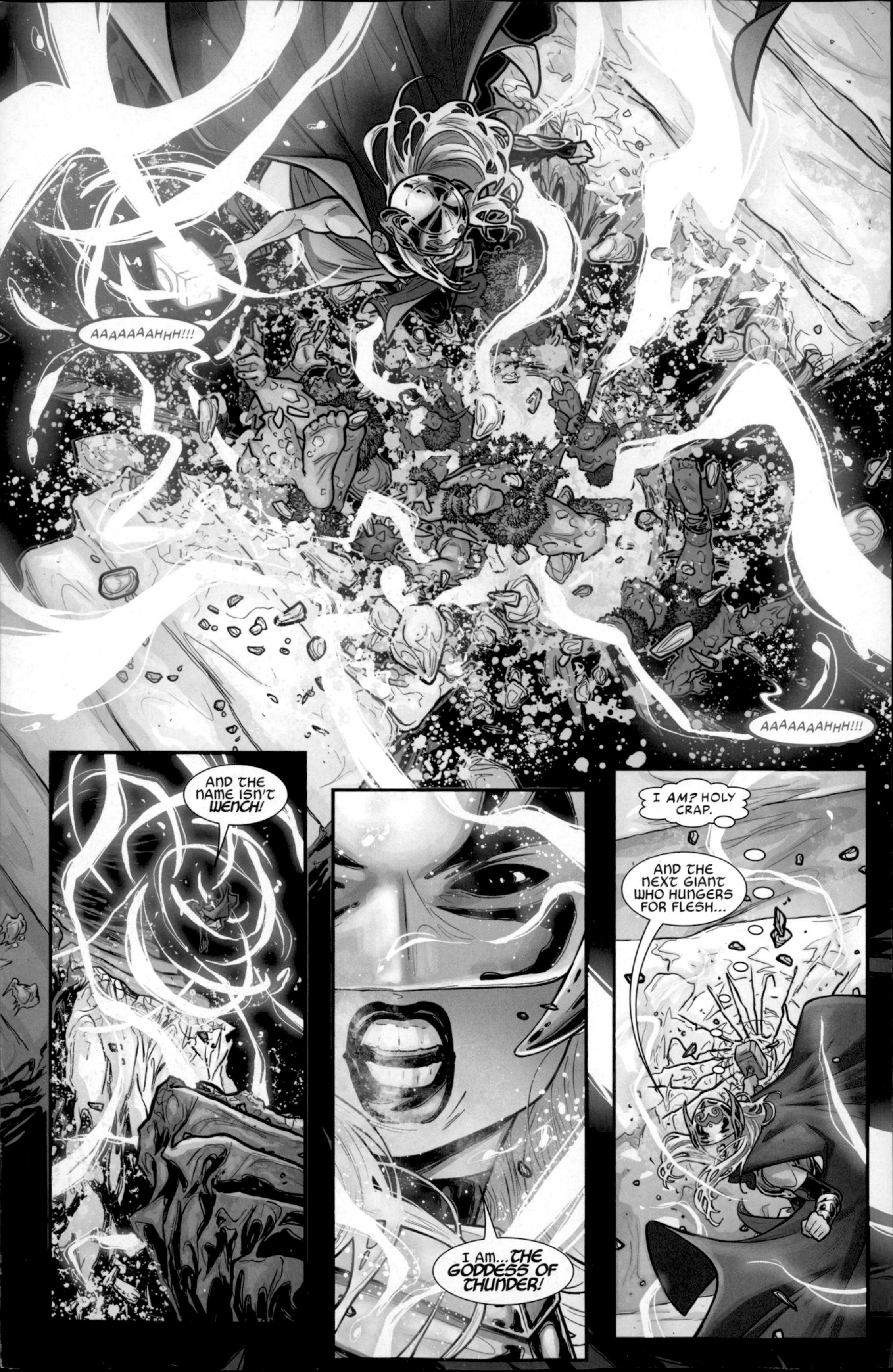
AAAAAAAHHH!!!
AAAAAAAAHHH!!!
AND THE NAME ISN'T WENCH!
I AM... THE GODDESS OF THUNDER!
I AM? HOLY CRAP.
AND THE NEXT GIANT WHO HUNGERS FOR FLESH...

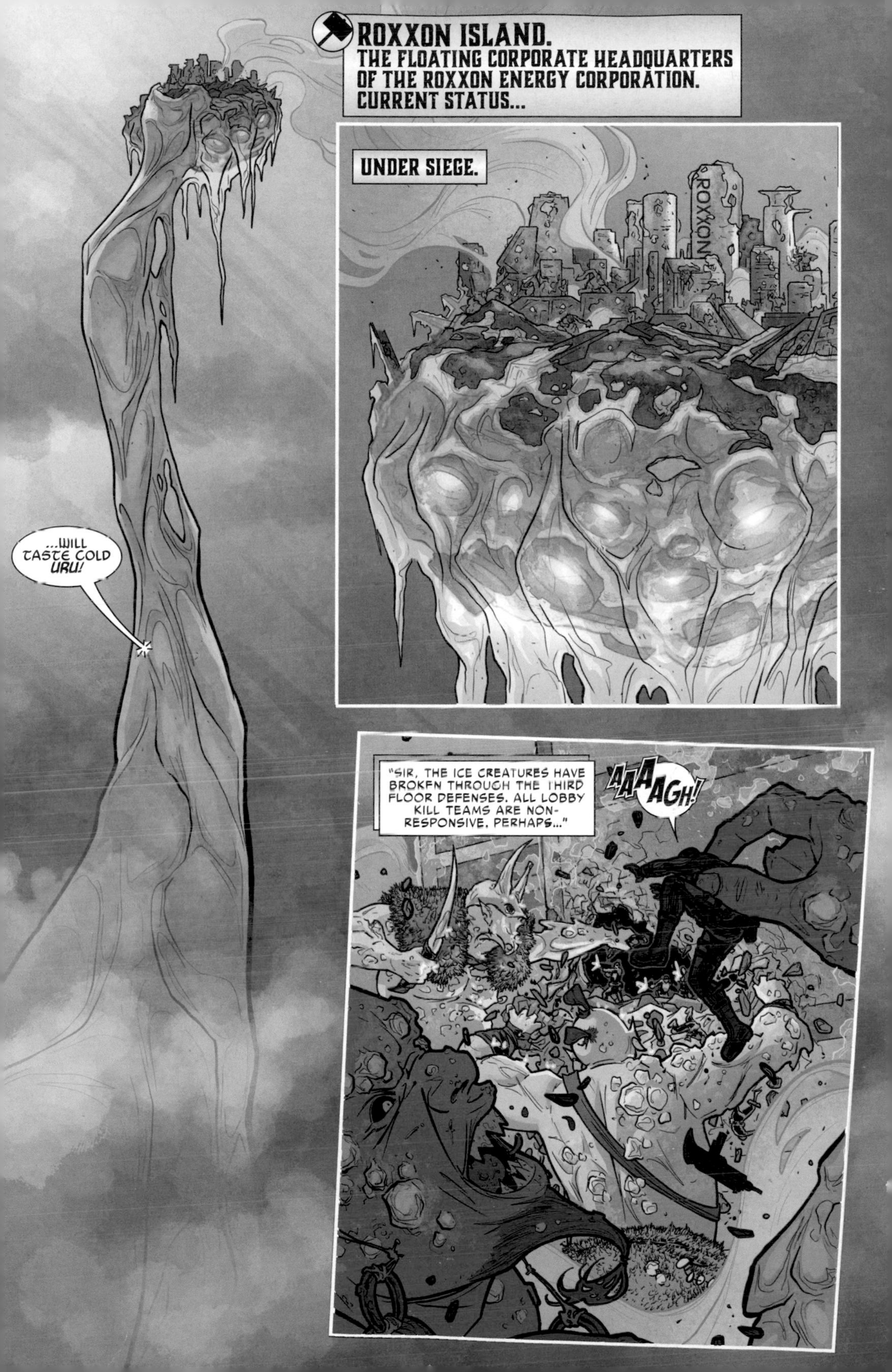
ROXXON ISLAND.
THE FLOATING CORPORATE HEADQUARTERS OF THE ROXXON ENERGY CORPORATION. CURRENT STATUS...
UNDER SIEGE.
ROXXON
...WILL TASTE COLD URU!
"SIR, THE ICE CREATURES HAVE BROKFN THROUGH THE THIRD FLOOR DEFENSES. ALL LOBBY KILL TEAMS ARE NON-RESPONSIVE. PERHAPS..."
AAAAGH!

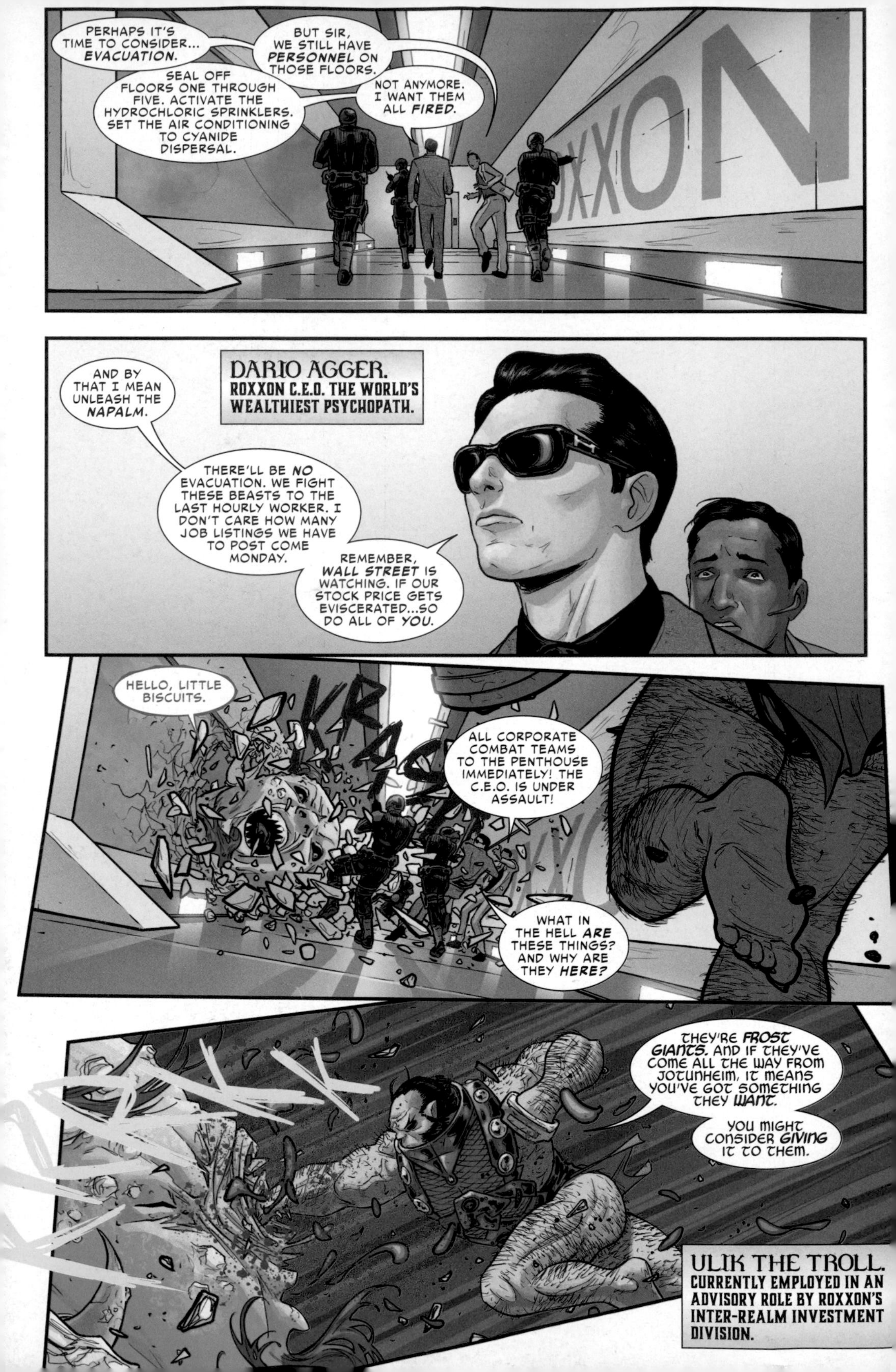
PERHAPS IT'S TIME TO CONSIDER... EVACUATION.
BUT SIR, WE STILL HAVE PERSONNEL ON THOSE FLOORS.
NOT ANYMORE. I WANT THEM ALL FIRED.
SEAL OFF FLOORS ONE THROUGH FIVE. ACTIVATE THE HYDROCHLORIC SPRINKLERS. SET THE AIR CONDITIONING TO CYANIDE DISPERSAL.
ROXXON
DARIO AGGER. ROXXON C.E.O. THE WORLD'S WEALTHIEST PSYCHOPATH.
AND BY THAT I MEAN UNLEASH THE NAPALM.
THERE'LL BE NO EVACUATION. WE FIGHT THESE BEASTS TO THE LAST HOURLY WORKER. I DON'T CARE HOW MANY JOB LISTINGS WE HAVE TO POST COME MONDAY.
REMEMBER, WALL STREET IS WATCHING. IF OUR STOCK PRICE GETS EVISCERATED...SO DO ALL OF YOU.
HELLO, LITTLE BISCUITS.
KRASH
ALL CORPORATE COMBAT TEAMS TO THE PENTHOUSE IMMEDIATELY! THE C.E.O. IS UNDER ASSAULT!
WHAT IN THE HELL ARE THESE THINGS? AND WHY ARE THEY HERE?
THEY'RE FROST GIANTS. AND IF THEY'VE COME ALL THE WAY FROM JOTUNHEIM, IT MEANS YOU'VE GOT SOMETHING THEY WANT.
YOU MIGHT CONSIDER GIVING IT TO THEM.
ULIK THE TROLL. CURRENTLY EMPLOYED IN AN ADVISORY ROLE BY ROXXON'S INTER-REALM INVESTMENT DIVISION.

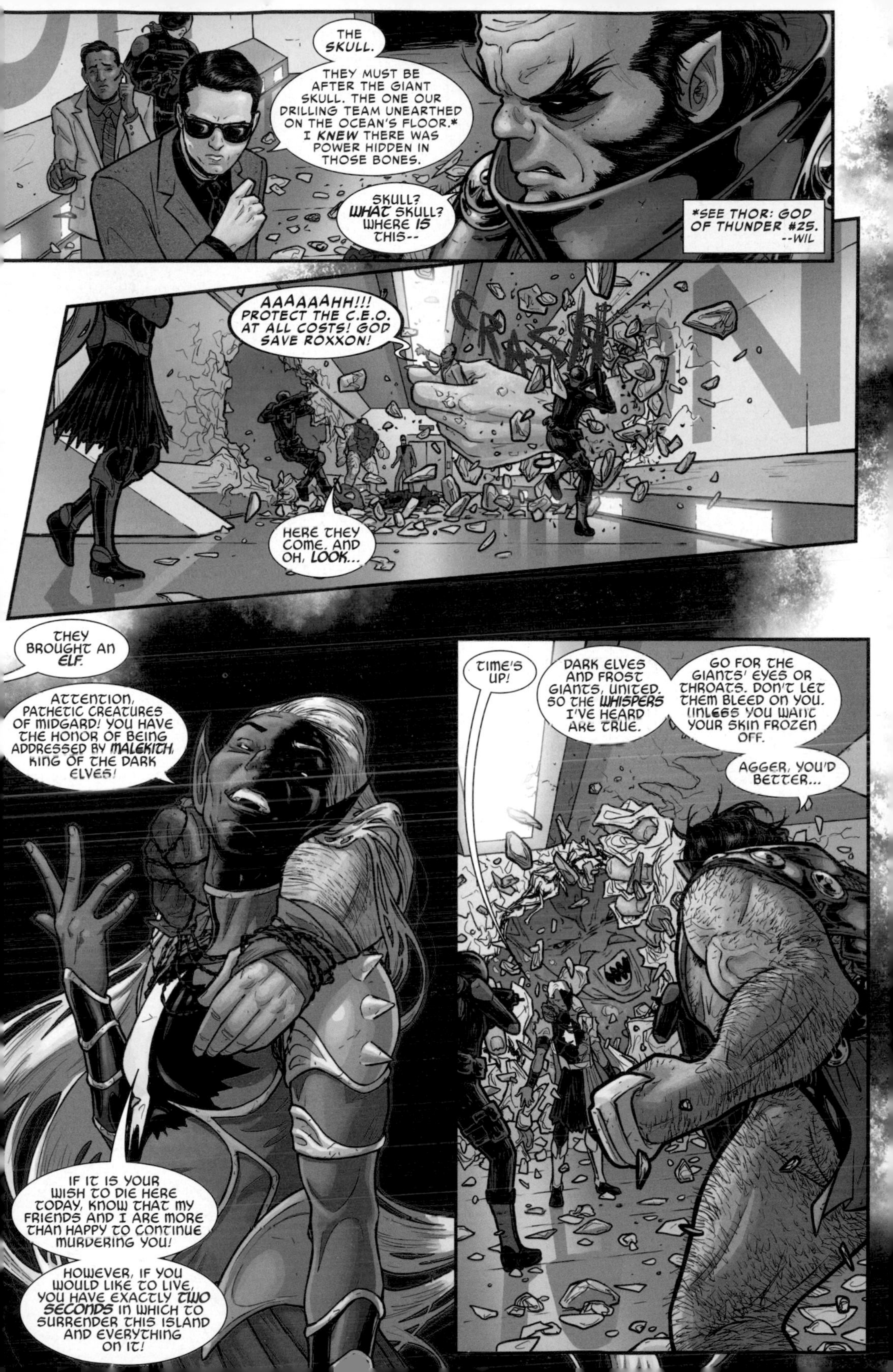
THE SKULL.
THEY MUST BE AFTER THE GIANT SKULL. THE ONE OUR DRILLING TEAM UNEARTHED ON THE OCEAN'S FLOOR.* I KNEW THERE WAS POWER HIDDEN IN THOSE BONES.
SKULL? WHAT SKULL? WHERE IS THIS--
*SEE THOR: GOD OF THUNDER #25. --WIL
AAAAAAHH!!! PROTECT THE C.E.O. AT ALL COSTS! GOD SAVE ROXXON!
CRASH
HERE THEY COME. AND OH, LOOK...
THEY BROUGHT AN ELF.
ATTENTION, PATHETIC CREATURES OF MIDGARD! YOU HAVE THE HONOR OF BEING ADDRESSED BY MALEKITH, KING OF THE DARK ELVES!
IF IT IS YOUR WISH TO DIE HERE TODAY, KNOW THAT MY FRIENDS AND I ARE MORE THAN HAPPY TO CONTINUE MURDERING YOU!
HOWEVER, IF YOU WOULD LIKE TO LIVE, YOU HAVE EXACTLY TWO SECONDS IN WHICH TO SURRENDER THIS ISLAND AND EVERYTHING ON IT!
TIME'S UP!
DARK ELVES AND FROST GIANTS, UNITED. SO THE WHISPERS I'VE HEARD ARE TRUE.
GO FOR THE GIANTS' EYES OR THROATS. DON'T LET THEM BLEED ON YOU. UNLESS YOU WANT YOUR SKIN FROZEN OFF.
AGGER, YOU'D BETTER...

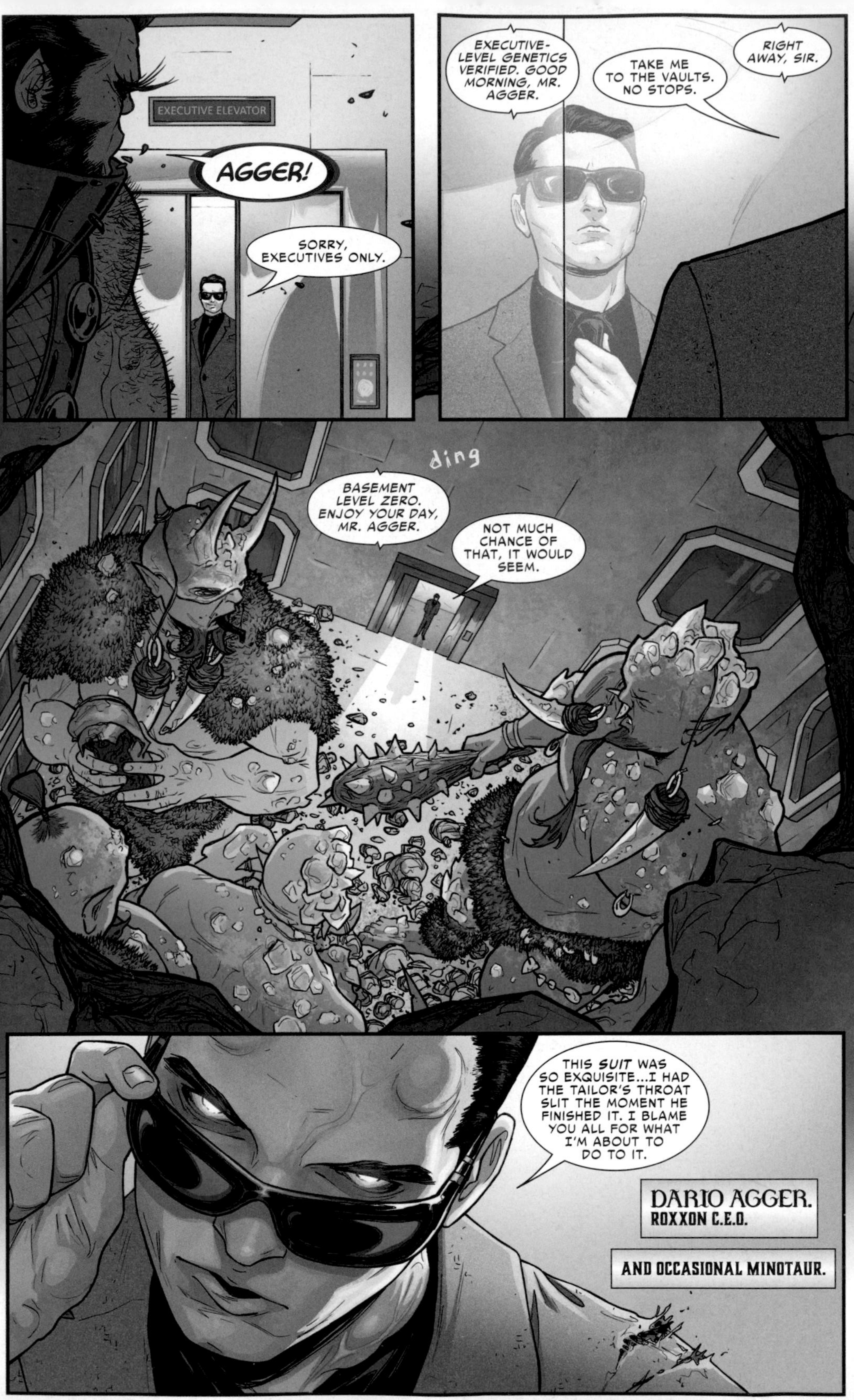
EXECUTIVE ELEVATOR
AGGER!
SORRY, EXECUTIVES ONLY.
EXECUTIVE-LEVEL GENETICS VERIFIED. GOOD MORNING, MR. AGGER.
TAKE ME TO THE VAULTS. NO STOPS.
RIGHT AWAY, SIR.
ding
BASEMENT LEVEL ZERO. ENJOY YOUR DAY, MR. AGGER.
NOT MUCH CHANCE OF THAT, IT WOULD SEEM.
THIS SUIT WAS SO EXQUISITE...I HAD THE TAILOR'S THROAT SLIT THE MOMENT HE FINISHED IT. I BLAME YOU ALL FOR WHAT I'M ABOUT TO DO TO IT.
DARIO AGGER.
ROXXON C.E.O.
AND OCCASIONAL MINOTAUR.

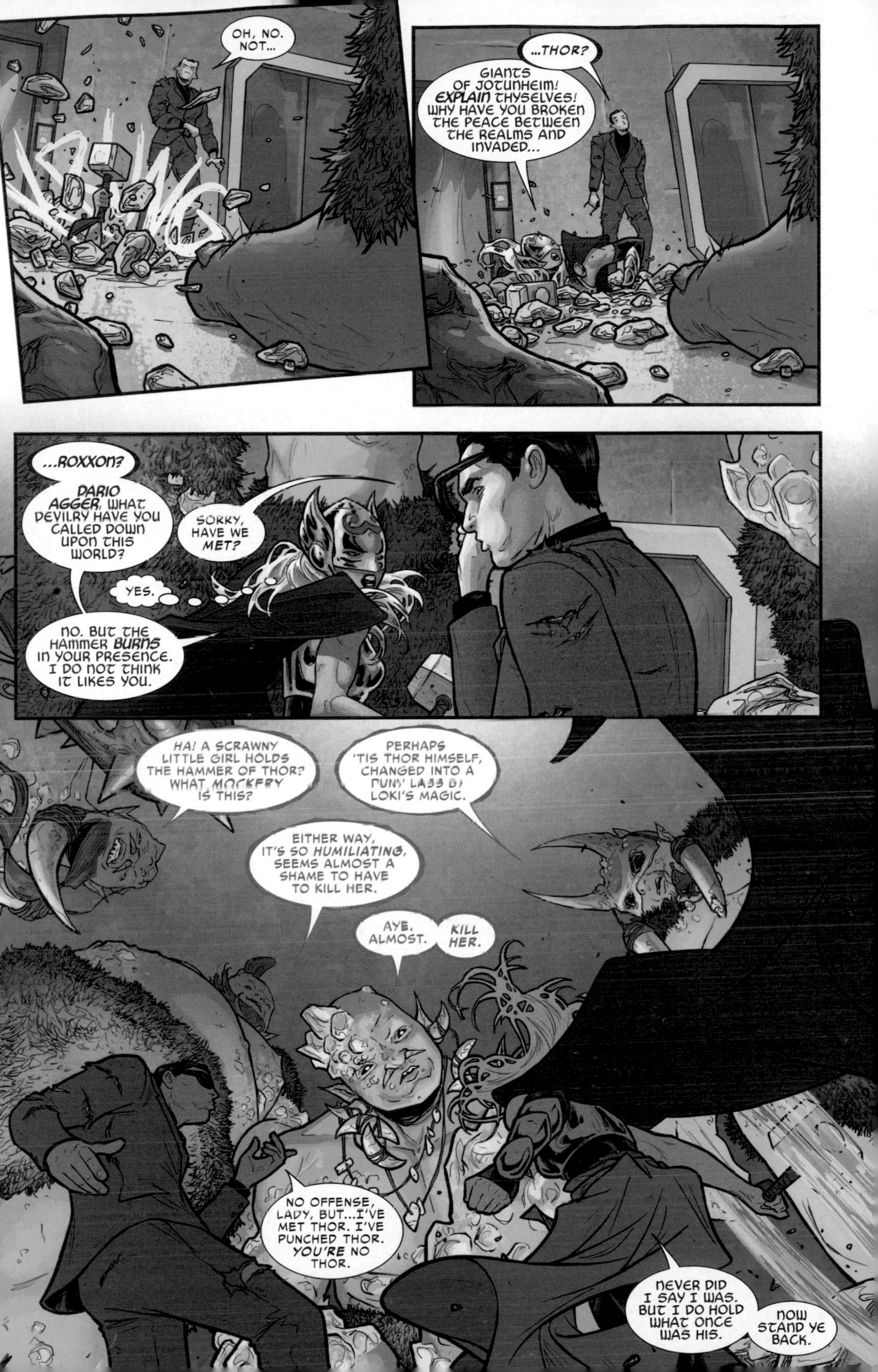

OH, NO. NOT...
...THOR?
GIANTS OF JOTUNHEIM! EXPLAIN THYSELVES! WHY HAVE YOU BROKEN THE PEACE BETWEEN THE REALMS AND INVADED...
...ROXXON?
DARIO AGGER, WHAT DEVILRY HAVE YOU CALLED DOWN UPON THIS WORLD?
SORRY, HAVE WE MET?
YES.
NO. BUT THE HAMMER BURNS IN YOUR PRESENCE. I DO NOT THINK IT LIKES YOU.
HA! A SCRAWNY LITTLE GIRL HOLDS THE HAMMER OF THOR? WHAT MOCKERY IS THIS?
PERHAPS 'TIS THOR HIMSELF, CHANGED INTO A PUNY LASS BY LOKI'S MAGIC.
EITHER WAY, IT'S SO HUMILIATING, SEEMS ALMOST A SHAME TO HAVE TO KILL HER.
AYE. ALMOST.
KILL HER.
NO OFFENSE, LADY, BUT...I'VE MET THOR. I'VE PUNCHED THOR. YOU'RE NO THOR.
NEVER DID I SAY I WAS. BUT I DO HOLD WHAT ONCE WAS HIS.
NOW STAND YE BACK.

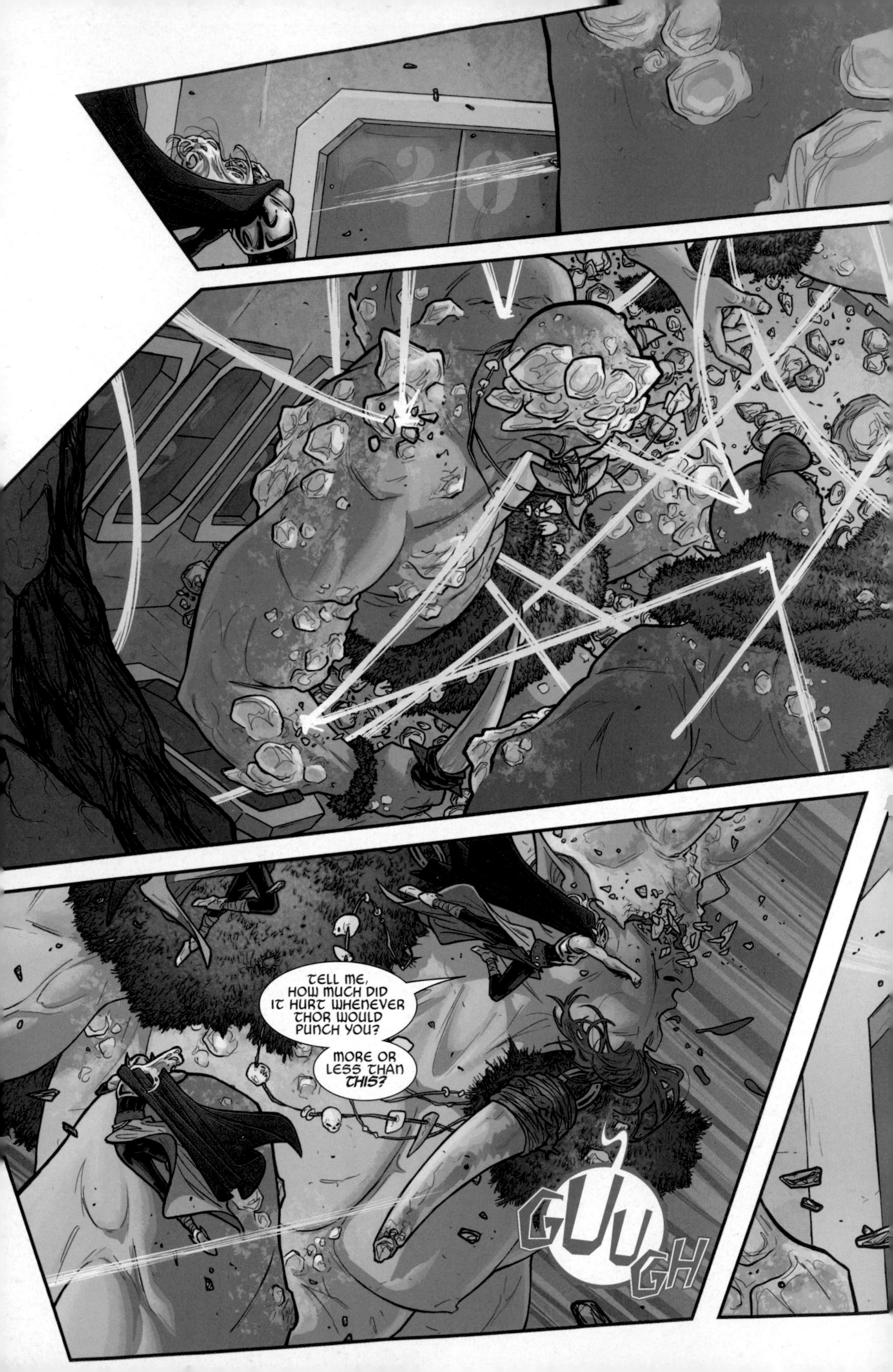
TELL ME, HOW MUCH DID IT HURT WHENEVER THOR WOULD PUNCH YOU?
MORE OR LESS THAN *THIS?*
GUUGH

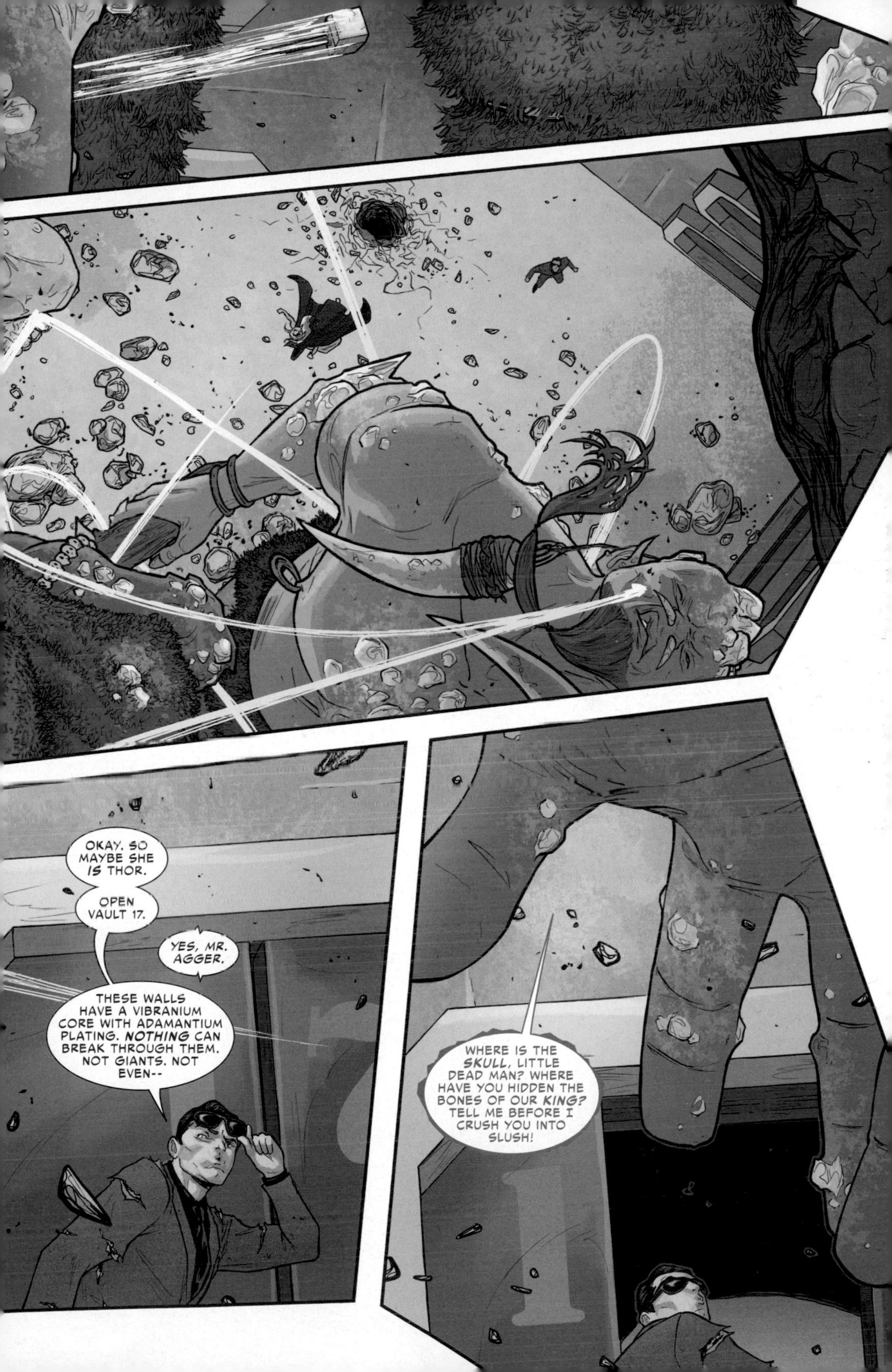

OKAY. SO MAYBE SHE *IS* THOR.
OPEN VAULT 17.
YES, MR. AGGER.
THESE WALLS HAVE A VIBRANIUM CORE WITH ADAMANTIUM PLATING. *NOTHING* CAN BREAK THROUGH THEM. NOT GIANTS. NOT EVEN--
WHERE IS THE *SKULL*, LITTLE DEAD MAN? WHERE HAVE YOU HIDDEN THE BONES OF OUR *KING?* TELL ME BEFORE I CRUSH YOU INTO SLUSH!

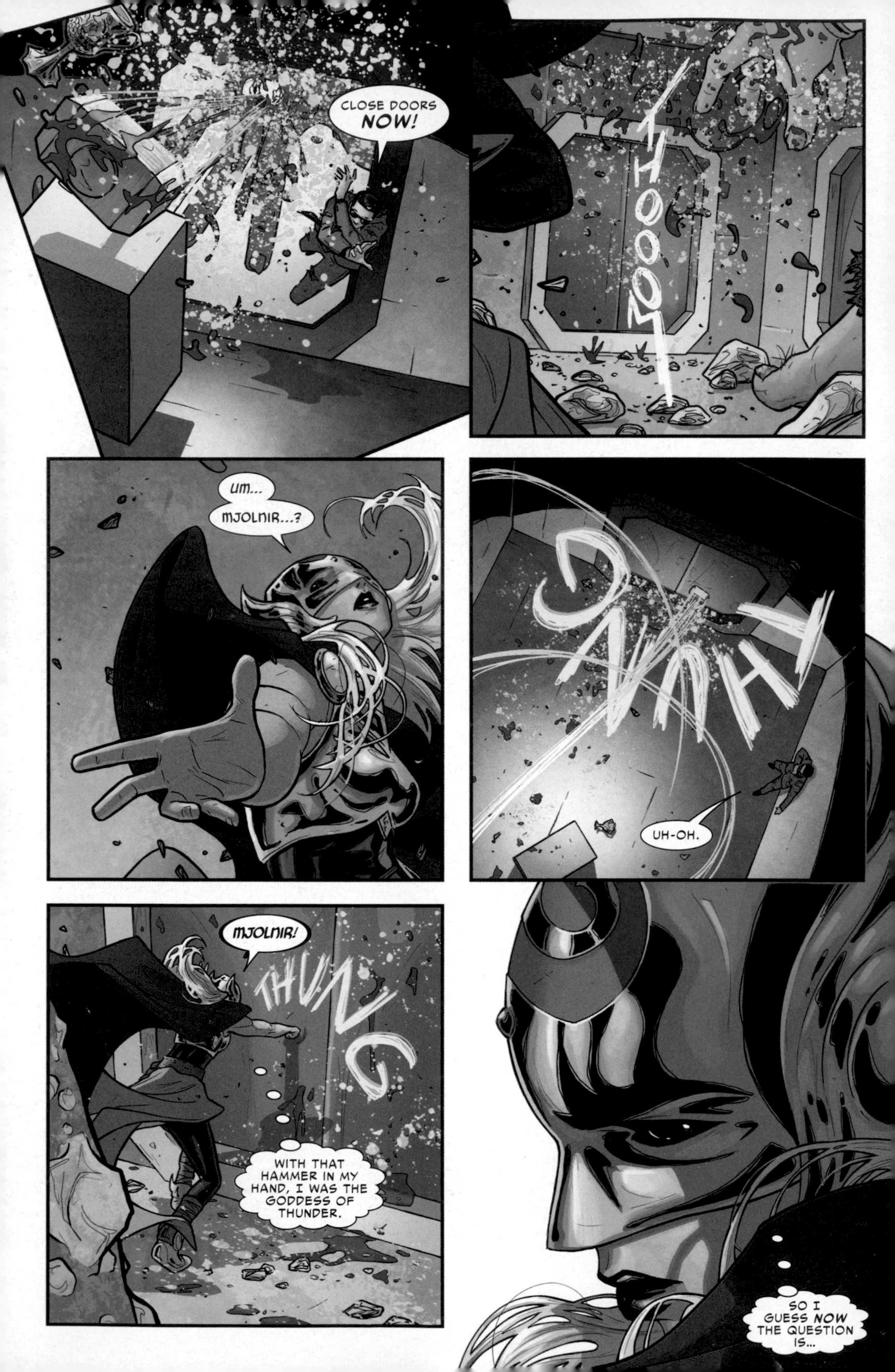
CLOSE DOORS NOW!
THOOOM
UM... MJOLNIR...?
DWAHY
UH-OH.
MJOLNIR!
THUNG
WITH THAT HAMMER IN MY HAND, I WAS THE GODDESS OF THUNDER.
SO I GUESS NOW THE QUESTION IS...

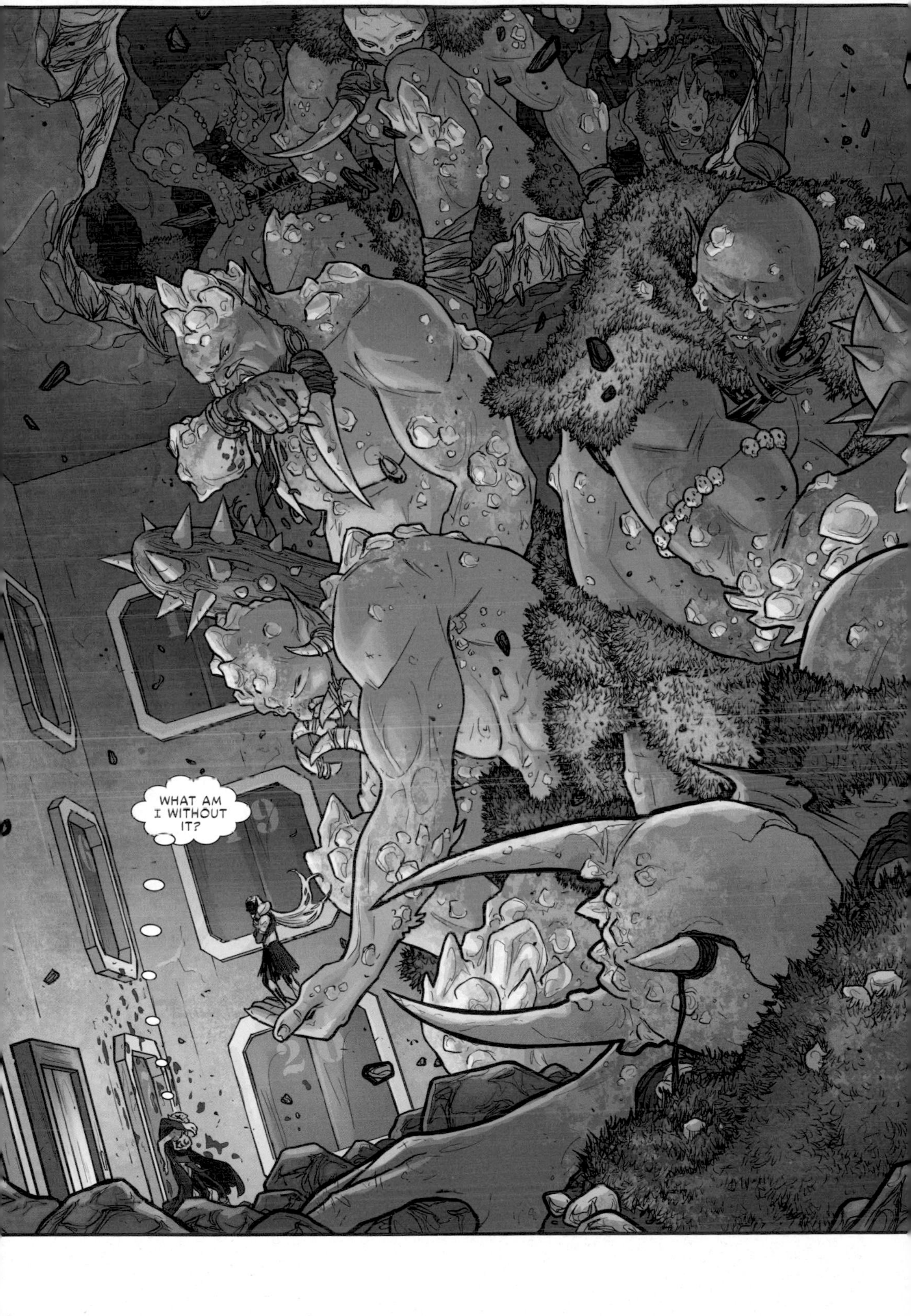
WHAT AM I WITHOUT IT?

THOR ANNUAL #1

THERE'S A NEW THOR IN ASGARDIA — AND NOT EVERYONE IS
HAPPY ABOUT IT! THE WARRIORS THREE SET OUT TO SEE IF SHE IS
WORTHY OF THE MANTLE!

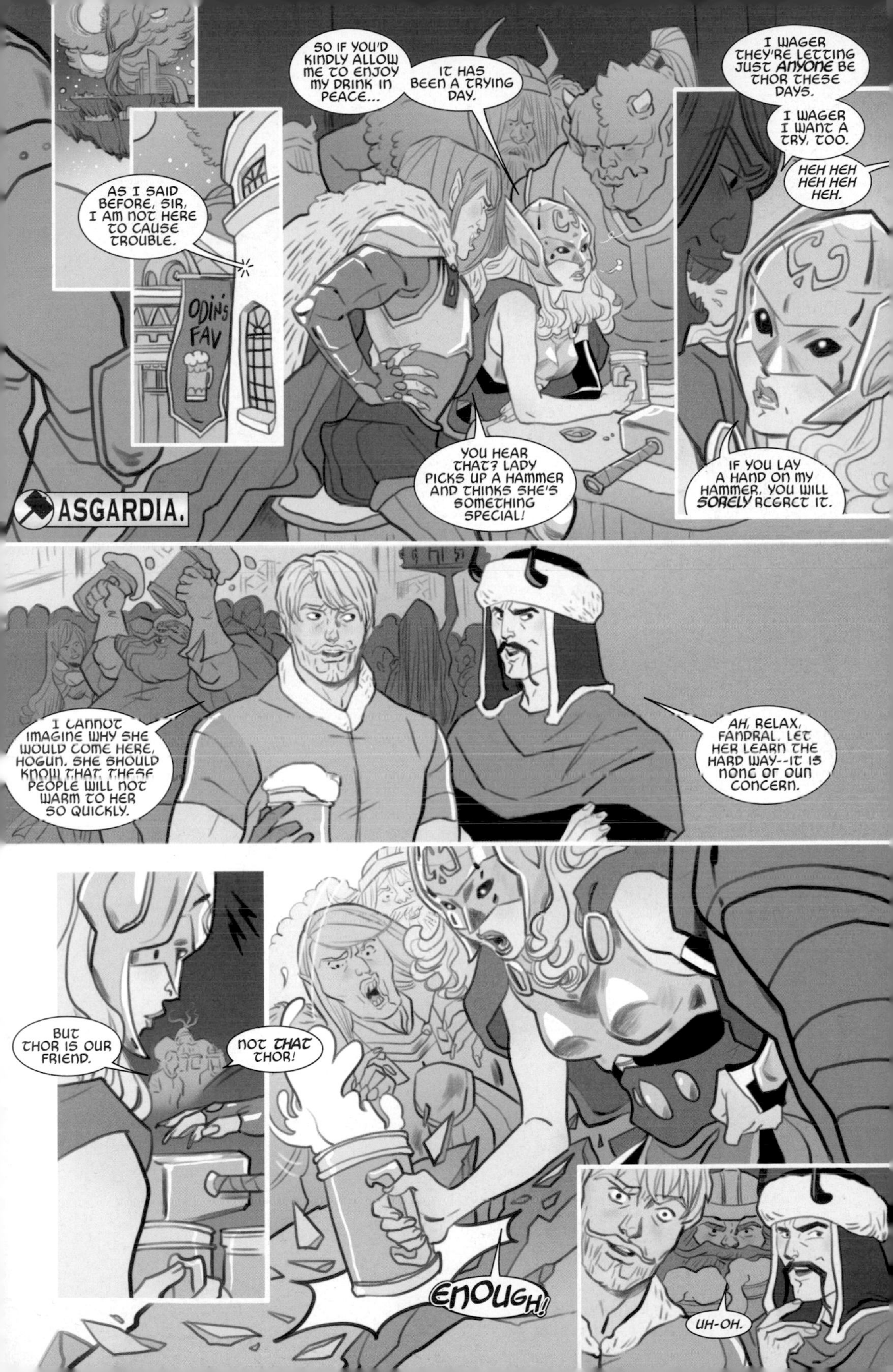
AS I SAID BEFORE, SIR, I AM NOT HERE TO CAUSE TROUBLE.
ODIN'S FAV
ASGARDIA.
SO IF YOU'D KINDLY ALLOW ME TO ENJOY MY DRINK IN PEACE...
IT HAS BEEN A TRYING DAY.
YOU HEAR THAT? LADY PICKS UP A HAMMER AND THINKS SHE'S SOMETHING SPECIAL!
I WAGER THEY'RE LETTING JUST ANYONE BE THOR THESE DAYS.
I WAGER I WANT A TRY, TOO.
HEH HEH HEH HEH HEH.
IF YOU LAY A HAND ON MY HAMMER, YOU WILL SORELY REGRET IT.
I CANNOT IMAGINE WHY SHE WOULD COME HERE, HOGUN. SHE SHOULD KNOW THAT THESE PEOPLE WILL NOT WARM TO HER SO QUICKLY.
AH, RELAX, FANDRAL. LET HER LEARN THE HARD WAY--IT IS NONE OF OUR CONCERN.
BUT THOR IS OUR FRIEND.
NOT THAT THOR!
ENOUGH!
UH-OH.

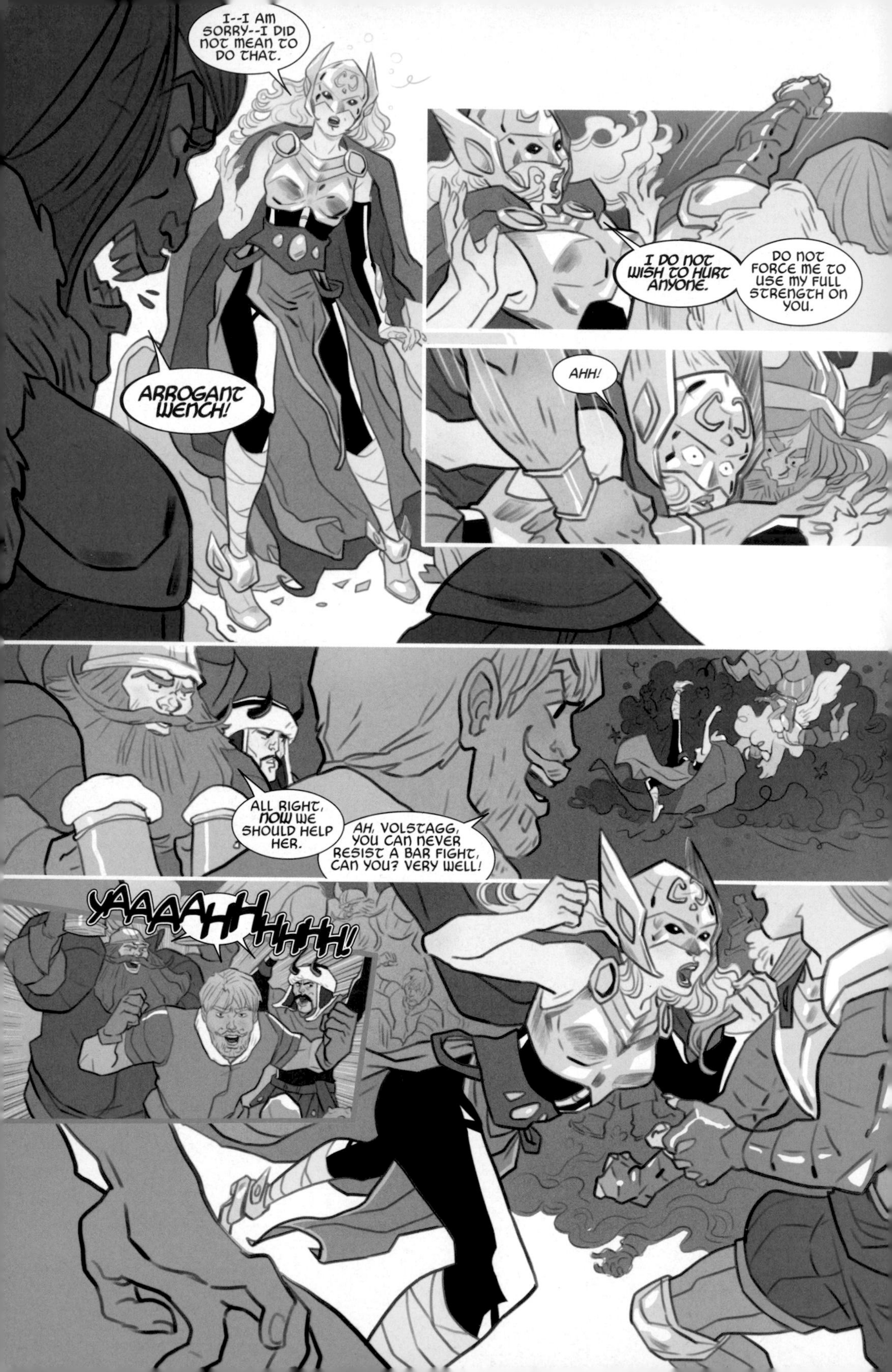
I--I AM SORRY--I DID NOT MEAN TO DO THAT.
ARROGANT WENCH!
I DO NOT WISH TO HURT ANYONE.
DO NOT FORCE ME TO USE MY FULL STRENGTH ON YOU.
AHH!
ALL RIGHT, NOW WE SHOULD HELP HER.
AH, VOLSTAGG, YOU CAN NEVER RESIST A BAR FIGHT, CAN YOU? VERY WELL!
YAAAAHHHHHH!

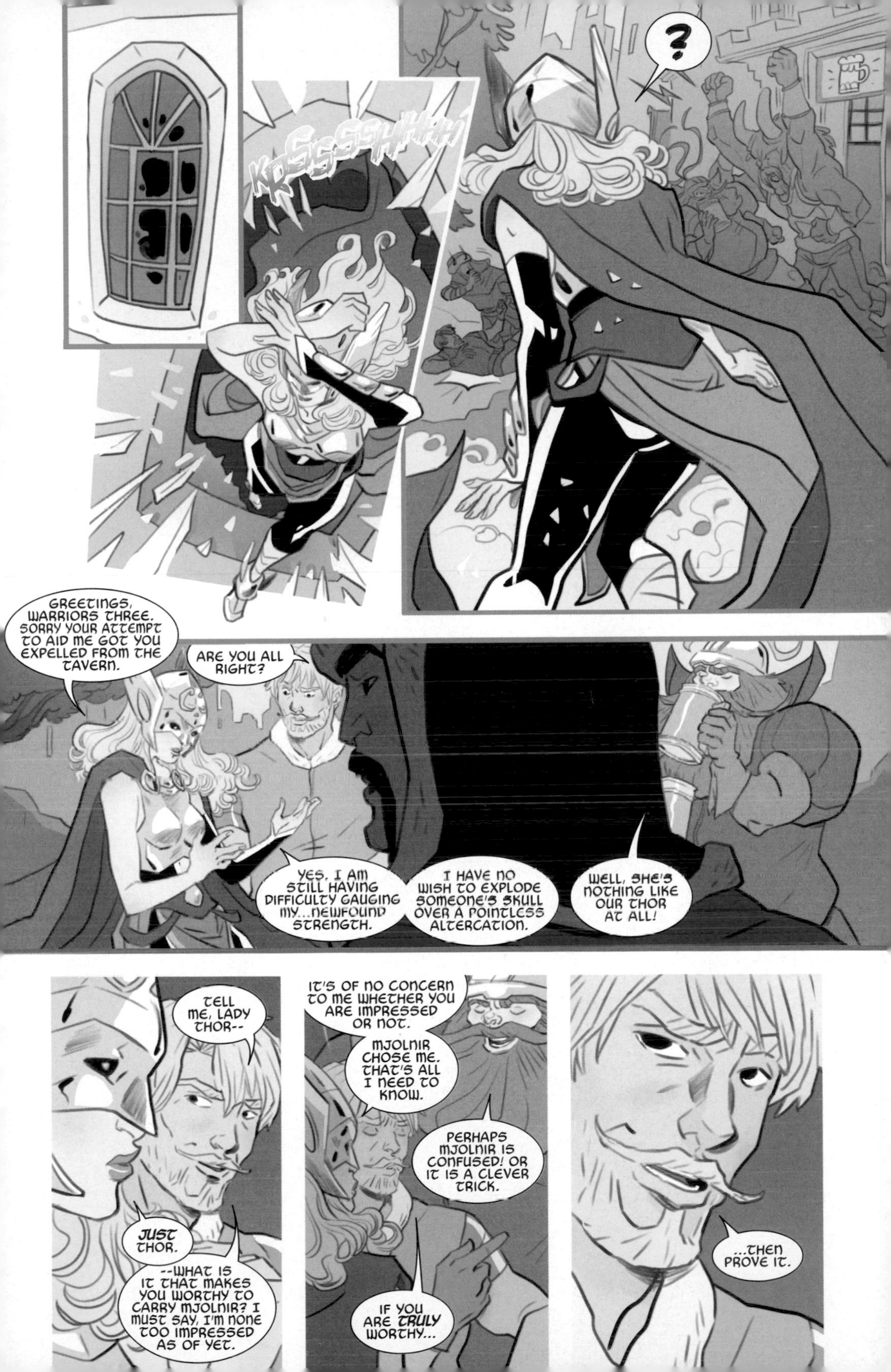
KRSSSSHHHH
?
GREETINGS, WARRIORS THREE. SORRY YOUR ATTEMPT TO AID ME GOT YOU EXPELLED FROM THE TAVERN.
ARE YOU ALL RIGHT?
YES. I AM STILL HAVING DIFFICULTY GAUGING MY...NEWFOUND STRENGTH.
I HAVE NO WISH TO EXPLODE SOMEONE'S SKULL OVER A POINTLESS ALTERCATION.
WELL, SHE'S NOTHING LIKE OUR THOR AT ALL!
TELL ME, LADY THOR--
JUST THOR.
--WHAT IS IT THAT MAKES YOU WORTHY TO CARRY MJOLNIR? I MUST SAY, I'M NONE TOO IMPRESSED AS OF YET.
IT'S OF NO CONCERN TO ME WHETHER YOU ARE IMPRESSED OR NOT.
MJOLNIR CHOSE ME. THAT'S ALL I NEED TO KNOW.
PERHAPS MJOLNIR IS CONFUSED! OR IT IS A CLEVER TRICK.
IF YOU ARE TRULY WORTHY...
...THEN PROVE IT.

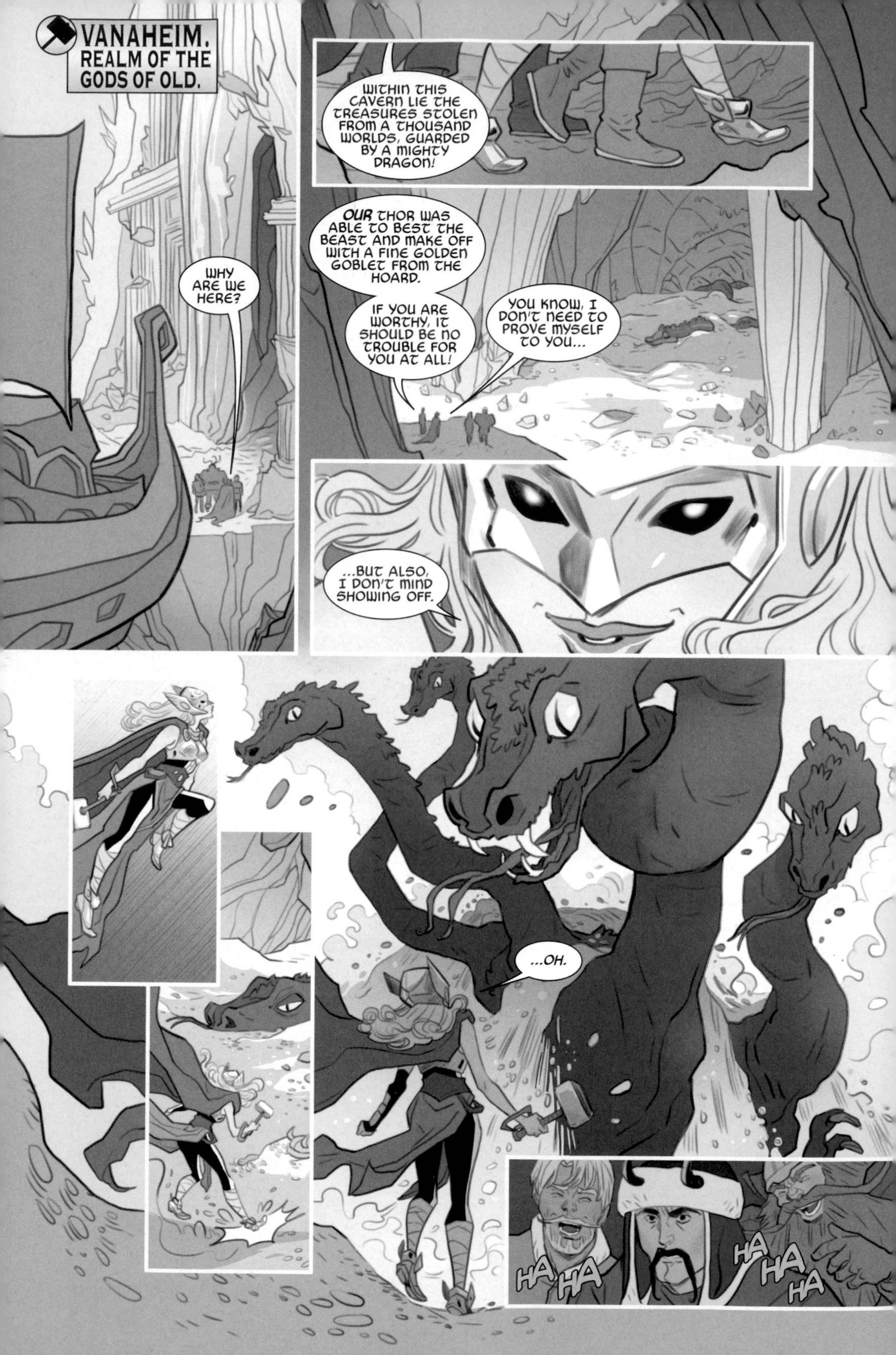
VANAHEIM. REALM OF THE GODS OF OLD.
WHY ARE WE HERE?
WITHIN THIS CAVERN LIE THE TREASURES STOLEN FROM A THOUSAND WORLDS, GUARDED BY A MIGHTY DRAGON!
OUR THOR WAS ABLE TO BEST THE BEAST AND MAKE OFF WITH A FINE GOLDEN GOBLET FROM THE HOARD.
IF YOU ARE WORTHY, IT SHOULD BE NO TROUBLE FOR YOU AT ALL!
YOU KNOW, I DON'T NEED TO PROVE MYSELF TO YOU...
...BUT ALSO, I DON'T MIND SHOWING OFF.
...OH.
HA HA
HA HA HA

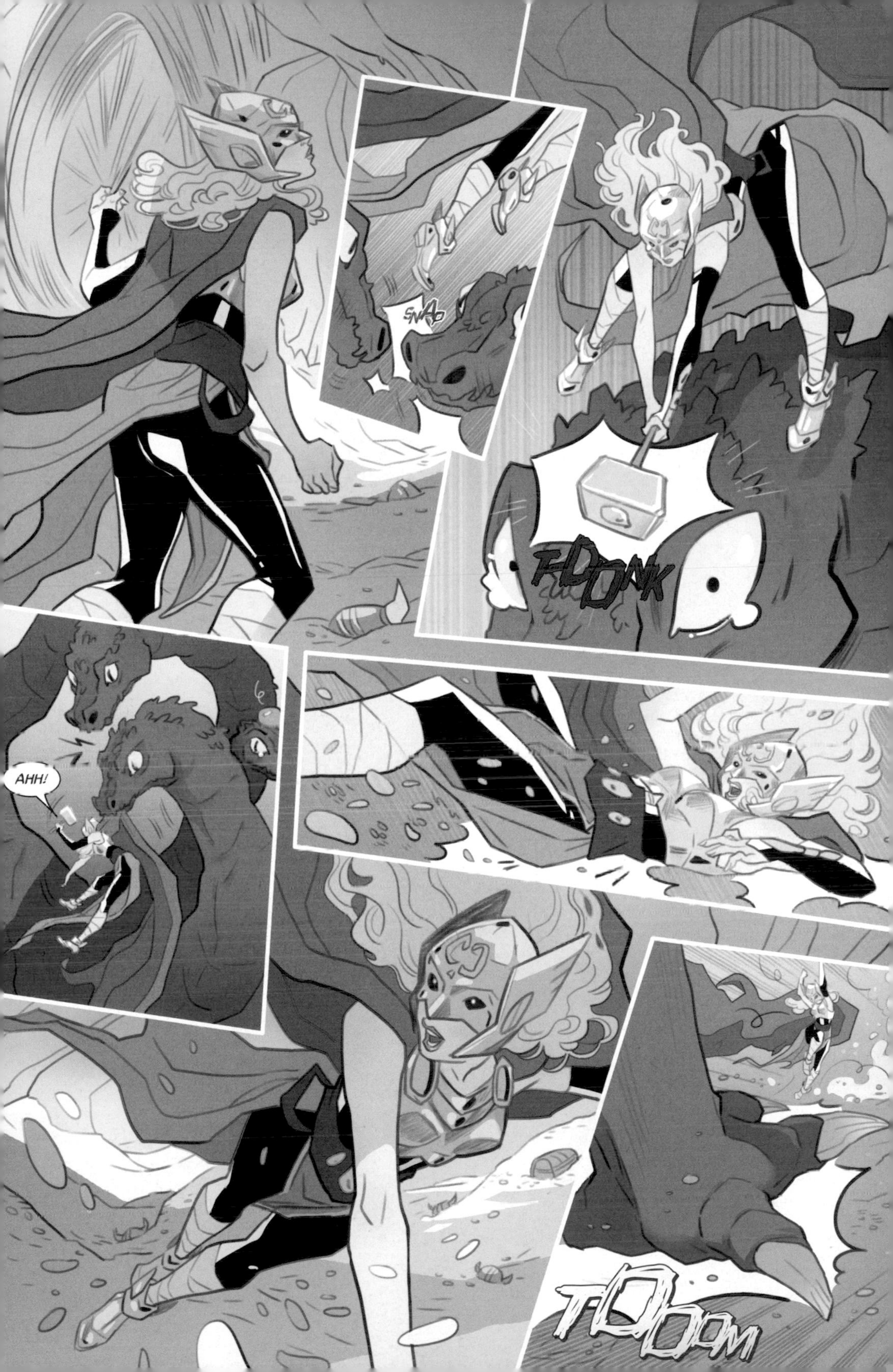
SNAP
TDOONK
AHH!
TOOOM

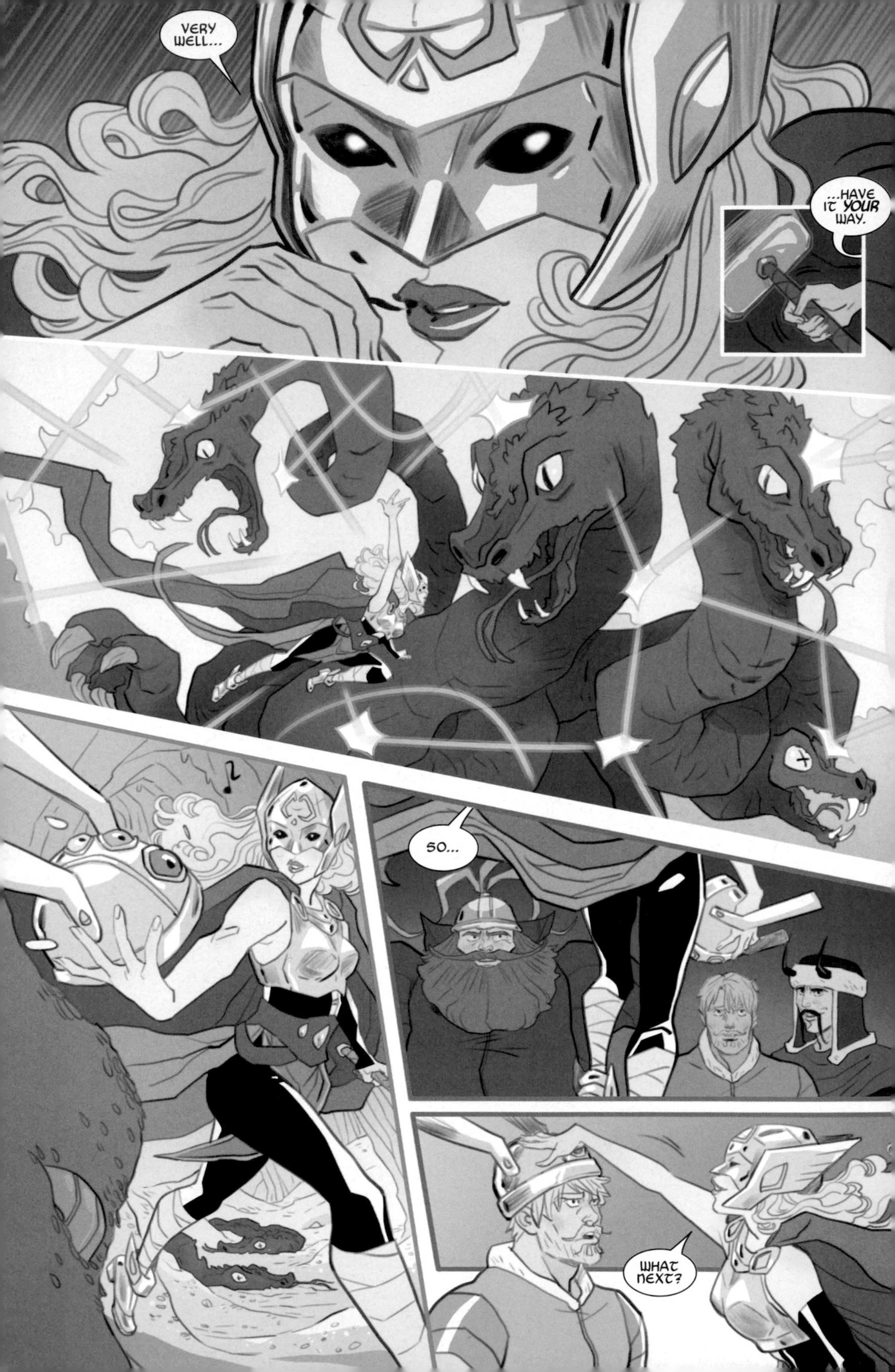
VERY WELL...
...HAVE IT YOUR WAY.
SO...
WHAT NEXT?

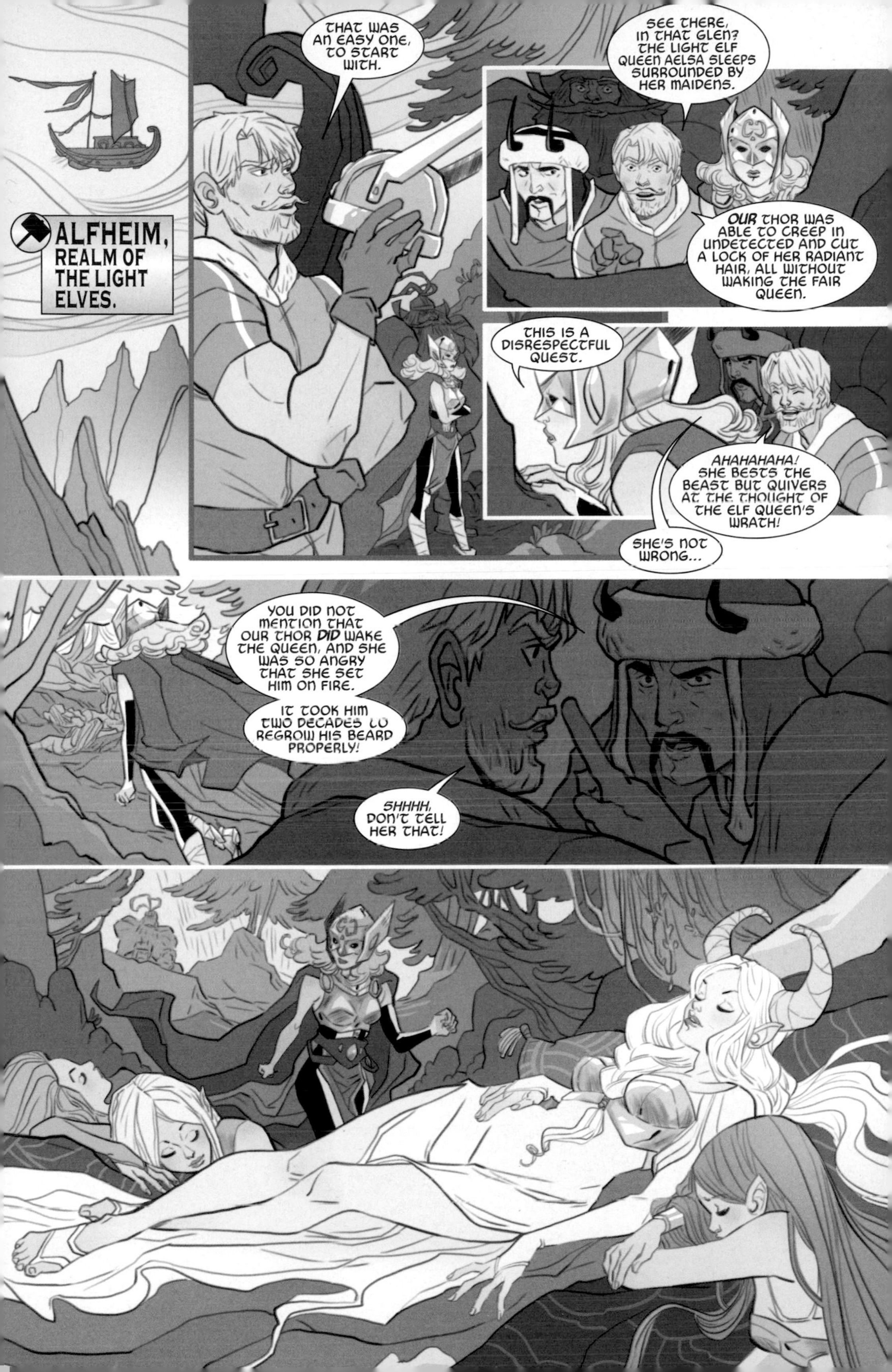
ALFHEIM, REALM OF THE LIGHT ELVES.
THAT WAS AN EASY ONE, TO START WITH.
SEE THERE, IN THAT GLEN? THE LIGHT ELF QUEEN AELSA SLEEPS SURROUNDED BY HER MAIDENS.
OUR THOR WAS ABLE TO CREEP IN UNDETECTED AND CUT A LOCK OF HER RADIANT HAIR, ALL WITHOUT WAKING THE FAIR QUEEN.
THIS IS A DISRESPECTFUL QUEST.
AHAHAHAHA! SHE BESTS THE BEAST BUT QUIVERS AT THE THOUGHT OF THE ELF QUEEN'S WRATH!
SHE'S NOT WRONG...
YOU DID NOT MENTION THAT OUR THOR DID WAKE THE QUEEN, AND SHE WAS SO ANGRY THAT SHE SET HIM ON FIRE.
IT TOOK HIM TWO DECADES TO REGROW HIS BEARD PROPERLY!
SHHHH, DON'T TELL HER THAT!

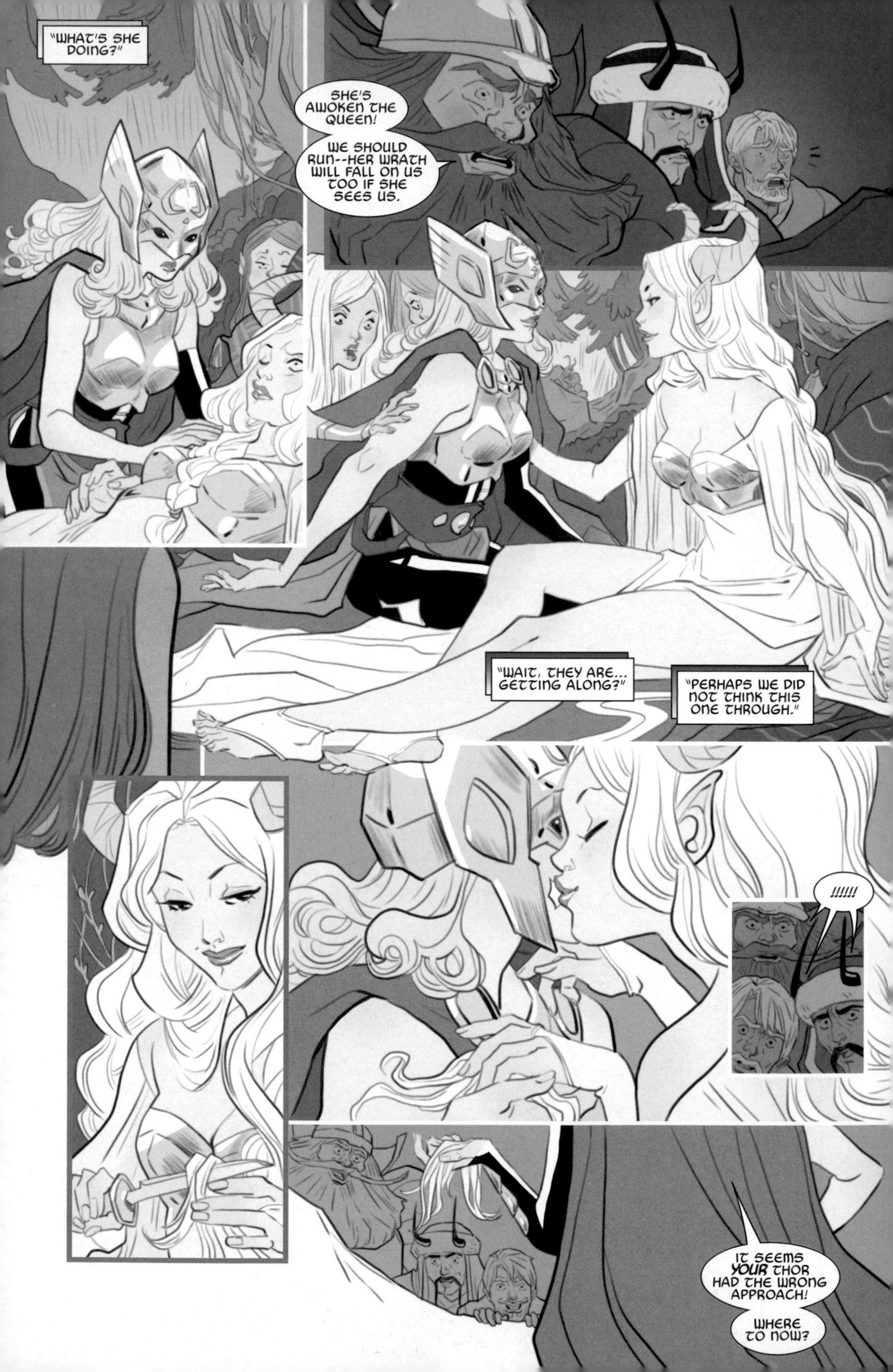
"WHAT'S SHE DOING?"
SHE'S AWOKEN THE QUEEN!
WE SHOULD RUN--HER WRATH WILL FALL ON US TOO IF SHE SEES US.
"WAIT, THEY ARE... GETTING ALONG?"
"PERHAPS WE DID NOT THINK THIS ONE THROUGH."
!!!!!!
IT SEEMS YOUR THOR HAD THE WRONG APPROACH!
WHERE TO NOW?

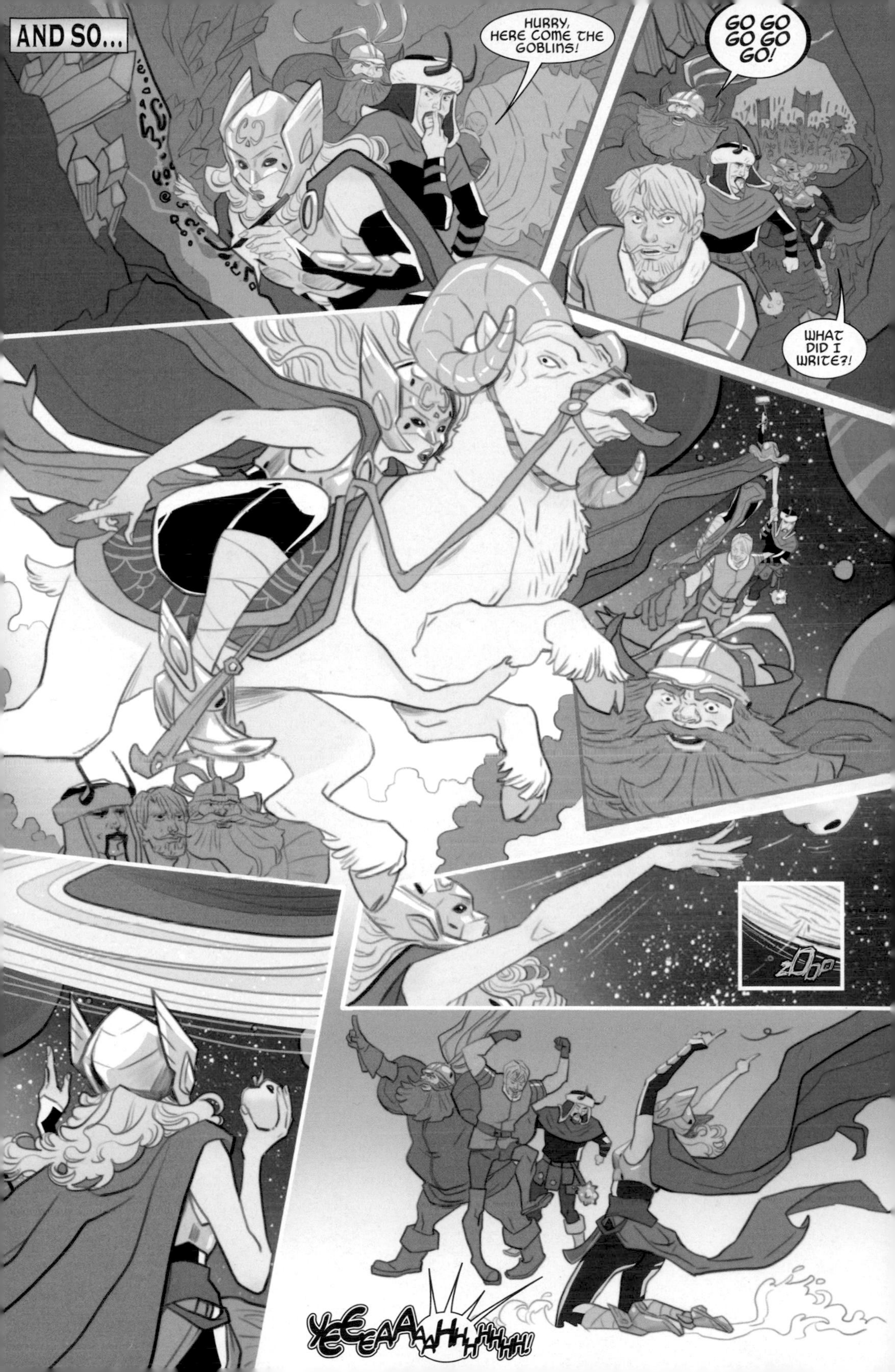
AND SO...
HURRY, HERE COME THE GOBLINS!
GO GO GO GO GO!
WHAT DID I WRITE?!
ZOOP
YEEEAAAAHHHHHHH!

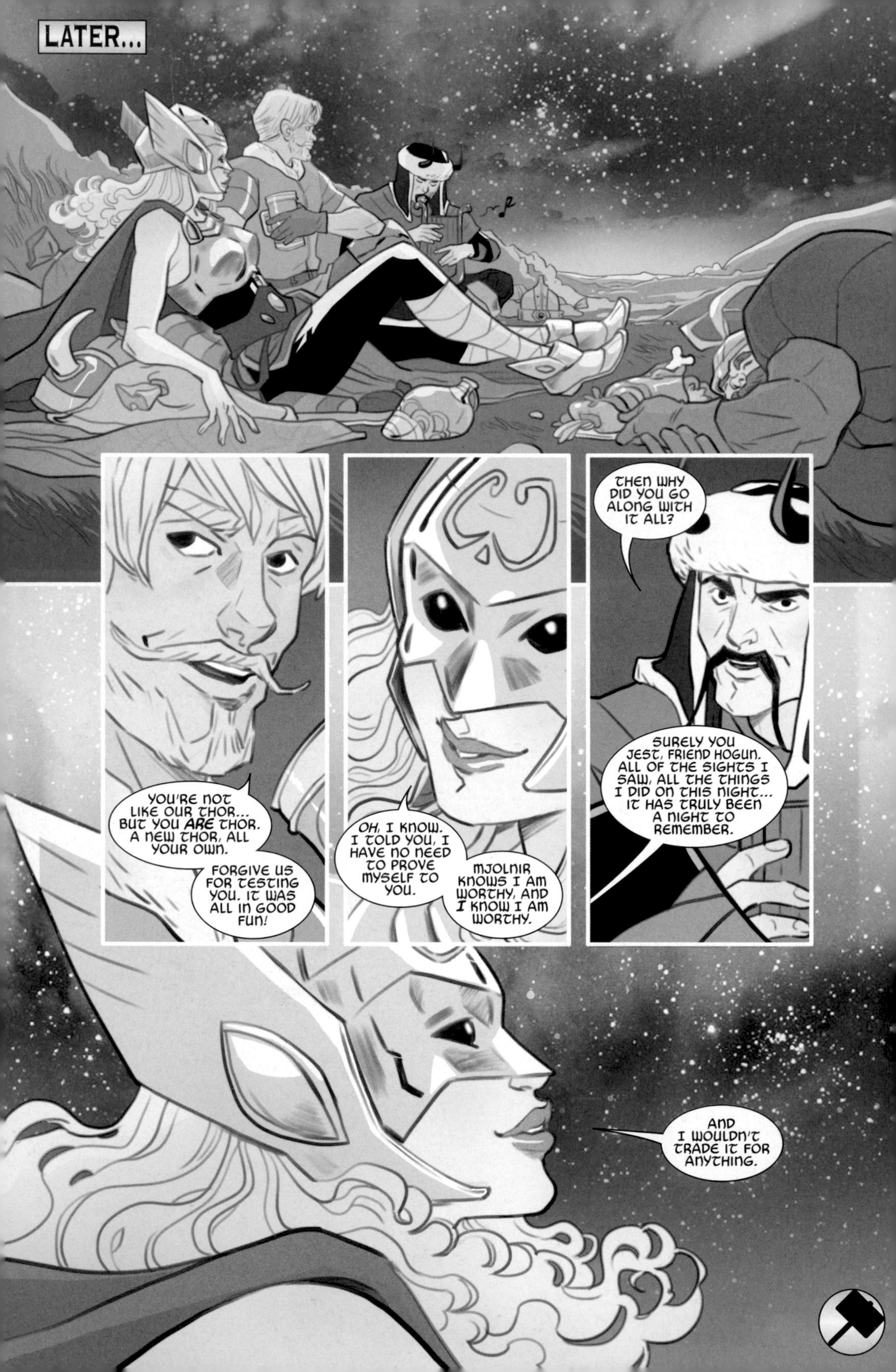
LATER...
YOU'RE NOT LIKE OUR THOR... BUT YOU ARE THOR. A NEW THOR, ALL YOUR OWN.
FORGIVE US FOR TESTING YOU. IT WAS ALL IN GOOD FUN!
OH, I KNOW. I TOLD YOU, I HAVE NO NEED TO PROVE MYSELF TO YOU.
MJOLNIR KNOWS I AM WORTHY, AND I KNOW I AM WORTHY.
THEN WHY DID YOU GO ALONG WITH IT ALL?
SURELY YOU JEST, FRIEND HOGUN. ALL OF THE SIGHTS I SAW, ALL THE THINGS I DID ON THIS NIGHT... IT HAS TRULY BEEN A NIGHT TO REMEMBER.
AND I WOULDN'T TRADE IT FOR ANYTHING.

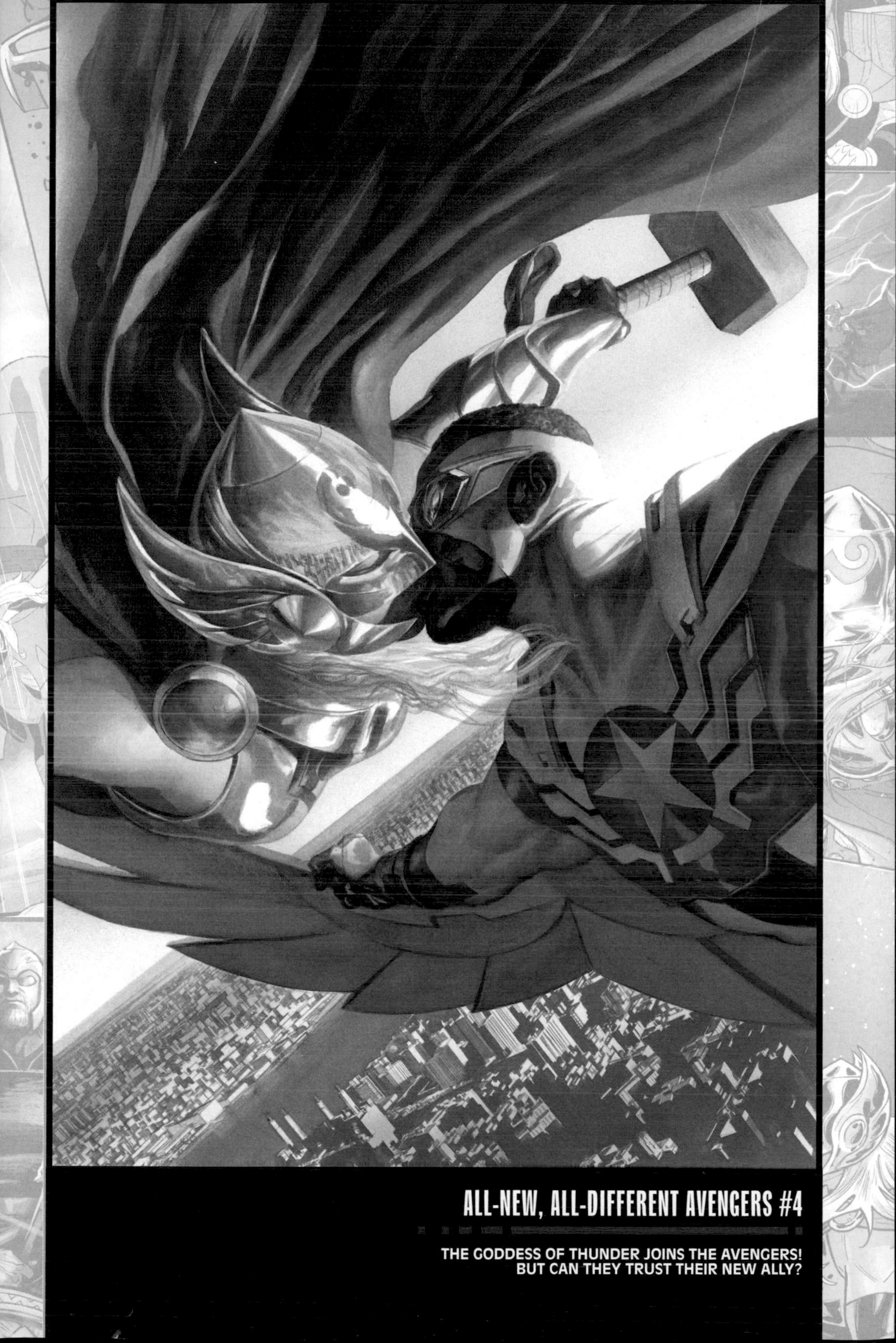

ALL-NEW, ALL-DIFFERENT AVENGERS #4

THE GODDESS OF THUNDER JOINS THE AVENGERS!
BUT CAN THEY TRUST THEIR NEW ALLY?

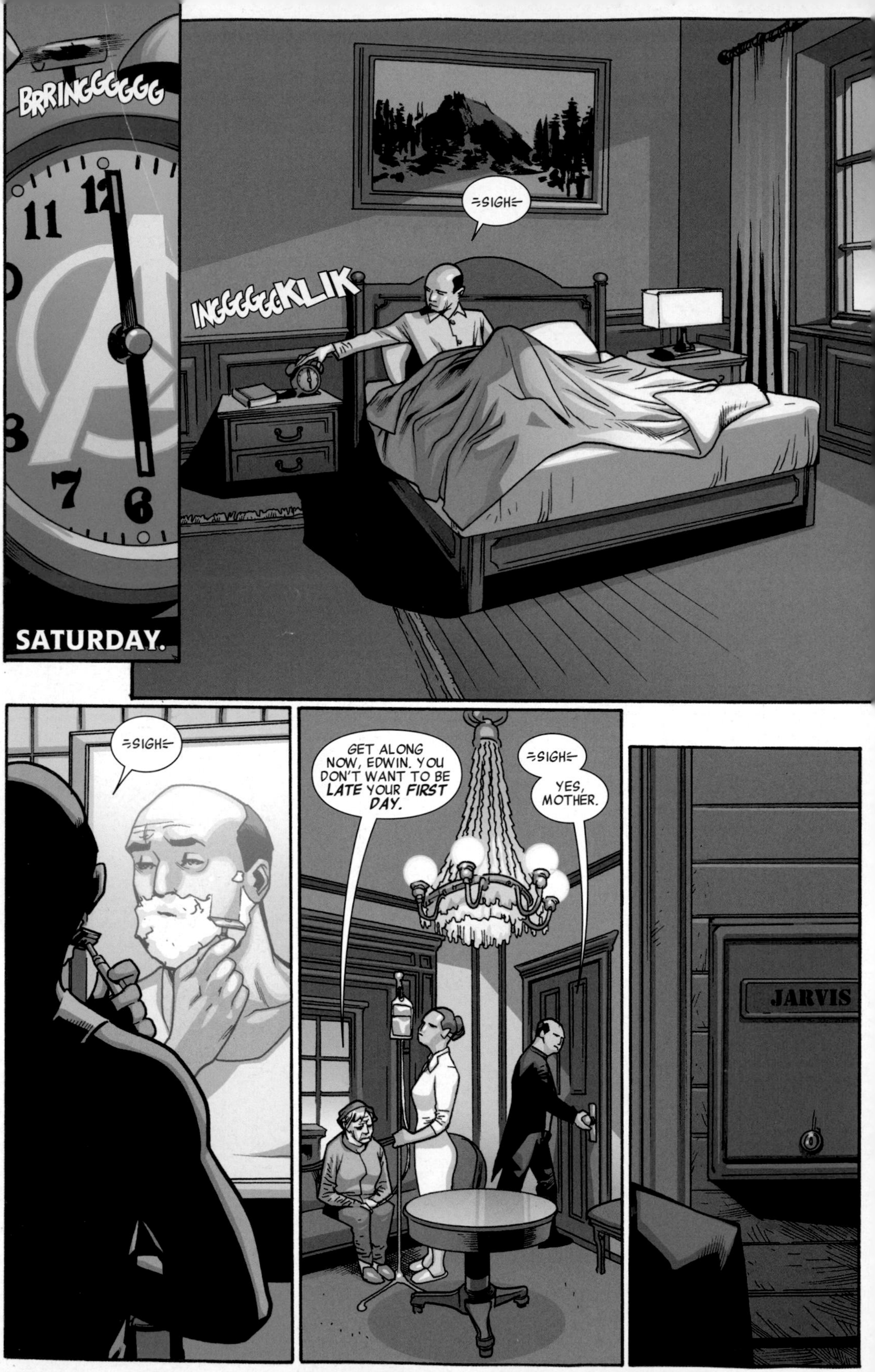
BRRINGGGGGG
SATURDAY.
INGGGGGGKLIK
=SIGH=
=SIGH=
GET ALONG NOW, EDWIN. YOU DON'T WANT TO BE LATE YOUR FIRST DAY.
=SIGH= YES, MOTHER.
JARVIS

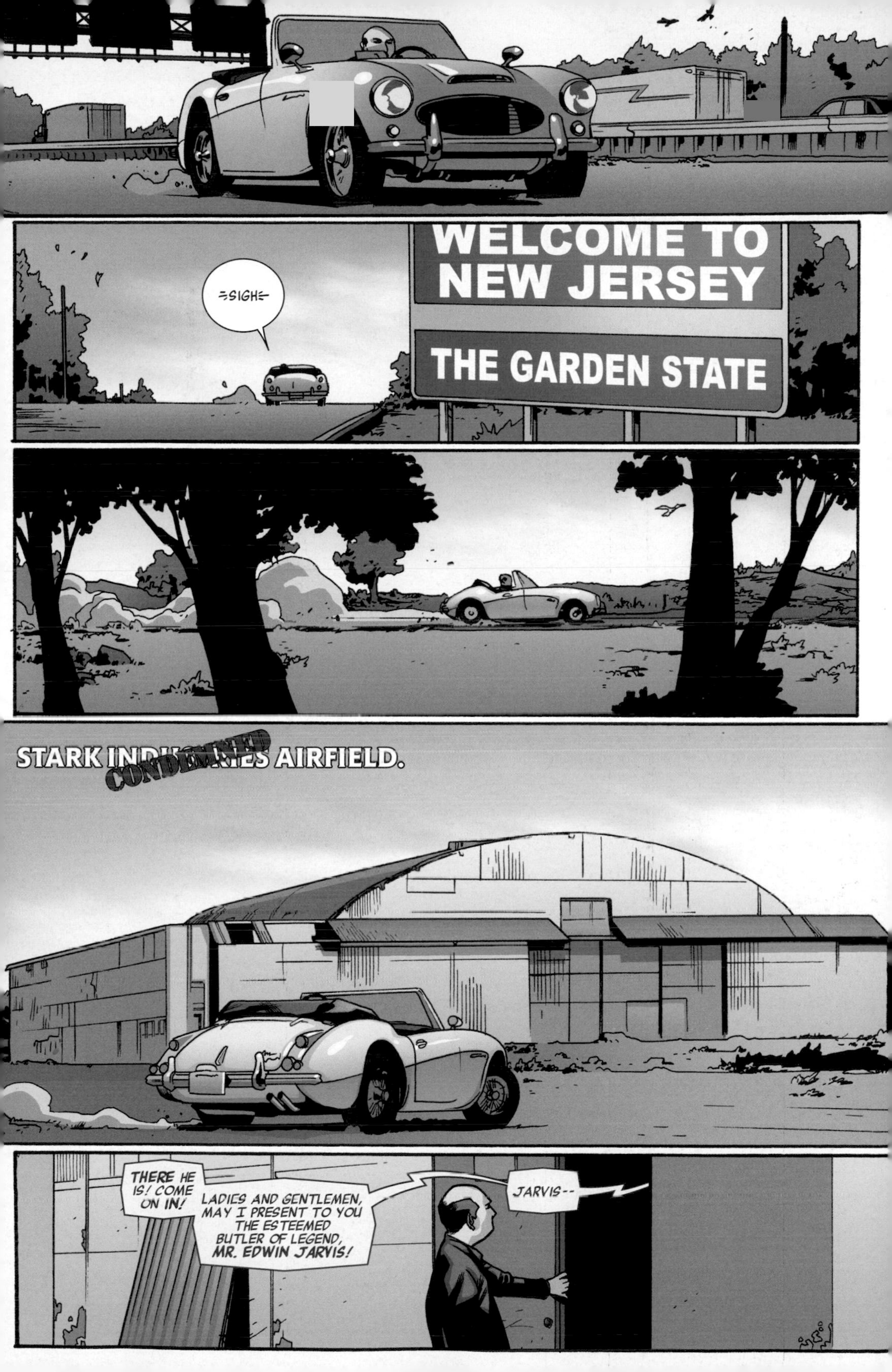
WELCOME TO NEW JERSEY
THE GARDEN STATE
=SIGH=
STARK INDUSTRIES AIRFIELD.
CONDEMNED
THERE HE IS! COME ON IN!
LADIES AND GENTLEMEN, MAY I PRESENT TO YOU THE ESTEEMED BUTLER OF LEGEND, MR. EDWIN JARVIS!
JARVIS--

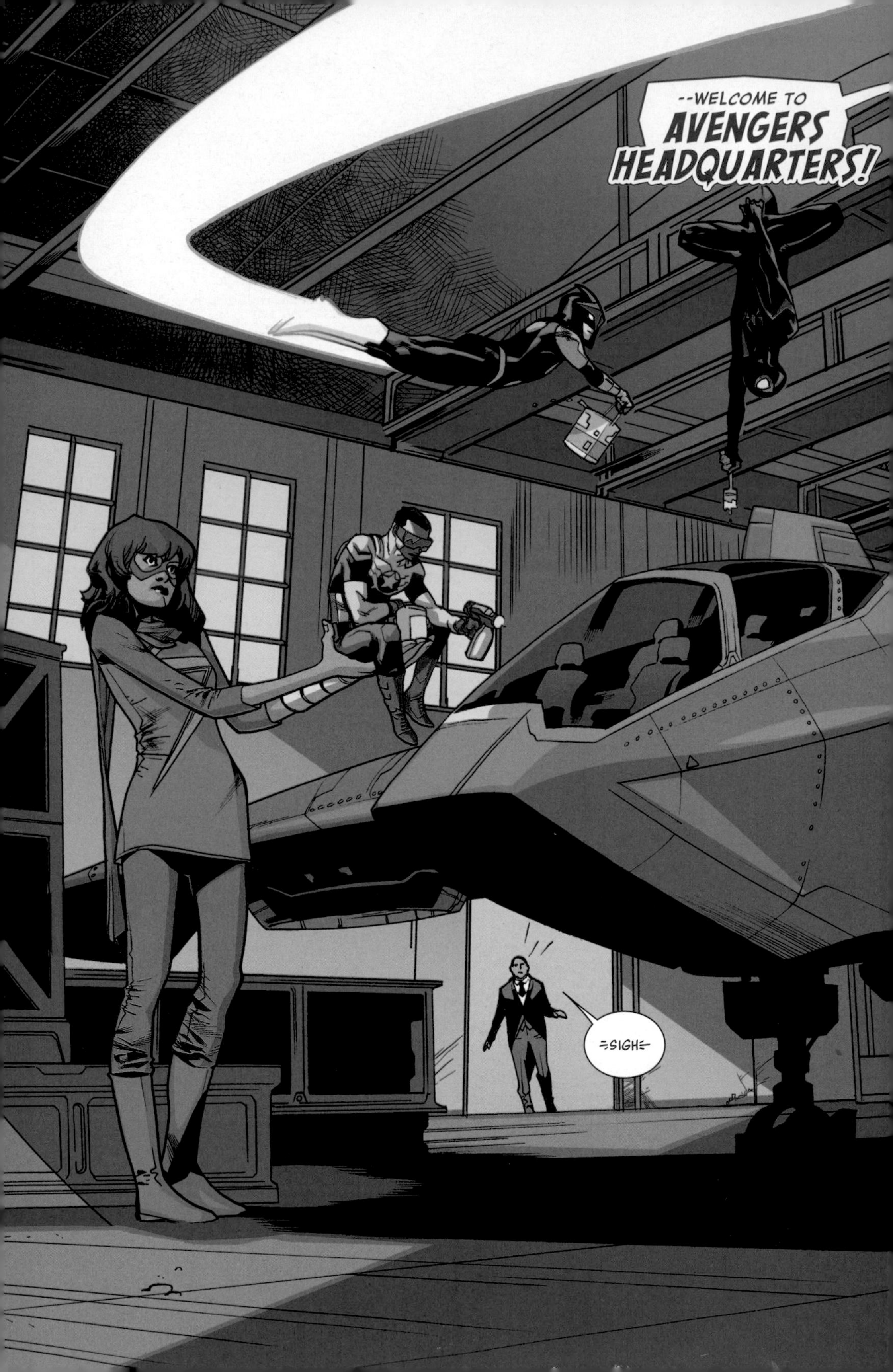
--WELCOME TO
AVENGERS HEADQUARTERS!
=SIGH=

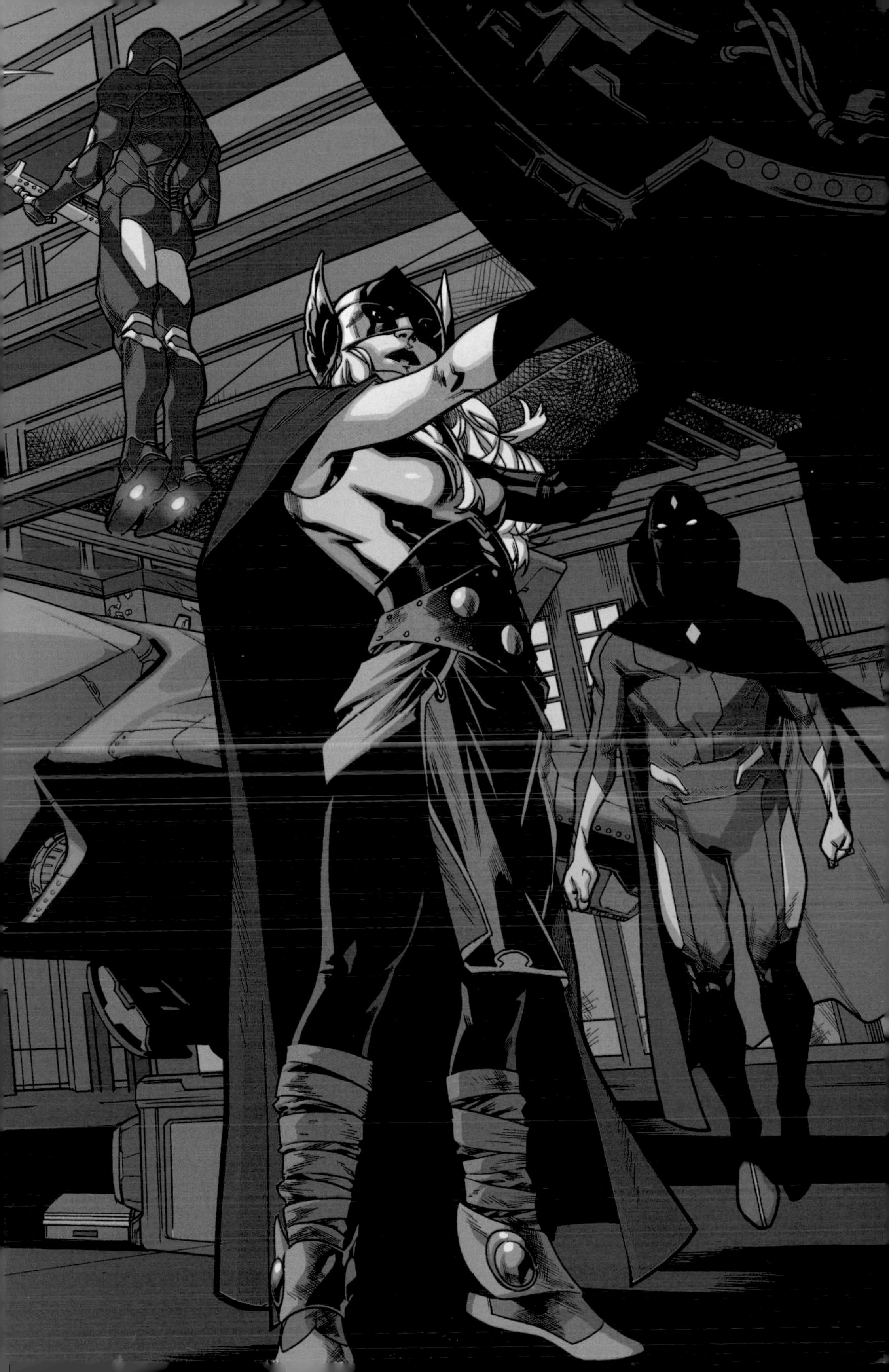

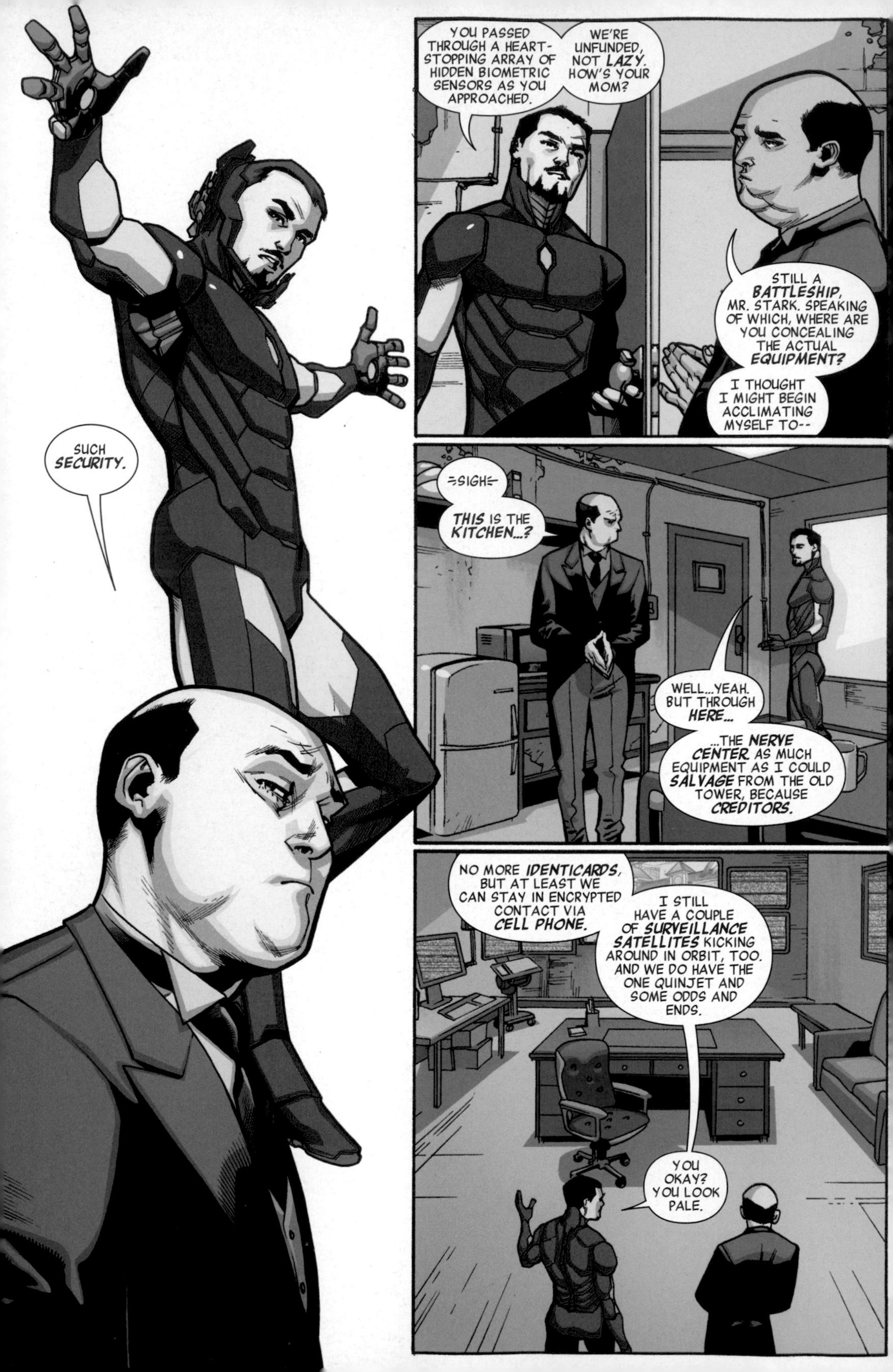

SUCH SECURITY.
YOU PASSED THROUGH A HEART-STOPPING ARRAY OF HIDDEN BIOMETRIC SENSORS AS YOU APPROACHED.
WE'RE UNFUNDED, NOT LAZY. HOW'S YOUR MOM?
STILL A BATTLESHIP, MR. STARK. SPEAKING OF WHICH, WHERE ARE YOU CONCEALING THE ACTUAL EQUIPMENT?
I THOUGHT I MIGHT BEGIN ACCLIMATING MYSELF TO--
=SIGH=
THIS IS THE KITCHEN...?
WELL...YEAH. BUT THROUGH HERE...
...THE NERVE CENTER. AS MUCH EQUIPMENT AS I COULD SALVAGE FROM THE OLD TOWER, BECAUSE CREDITORS.
NO MORE IDENTICARDS, BUT AT LEAST WE CAN STAY IN ENCRYPTED CONTACT VIA CELL PHONE.
I STILL HAVE A COUPLE OF SURVEILLANCE SATELLITES KICKING AROUND IN ORBIT, TOO. AND WE DO HAVE THE ONE QUINJET AND SOME ODDS AND ENDS.
YOU OKAY? YOU LOOK PALE.

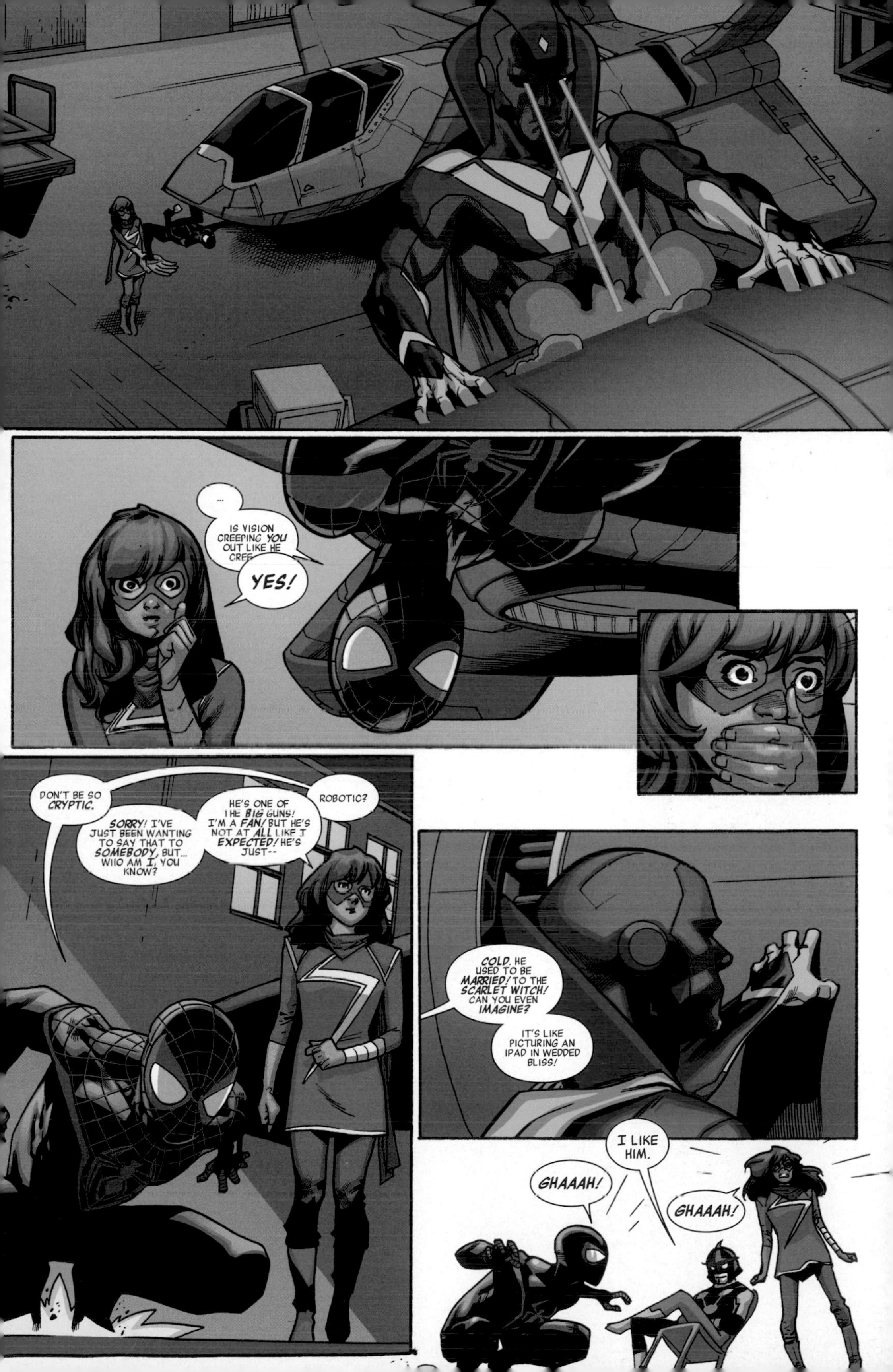
...
IS VISION CREEPING YOU OUT LIKE HE CREE
YES!
DON'T BE SO CRYPTIC.
SORRY! I'VE JUST BEEN WANTING TO SAY THAT TO SOMEBODY, BUT... WHO AM I, YOU KNOW?
HE'S ONE OF THE BIG GUNS! I'M A FAN! BUT HE'S NOT AT ALL LIKE I EXPECTED! HE'S JUST--
ROBOTIC?
COLD. HE USED TO BE MARRIED! TO THE SCARLET WITCH! CAN YOU EVEN IMAGINE?
IT'S LIKE PICTURING AN IPAD IN WEDDED BLISS!
I LIKE HIM.
GHAAAH!
GHAAAH!

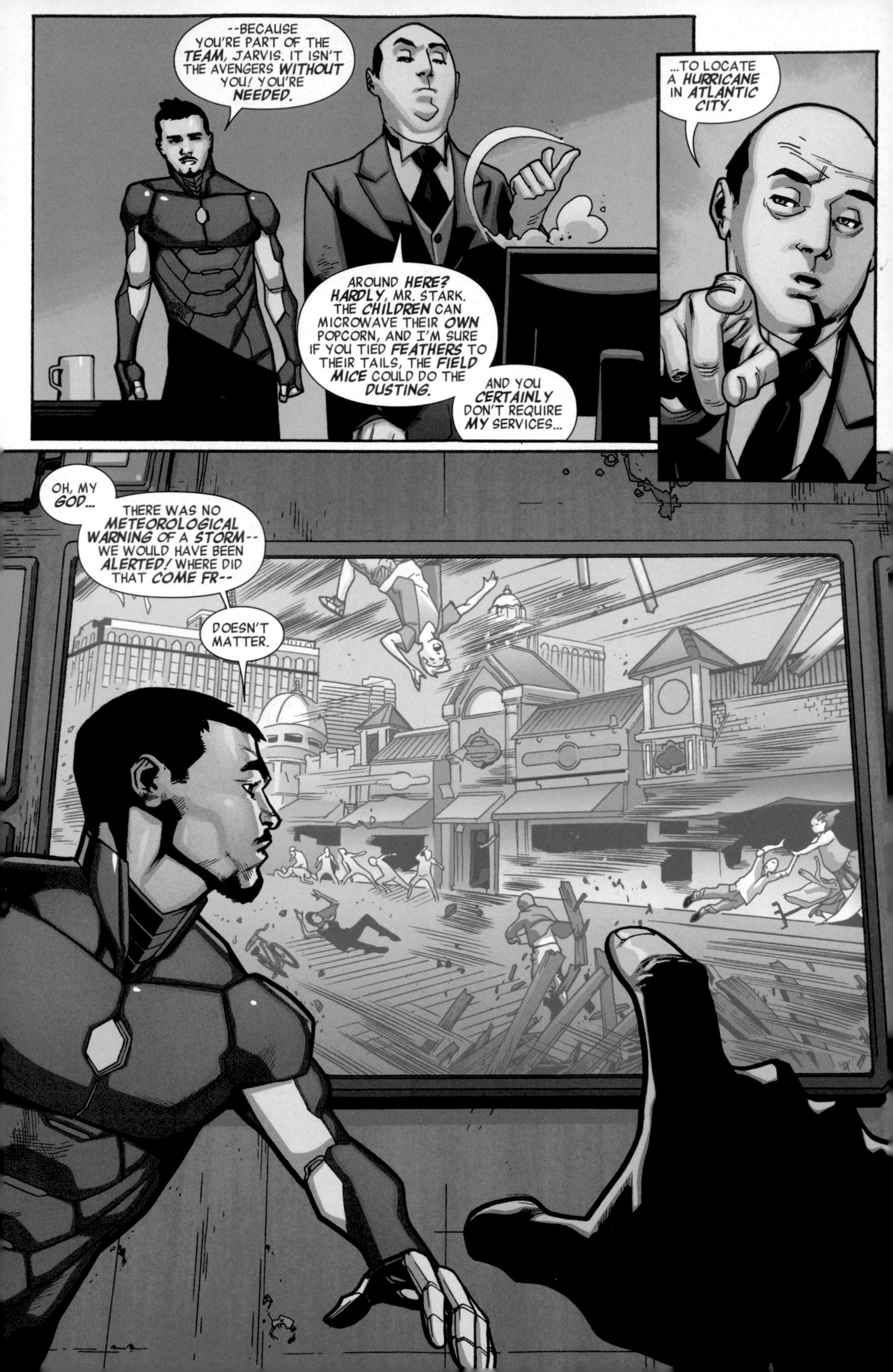
--BECAUSE YOU'RE PART OF THE TEAM, JARVIS. IT ISN'T THE AVENGERS WITHOUT YOU! YOU'RE NEEDED.
AROUND HERE? HARDLY, MR. STARK. THE CHILDREN CAN MICROWAVE THEIR OWN POPCORN, AND I'M SURE IF YOU TIED FEATHERS TO THEIR TAILS, THE FIELD MICE COULD DO THE DUSTING.
AND YOU CERTAINLY DON'T REQUIRE MY SERVICES...
...TO LOCATE A HURRICANE IN ATLANTIC CITY.
OH, MY GOD...
THERE WAS NO METEOROLOGICAL WARNING OF A STORM--WE WOULD HAVE BEEN ALERTED! WHERE DID THAT COME FR--
DOESN'T MATTER.

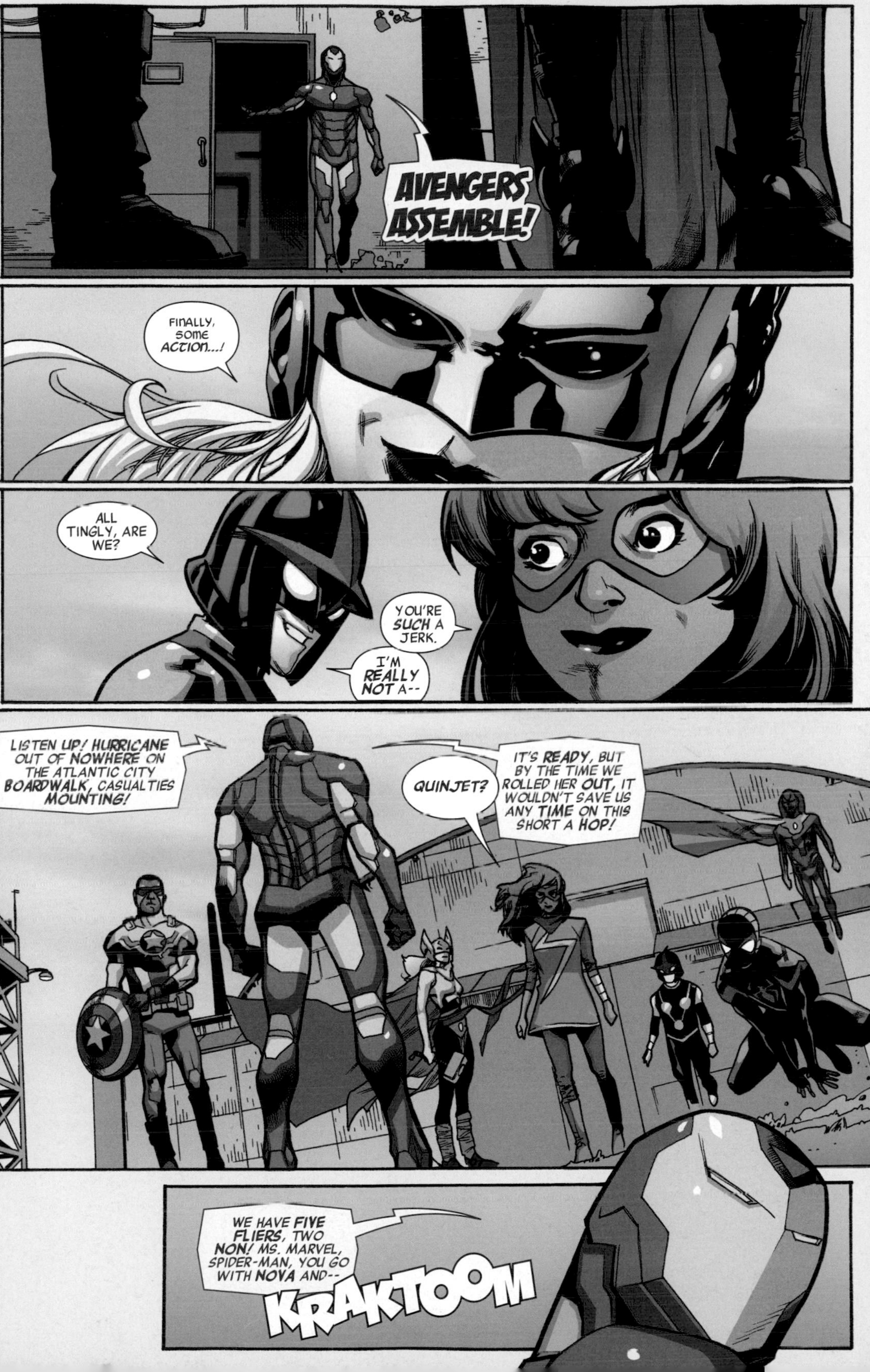
AVENGERS ASSEMBLE!
FINALLY, SOME ACTION...!
ALL TINGLY, ARE WE?
YOU'RE SUCH A JERK.
I'M REALLY NOT A--
LISTEN UP! HURRICANE OUT OF NOWHERE ON THE ATLANTIC CITY BOARDWALK, CASUALTIES MOUNTING!
QUINJET?
IT'S READY, BUT BY THE TIME WE ROLLED HER OUT, IT WOULDN'T SAVE US ANY TIME ON THIS SHORT A HOP!
WE HAVE FIVE FLIERS, TWO NON! MS. MARVEL, SPIDER-MAN, YOU GO WITH NOVA AND--
KRAKTOOM

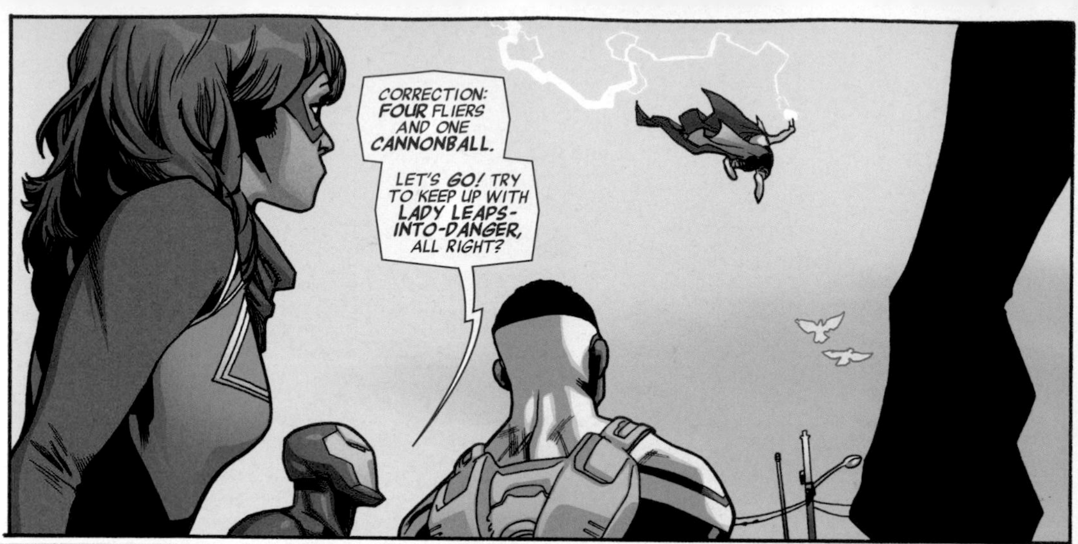
CORRECTION: FOUR FLIERS AND ONE CANNONBALL.
LET'S GO! TRY TO KEEP UP WITH LADY LEAPS-INTO-DANGER, ALL RIGHT?

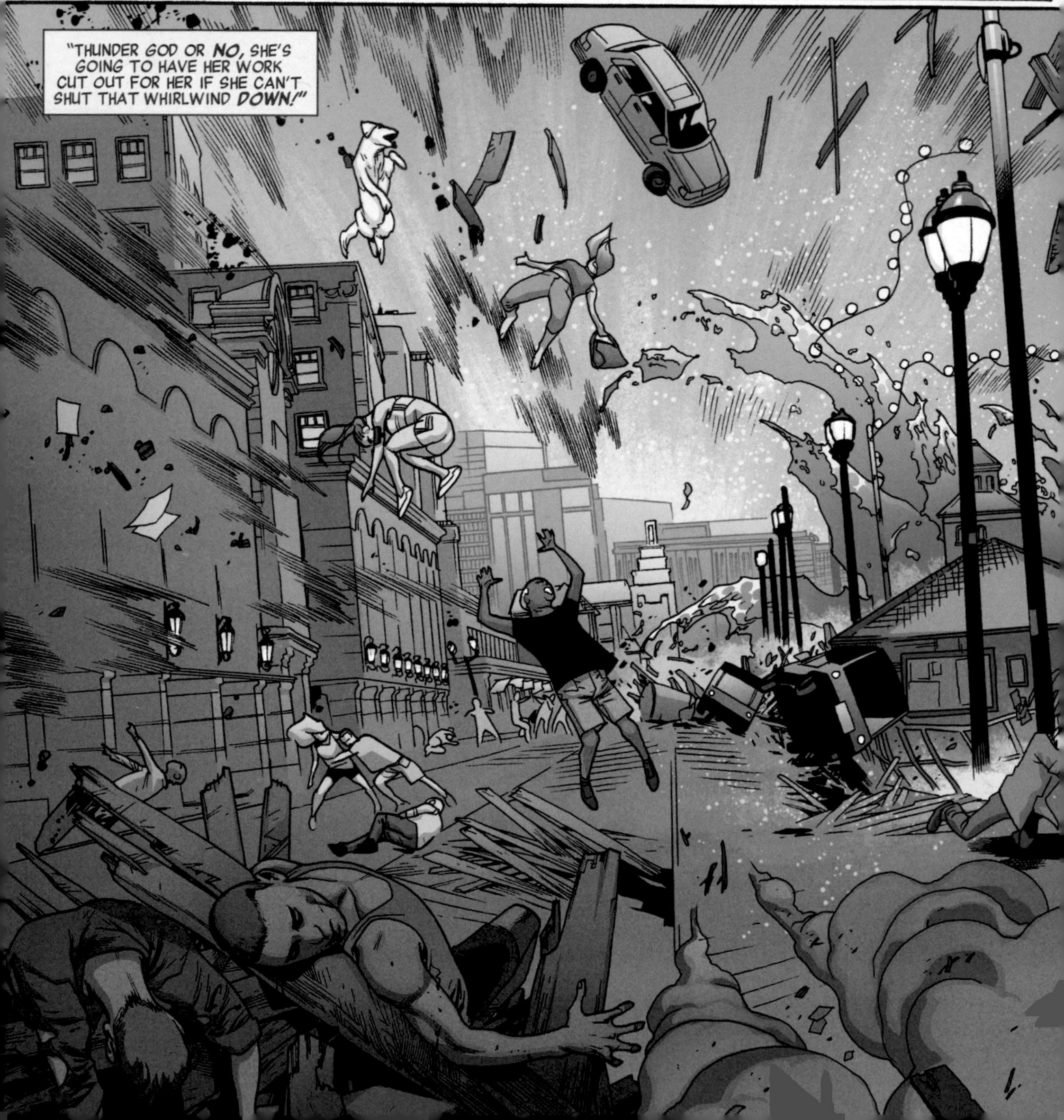
"THUNDER GOD OR NO, SHE'S GOING TO HAVE HER WORK CUT OUT FOR HER IF SHE CAN'T SHUT THAT WHIRLWIND DOWN!"

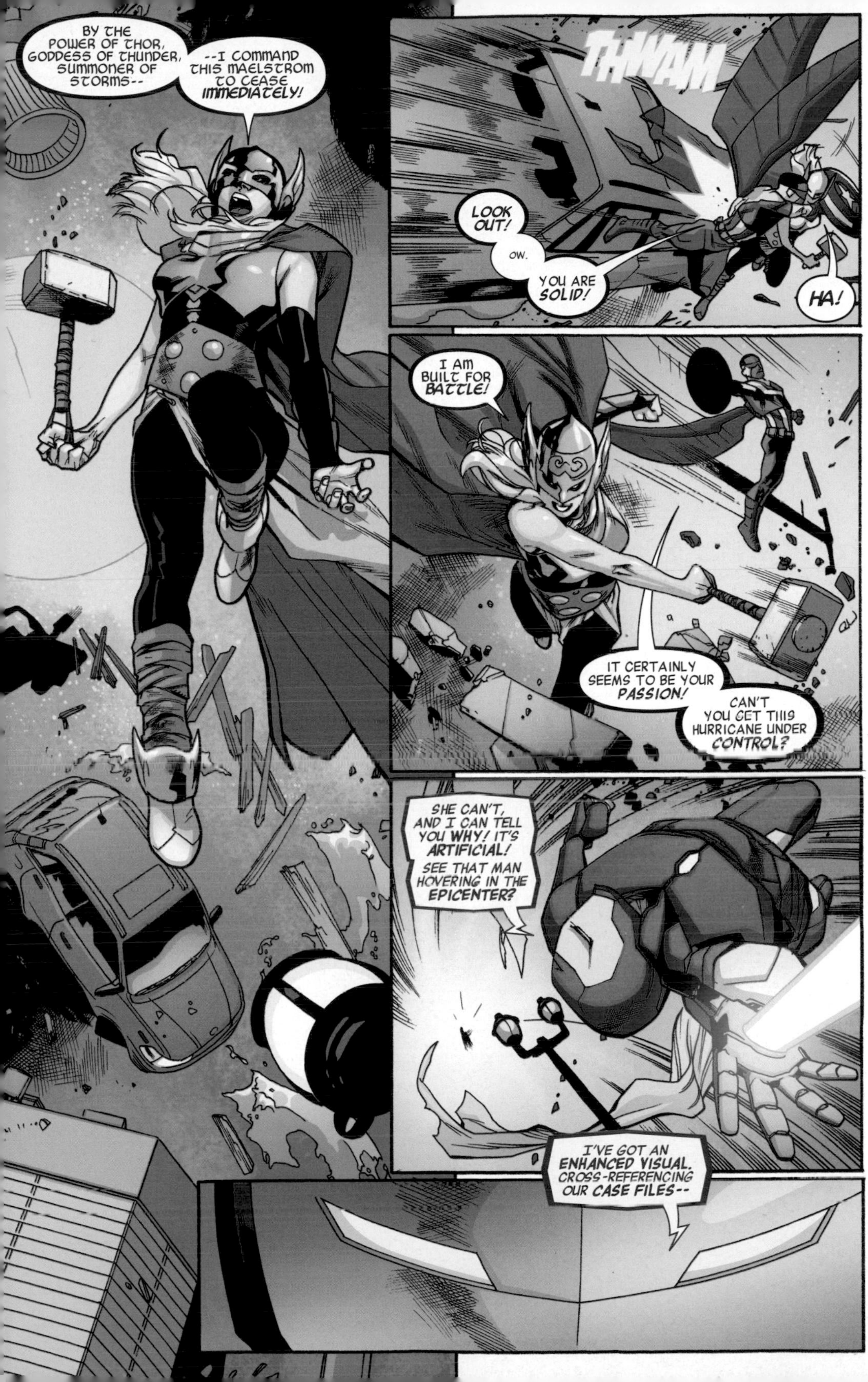
BY THE POWER OF THOR, GODDESS OF THUNDER, SUMMONER OF STORMS--
--I COMMAND THIS MAELSTROM TO CEASE IMMEDIATELY!
THWAM
LOOK OUT!
OW.
YOU ARE SOLID!
HA!
I AM BUILT FOR BATTLE!
IT CERTAINLY SEEMS TO BE YOUR PASSION!
CAN'T YOU GET THIS HURRICANE UNDER CONTROL?
SHE CAN'T, AND I CAN TELL YOU WHY! IT'S ARTIFICIAL!
SEE THAT MAN HOVERING IN THE EPICENTER?
I'VE GOT AN ENHANCED VISUAL. CROSS-REFERENCING OUR CASE FILES--

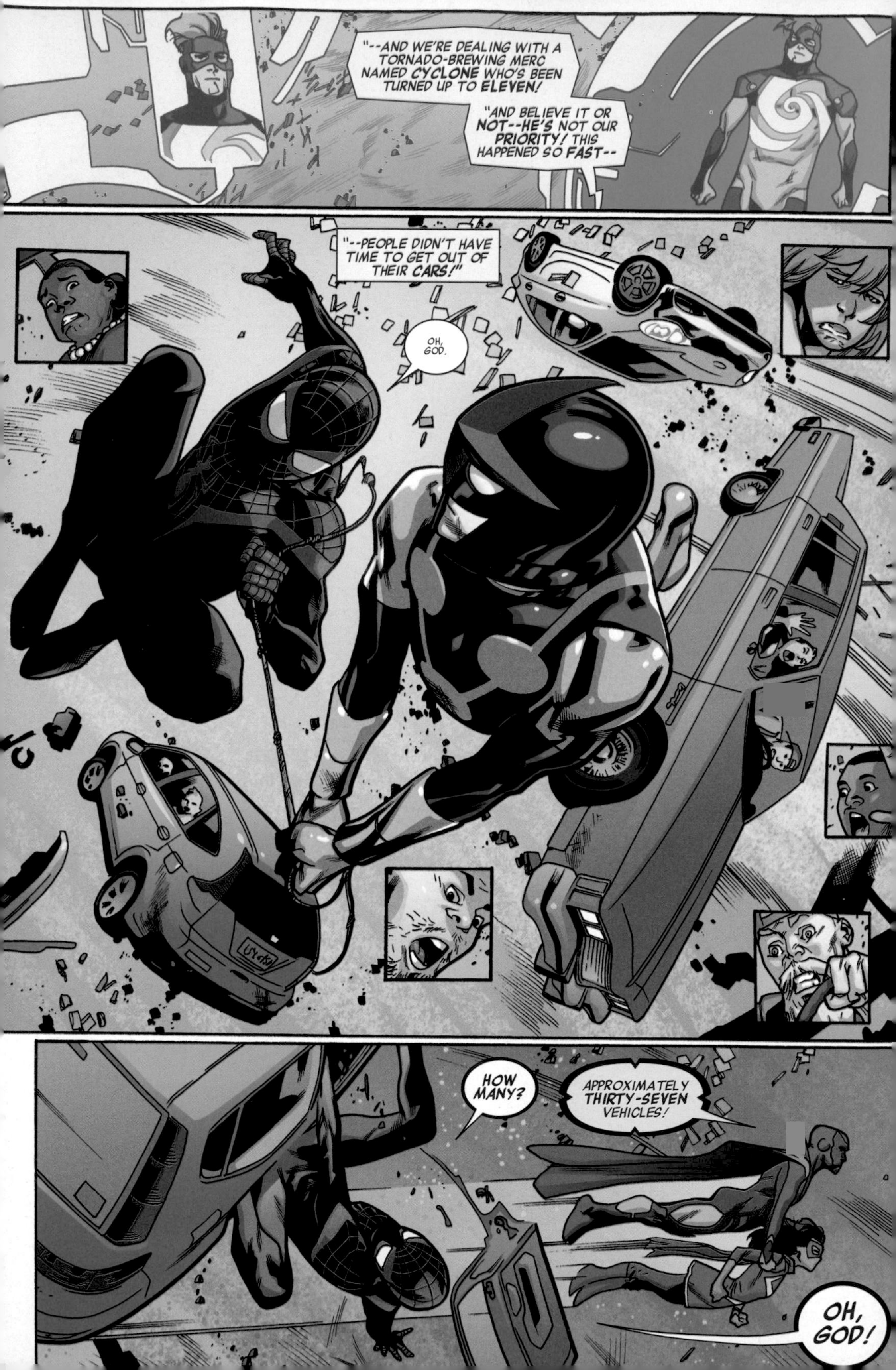
"--AND WE'RE DEALING WITH A TORNADO-BREWING MERC NAMED CYCLONE WHO'S BEEN TURNED UP TO ELEVEN!
"AND BELIEVE IT OR NOT--HE'S NOT OUR PRIORITY! THIS HAPPENED SO FAST--
"--PEOPLE DIDN'T HAVE TIME TO GET OUT OF THEIR CARS!"
OH, GOD.
HOW MANY?
APPROXIMATELY THIRTY-SEVEN VEHICLES!
OH, GOD!

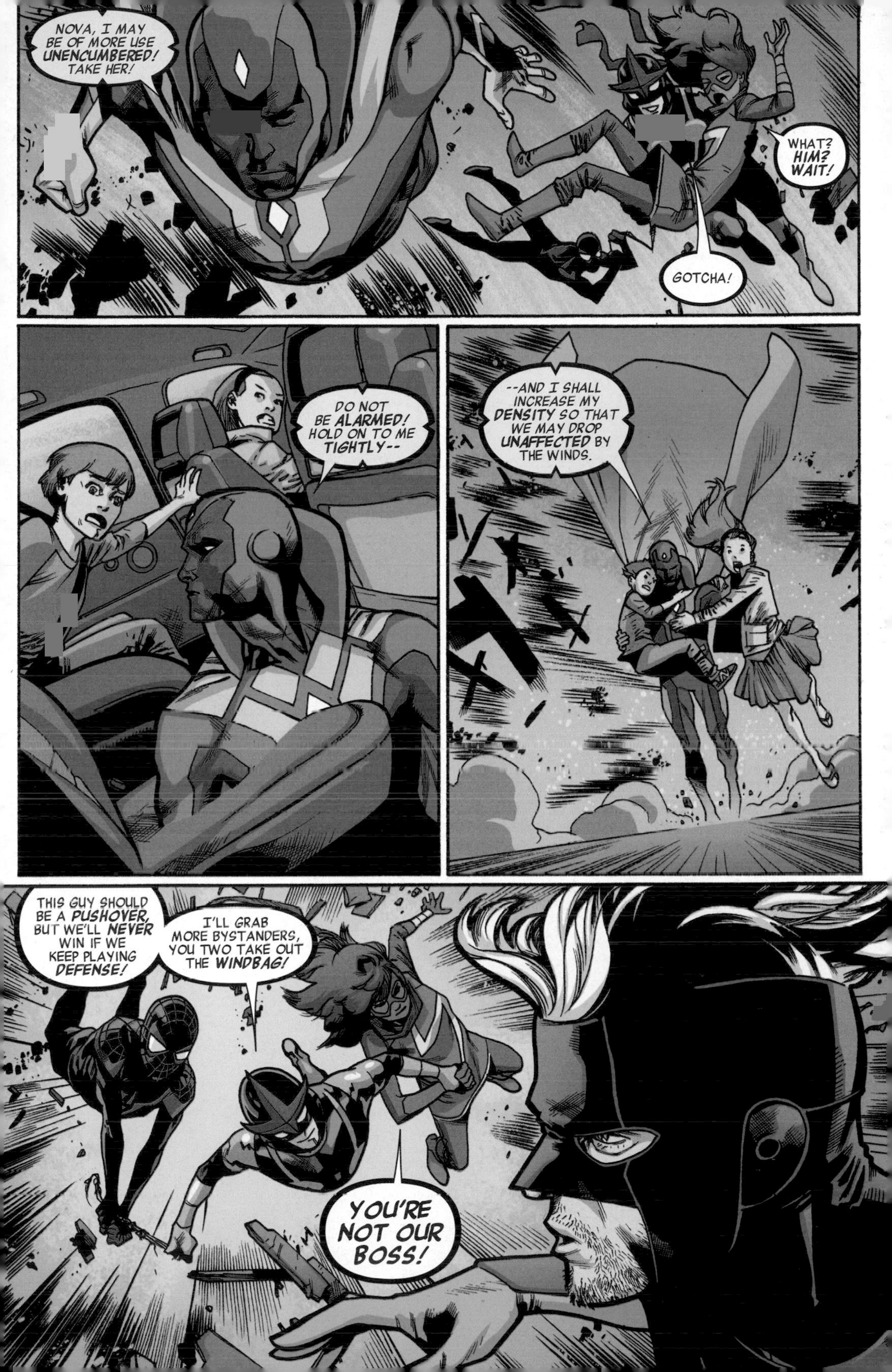
NOVA, I MAY BE OF MORE USE UNENCUMBERED! TAKE HER!
WHAT? HIM? WAIT!
GOTCHA!
DO NOT BE ALARMED! HOLD ON TO ME TIGHTLY--
--AND I SHALL INCREASE MY DENSITY SO THAT WE MAY DROP UNAFFECTED BY THE WINDS.
THIS GUY SHOULD BE A PUSHOVER, BUT WE'LL NEVER WIN IF WE KEEP PLAYING DEFENSE!
I'LL GRAB MORE BYSTANDERS, YOU TWO TAKE OUT THE WINDBAG!
YOU'RE NOT OUR BOSS!

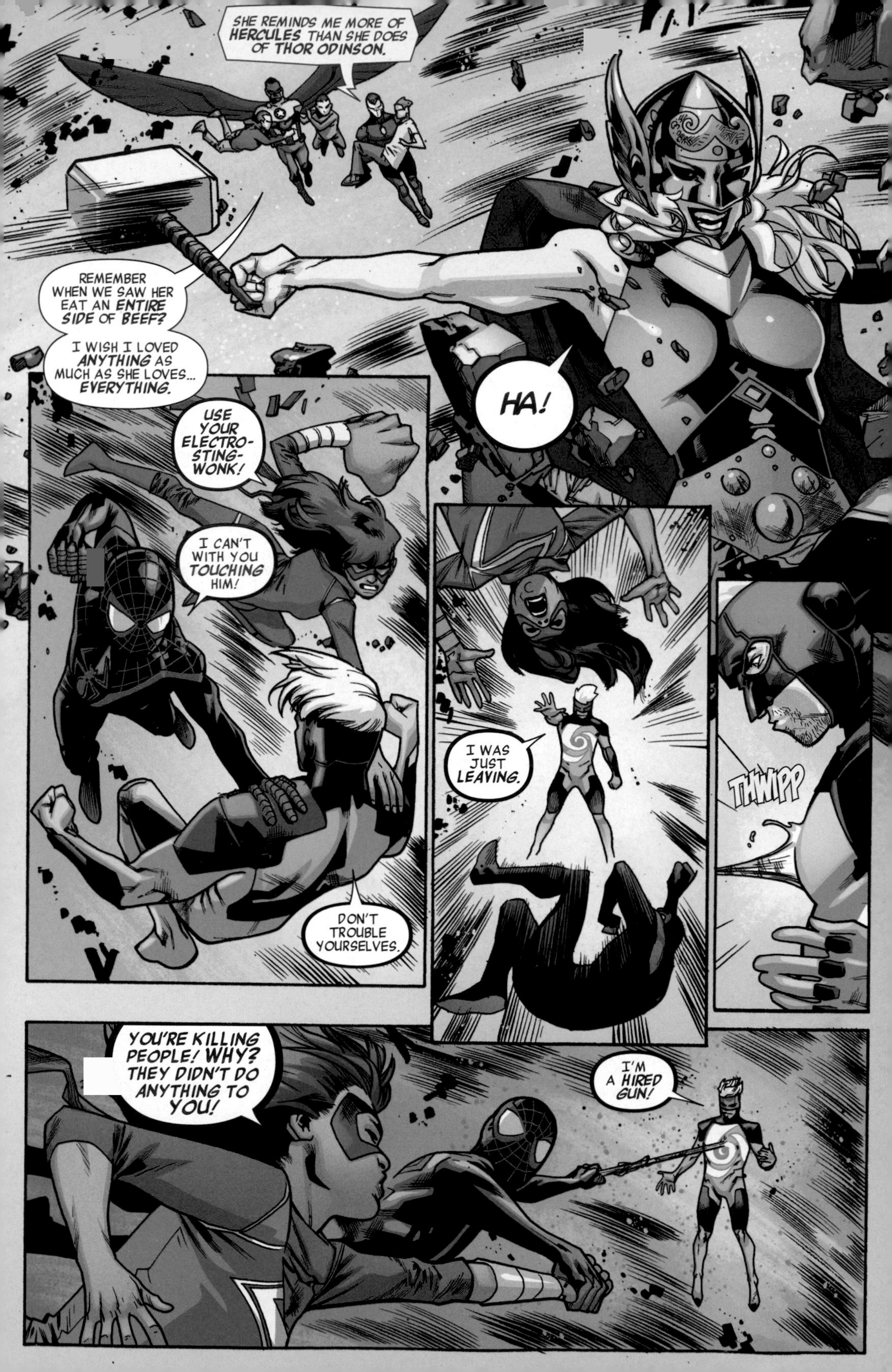
SHE REMINDS ME MORE OF HERCULES THAN SHE DOES OF THOR ODINSON.
REMEMBER WHEN WE SAW HER EAT AN ENTIRE SIDE OF BEEF?
I WISH I LOVED ANYTHING AS MUCH AS SHE LOVES... EVERYTHING.
HA!
USE YOUR ELECTRO-STING-WONK!
I CAN'T WITH YOU TOUCHING HIM!
DON'T TROUBLE YOURSELVES.
I WAS JUST LEAVING.
THWIPP
YOU'RE KILLING PEOPLE! WHY? THEY DIDN'T DO ANYTHING TO YOU!
I'M A HIRED GUN!

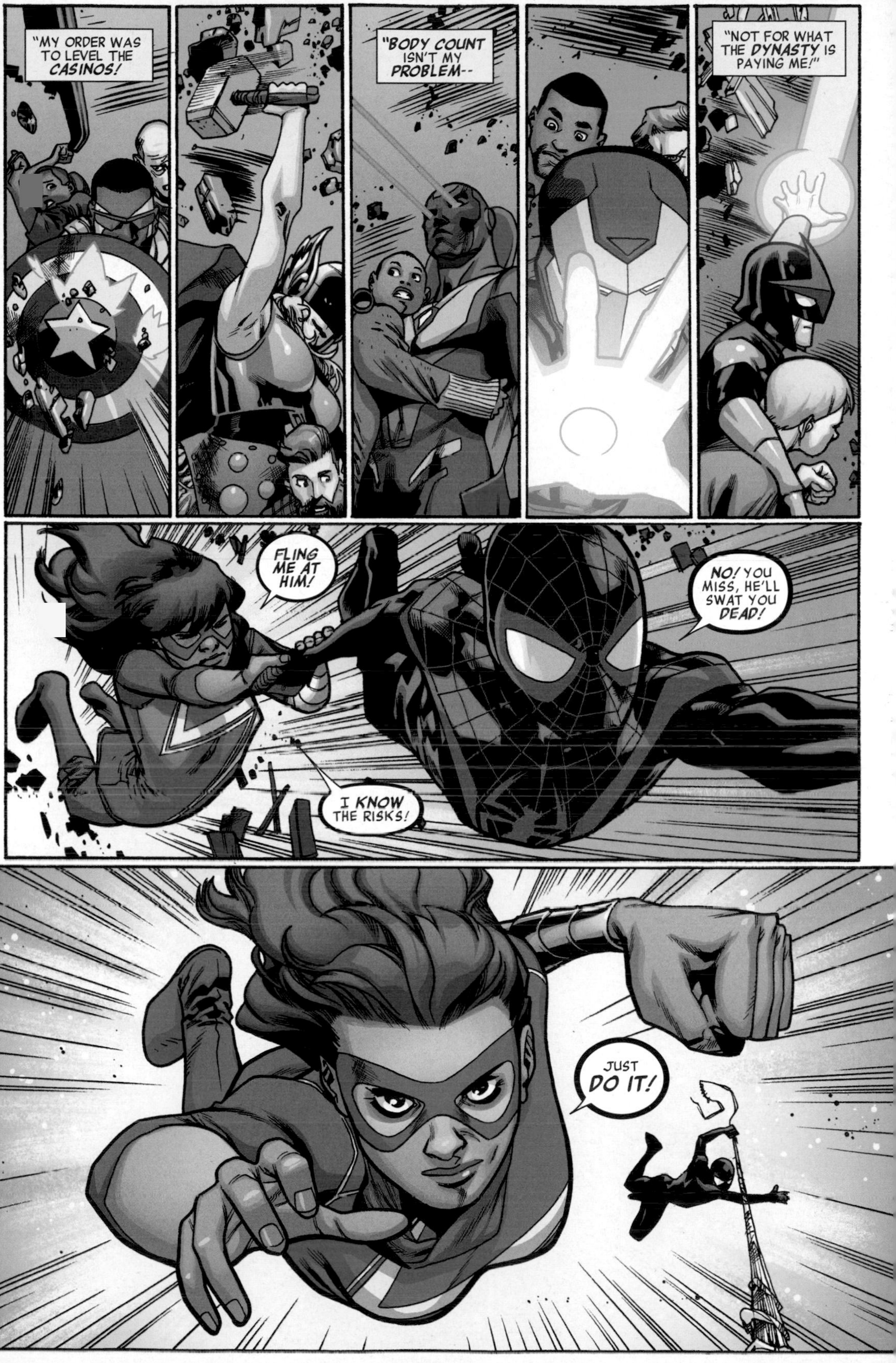
"MY ORDER WAS TO LEVEL THE CASINOS!
"BODY COUNT ISN'T MY PROBLEM--
"NOT FOR WHAT THE DYNASTY IS PAYING ME!"
FLING ME AT HIM!
NO! YOU MISS, HE'LL SWAT YOU DEAD!
I KNOW THE RISKS!
JUST DO IT!

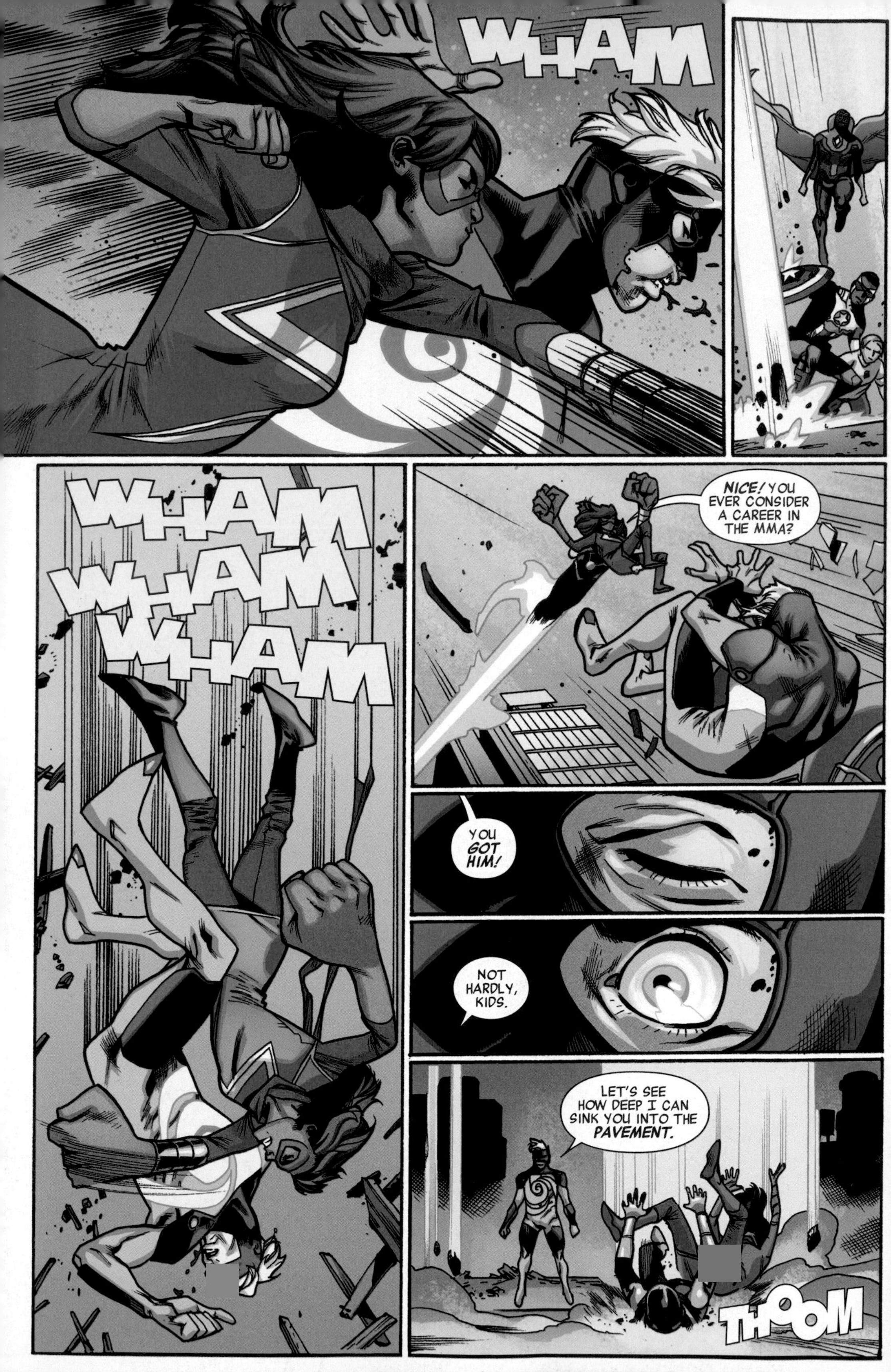
WHAM
WHAM
WHAM
WHAM
NICE! YOU EVER CONSIDER A CAREER IN THE MMA?
YOU GOT HIM!
NOT HARDLY, KIDS.
LET'S SEE HOW DEEP I CAN SINK YOU INTO THE PAVEMENT.
THOOOM

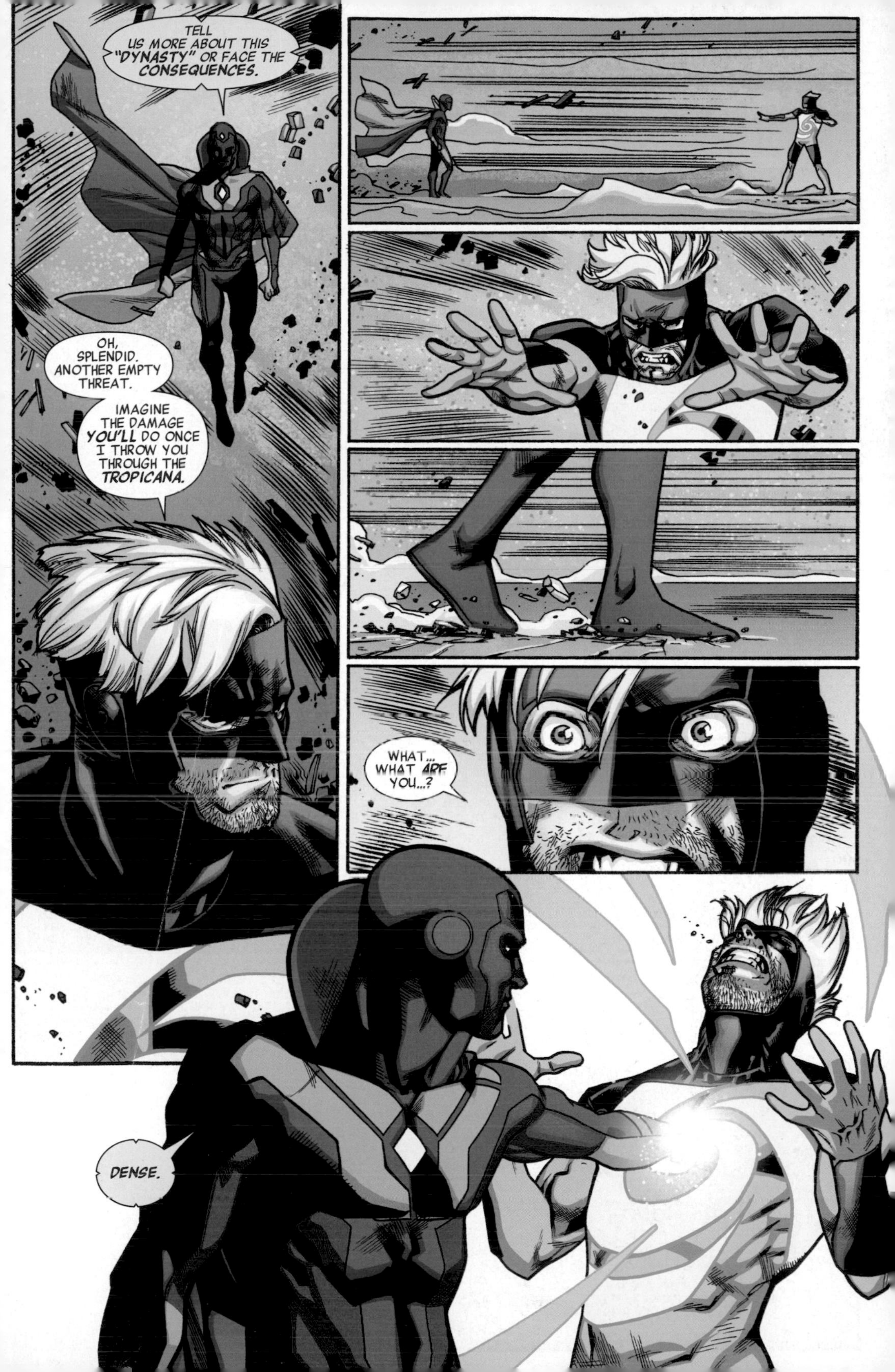
TELL US MORE ABOUT THIS "DYNASTY" OR FACE THE CONSEQUENCES.
OH, SPLENDID. ANOTHER EMPTY THREAT.
IMAGINE THE DAMAGE YOU'LL DO ONCE I THROW YOU THROUGH THE TROPICANA.
WHAT... WHAT ARE YOU...?
DENSE.

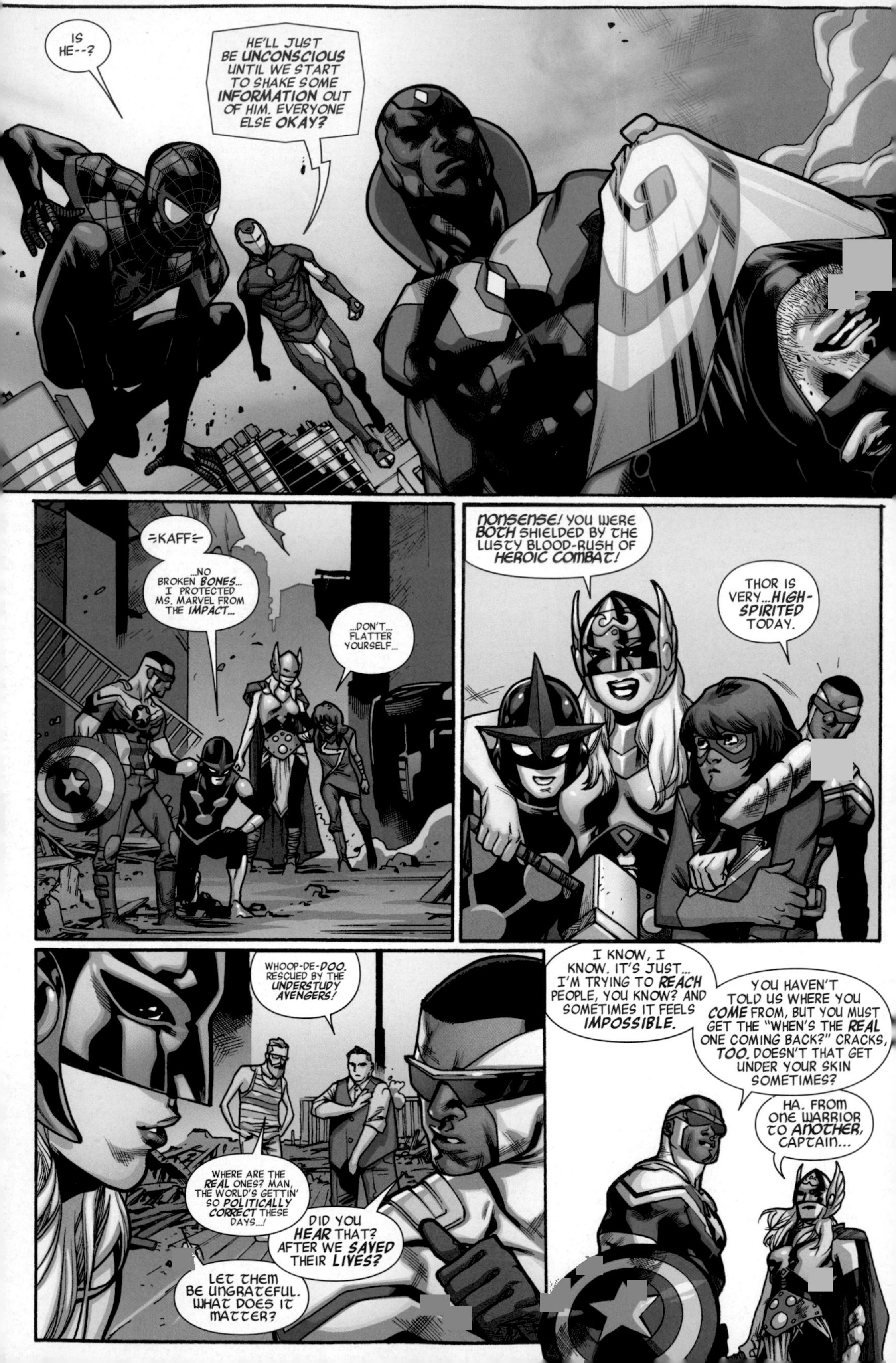
IS HE--?
HE'LL JUST BE UNCONSCIOUS UNTIL WE START TO SHAKE SOME INFORMATION OUT OF HIM. EVERYONE ELSE OKAY?
=KAFF=
...NO BROKEN BONES... I PROTECTED MS. MARVEL FROM THE IMPACT...
...DON'T... FLATTER YOURSELF...
NONSENSE! YOU WERE BOTH SHIELDED BY THE LUSTY BLOOD-RUSH OF HEROIC COMBAT!
THOR IS VERY...HIGH-SPIRITED TODAY.
WHOOP-DE-DOO. RESCUED BY THE UNDERSTUDY AVENGERS!
WHERE ARE THE REAL ONES? MAN, THE WORLD'S GETTIN' SO POLITICALLY CORRECT THESE DAYS...!
DID YOU HEAR THAT? AFTER WE SAVED THEIR LIVES?
LET THEM BE UNGRATEFUL. WHAT DOES IT MATTER?
I KNOW, I KNOW. IT'S JUST... I'M TRYING TO REACH PEOPLE, YOU KNOW? AND SOMETIMES IT FEELS IMPOSSIBLE.
YOU HAVEN'T TOLD US WHERE YOU COME FROM, BUT YOU MUST GET THE "WHEN'S THE REAL ONE COMING BACK?" CRACKS, TOO. DOESN'T THAT GET UNDER YOUR SKIN SOMETIMES?
HA. FROM ONE WARRIOR TO ANOTHER, CAPTAIN...

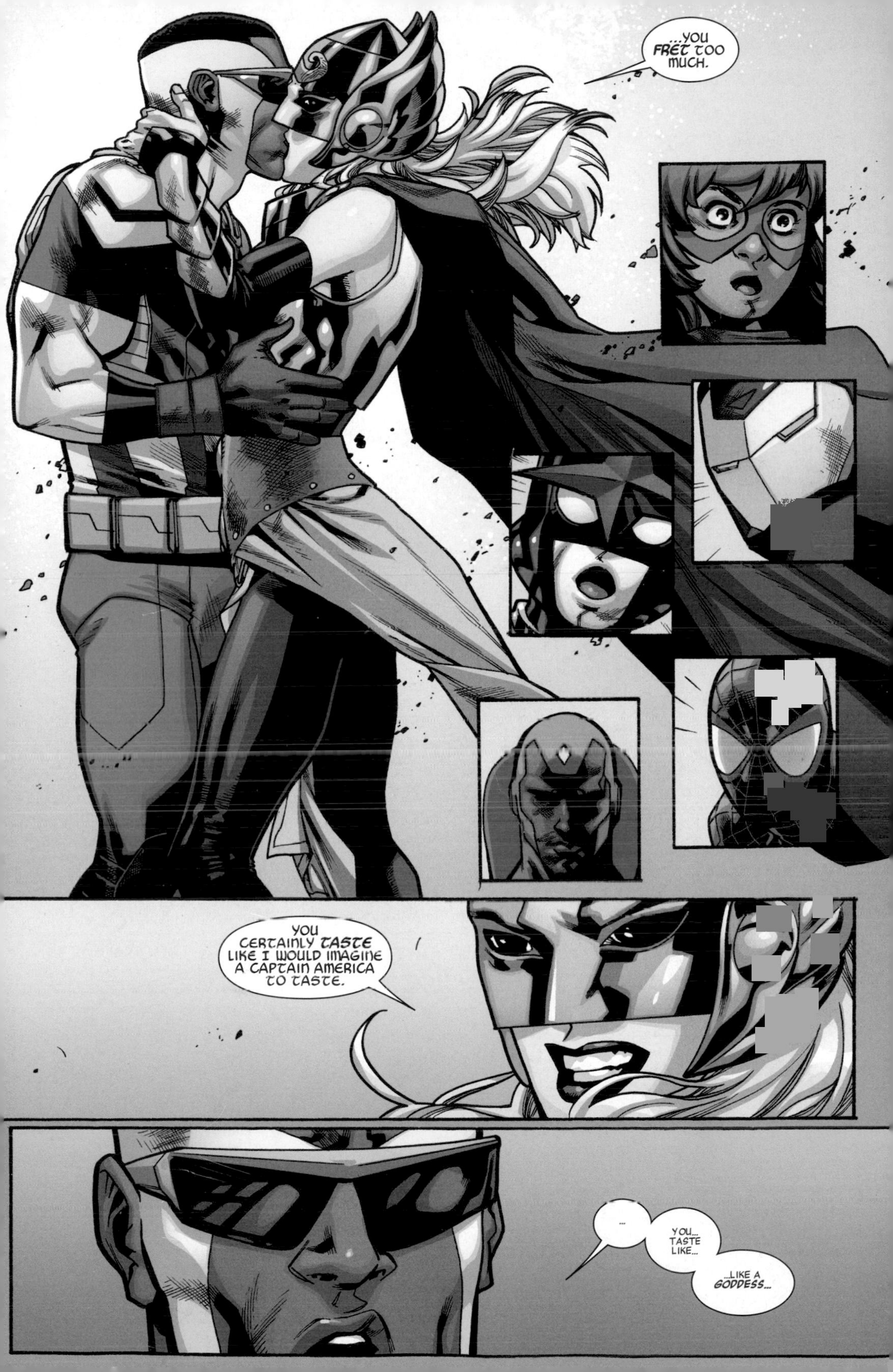
...YOU FRET TOO MUCH.
YOU CERTAINLY TASTE LIKE I WOULD IMAGINE A CAPTAIN AMERICA TO TASTE.
...
YOU... TASTE LIKE...
...LIKE A GODDESS...

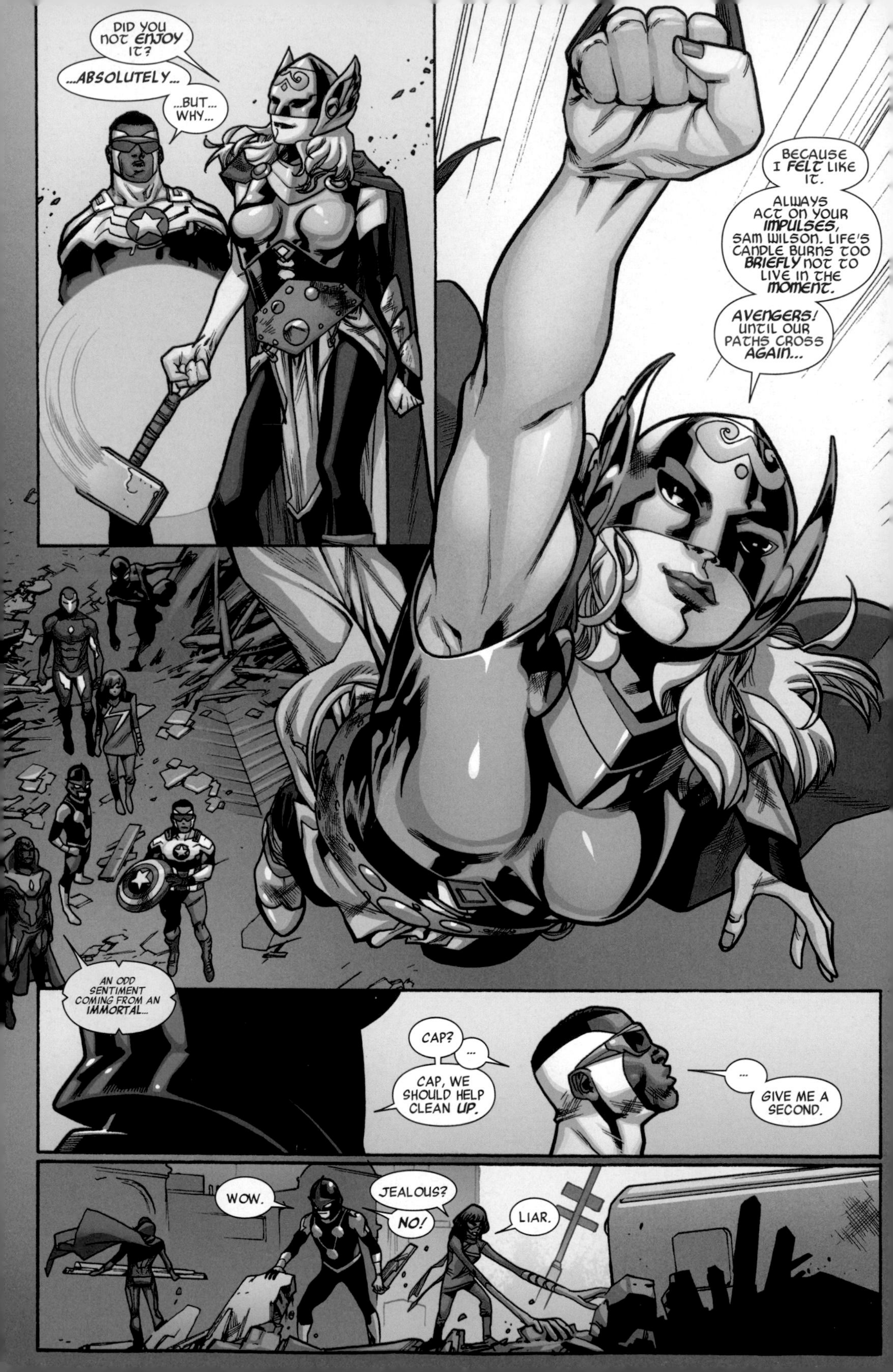
DID YOU NOT ENJOY IT?
...ABSOLUTELY...
...BUT... WHY...
BECAUSE I FELT LIKE IT.
ALWAYS ACT ON YOUR IMPULSES, SAM WILSON. LIFE'S CANDLE BURNS TOO BRIEFLY NOT TO LIVE IN THE MOMENT.
AVENGERS! UNTIL OUR PATHS CROSS AGAIN...
AN ODD SENTIMENT COMING FROM AN IMMORTAL...
CAP?
...
CAP, WE SHOULD HELP CLEAN UP.
...
GIVE ME A SECOND.
WOW.
JEALOUS?
NO!
LIAR.

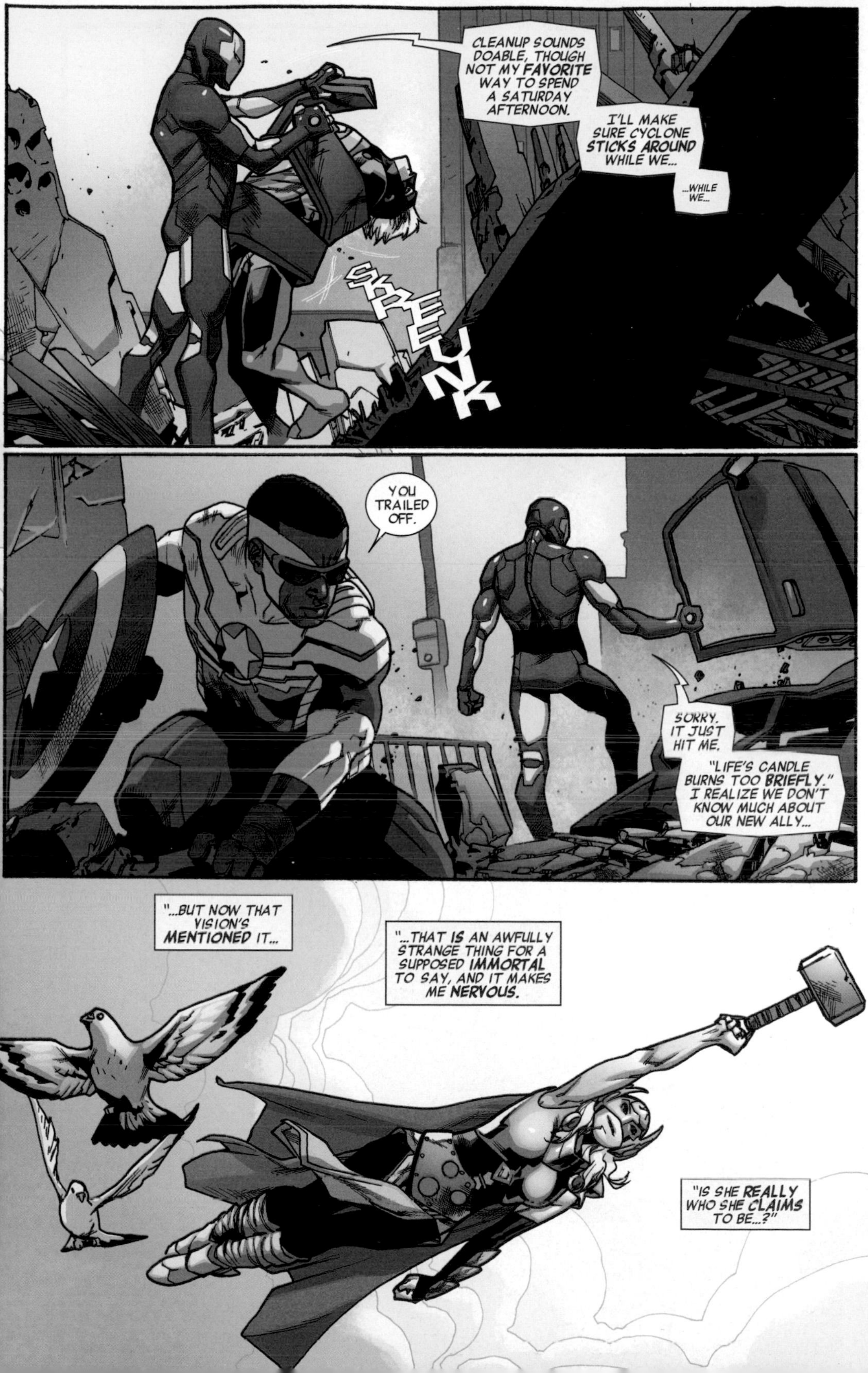
CLEANUP SOUNDS DOABLE, THOUGH NOT MY FAVORITE WAY TO SPEND A SATURDAY AFTERNOON.
I'LL MAKE SURE CYCLONE STICKS AROUND WHILE WE...
...WHILE WE...
SKREEUNK
YOU TRAILED OFF.
SORRY. IT JUST HIT ME.
"LIFE'S CANDLE BURNS TOO BRIEFLY." I REALIZE WE DON'T KNOW MUCH ABOUT OUR NEW ALLY...
"...BUT NOW THAT VISION'S MENTIONED IT...
"...THAT IS AN AWFULLY STRANGE THING FOR A SUPPOSED IMMORTAL TO SAY, AND IT MAKES ME NERVOUS.
"IS SHE REALLY WHO SHE CLAIMS TO BE...?"

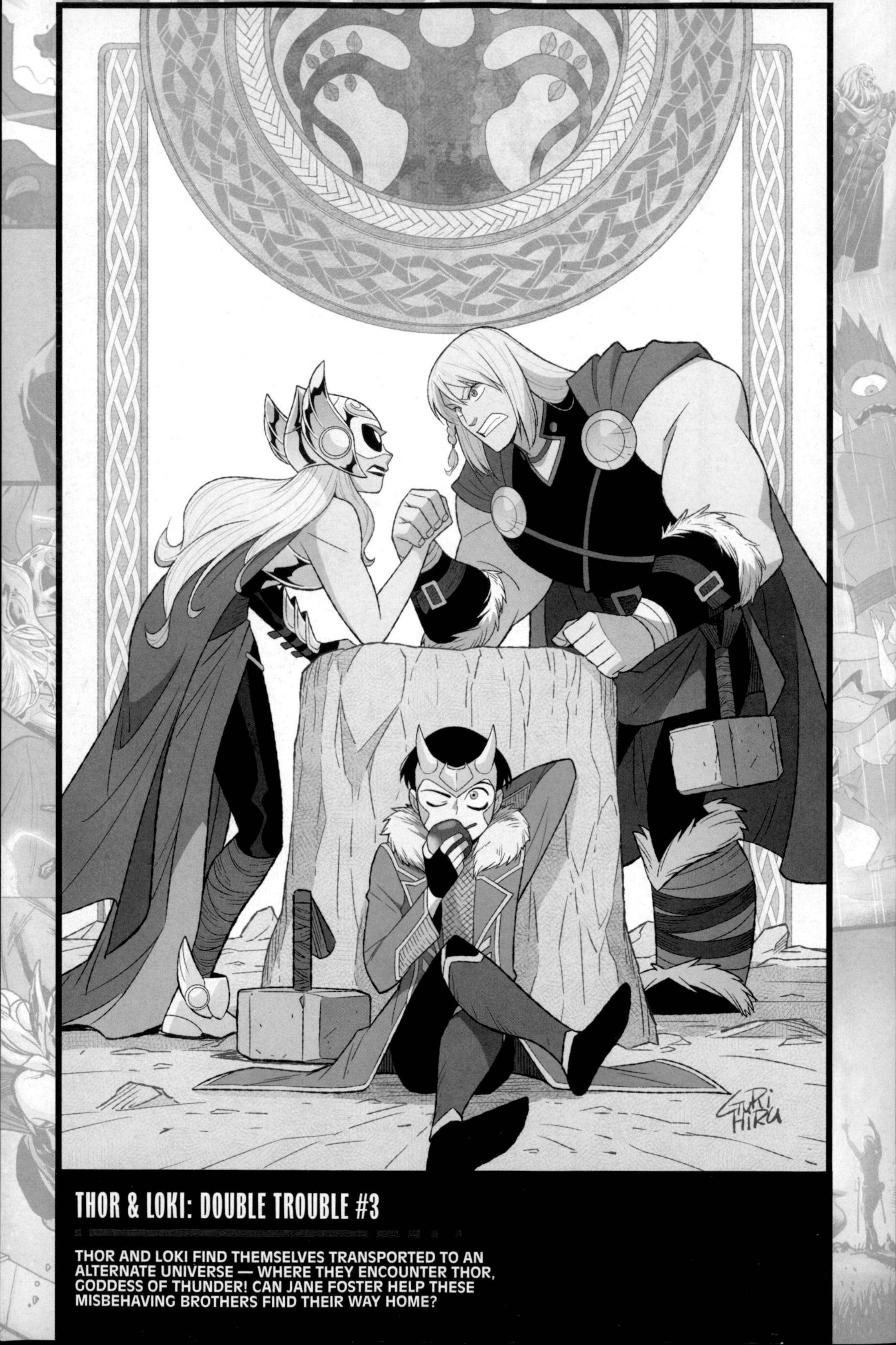
GURI HIRU

THOR & LOKI: DOUBLE TROUBLE #3

THOR AND LOKI FIND THEMSELVES TRANSPORTED TO AN ALTERNATE UNIVERSE — WHERE THEY ENCOUNTER THOR, GODDESS OF THUNDER! CAN JANE FOSTER HELP THESE MISBEHAVING BROTHERS FIND THEIR WAY HOME?

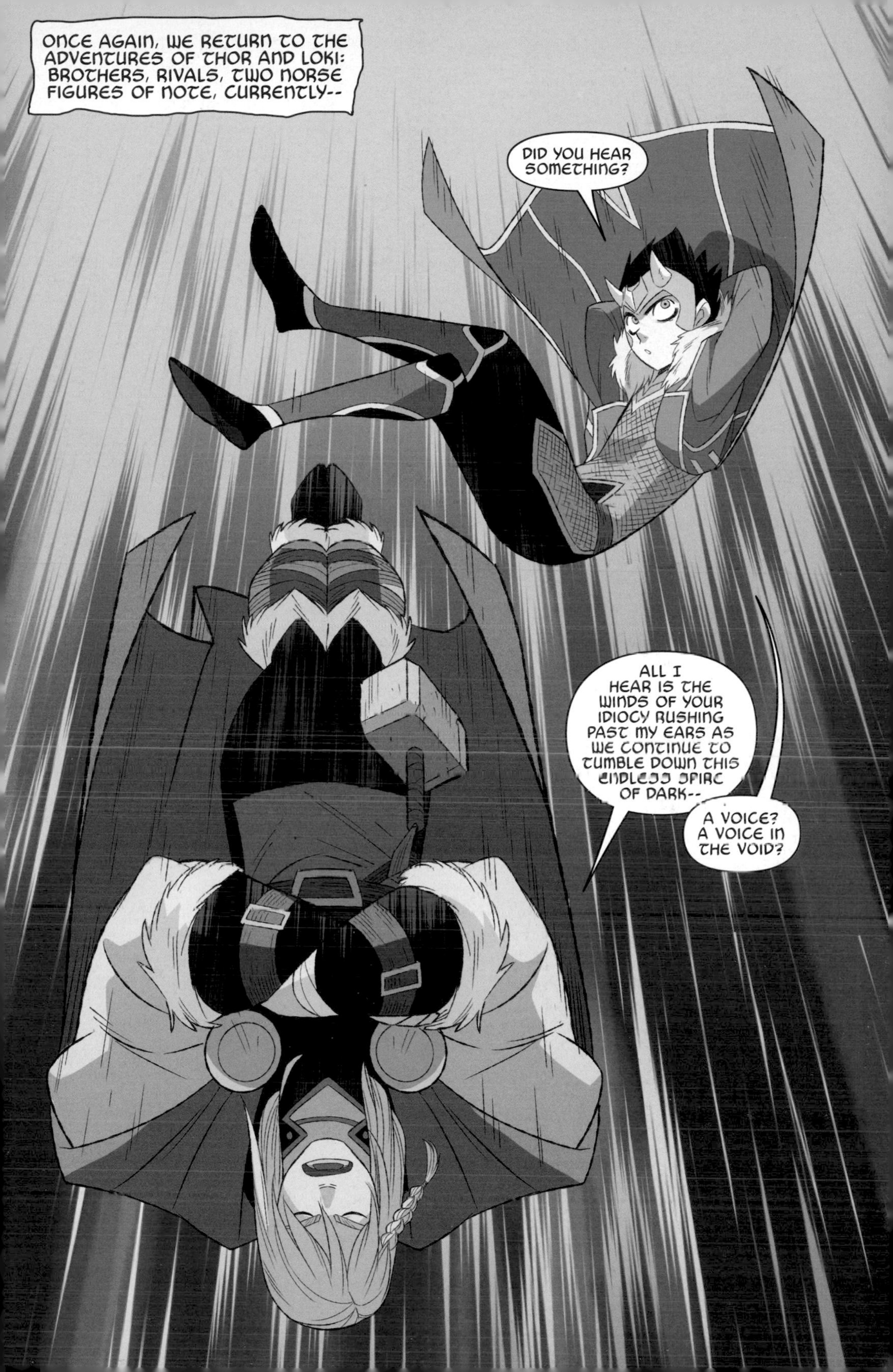
ONCE AGAIN, WE RETURN TO THE ADVENTURES OF THOR AND LOKI: BROTHERS, RIVALS, TWO NORSE FIGURES OF NOTE, CURRENTLY--
DID YOU HEAR SOMETHING?
ALL I HEAR IS THE WINDS OF YOUR IDIOCY RUSHING PAST MY EARS AS WE CONTINUE TO TUMBLE DOWN THIS ENDLESS SPIRE OF DARK--
A VOICE? A VOICE IN THE VOID?

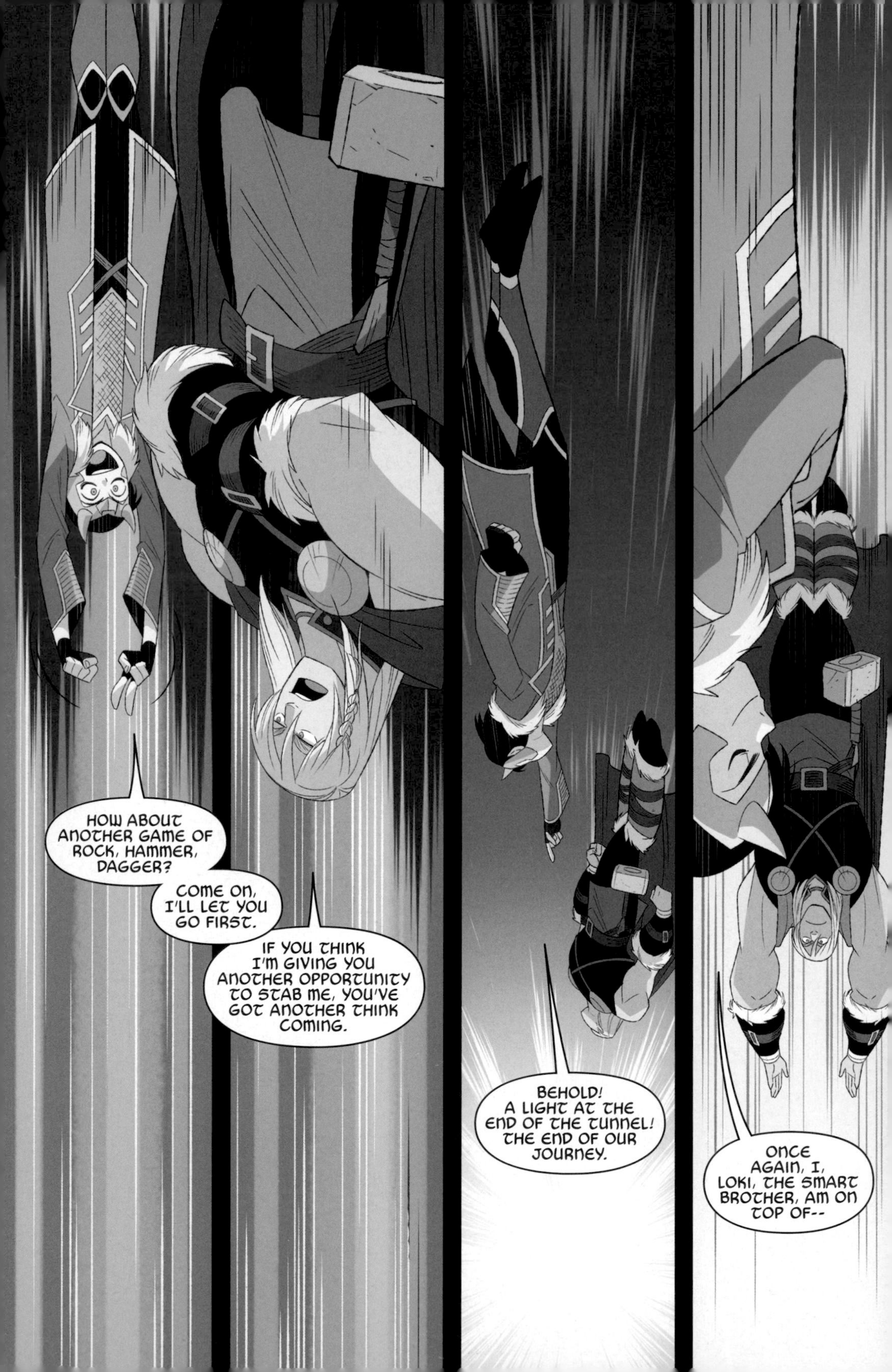
HOW ABOUT ANOTHER GAME OF ROCK, HAMMER, DAGGER?
COME ON, I'LL LET YOU GO FIRST.
IF YOU THINK I'M GIVING YOU ANOTHER OPPORTUNITY TO STAB ME, YOU'VE GOT ANOTHER THINK COMING.
BEHOLD! A LIGHT AT THE END OF THE TUNNEL! THE END OF OUR JOURNEY.
ONCE AGAIN, I, LOKI, THE SMART BROTHER, AM ON TOP OF--

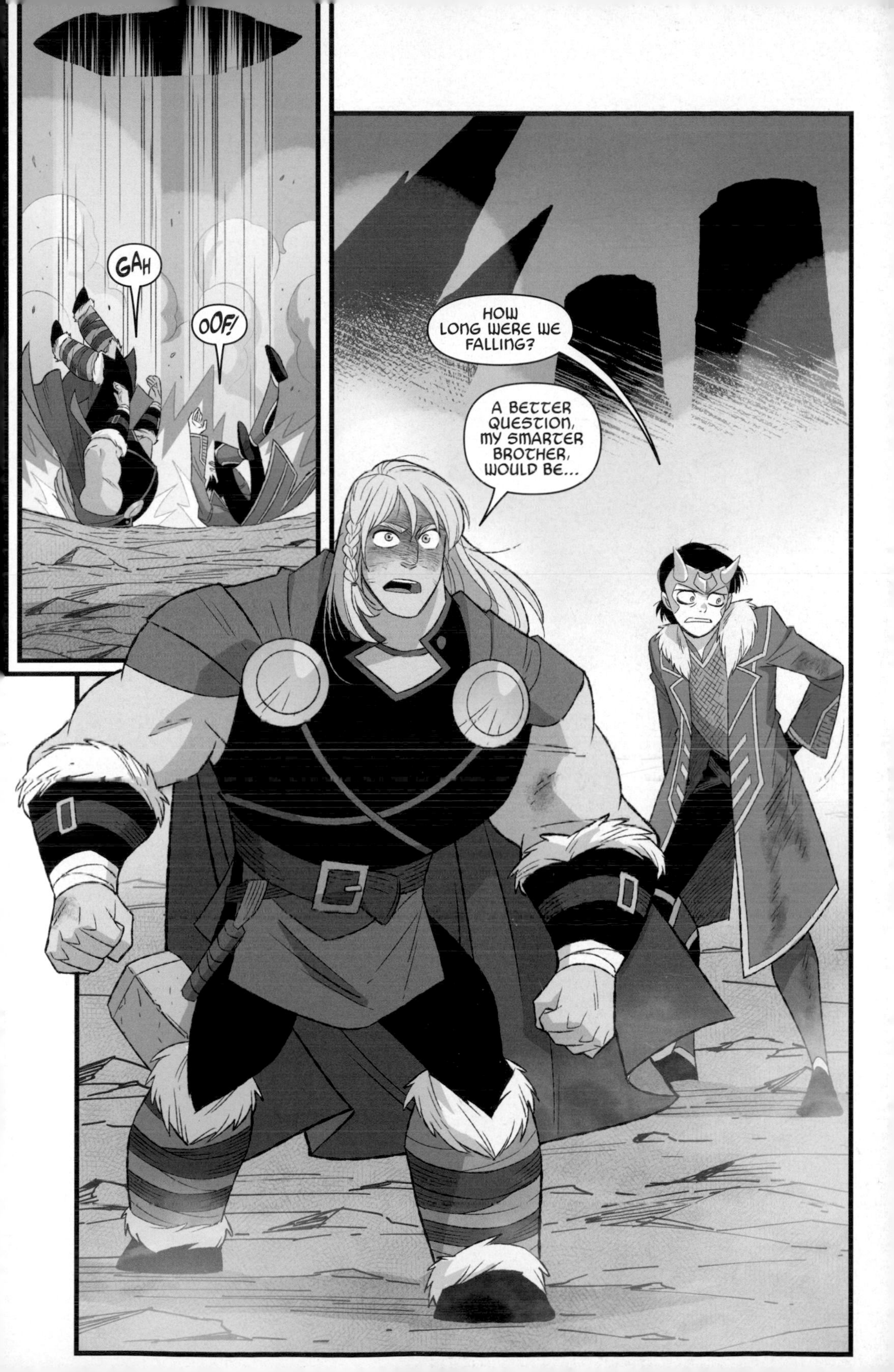
GAH
OOF!
HOW LONG WERE WE FALLING?
A BETTER QUESTION, MY SMARTER BROTHER, WOULD BE...

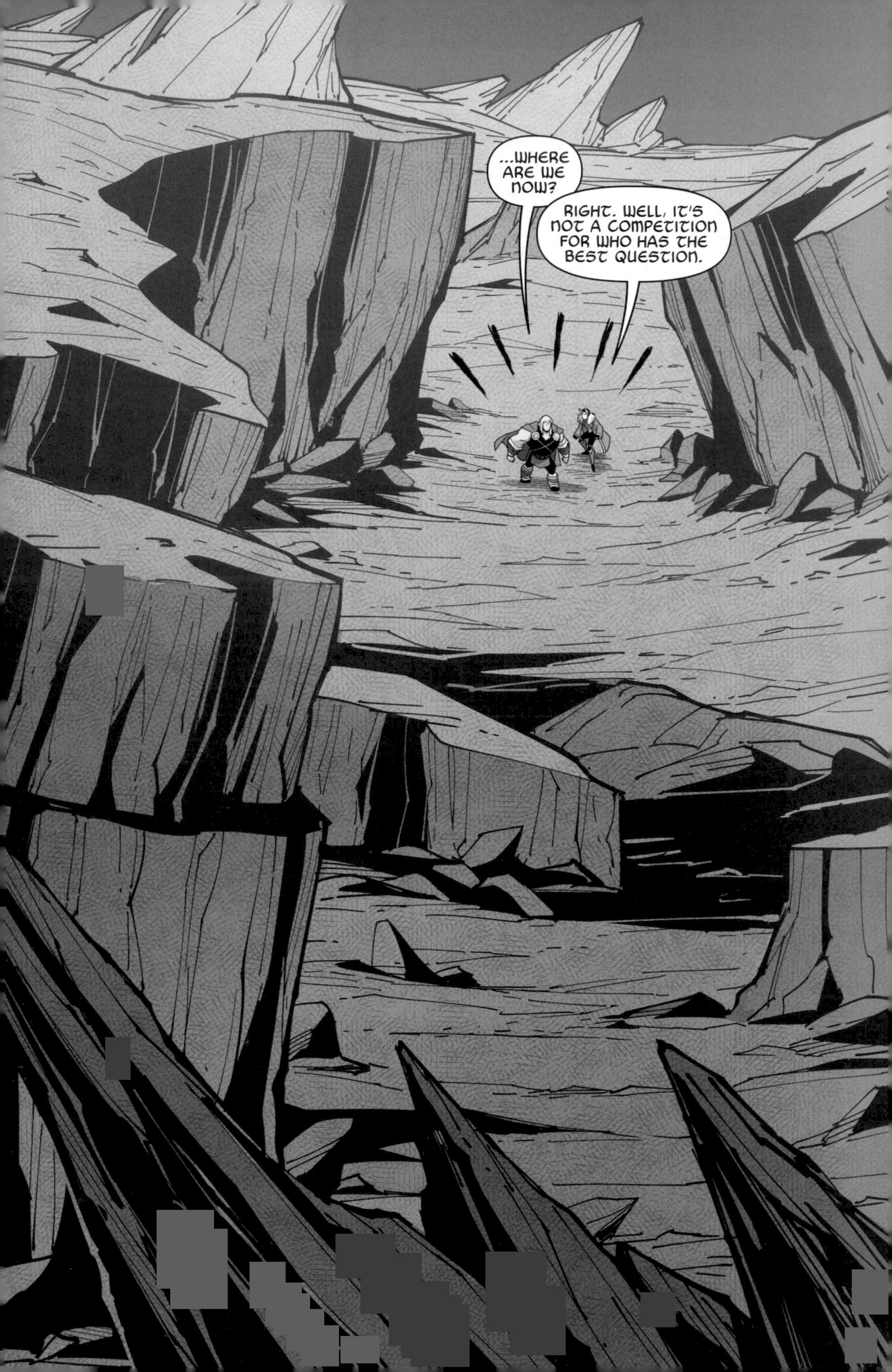
...WHERE ARE WE NOW?
RIGHT. WELL, IT'S NOT A COMPETITION FOR WHO HAS THE BEST QUESTION.

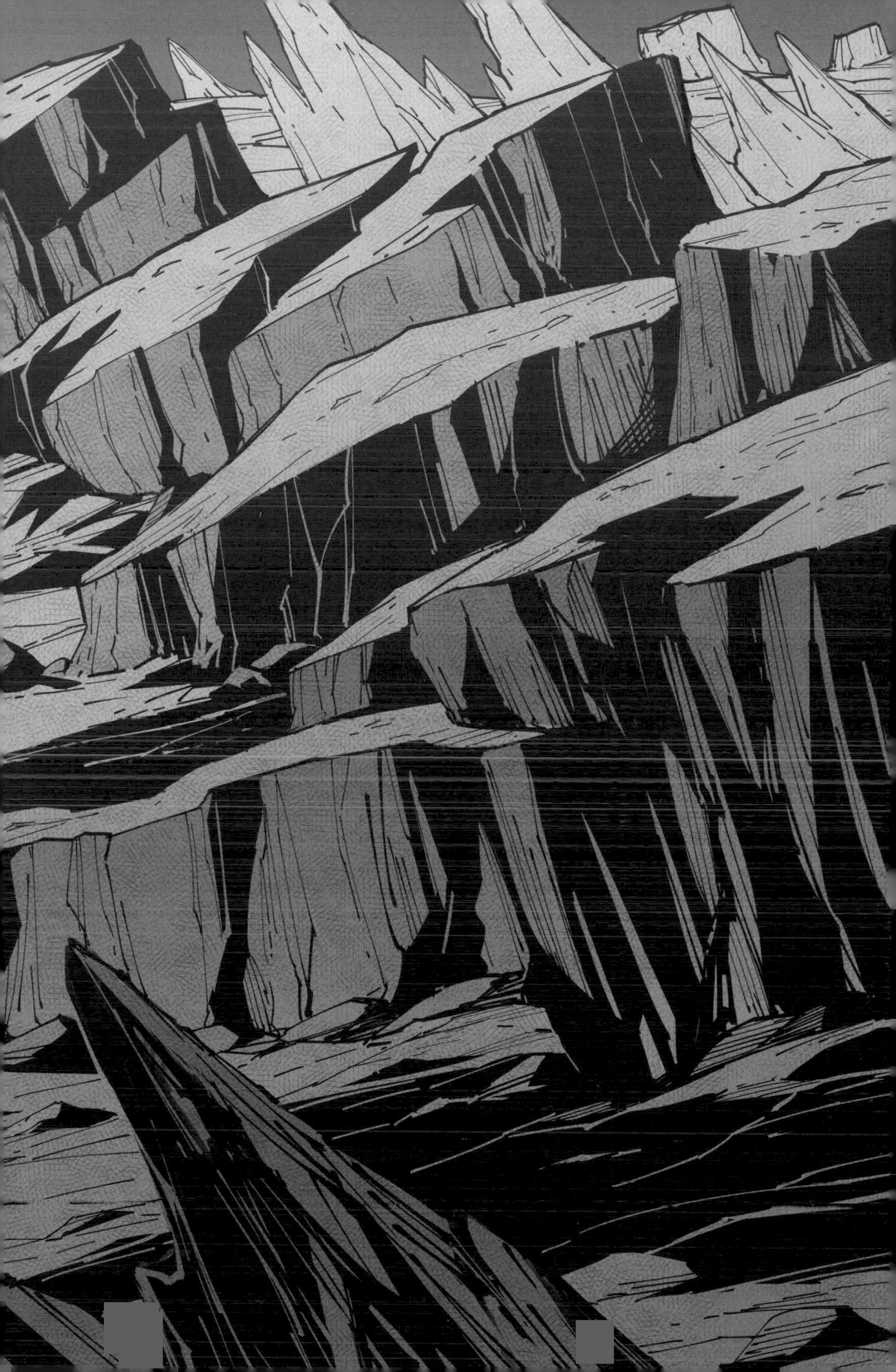

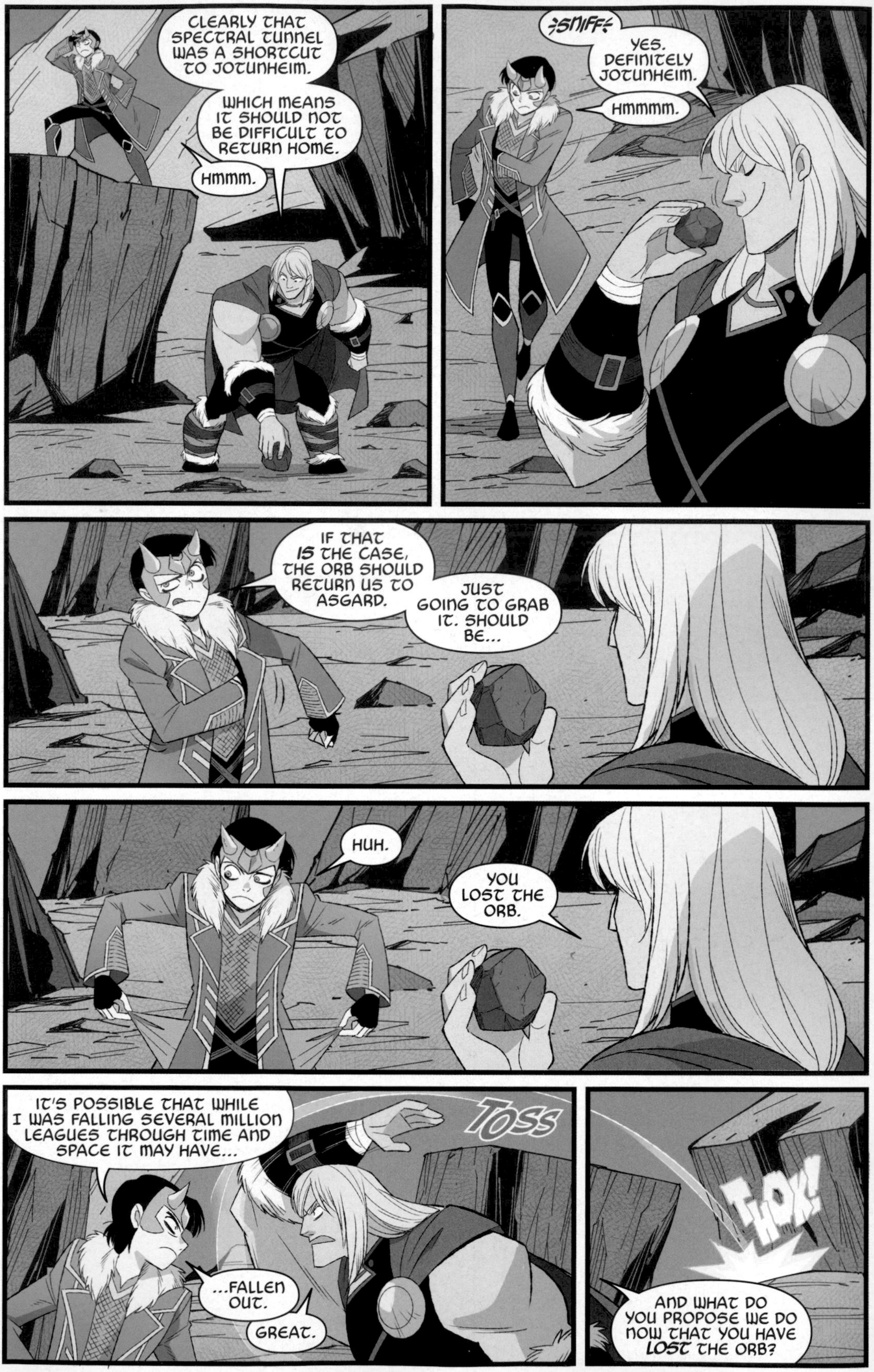
CLEARLY THAT SPECTRAL TUNNEL WAS A SHORTCUT TO JOTUNHEIM.
WHICH MEANS IT SHOULD NOT BE DIFFICULT TO RETURN HOME.
HMMM.
SNIFF
YES. DEFINITELY JOTUNHEIM.
HMMMM.
IF THAT IS THE CASE, THE ORB SHOULD RETURN US TO ASGARD.
JUST GOING TO GRAB IT. SHOULD BE...
HUH.
YOU LOST THE ORB.
IT'S POSSIBLE THAT WHILE I WAS FALLING SEVERAL MILLION LEAGUES THROUGH TIME AND SPACE IT MAY HAVE...
...FALLEN OUT.
GREAT.
TOSS
THOK!
AND WHAT DO YOU PROPOSE WE DO NOW THAT YOU HAVE LOST THE ORB?

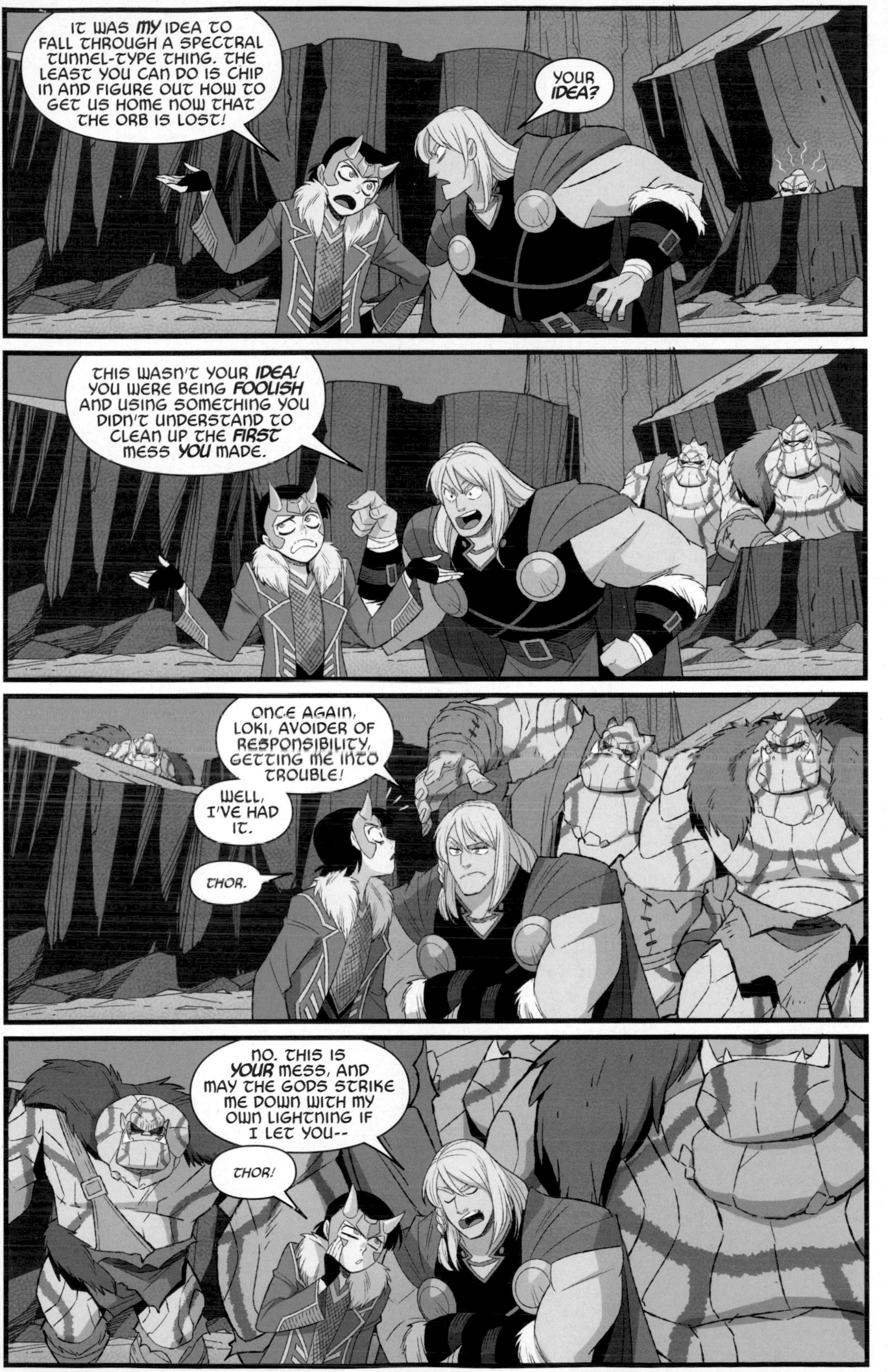
IT WAS MY IDEA TO FALL THROUGH A SPECTRAL TUNNEL-TYPE THING. THE LEAST YOU CAN DO IS CHIP IN AND FIGURE OUT HOW TO GET US HOME NOW THAT THE ORB IS LOST!
YOUR IDEA?
THIS WASN'T YOUR IDEA! YOU WERE BEING FOOLISH AND USING SOMETHING YOU DIDN'T UNDERSTAND TO CLEAN UP THE FIRST MESS YOU MADE.
ONCE AGAIN, LOKI, AVOIDER OF RESPONSIBILITY, GETTING ME INTO TROUBLE!
WELL, I'VE HAD IT.
THOR.
NO. THIS IS YOUR MESS, AND MAY THE GODS STRIKE ME DOWN WITH MY OWN LIGHTNING IF I LET YOU--
THOR!

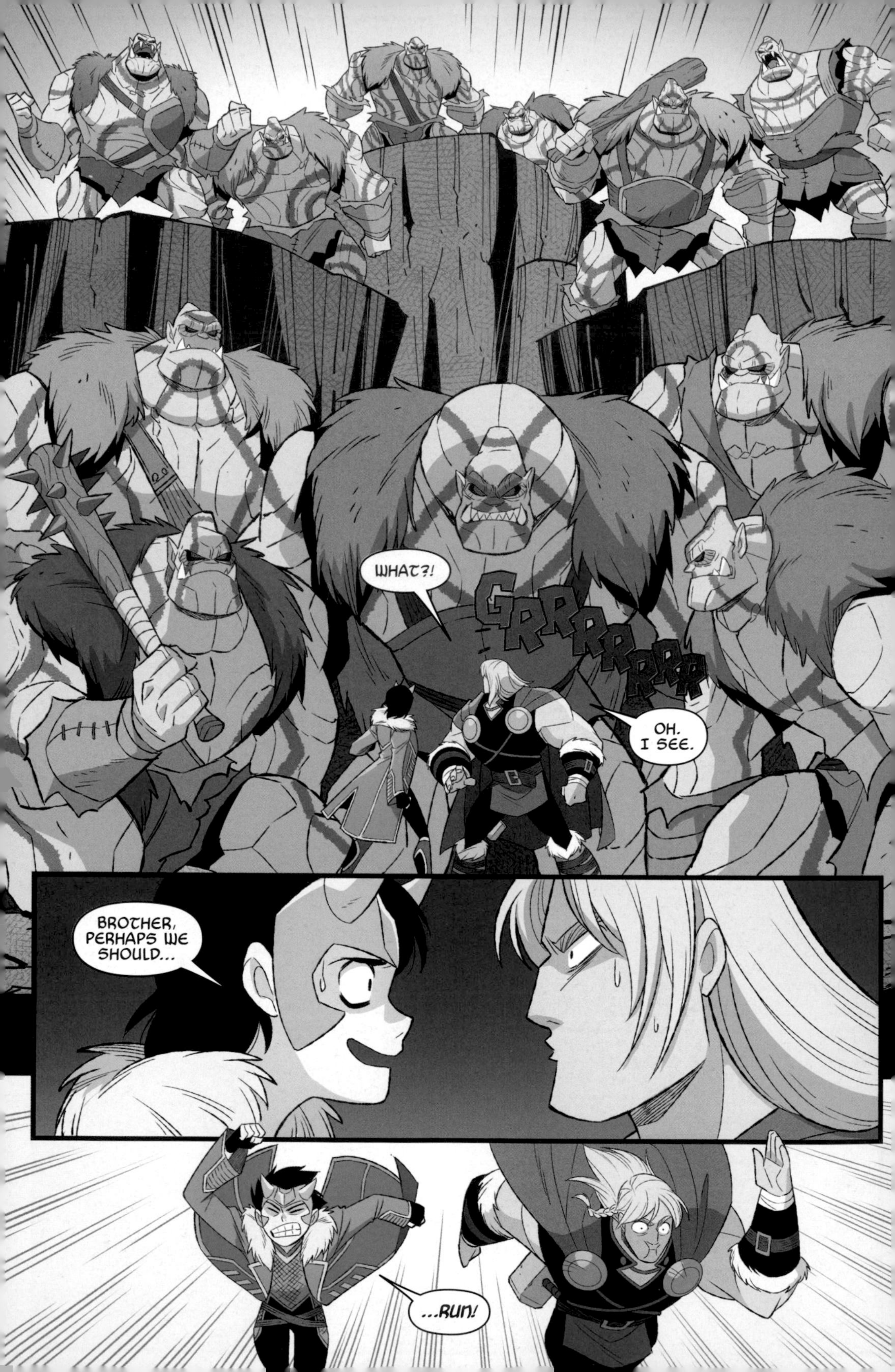
WHAT?!
GRRRRRRR
OH. I SEE.
BROTHER, PERHAPS WE SHOULD...
...RUN!

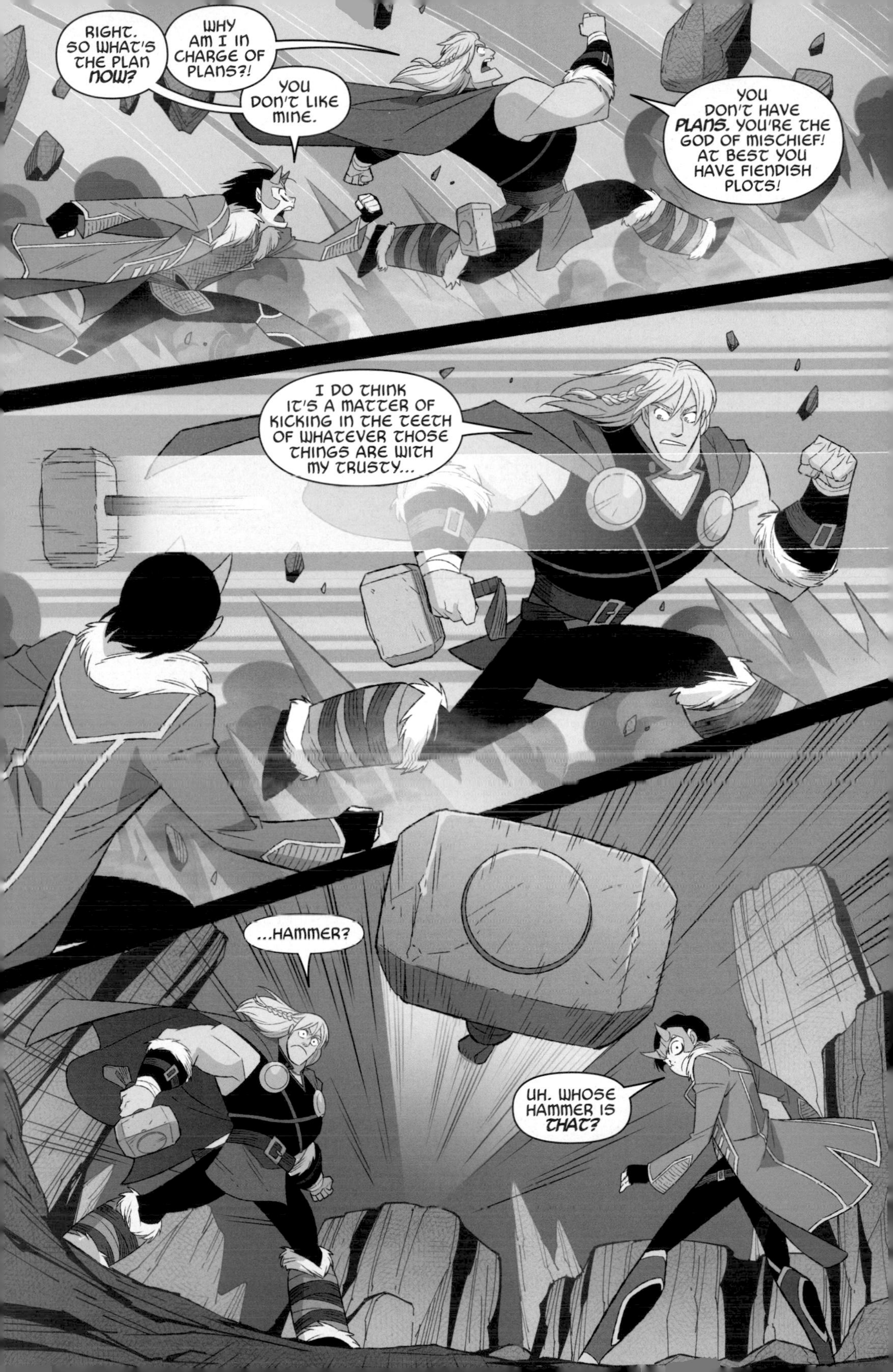
RIGHT. SO WHAT'S THE PLAN *NOW?*
WHY AM I IN CHARGE OF PLANS?!
YOU DON'T LIKE MINE.
YOU DON'T HAVE **PLANS.** YOU'RE THE GOD OF MISCHIEF! AT BEST YOU HAVE FIENDISH PLOTS!
I DO THINK IT'S A MATTER OF KICKING IN THE TEETH OF WHATEVER THOSE THINGS ARE WITH MY TRUSTY...
...HAMMER?
UH. WHOSE HAMMER IS *THAT?*

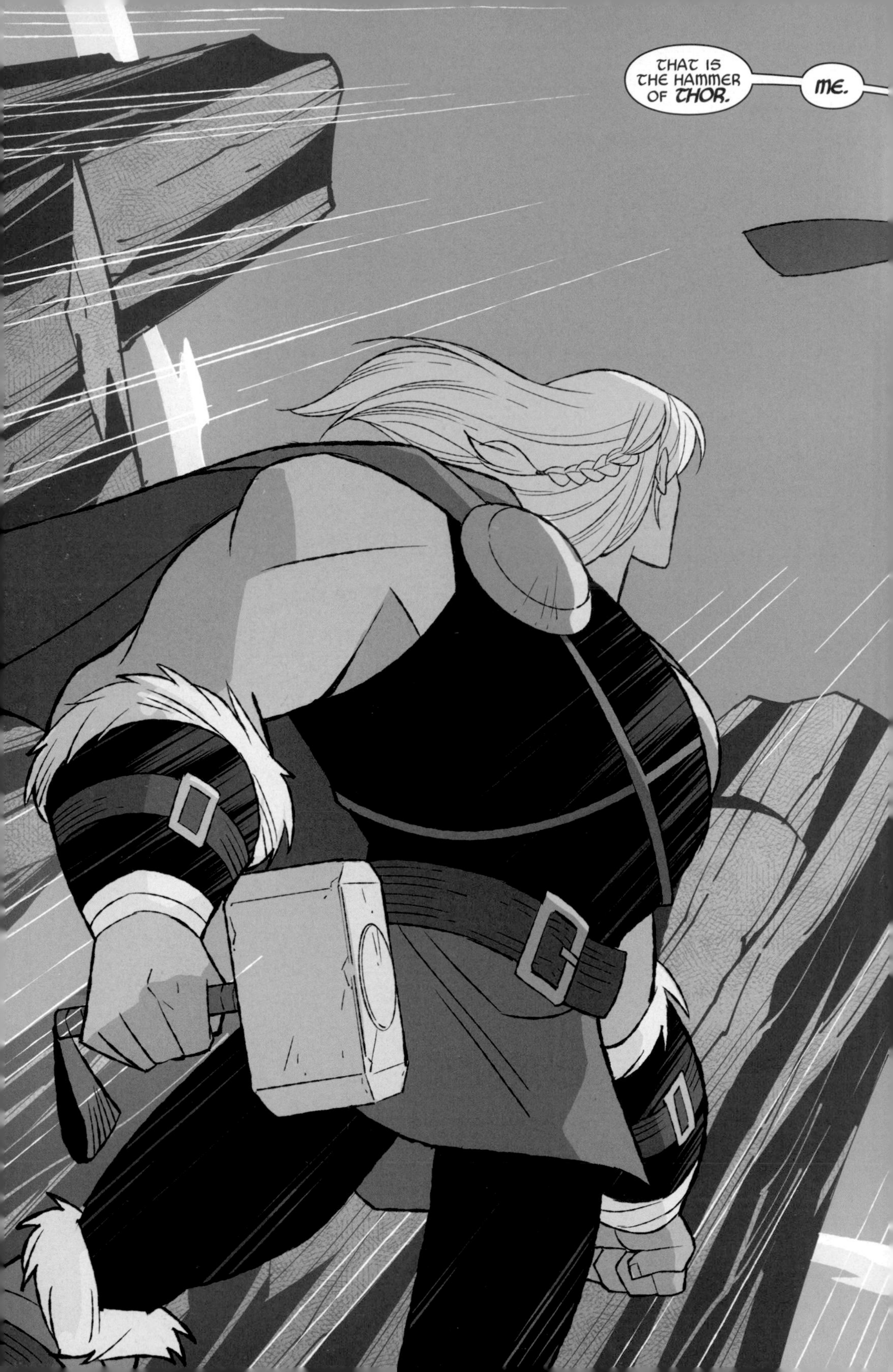
THAT IS THE HAMMER OF THOR.
ME.

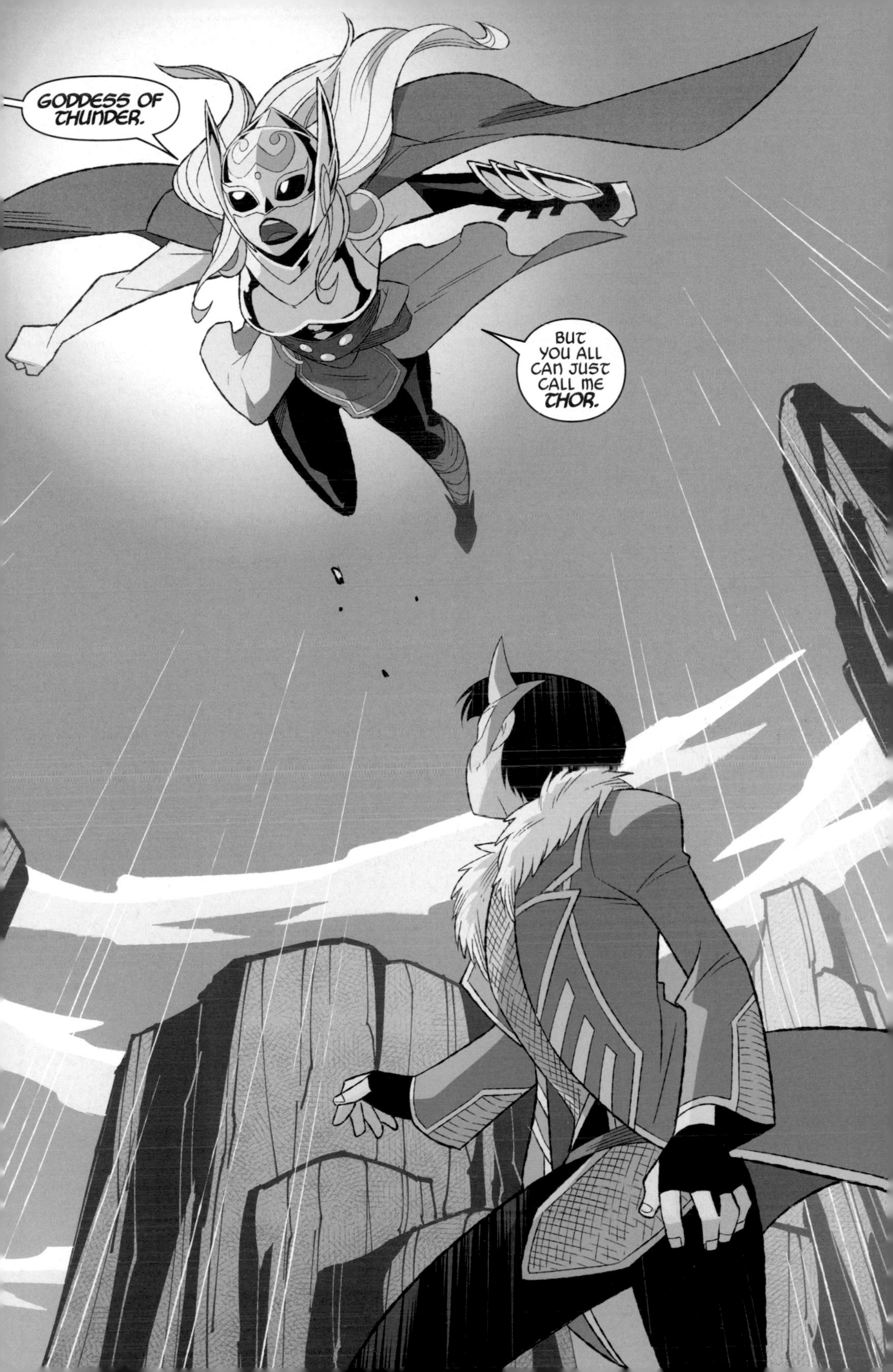
GODDESS OF THUNDER.
BUT YOU ALL CAN JUST CALL ME THOR.

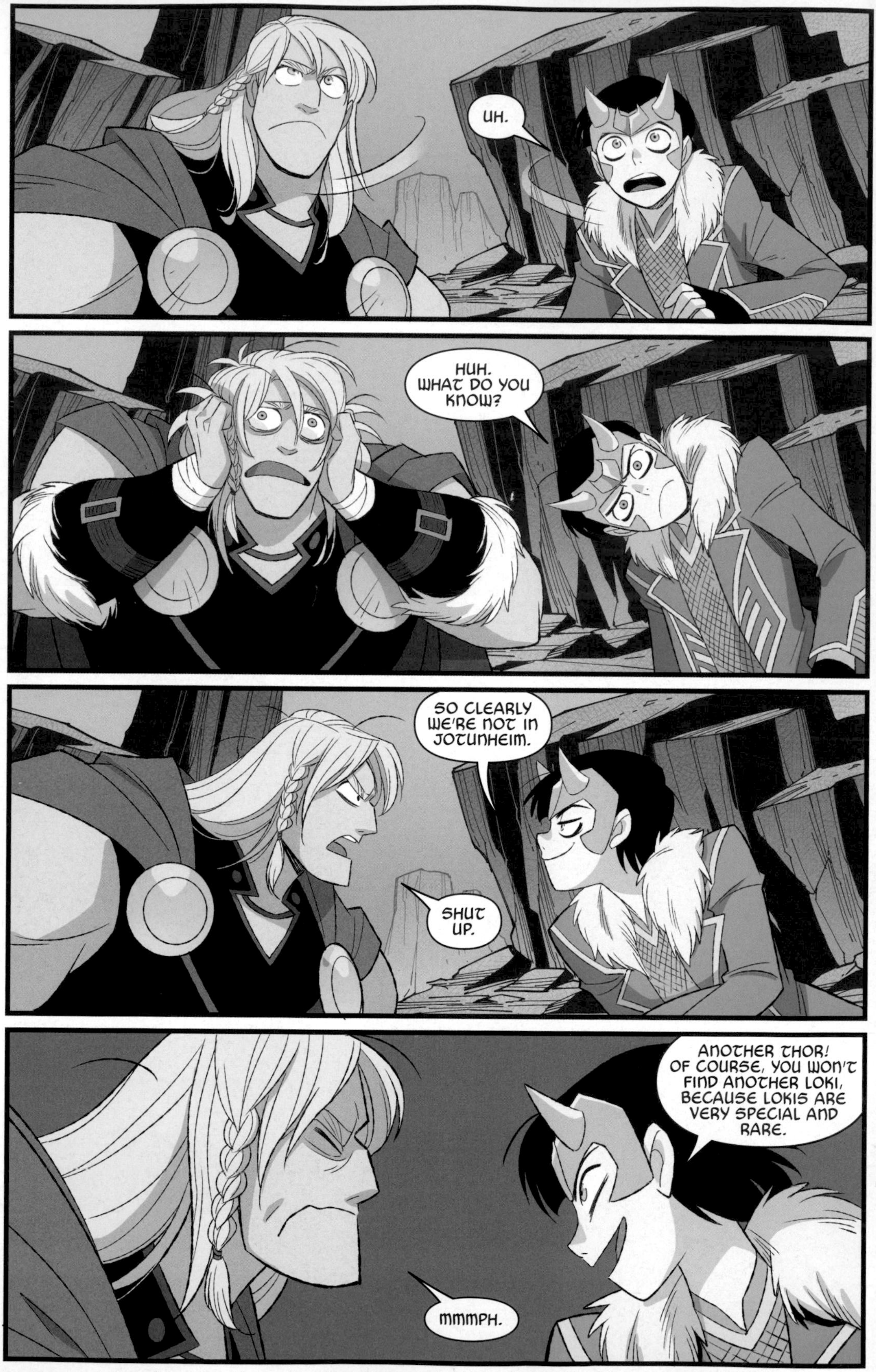
UH.
HUH. WHAT DO YOU KNOW?
SO CLEARLY WE'RE NOT IN JOTUNHEIM.
SHUT UP.
ANOTHER THOR! OF COURSE, YOU WON'T FIND ANOTHER LOKI, BECAUSE LOKIS ARE VERY SPECIAL AND RARE.
MMMPH.

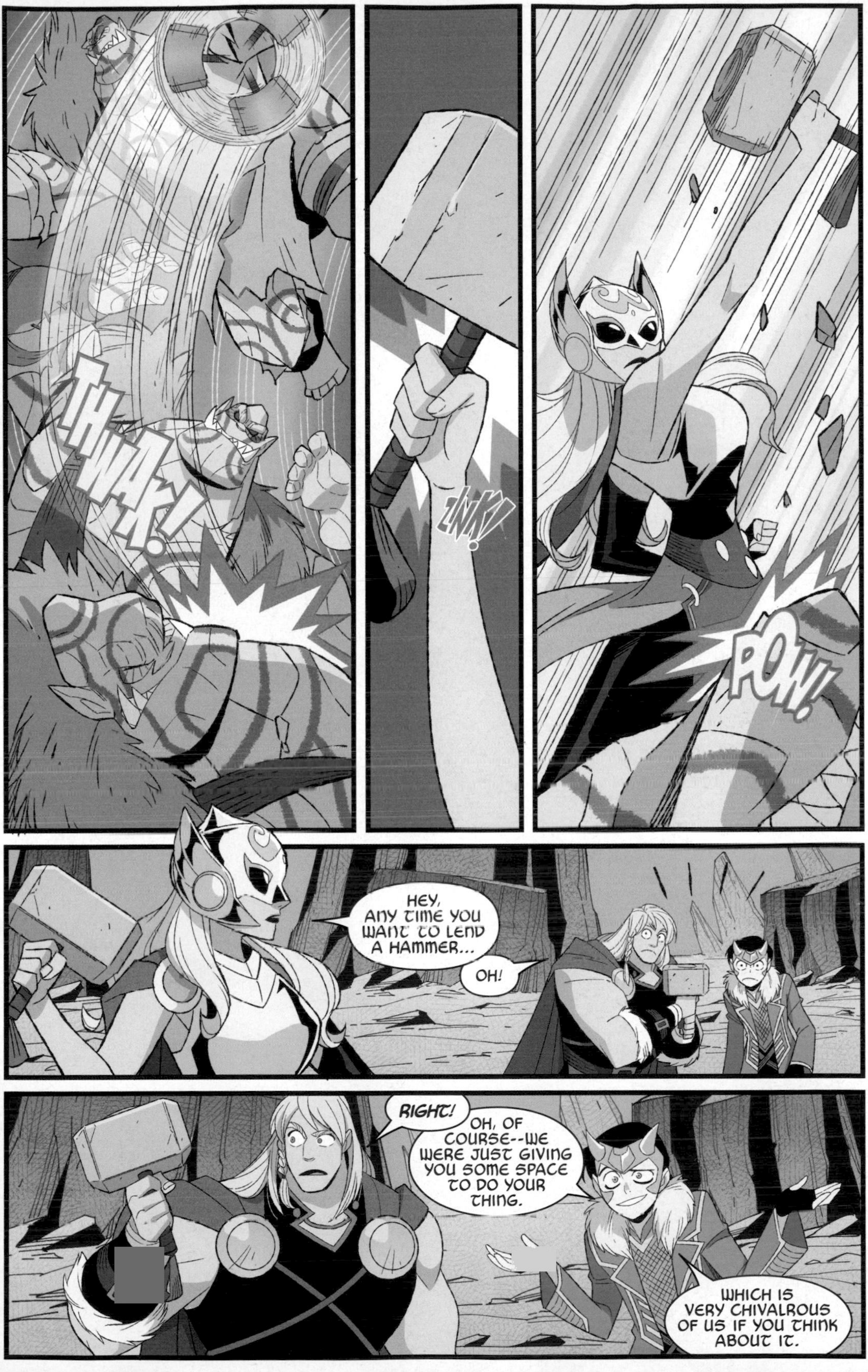
THWAK!
ZNAK!
POW!
HEY, ANY TIME YOU WANT TO LEND A HAMMER...
OH!
RIGHT!
OH, OF COURSE--WE WERE JUST GIVING YOU SOME SPACE TO DO YOUR THING.
WHICH IS VERY CHIVALROUS OF US IF YOU THINK ABOUT IT.

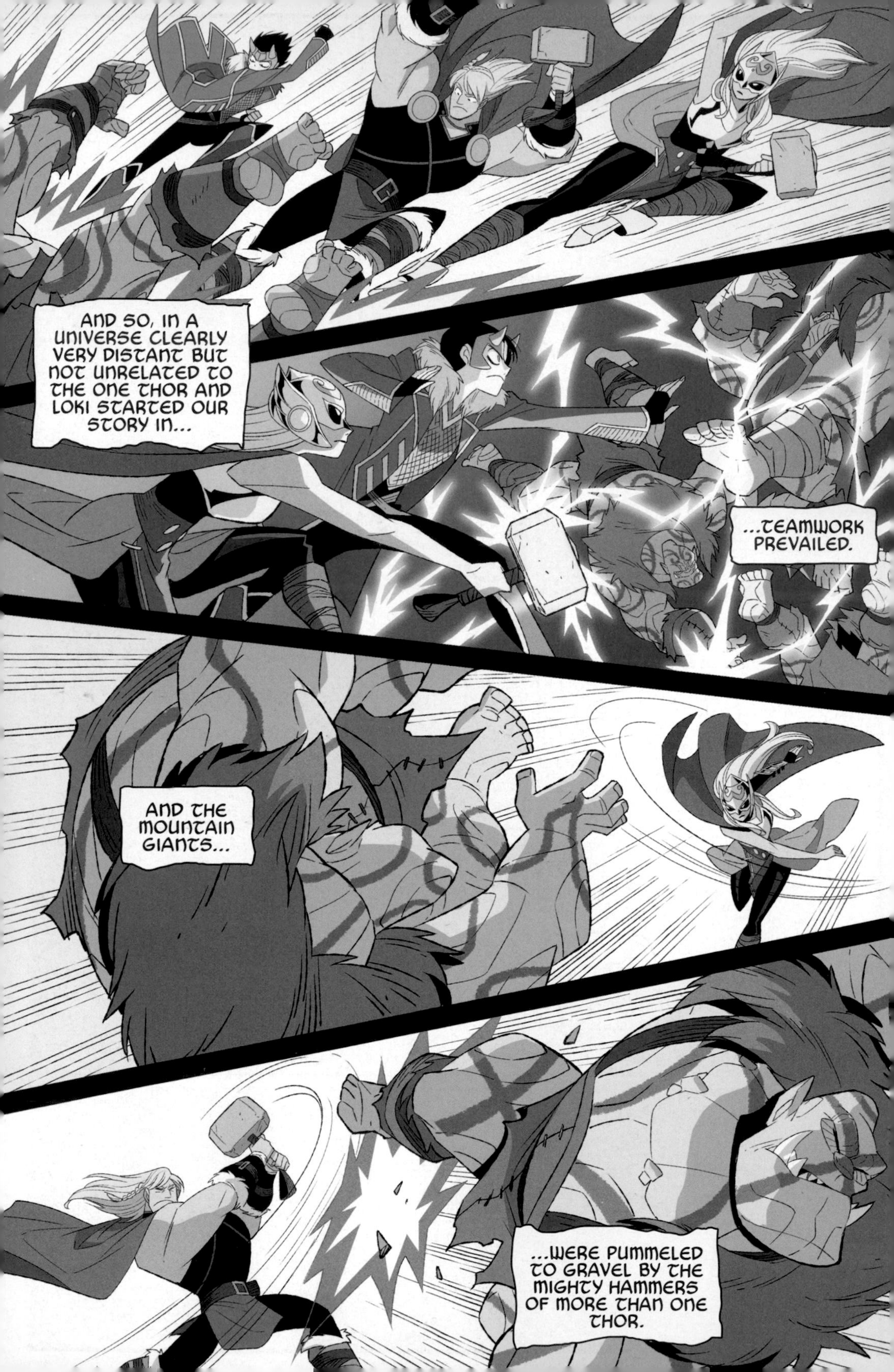

AND SO, IN A UNIVERSE CLEARLY VERY DISTANT BUT NOT UNRELATED TO THE ONE THOR AND LOKI STARTED OUR STORY IN...
...TEAMWORK PREVAILED.
AND THE MOUNTAIN GIANTS...
...WERE PUMMELED TO GRAVEL BY THE MIGHTY HAMMERS OF MORE THAN ONE THOR.

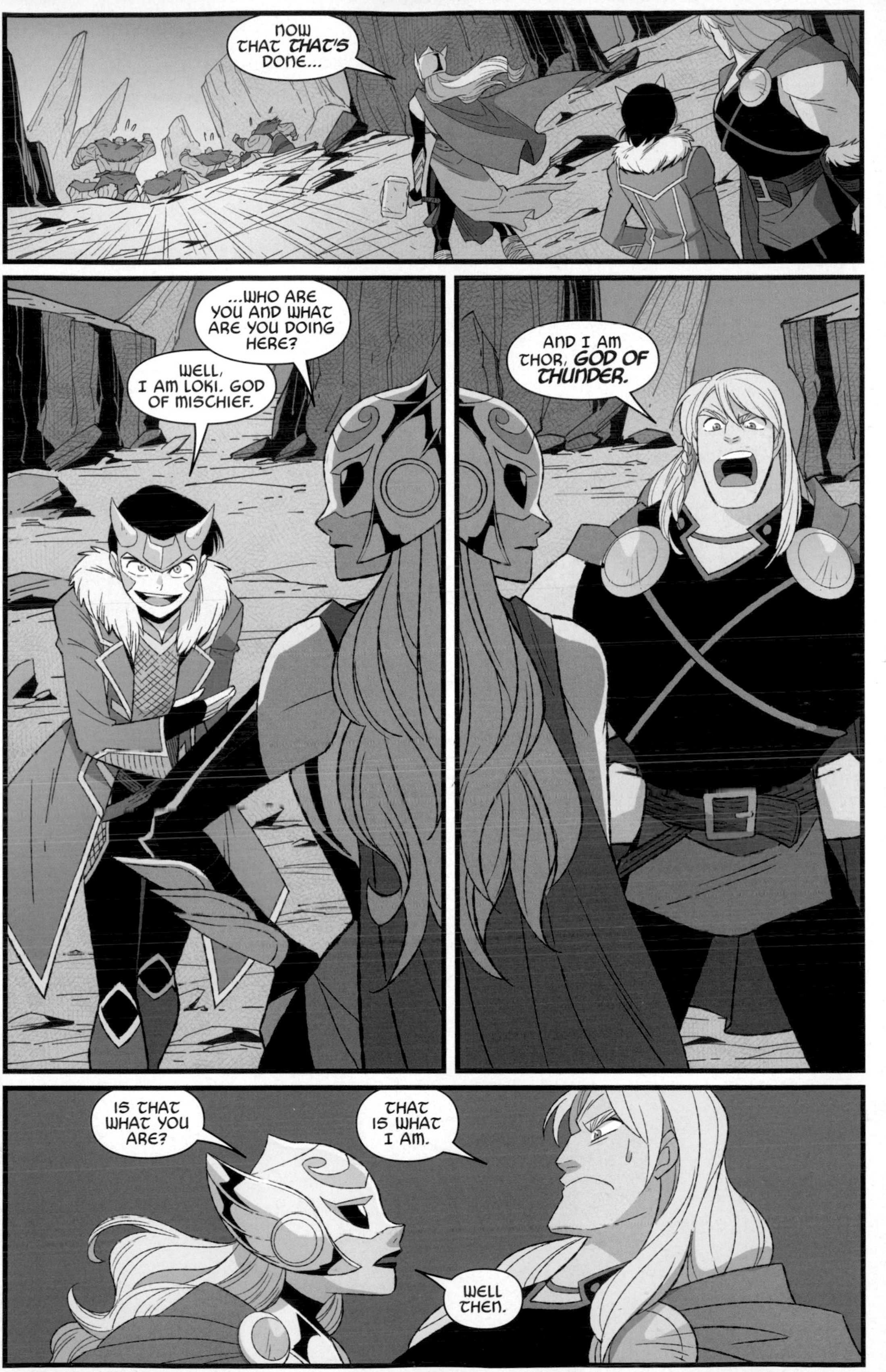
NOW THAT THAT'S DONE...
...WHO ARE YOU AND WHAT ARE YOU DOING HERE?
WELL, I AM LOKI. GOD OF MISCHIEF.
AND I AM THOR, GOD OF THUNDER.
IS THAT WHAT YOU ARE?
THAT IS WHAT I AM.
WELL THEN.

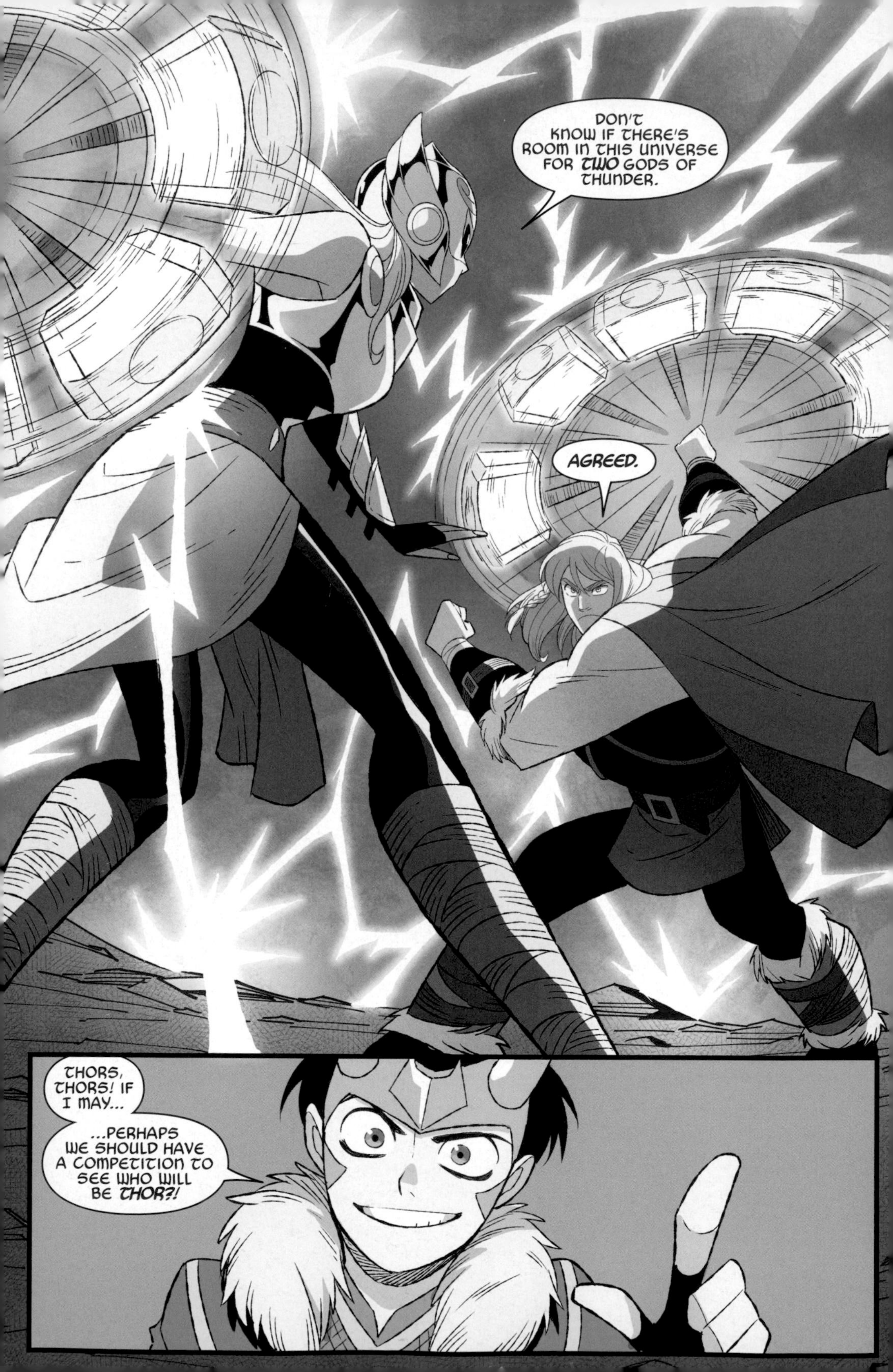
DON'T KNOW IF THERE'S ROOM IN THIS UNIVERSE FOR TWO GODS OF THUNDER.
AGREED.
THORS, THORS! IF I MAY...
...PERHAPS WE SHOULD HAVE A COMPETITION TO SEE WHO WILL BE THOR?!

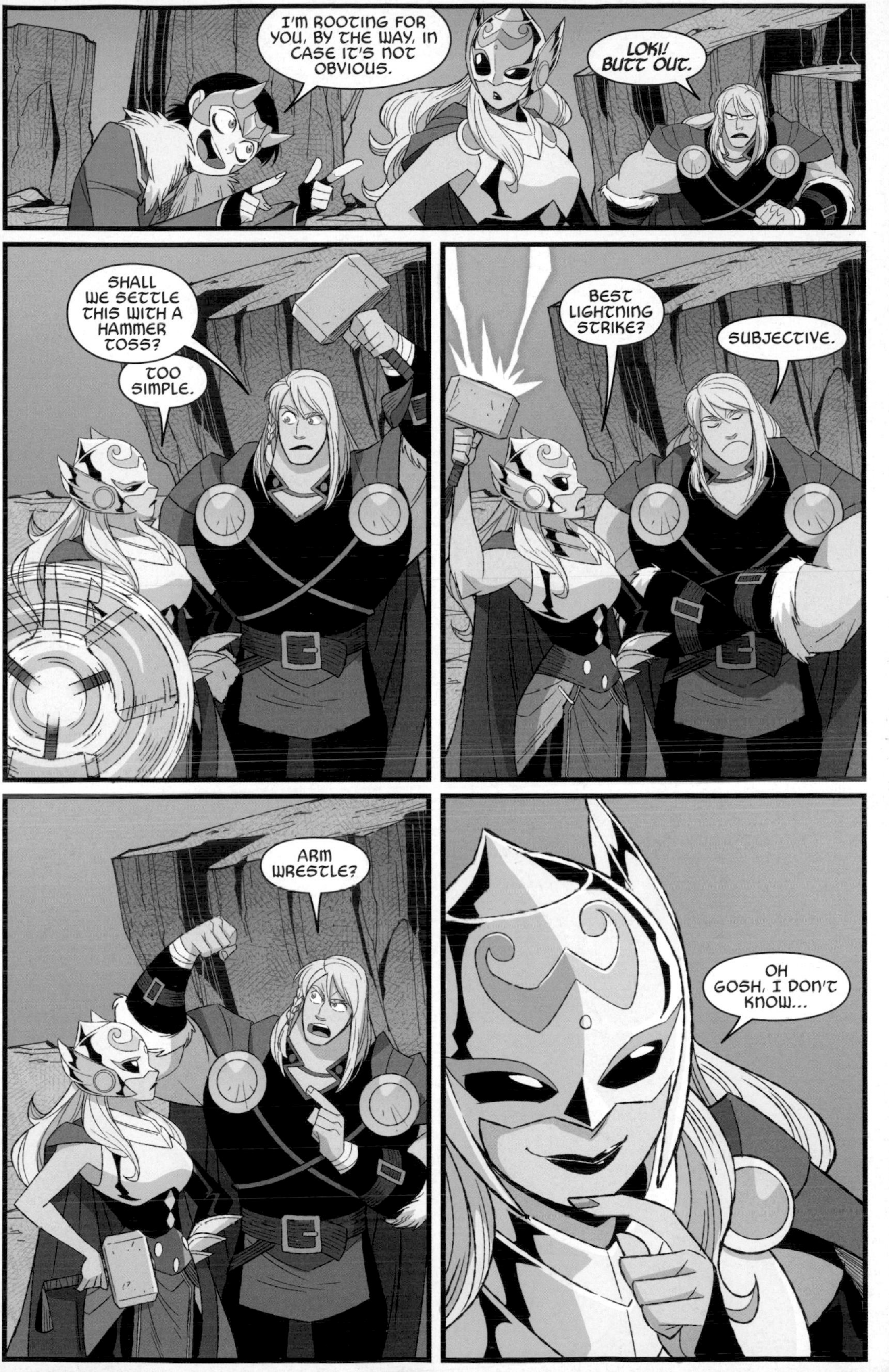
I'M ROOTING FOR YOU, BY THE WAY, IN CASE IT'S NOT OBVIOUS.
LOKI! BUTT OUT.
SHALL WE SETTLE THIS WITH A HAMMER TOSS?
TOO SIMPLE.
BEST LIGHTNING STRIKE?
SUBJECTIVE.
ARM WRESTLE?
OH GOSH, I DON'T KNOW...

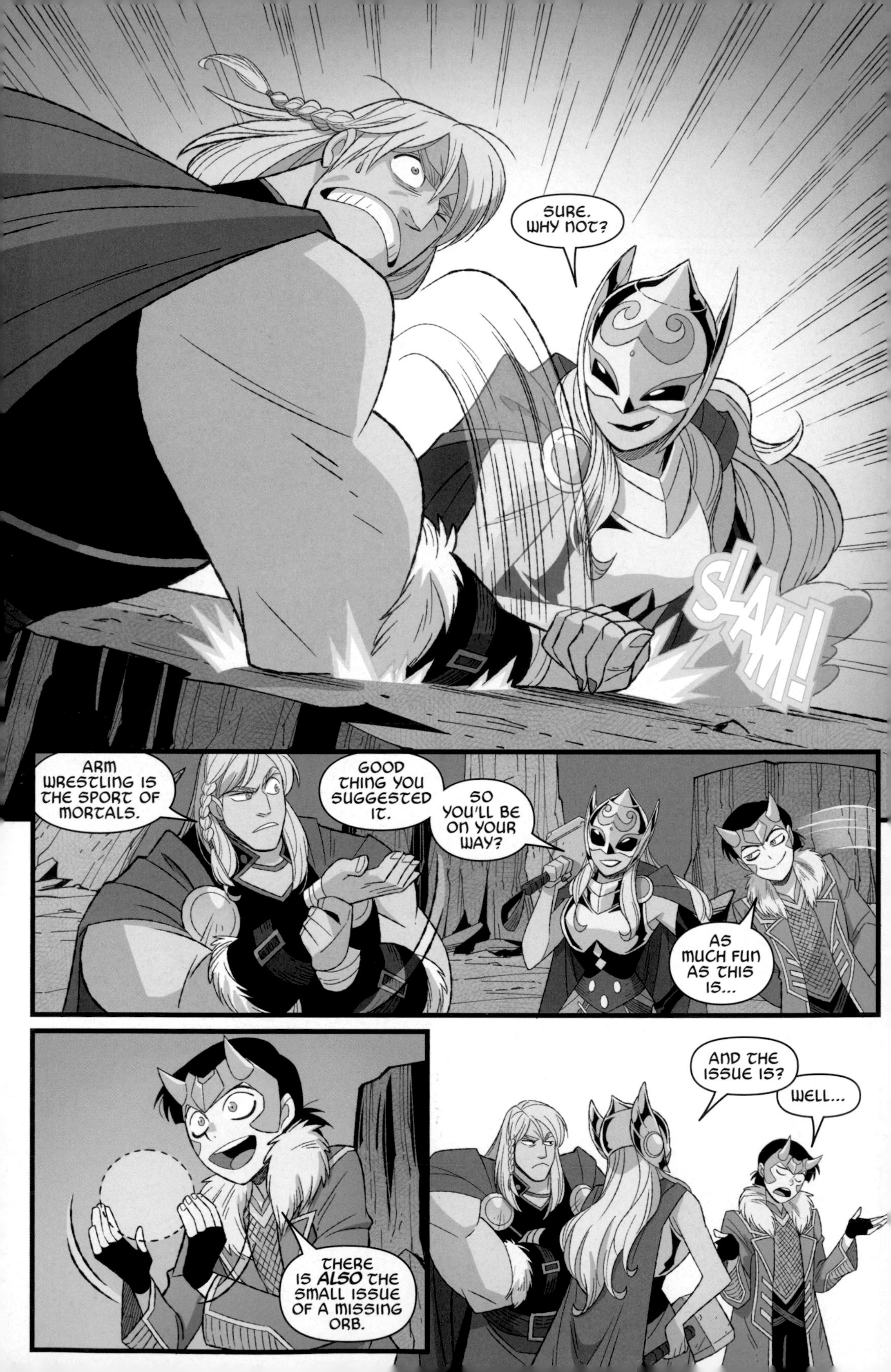
SURE. WHY NOT?
SLAM!
ARM WRESTLING IS THE SPORT OF MORTALS.
GOOD THING YOU SUGGESTED IT.
SO YOU'LL BE ON YOUR WAY?
AS MUCH FUN AS THIS IS...
THERE IS ALSO THE SMALL ISSUE OF A MISSING ORB.
AND THE ISSUE IS?
WELL...

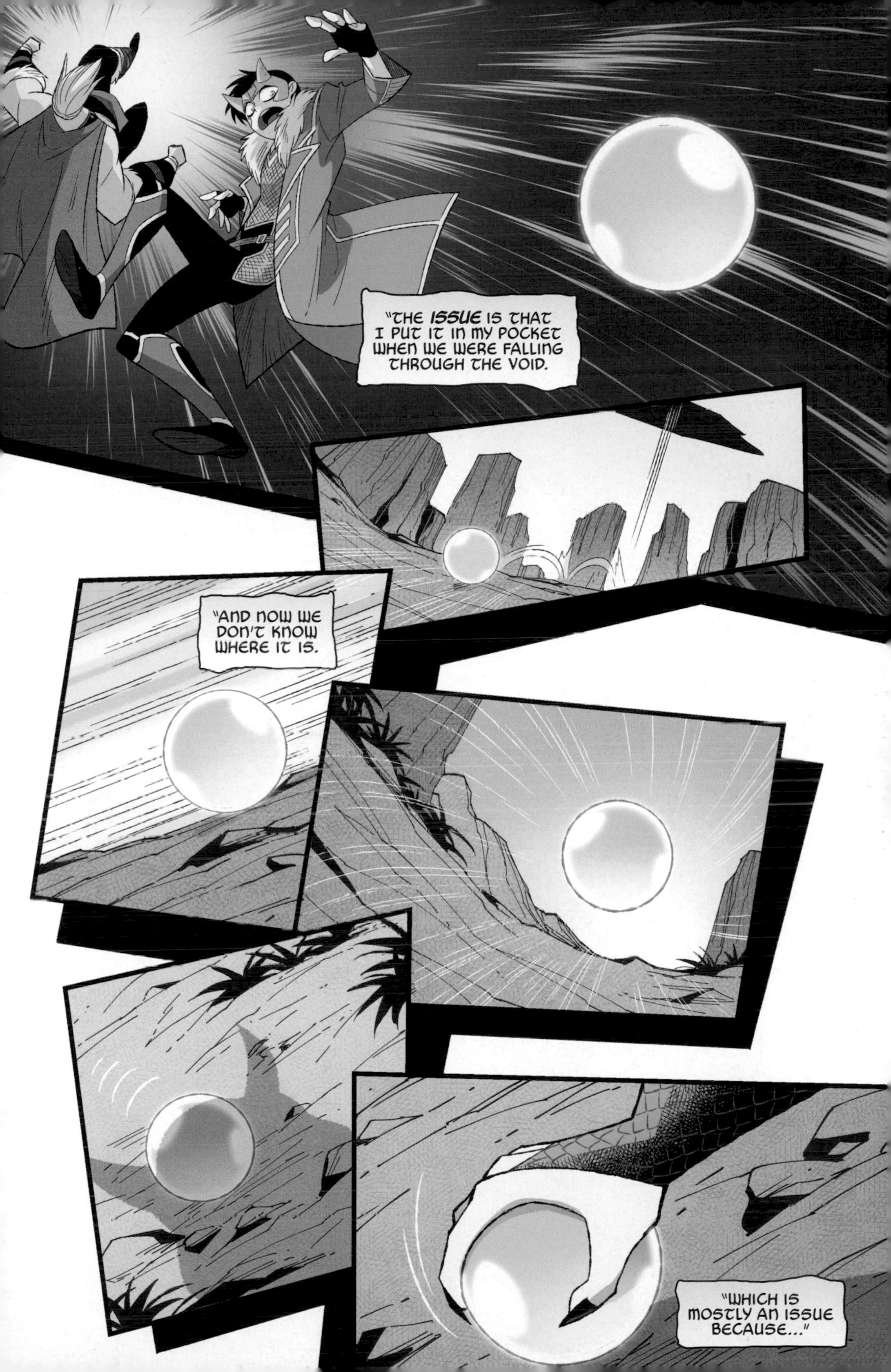
"THE ISSUE IS THAT I PUT IT IN MY POCKET WHEN WE WERE FALLING THROUGH THE VOID.
"AND NOW WE DON'T KNOW WHERE IT IS.
"WHICH IS MOSTLY AN ISSUE BECAUSE..."

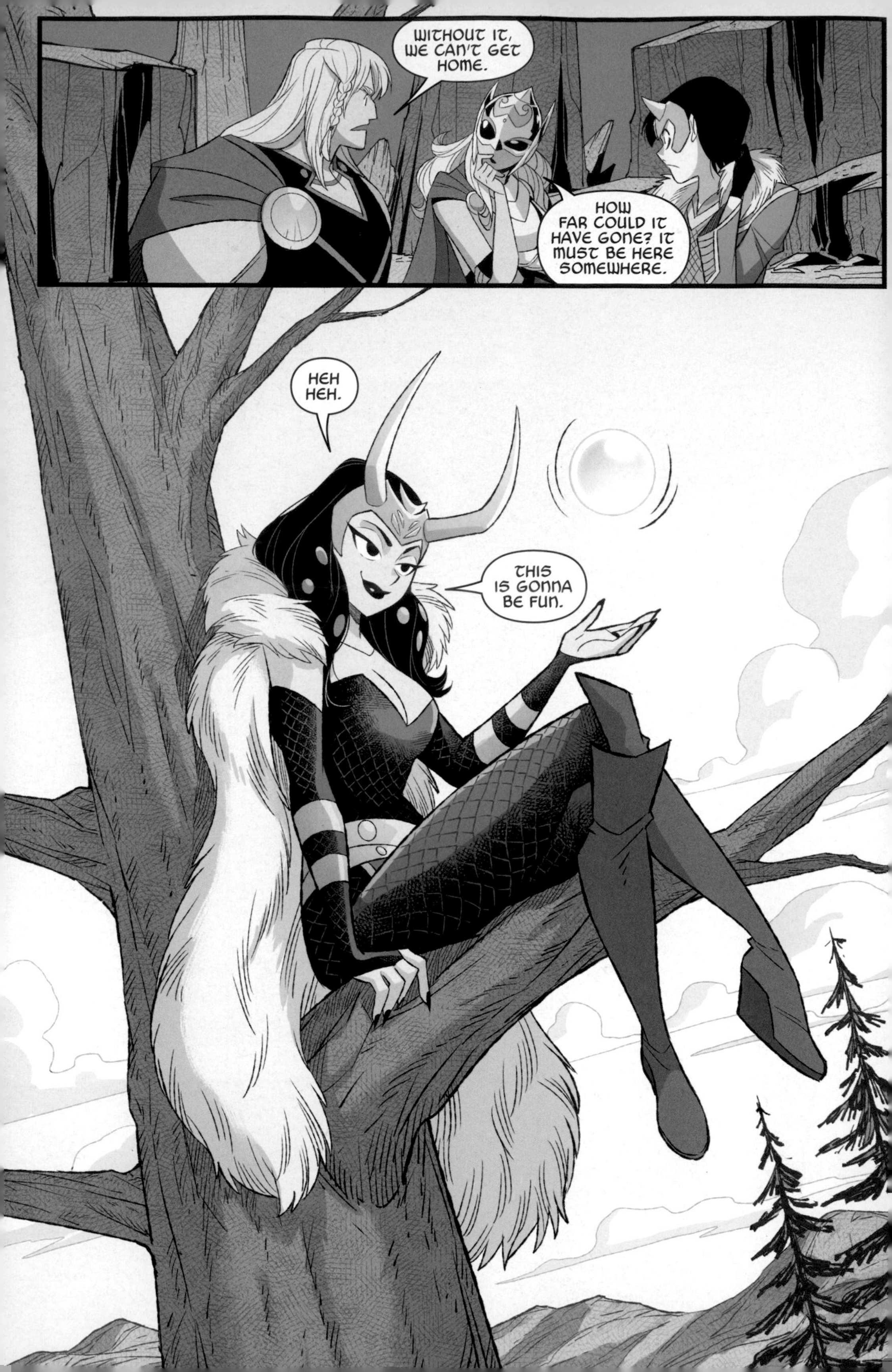
WITHOUT IT, WE CAN'T GET HOME.
HOW FAR COULD IT HAVE GONE? IT MUST BE HERE SOMEWHERE.
HEH HEH.
THIS IS GONNA BE FUN.

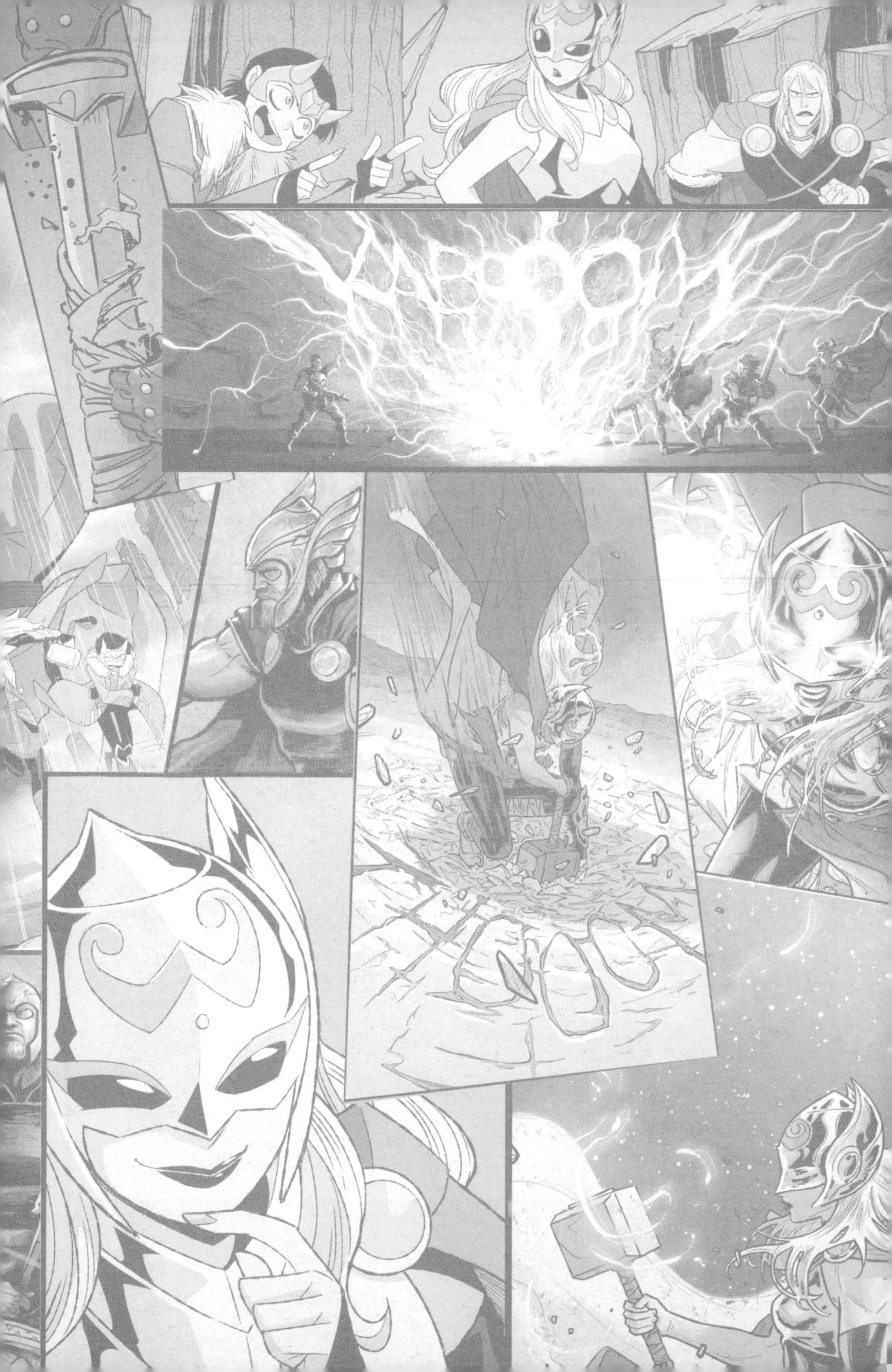

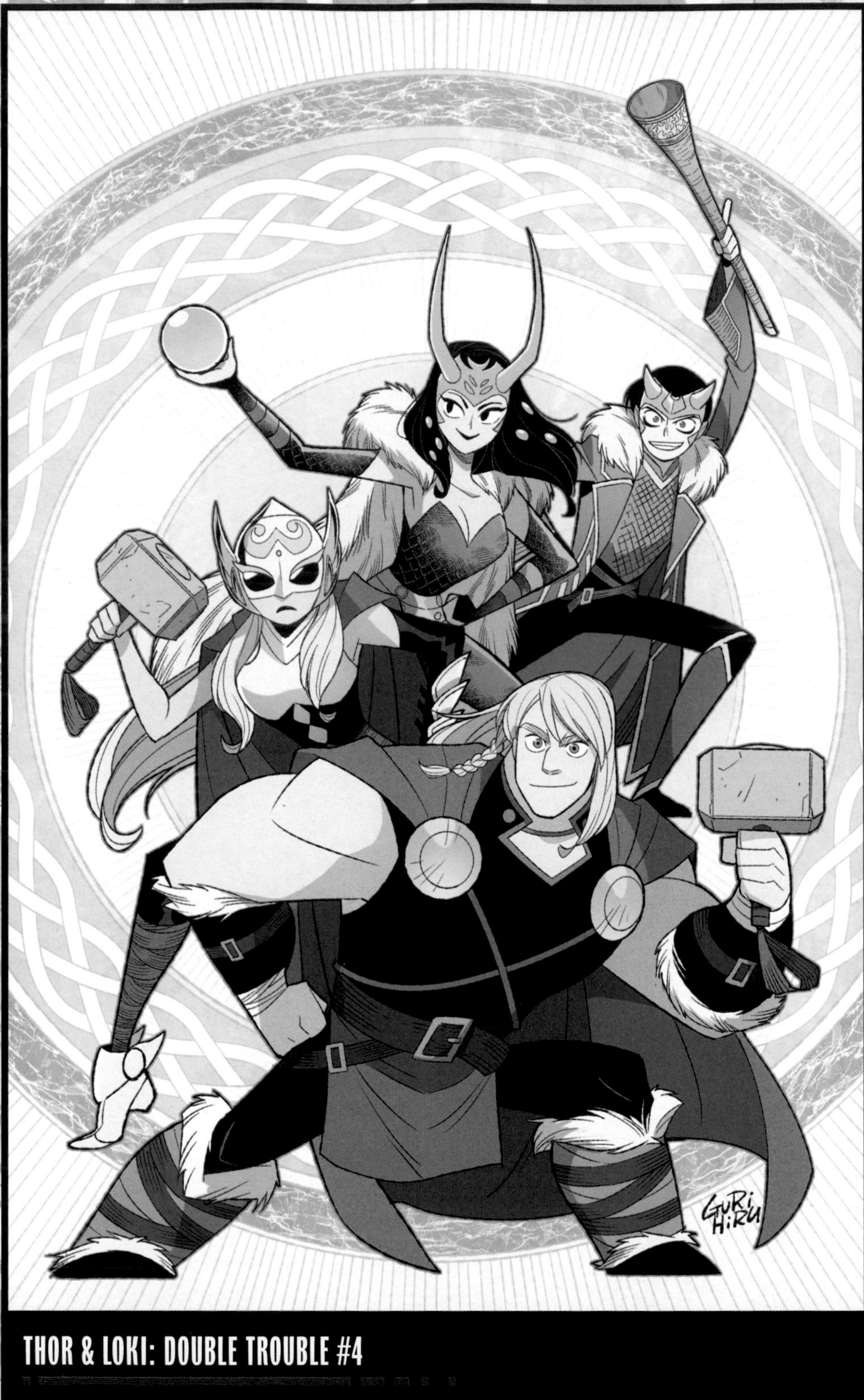
GURI HIRU

THOR & LOKI: DOUBLE TROUBLE #4

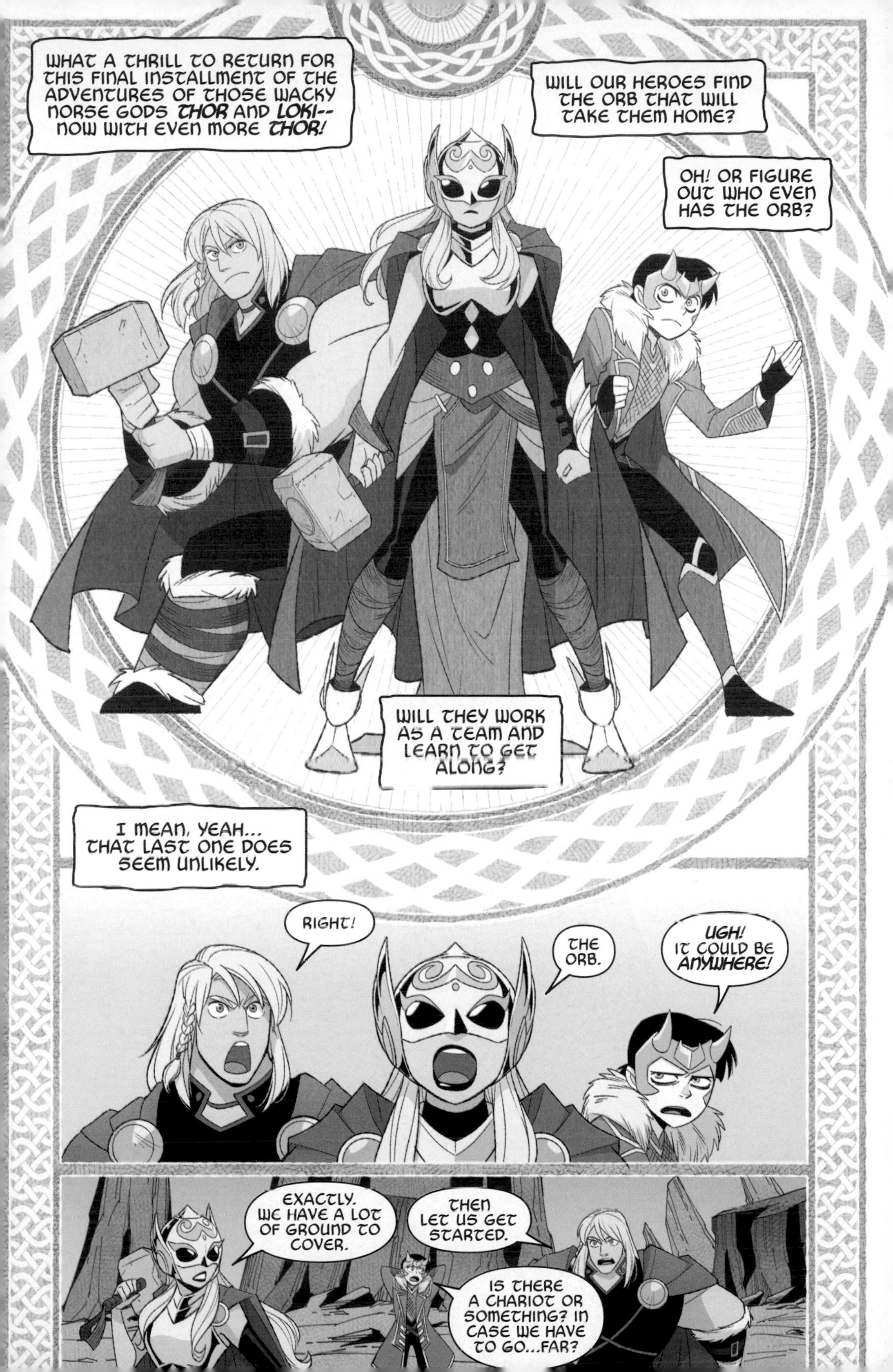
WHAT A THRILL TO RETURN FOR THIS FINAL INSTALLMENT OF THE ADVENTURES OF THOSE WACKY NORSE GODS THOR AND LOKI-- NOW WITH EVEN MORE THOR!
WILL OUR HEROES FIND THE ORB THAT WILL TAKE THEM HOME?
OH! OR FIGURE OUT WHO EVEN HAS THE ORB?
WILL THEY WORK AS A TEAM AND LEARN TO GET ALONG?
I MEAN, YEAH... THAT LAST ONE DOES SEEM UNLIKELY.
RIGHT!
THE ORB.
UGH! IT COULD BE ANYWHERE!
EXACTLY. WE HAVE A LOT OF GROUND TO COVER.
THEN LET US GET STARTED.
IS THERE A CHARIOT OR SOMETHING? IN CASE WE HAVE TO GO...FAR?

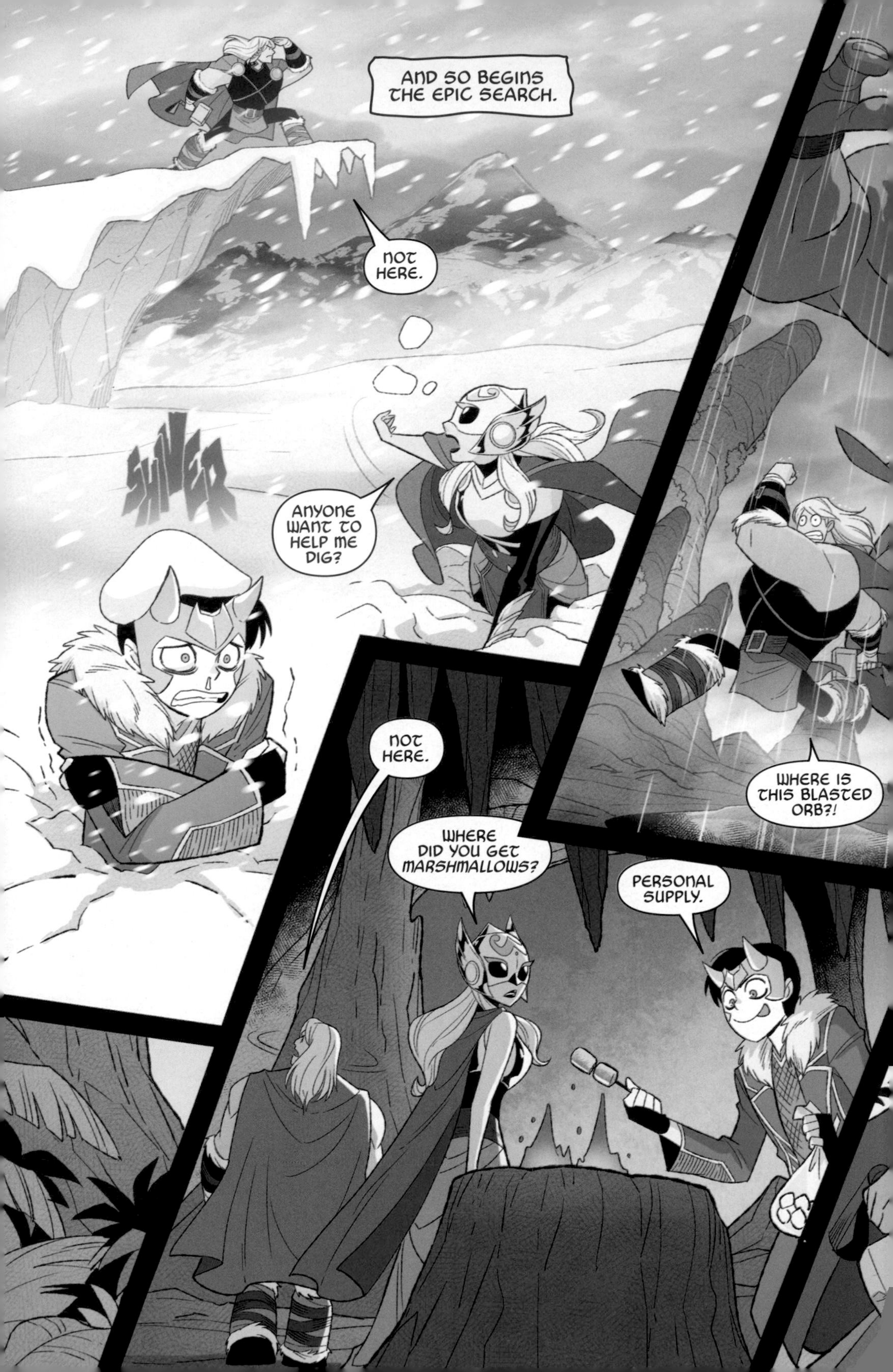
AND SO BEGINS THE EPIC SEARCH.
NOT HERE.
SHIVER
ANYONE WANT TO HELP ME DIG?
WHERE IS THIS BLASTED ORB?!
NOT HERE.
WHERE DID YOU GET MARSHMALLOWS?
PERSONAL SUPPLY.

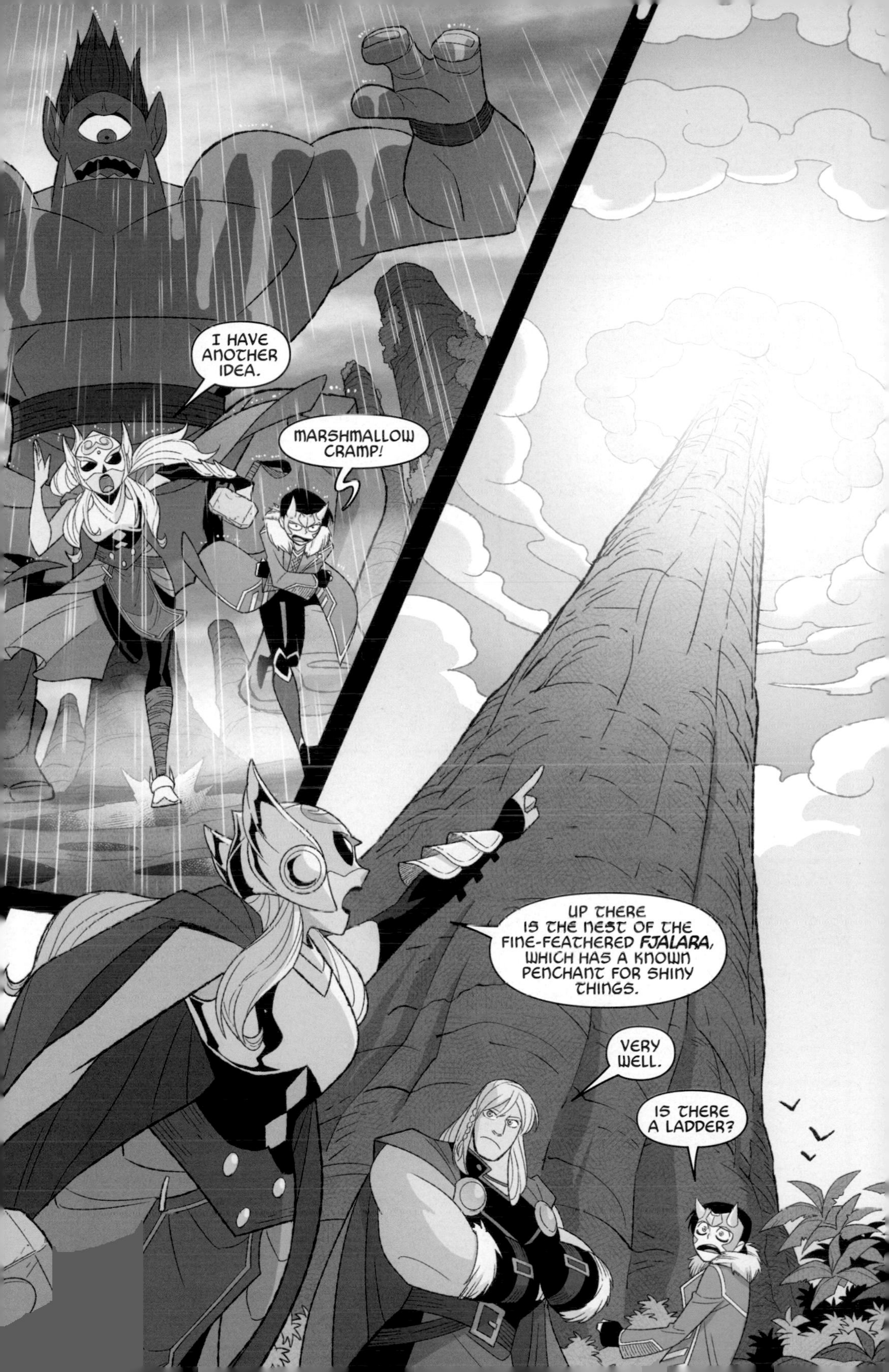
I HAVE ANOTHER IDEA.
MARSHMALLOW CRAMP!
UP THERE IS THE NEST OF THE FINE-FEATHERED FJALARA, WHICH HAS A KNOWN PENCHANT FOR SHINY THINGS.
VERY WELL.
IS THERE A LADDER?

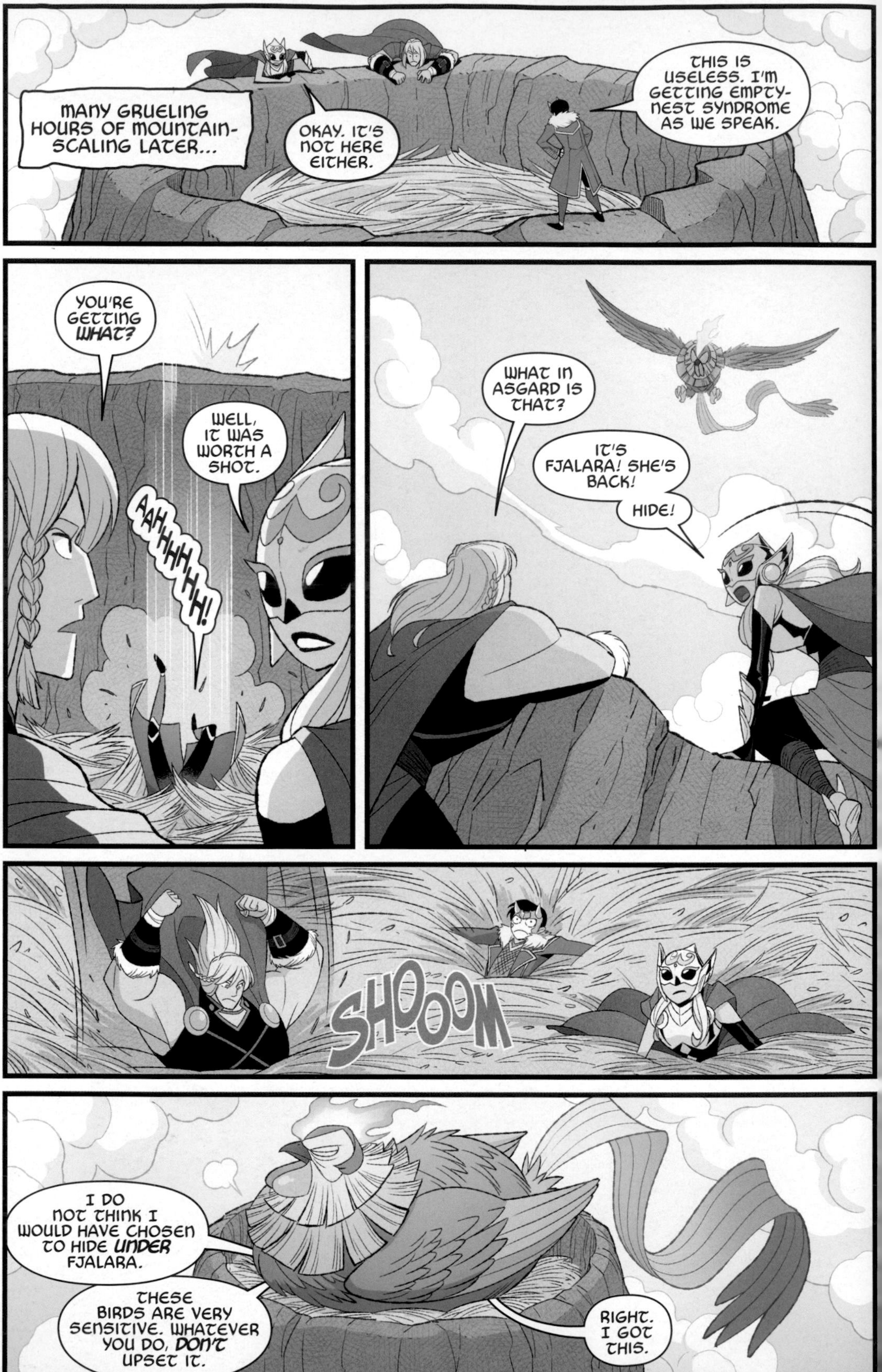

MANY GRUELING HOURS OF MOUNTAIN-SCALING LATER...
OKAY. IT'S NOT HERE EITHER.
THIS IS USELESS. I'M GETTING EMPTY-NEST SYNDROME AS WE SPEAK.
YOU'RE GETTING WHAT?
WELL, IT WAS WORTH A SHOT.
AAHHHHHHH!
WHAT IN ASGARD IS THAT?
IT'S FJALARA! SHE'S BACK!
HIDE!
SHOOOM
I DO NOT THINK I WOULD HAVE CHOSEN TO HIDE UNDER FJALARA.
THESE BIRDS ARE VERY SENSITIVE. WHATEVER YOU DO, DON'T UPSET IT.
RIGHT. I GOT THIS.

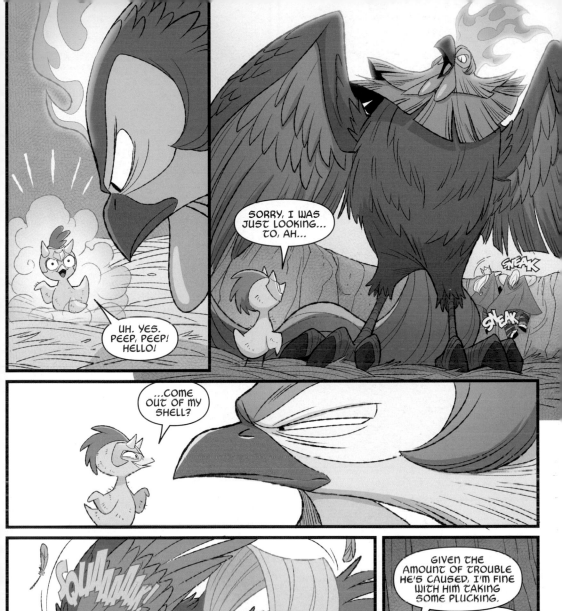

SORRY, I WAS JUST LOOKING... TO, AH...

UH. YES. PEEP, PEEP! HELLO!

SNEAK

SNEAK

...COME OUT OF MY SHELL?

SQUAAAAAK!

HEY THERE! EASY WITH THE TALONS!

SHOULD WE HELP HIM?

WHO, LOKI?

GIVEN THE AMOUNT OF TROUBLE HE'S CAUSED, I'M FINE WITH HIM TAKING SOME PLUCKING.

BUGBERRIES! OF COURSE!

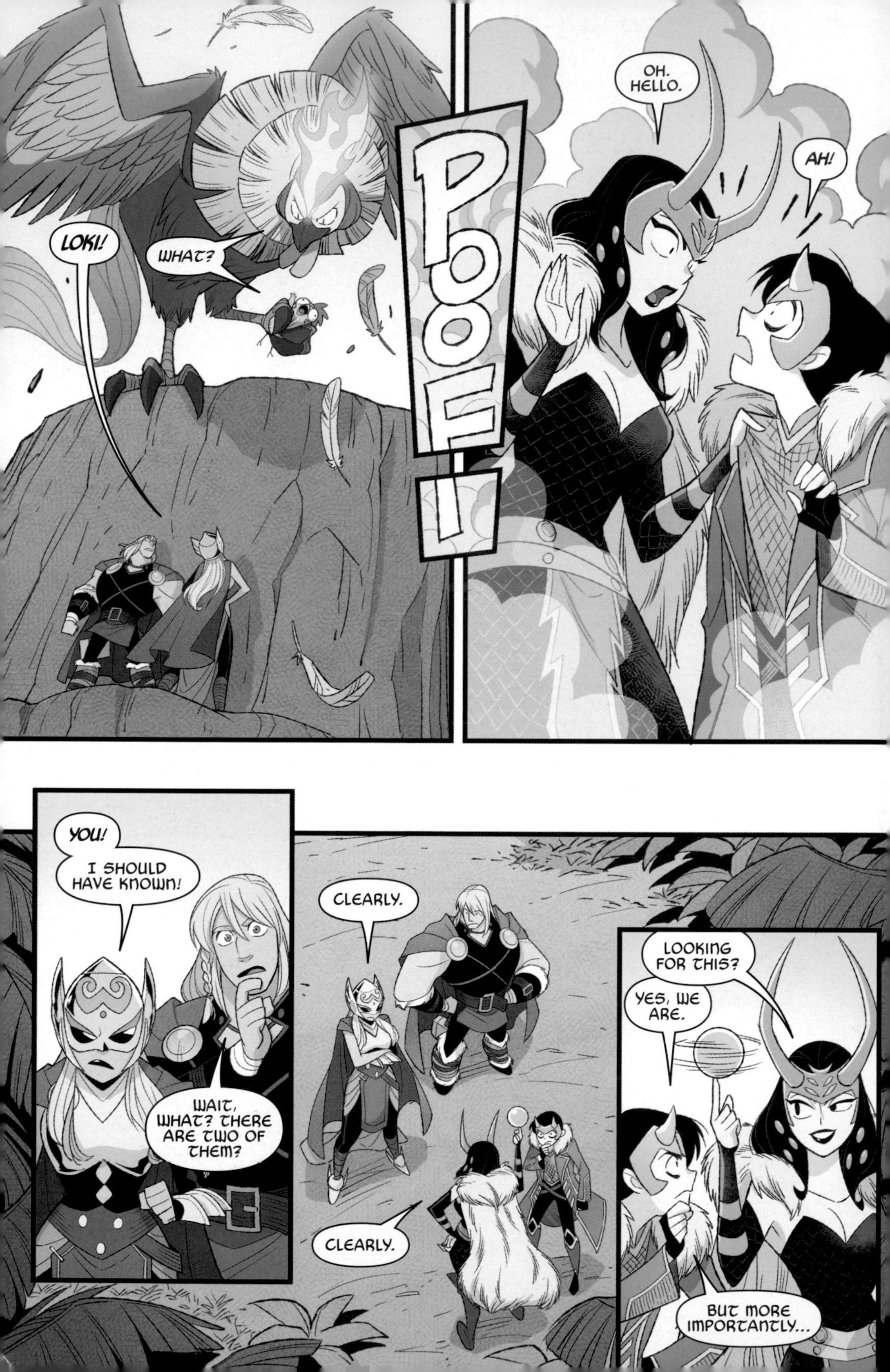
LOKI!
WHAT?
POOF!
OH. HELLO.
AH!
YOU!
I SHOULD HAVE KNOWN!
WAIT, WHAT? THERE ARE TWO OF THEM?
CLEARLY.
CLEARLY.
LOOKING FOR THIS?
YES, WE ARE.
BUT MORE IMPORTANTLY...

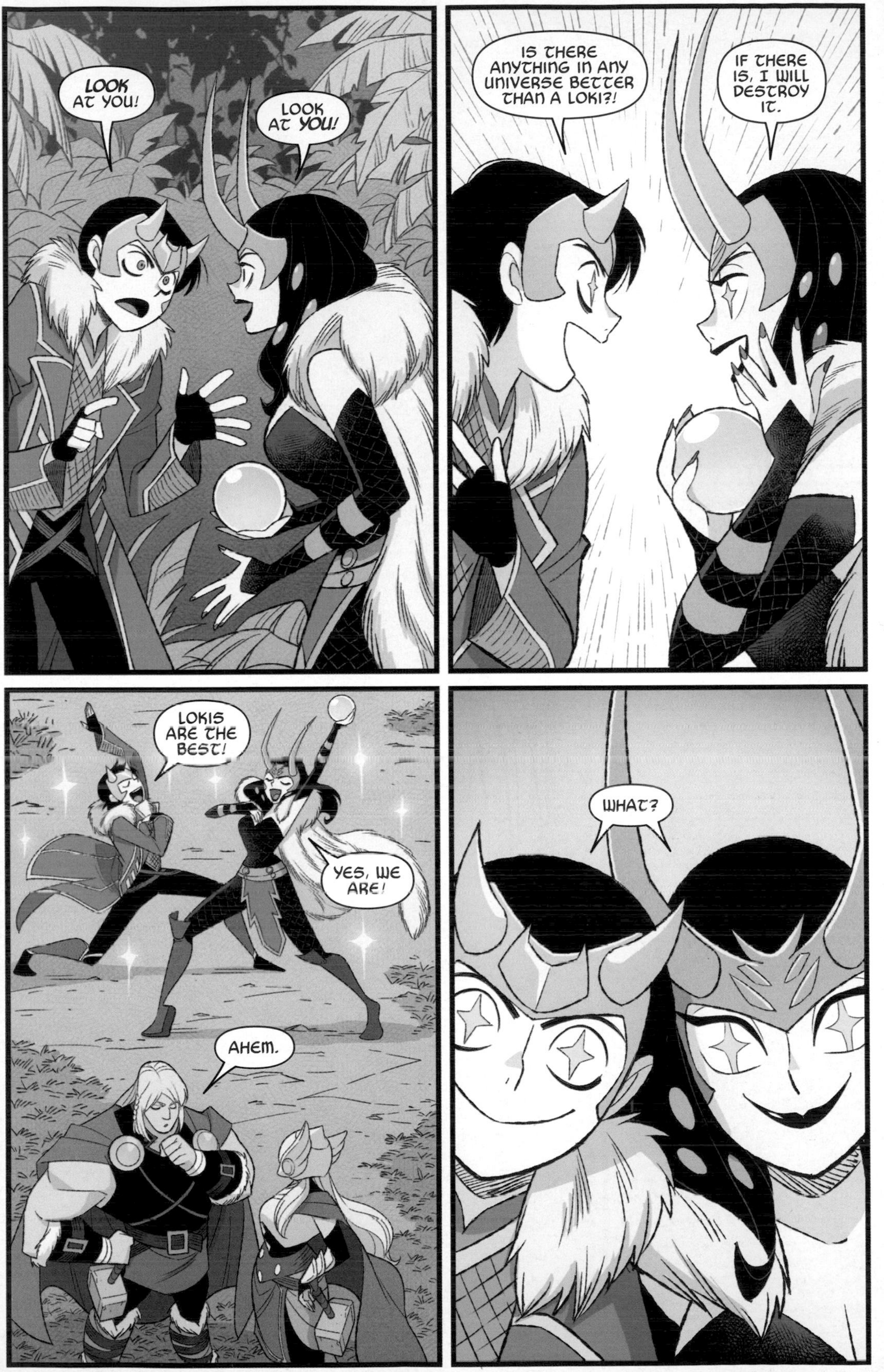
LOOK AT YOU!
LOOK AT YOU!
IS THERE ANYTHING IN ANY UNIVERSE BETTER THAN A LOKI?!
IF THERE IS, I WILL DESTROY IT.
LOKIS ARE THE BEST!
YES, WE ARE!
AHEM.
WHAT?

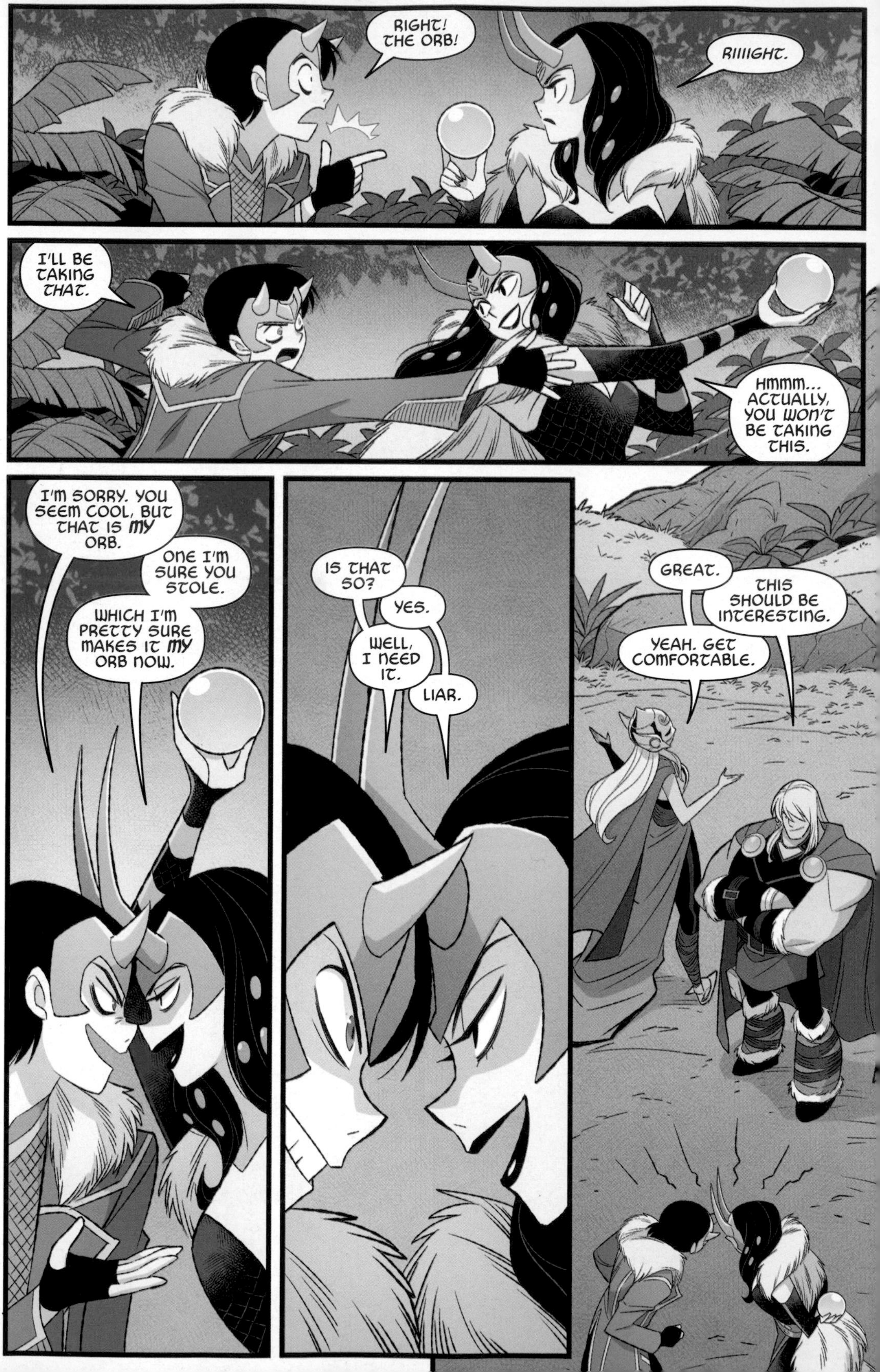
RIGHT! THE ORB!
RIIIIGHT.
I'LL BE TAKING *THAT.*
HMMM... ACTUALLY, YOU *WON'T* BE TAKING THIS.
I'M SORRY. YOU SEEM COOL, BUT THAT IS *MY* ORB.
ONE I'M SURE YOU STOLE.
WHICH I'M PRETTY SURE MAKES IT *MY* ORB NOW.
IS THAT SO?
YES.
WELL, I NEED IT.
LIAR.
GREAT.
THIS SHOULD BE INTERESTING.
YEAH. GET COMFORTABLE.

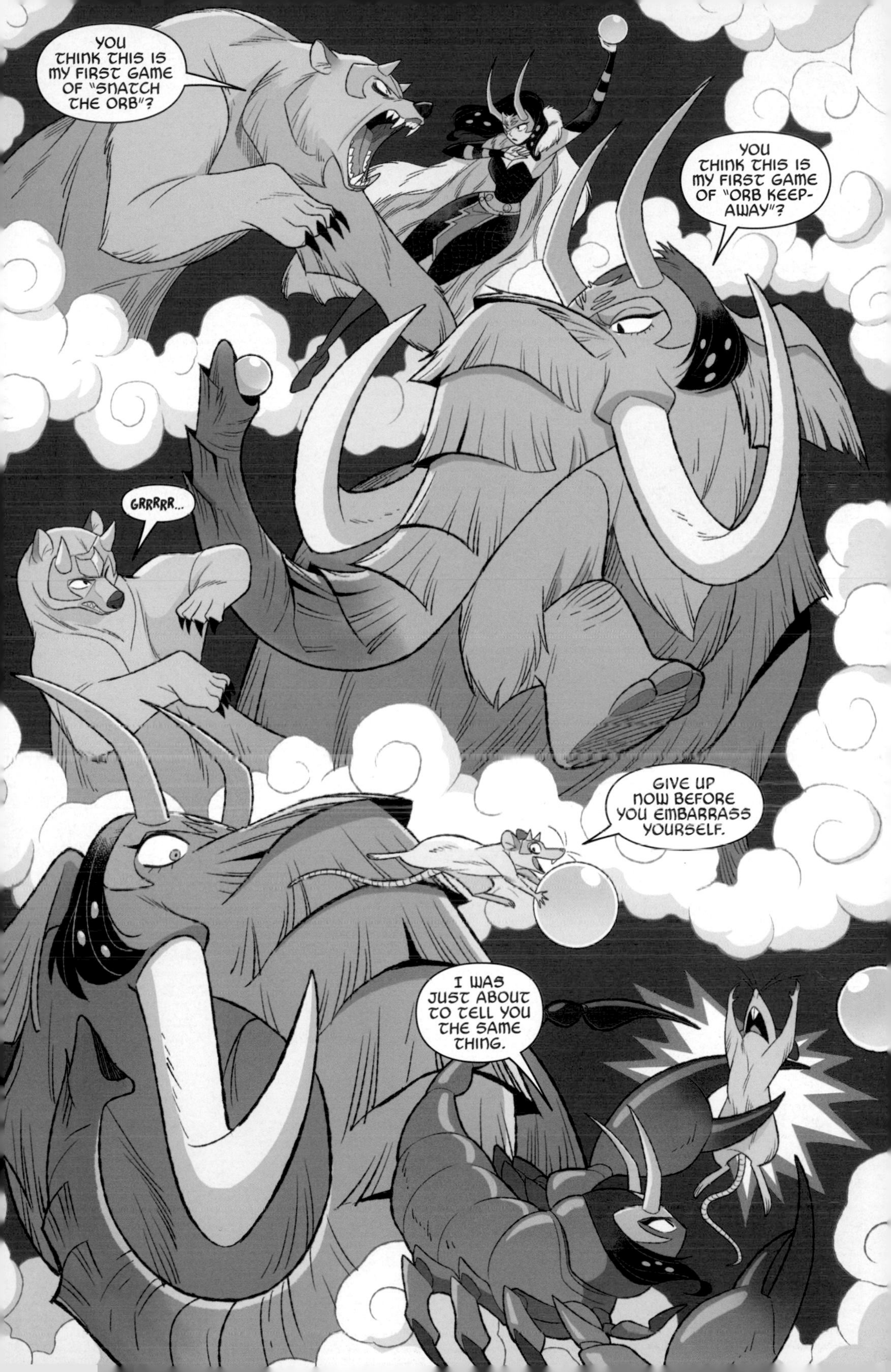
YOU THINK THIS IS MY FIRST GAME OF "SNATCH THE ORB"?
YOU THINK THIS IS MY FIRST GAME OF "ORB KEEP-AWAY"?
GRRRRR...
GIVE UP NOW BEFORE YOU EMBARRASS YOURSELF.
I WAS JUST ABOUT TO TELL YOU THE SAME THING.

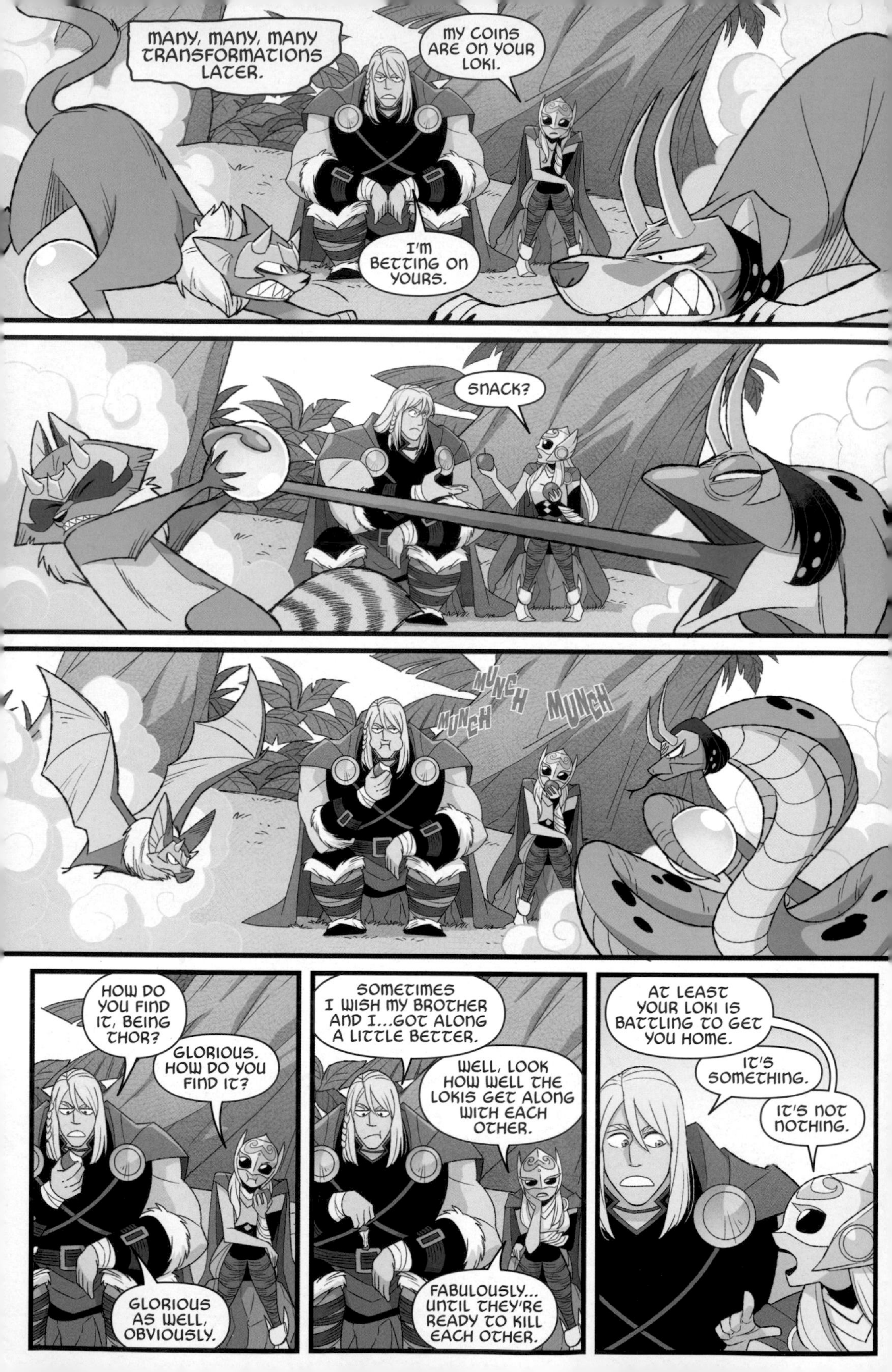
MANY, MANY, MANY TRANSFORMATIONS LATER.
MY COINS ARE ON YOUR LOKI.
I'M BETTING ON YOURS.
SNACK?
MUNCH
MUNCH
MUNCH
HOW DO YOU FIND IT, BEING THOR?
GLORIOUS. HOW DO YOU FIND IT?
GLORIOUS AS WELL, OBVIOUSLY.
SOMETIMES I WISH MY BROTHER AND I...GOT ALONG A LITTLE BETTER.
WELL, LOOK HOW WELL THE LOKIS GET ALONG WITH EACH OTHER.
FABULOUSLY... UNTIL THEY'RE READY TO KILL EACH OTHER.
AT LEAST YOUR LOKI IS BATTLING TO GET YOU HOME.
IT'S SOMETHING.
IT'S NOT NOTHING.

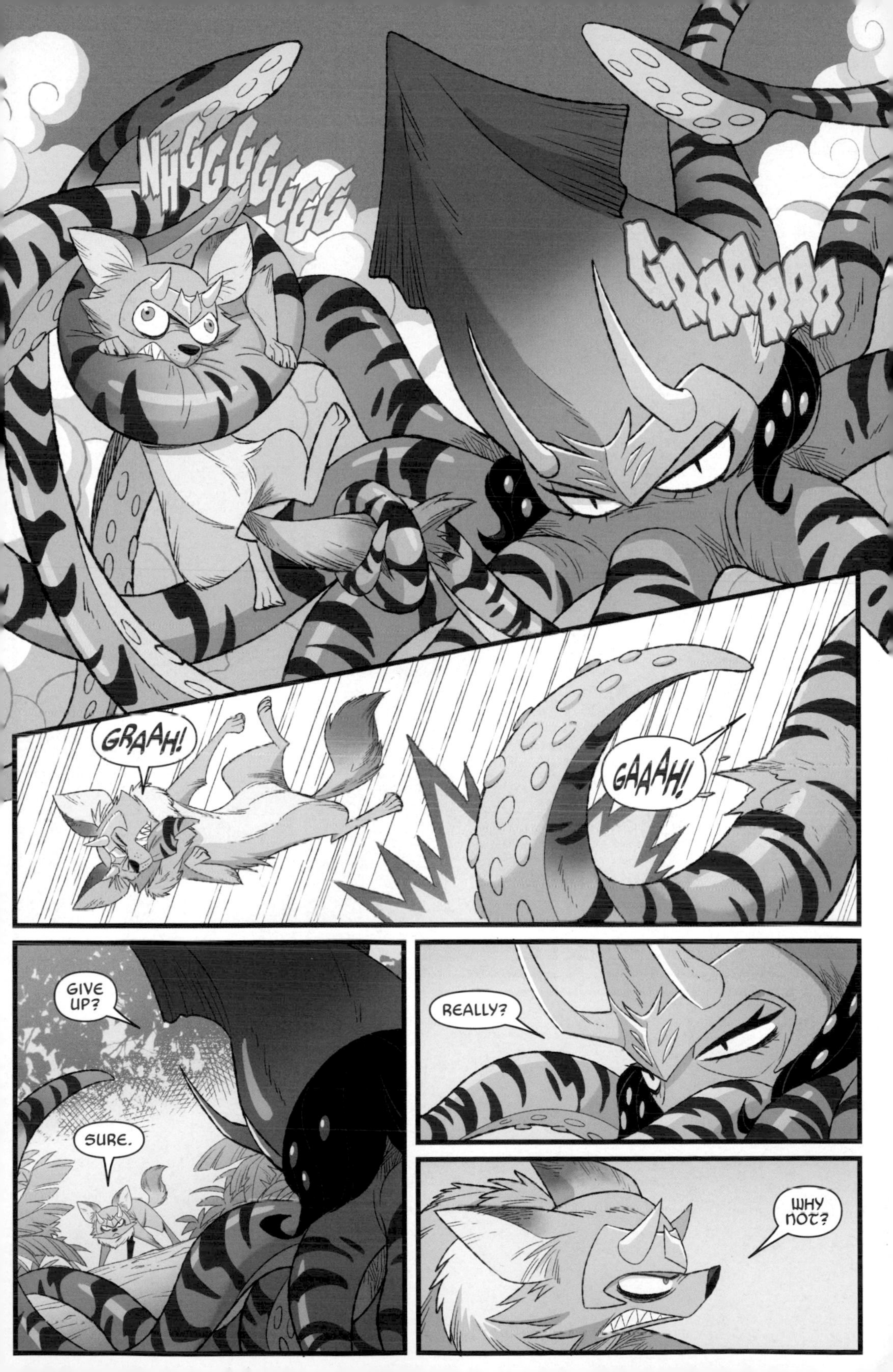
NHGGGGGGG
GRRRRRR
GRAAH!
GAAAH!
GIVE UP?
SURE.
REALLY?
WHY NOT?

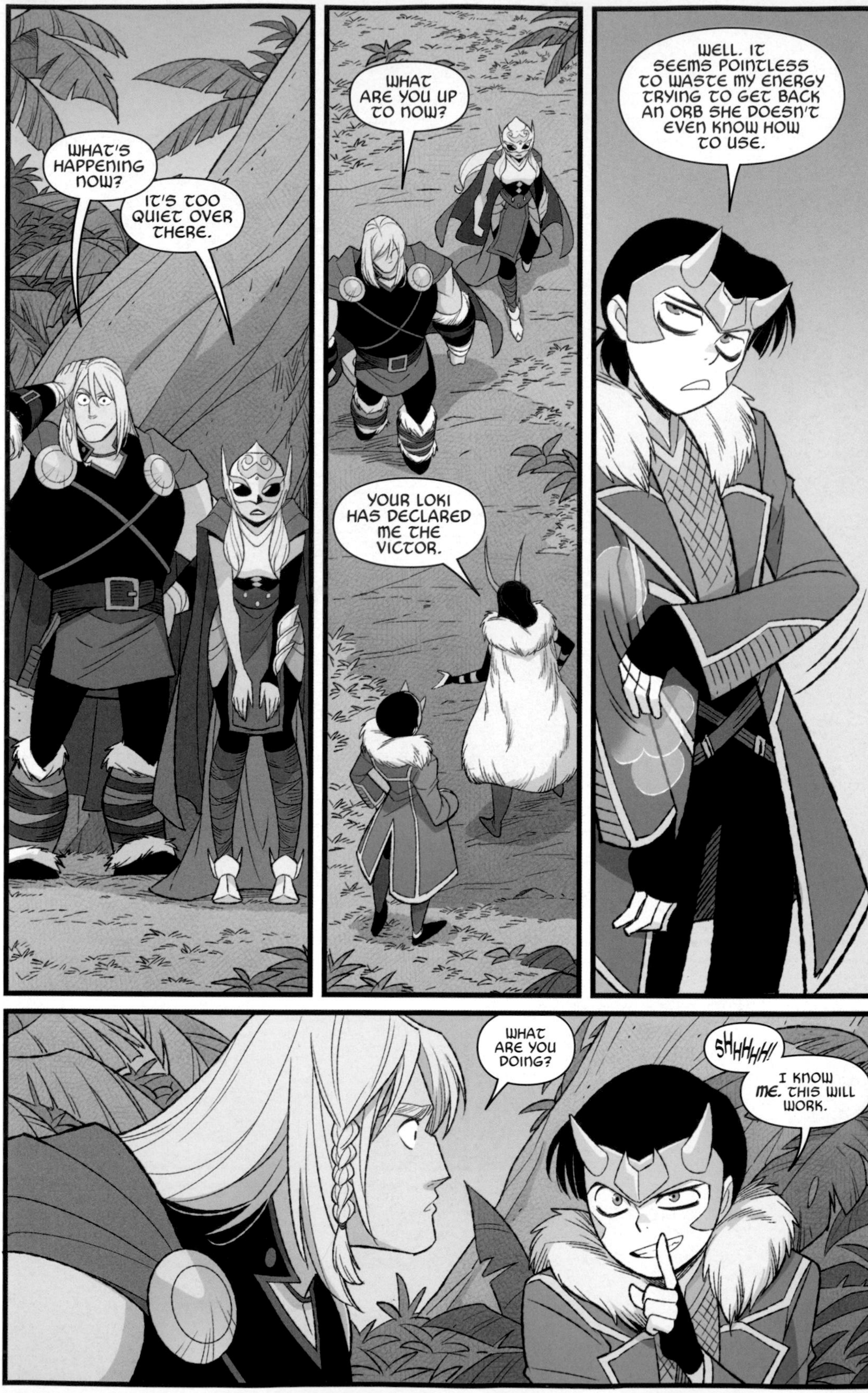
WHAT'S HAPPENING NOW?
IT'S TOO QUIET OVER THERE.
WHAT ARE YOU UP TO NOW?
YOUR LOKI HAS DECLARED ME THE VICTOR.
WELL. IT SEEMS POINTLESS TO WASTE MY ENERGY TRYING TO GET BACK AN ORB SHE DOESN'T EVEN KNOW HOW TO USE.
WHAT ARE YOU DOING?
SHHHHH!
I KNOW *ME.* THIS WILL WORK.

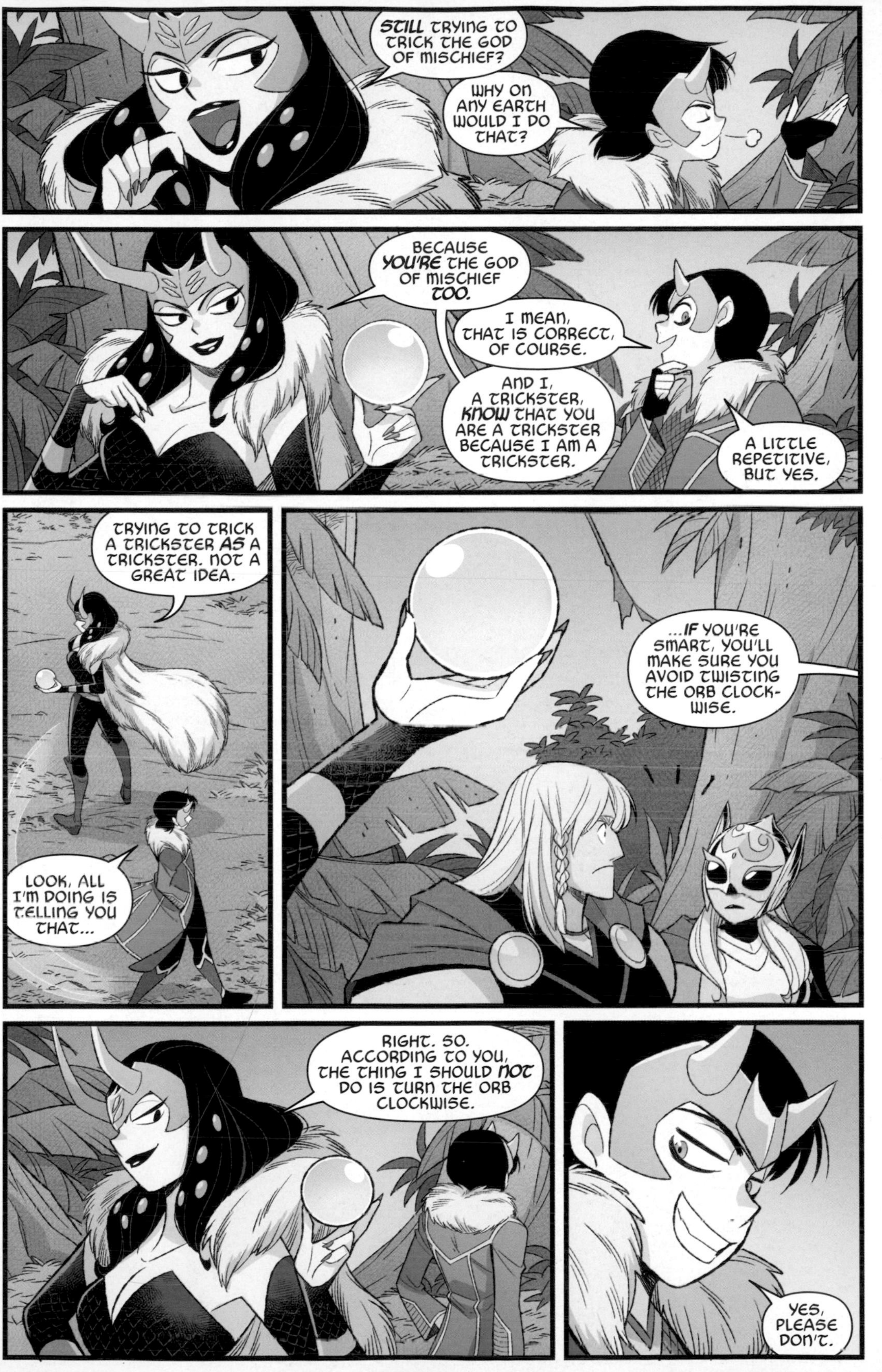
STILL TRYING TO TRICK THE GOD OF MISCHIEF?
WHY ON ANY EARTH WOULD I DO THAT?
BECAUSE YOU'RE THE GOD OF MISCHIEF TOO.
I MEAN, THAT IS CORRECT, OF COURSE.
AND I, A TRICKSTER, KNOW THAT YOU ARE A TRICKSTER BECAUSE I AM A TRICKSTER.
A LITTLE REPETITIVE, BUT YES.
TRYING TO TRICK A TRICKSTER AS A TRICKSTER. NOT A GREAT IDEA.
LOOK, ALL I'M DOING IS TELLING YOU THAT...
...IF YOU'RE SMART, YOU'LL MAKE SURE YOU AVOID TWISTING THE ORB CLOCK-WISE.
RIGHT. SO. ACCORDING TO YOU, THE THING I SHOULD NOT DO IS TURN THE ORB CLOCKWISE.
YES, PLEASE DON'T.

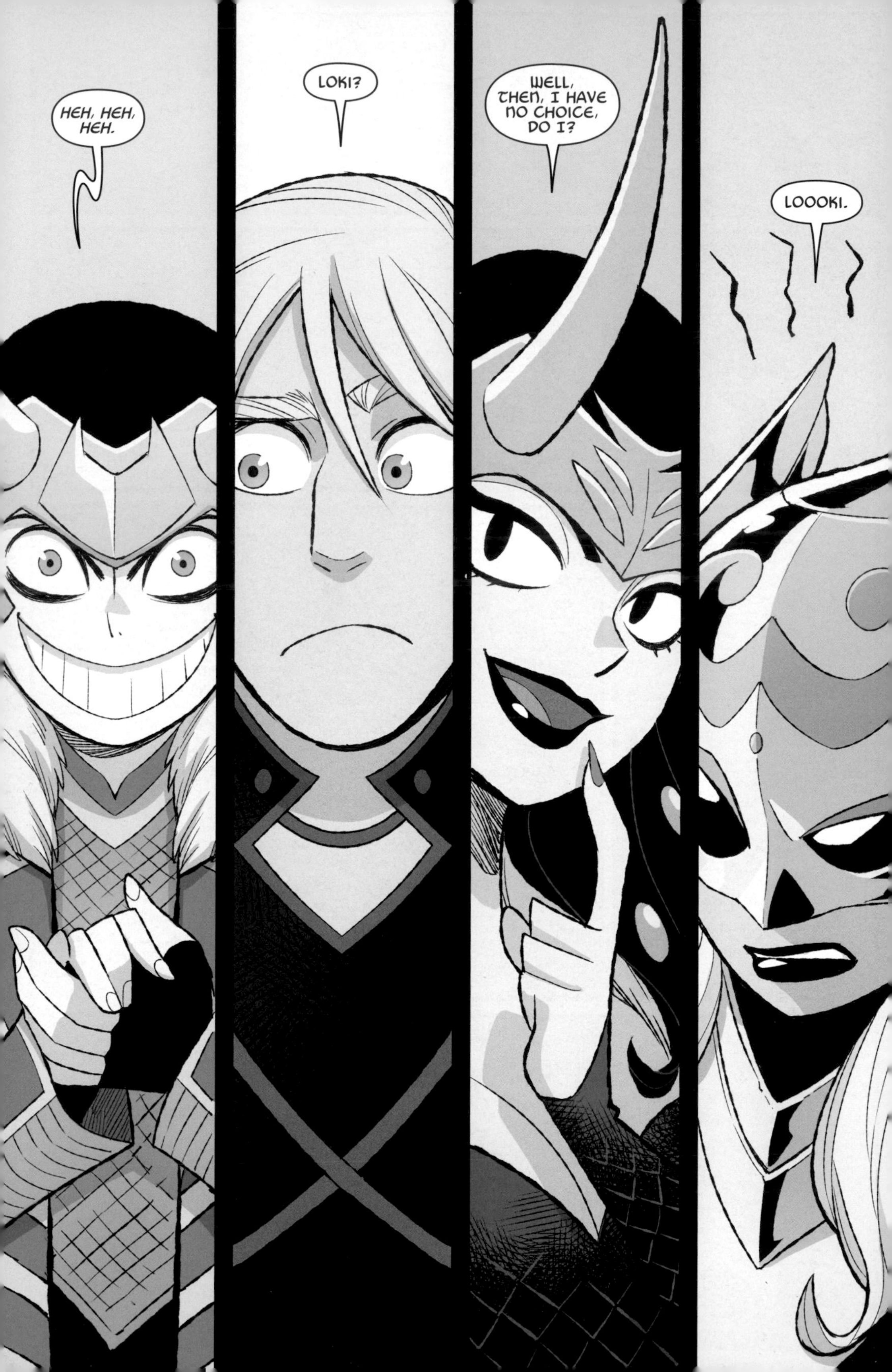
HEH, HEH, HEH.
LOKI?
WELL, THEN, I HAVE NO CHOICE, DO I?
LOOOKI.

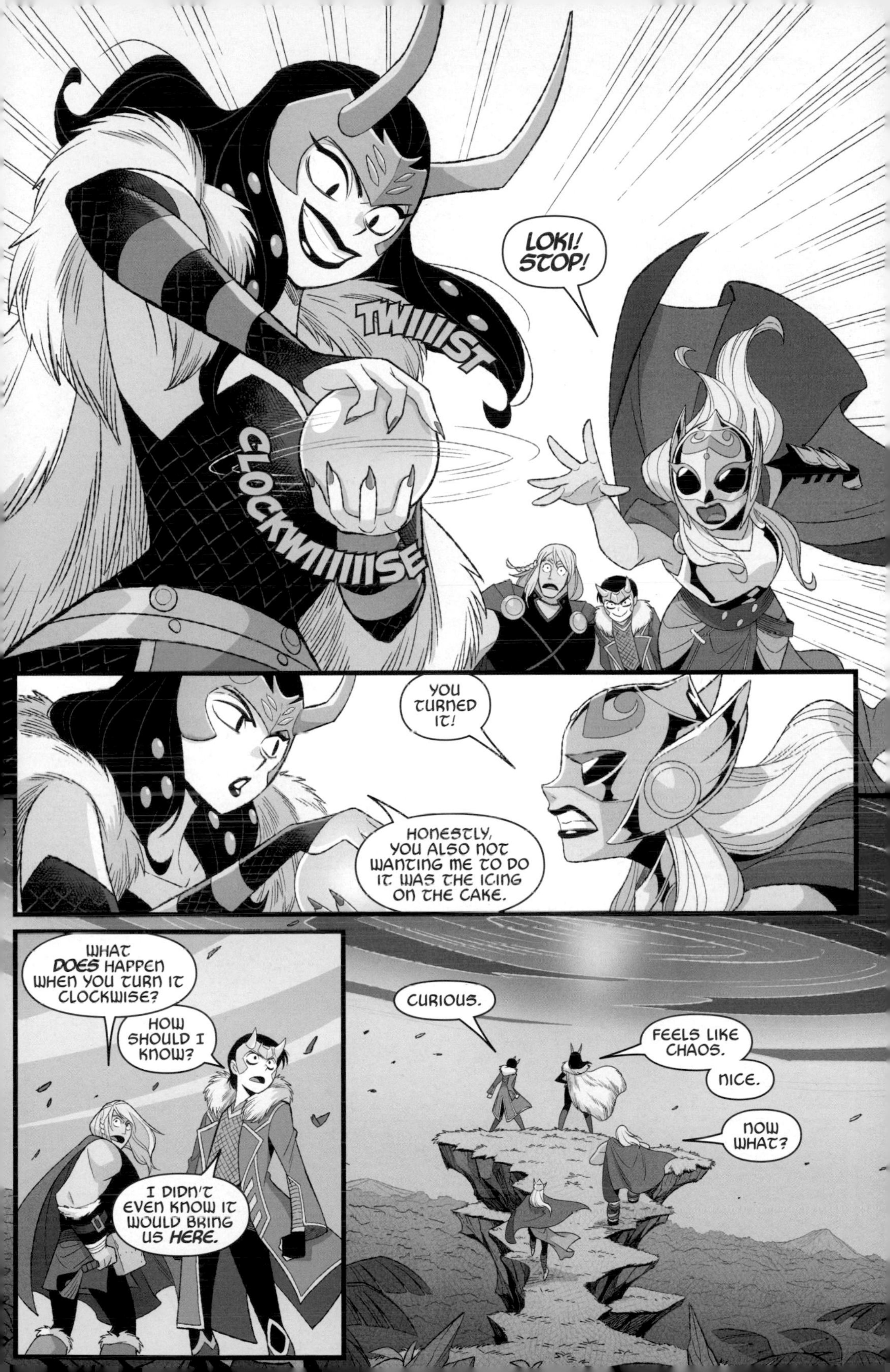
LOKI! STOP!
TWIIIIST
CLOCKWIIIIISE
YOU TURNED IT!
HONESTLY, YOU ALSO NOT WANTING ME TO DO IT WAS THE ICING ON THE CAKE.
WHAT DOES HAPPEN WHEN YOU TURN IT CLOCKWISE?
HOW SHOULD I KNOW?
I DIDN'T EVEN KNOW IT WOULD BRING US HERE.
CURIOUS.
FEELS LIKE CHAOS.
NICE.
NOW WHAT?

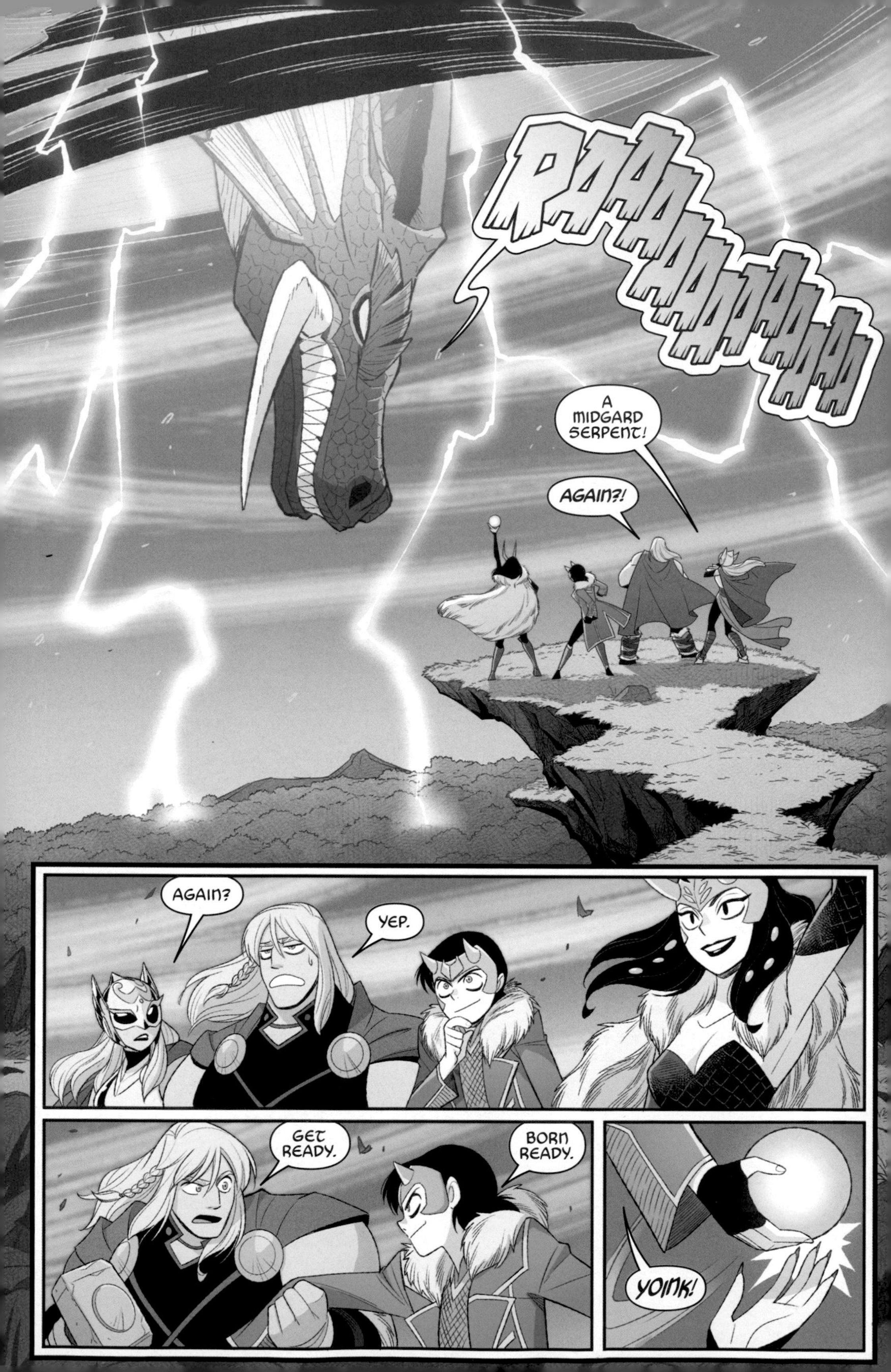
RAAAAAAAAAAAAAA
A MIDGARD SERPENT!
AGAIN?!
AGAIN?
YEP.
GET READY.
BORN READY.
YOINK!

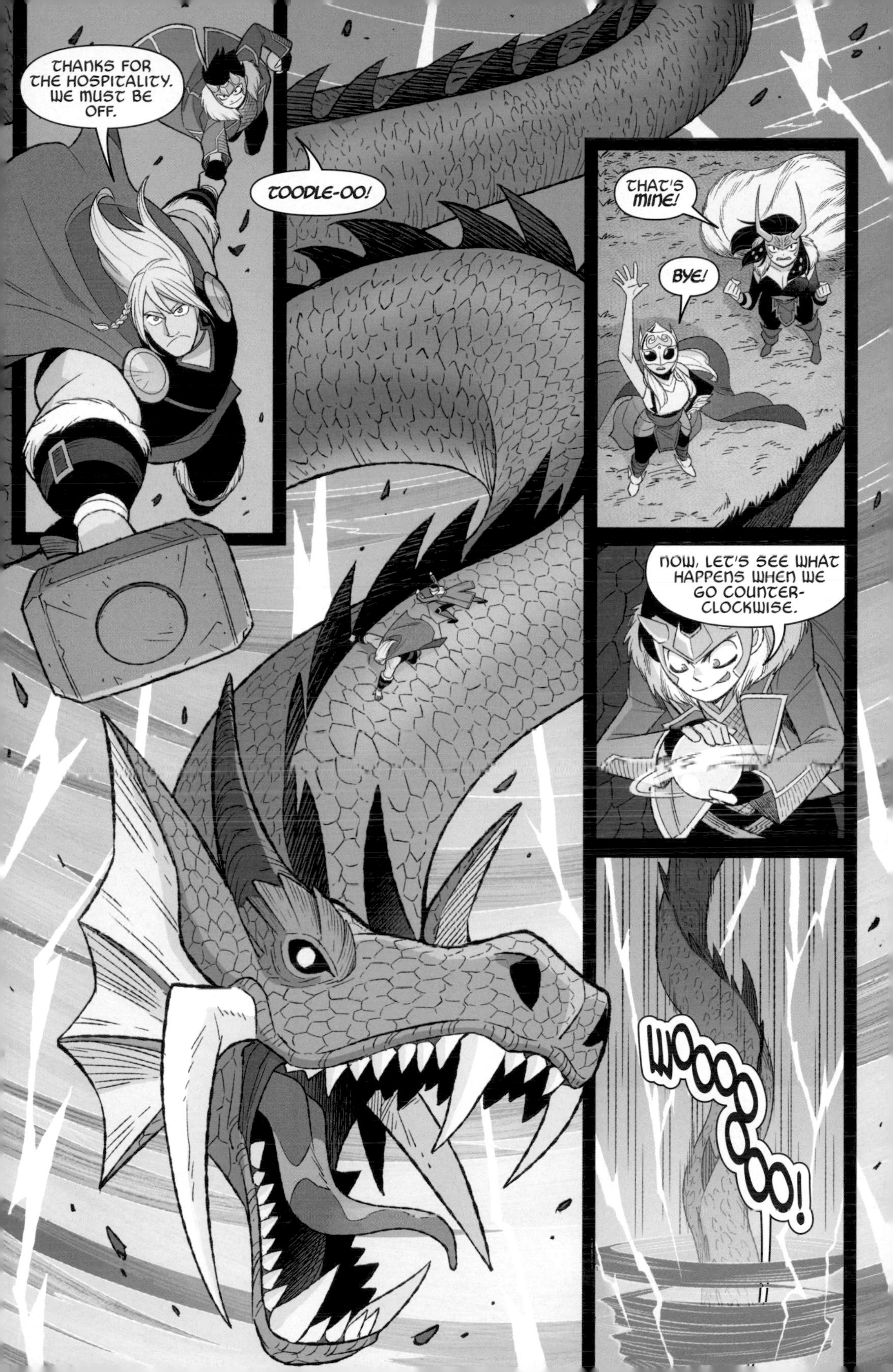
THANKS FOR THE HOSPITALITY. WE MUST BE OFF.
TOODLE-OO!
THAT'S MINE!
BYE!
NOW, LET'S SEE WHAT HAPPENS WHEN WE GO COUNTER-CLOCKWISE.
WOOOOOOOO!

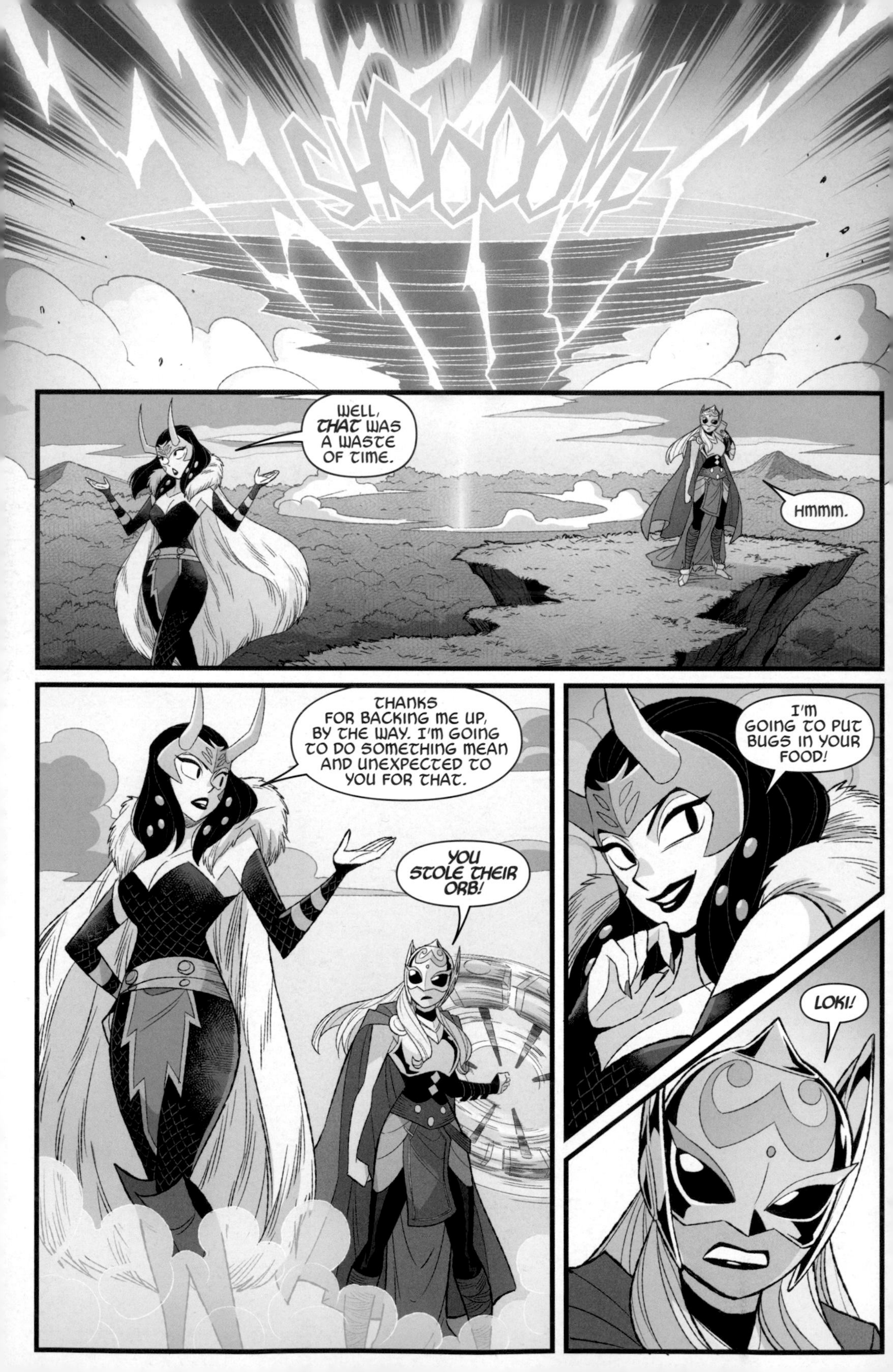
WELL, THAT WAS A WASTE OF TIME.
HMMM.
THANKS FOR BACKING ME UP, BY THE WAY. I'M GOING TO DO SOMETHING MEAN AND UNEXPECTED TO YOU FOR THAT.
YOU STOLE THEIR ORB!
I'M GOING TO PUT BUGS IN YOUR FOOD!
LOKI!

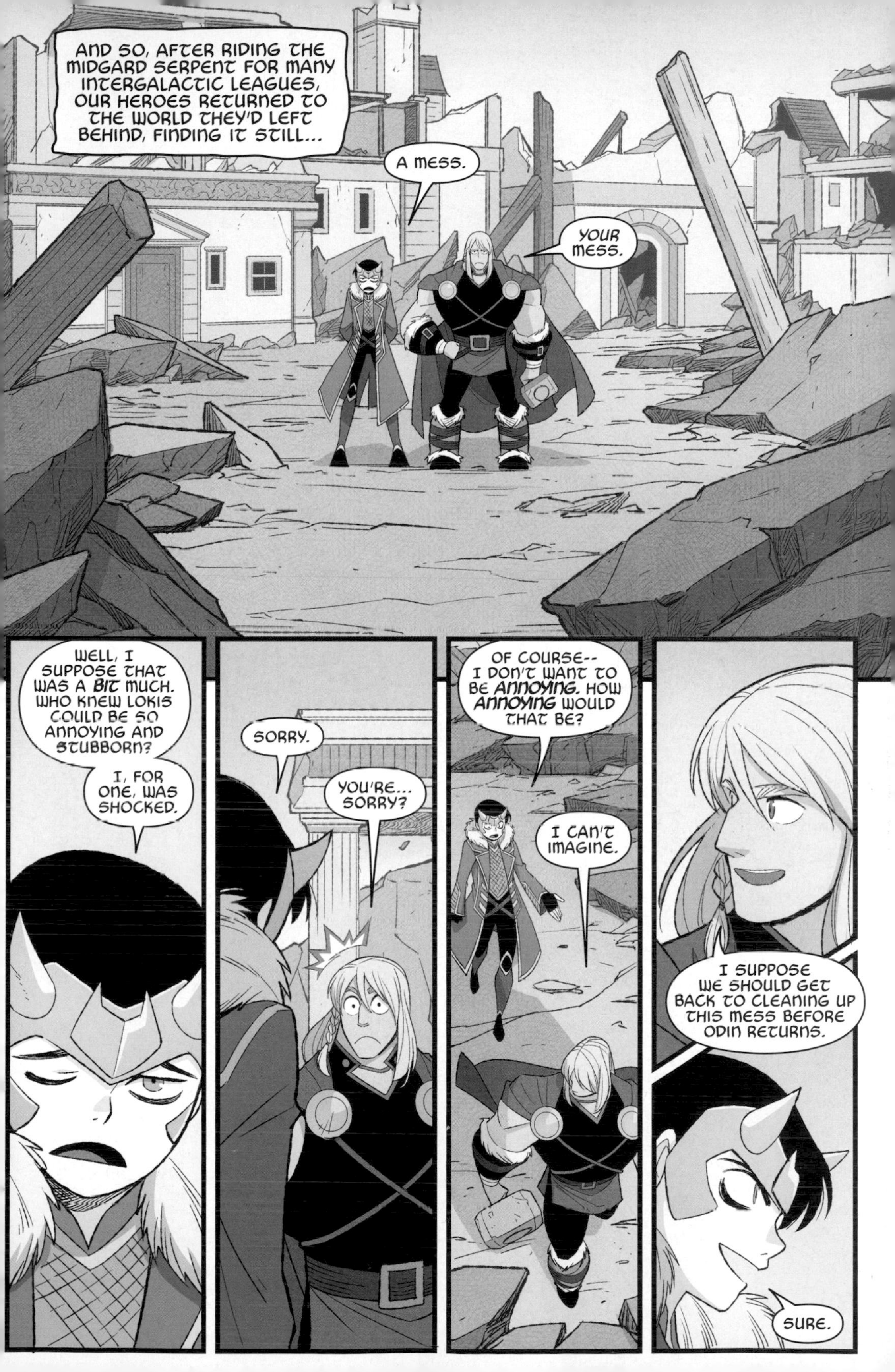
AND SO, AFTER RIDING THE MIDGARD SERPENT FOR MANY INTERGALACTIC LEAGUES, OUR HEROES RETURNED TO THE WORLD THEY'D LEFT BEHIND, FINDING IT STILL...
A MESS.
YOUR MESS.
WELL, I SUPPOSE THAT WAS A *BIT* MUCH. WHO KNEW LOKIS COULD BE SO ANNOYING AND STUBBORN?
I, FOR ONE, WAS SHOCKED.
SORRY.
YOU'RE... SORRY?
OF COURSE-- I DON'T WANT TO BE *ANNOYING*. HOW *ANNOYING* WOULD THAT BE?
I CAN'T IMAGINE.
I SUPPOSE WE SHOULD GET BACK TO CLEANING UP THIS MESS BEFORE ODIN RETURNS.
SURE.

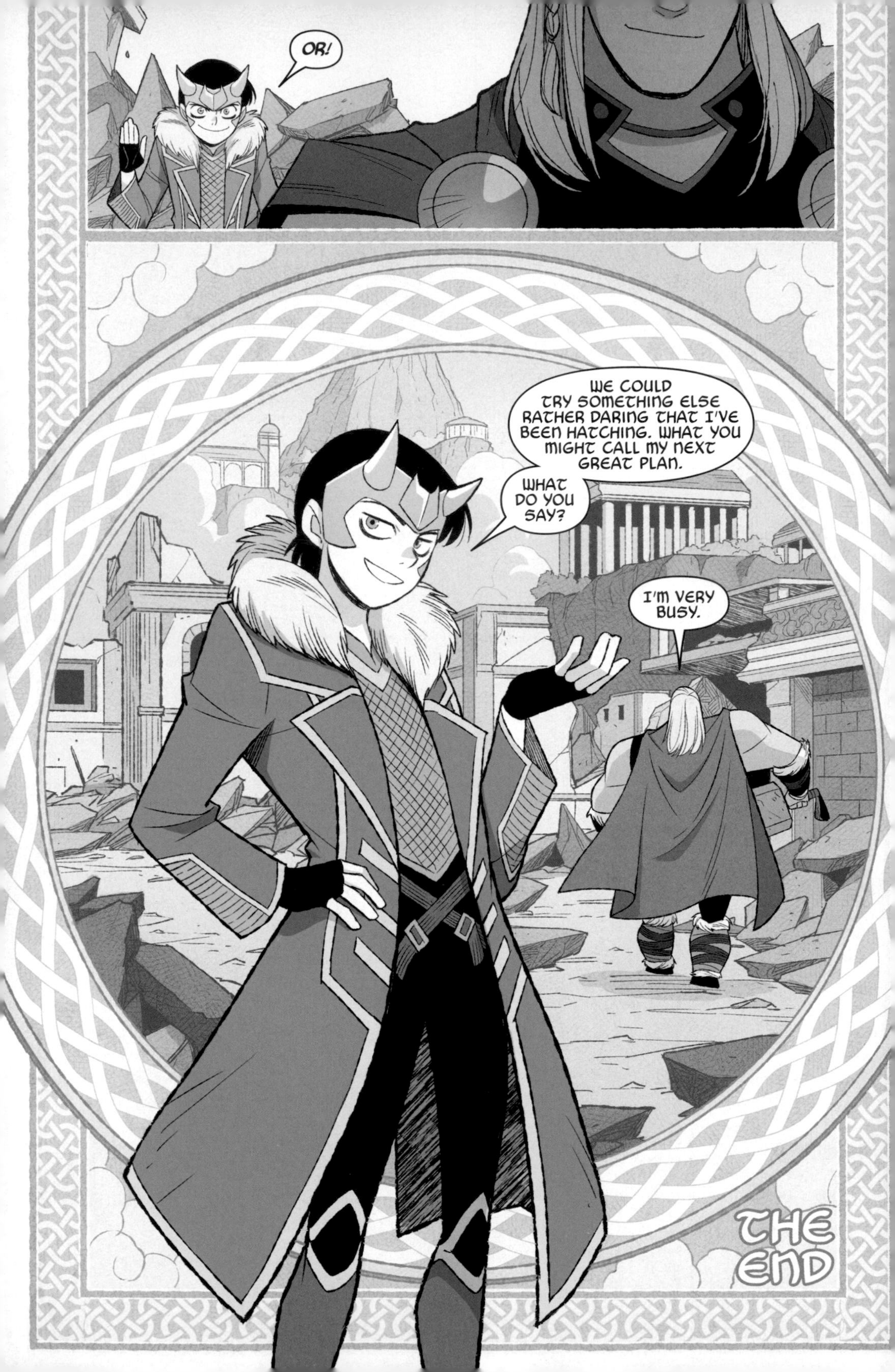
OR!
WE COULD TRY SOMETHING ELSE RATHER DARING THAT I'VE BEEN HATCHING. WHAT YOU MIGHT CALL MY NEXT GREAT PLAN.
WHAT DO YOU SAY?
I'M VERY BUSY.
THE END

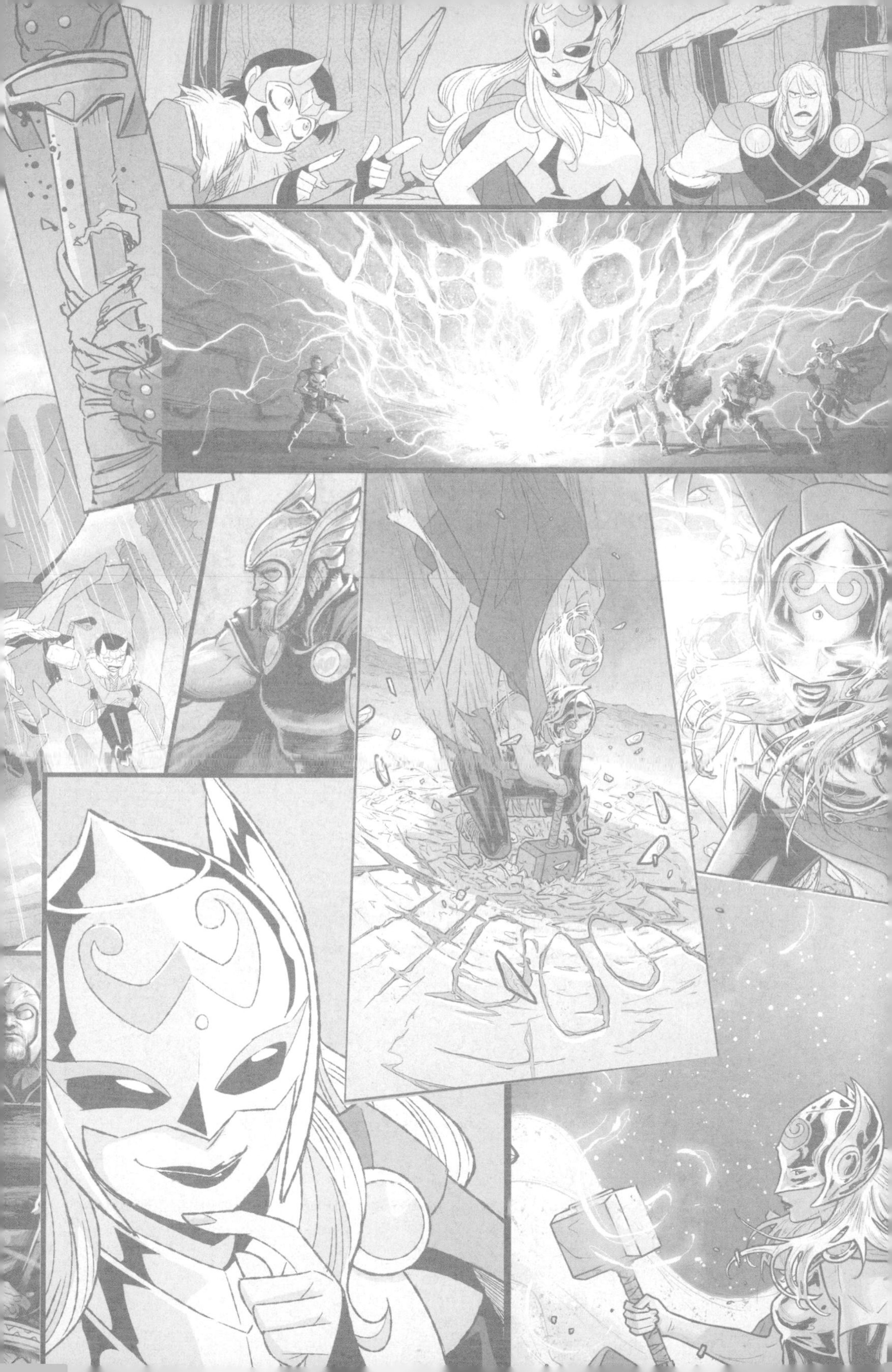

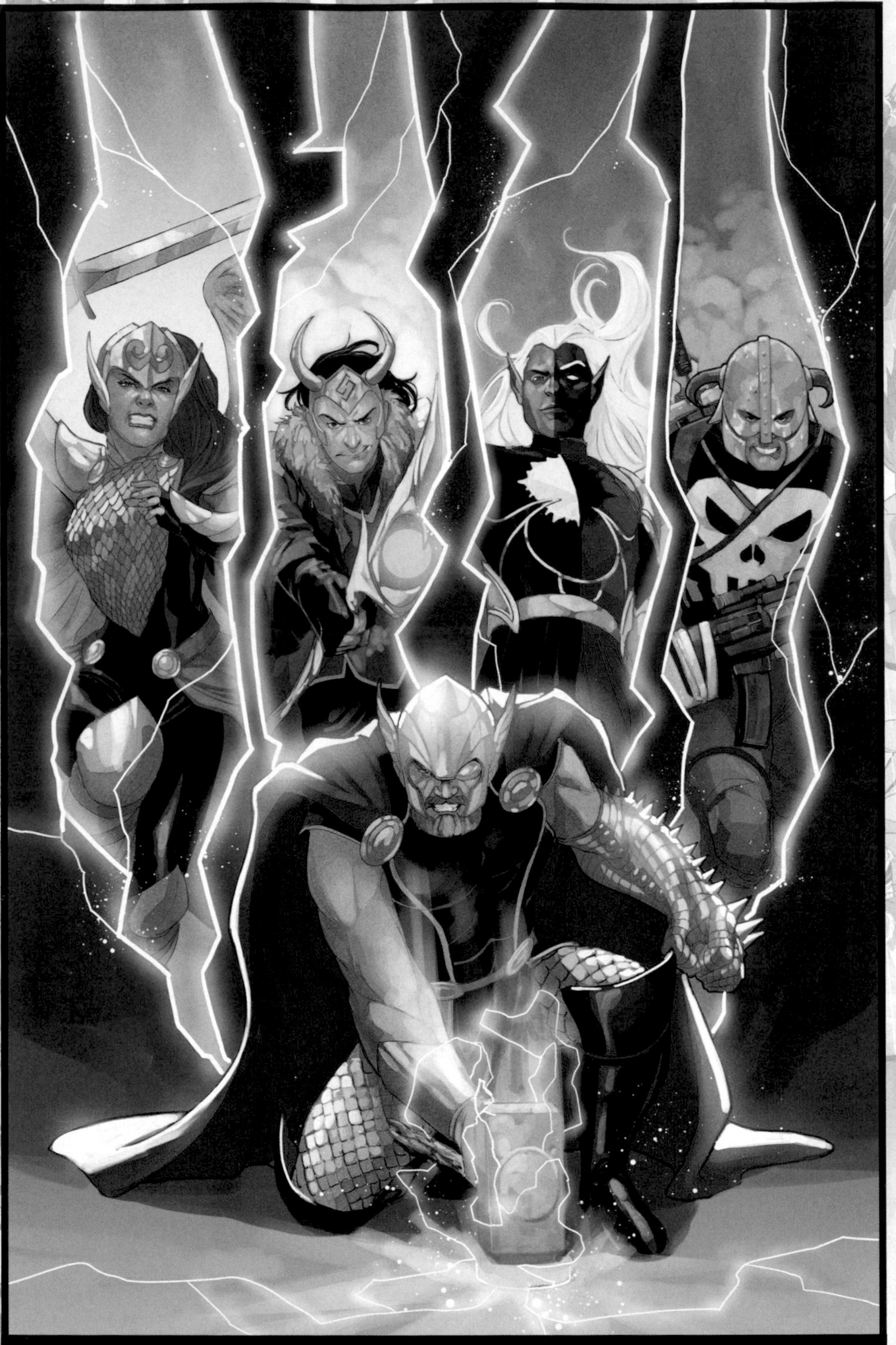

WAR OF THE REALMS OMEGA

JANE FOSTER'S TIME AS THE GODDESS OF THUNDER HAS COME TO AN END — BUT A NEW HEROIC LEGACY AWAITS HER AS THE LAST OF THE VALKYRIES!

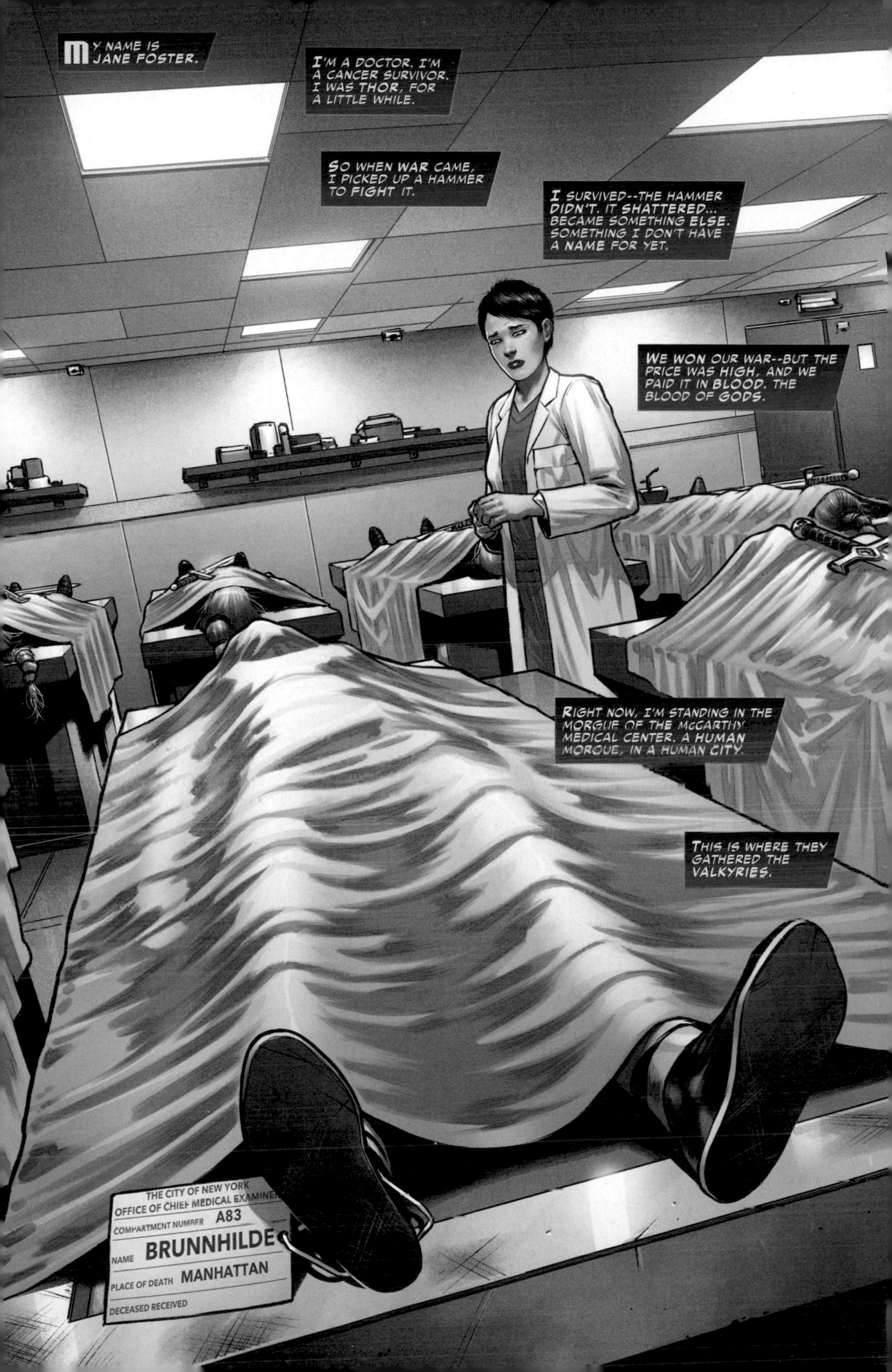
MY NAME IS JANE FOSTER.
I'M A DOCTOR. I'M A CANCER SURVIVOR. I WAS THOR, FOR A LITTLE WHILE.
SO WHEN WAR CAME, I PICKED UP A HAMMER TO FIGHT IT.
I SURVIVED--THE HAMMER DIDN'T. IT SHATTERED... BECAME SOMETHING ELSE. SOMETHING I DON'T HAVE A NAME FOR YET.
WE WON OUR WAR--BUT THE PRICE WAS HIGH, AND WE PAID IT IN BLOOD. THE BLOOD OF GODS.
RIGHT NOW, I'M STANDING IN THE MORGUE OF THE McCARTHY MEDICAL CENTER. A HUMAN MORGUE, IN A HUMAN CITY.
THIS IS WHERE THEY GATHERED THE VALKYRIES.
THE CITY OF NEW YORK
OFFICE OF CHIEF MEDICAL EXAMINER
COMPARTMENT NUMBER A83
NAME BRUNNHILDE
PLACE OF DEATH MANHATTAN
DECEASED RECEIVED

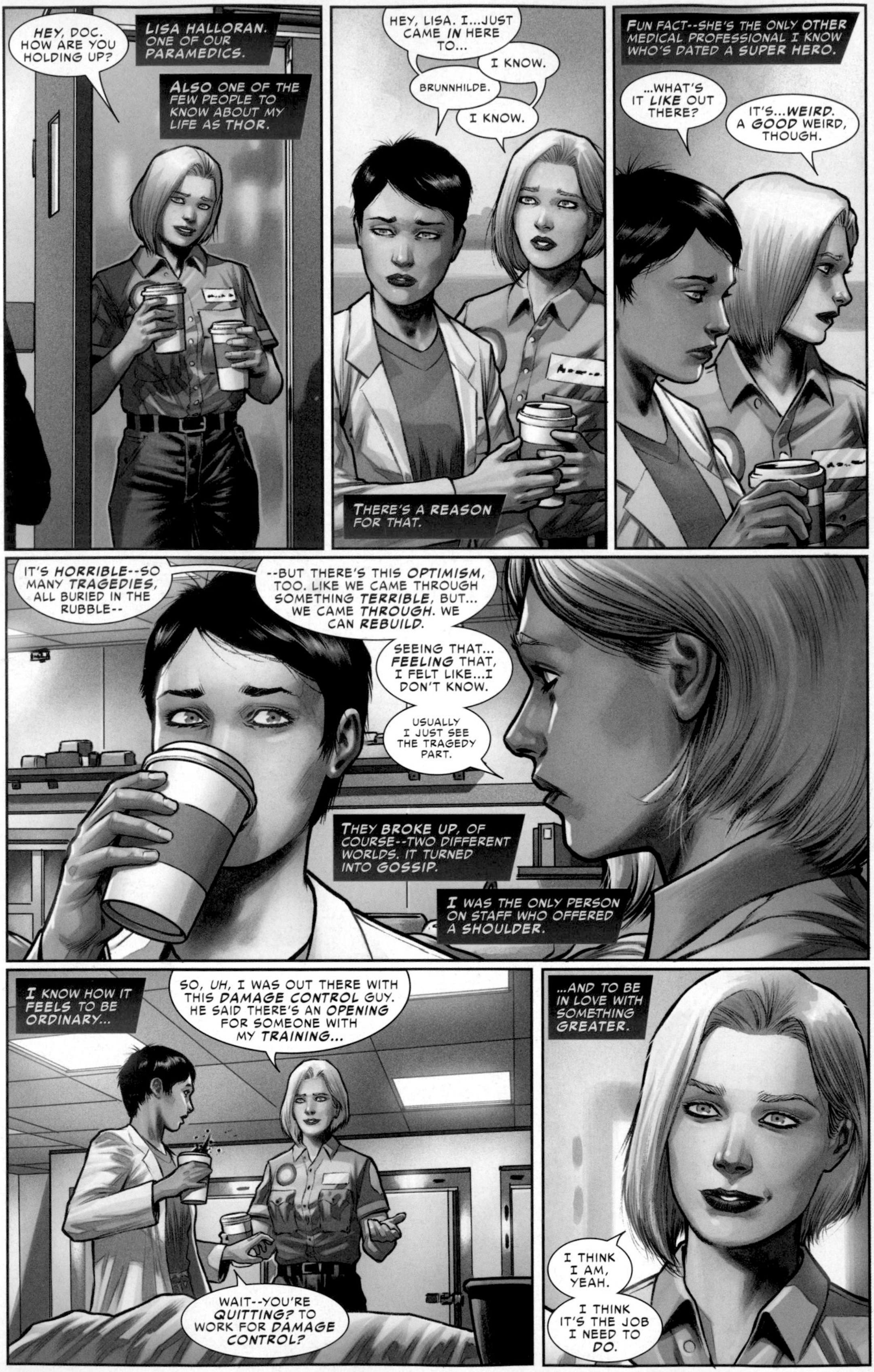
HEY, DOC. HOW ARE YOU HOLDING UP?
LISA HALLORAN. ONE OF OUR PARAMEDICS.
ALSO ONE OF THE FEW PEOPLE TO KNOW ABOUT MY LIFE AS THOR.
HEY, LISA. I...JUST CAME IN HERE TO...
I KNOW.
BRUNNHILDE.
I KNOW.
THERE'S A REASON FOR THAT.
FUN FACT--SHE'S THE ONLY OTHER MEDICAL PROFESSIONAL I KNOW WHO'S DATED A SUPER HERO.
...WHAT'S IT LIKE OUT THERE?
IT'S...WEIRD. A GOOD WEIRD, THOUGH.
IT'S HORRIBLE--SO MANY TRAGEDIES, ALL BURIED IN THE RUBBLE--
--BUT THERE'S THIS OPTIMISM, TOO. LIKE WE CAME THROUGH SOMETHING TERRIBLE, BUT... WE CAME THROUGH. WE CAN REBUILD.
SEEING THAT... FEELING THAT, I FELT LIKE...I DON'T KNOW.
USUALLY I JUST SEE THE TRAGEDY PART.
THEY BROKE UP, OF COURSE--TWO DIFFERENT WORLDS. IT TURNED INTO GOSSIP.
I WAS THE ONLY PERSON ON STAFF WHO OFFERED A SHOULDER.
I KNOW HOW IT FEELS TO BE ORDINARY...
SO, UH, I WAS OUT THERE WITH THIS DAMAGE CONTROL GUY. HE SAID THERE'S AN OPENING FOR SOMEONE WITH MY TRAINING...
WAIT--YOU'RE QUITTING? TO WORK FOR DAMAGE CONTROL?
...AND TO BE IN LOVE WITH SOMETHING GREATER.
I THINK I AM, YEAH.
I THINK IT'S THE JOB I NEED TO DO.

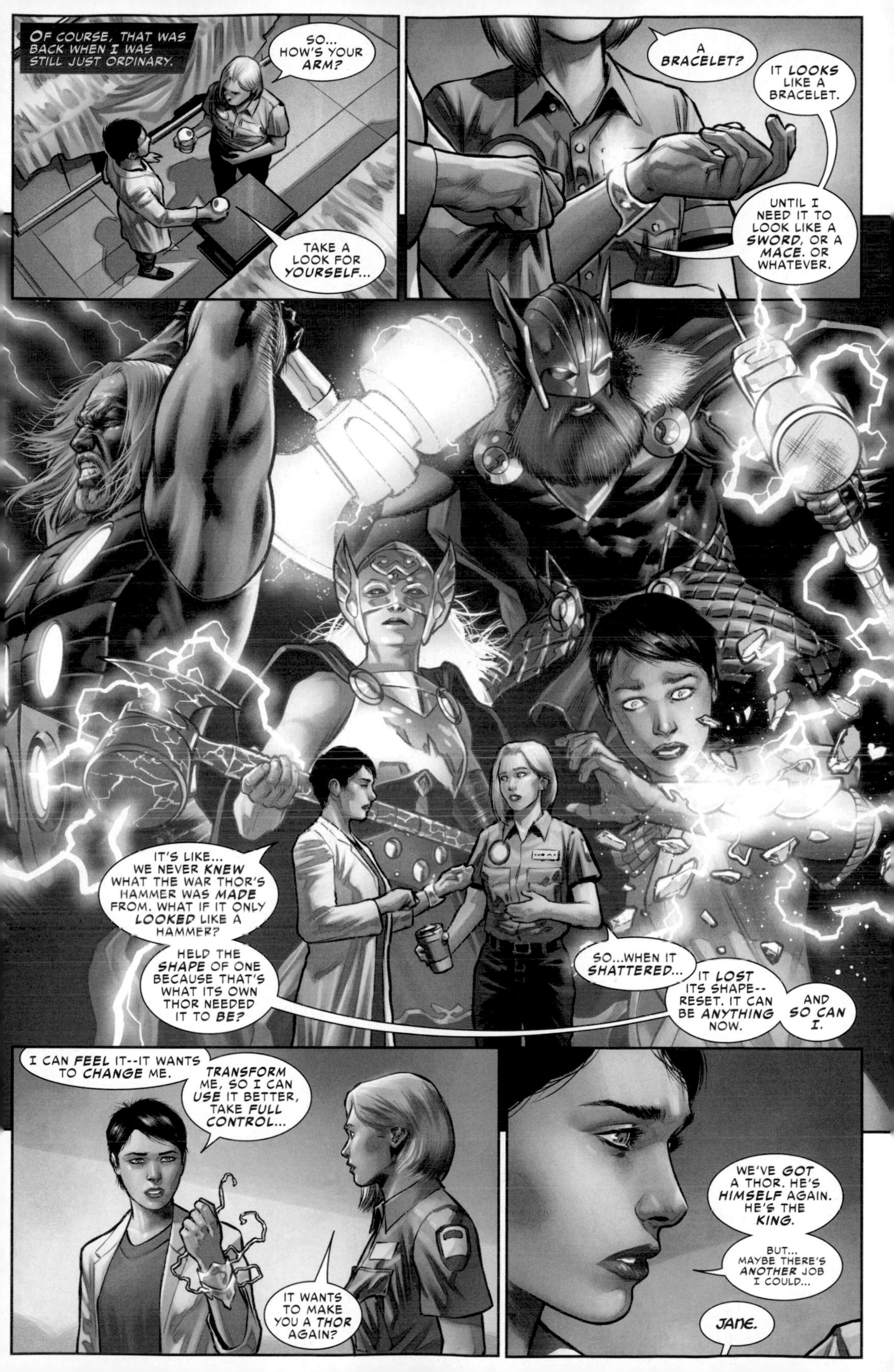
OF COURSE, THAT WAS BACK WHEN I WAS STILL JUST ORDINARY.
SO... HOW'S YOUR ARM?
TAKE A LOOK FOR YOURSELF...
A BRACELET?
IT LOOKS LIKE A BRACELET.
UNTIL I NEED IT TO LOOK LIKE A SWORD, OR A MACE. OR WHATEVER.
IT'S LIKE... WE NEVER KNEW WHAT THE WAR THOR'S HAMMER WAS MADE FROM. WHAT IF IT ONLY LOOKED LIKE A HAMMER?
HELD THE SHAPE OF ONE BECAUSE THAT'S WHAT ITS OWN THOR NEEDED IT TO BE?
SO...WHEN IT SHATTERED...
IT LOST ITS SHAPE-- RESET. IT CAN BE ANYTHING NOW.
AND SO CAN I.
I CAN FEEL IT--IT WANTS TO CHANGE ME.
TRANSFORM ME, SO I CAN USE IT BETTER, TAKE FULL CONTROL...
IT WANTS TO MAKE YOU A THOR AGAIN?
WE'VE GOT A THOR. HE'S HIMSELF AGAIN. HE'S THE KING.
BUT... MAYBE THERE'S ANOTHER JOB I COULD...
JANE.

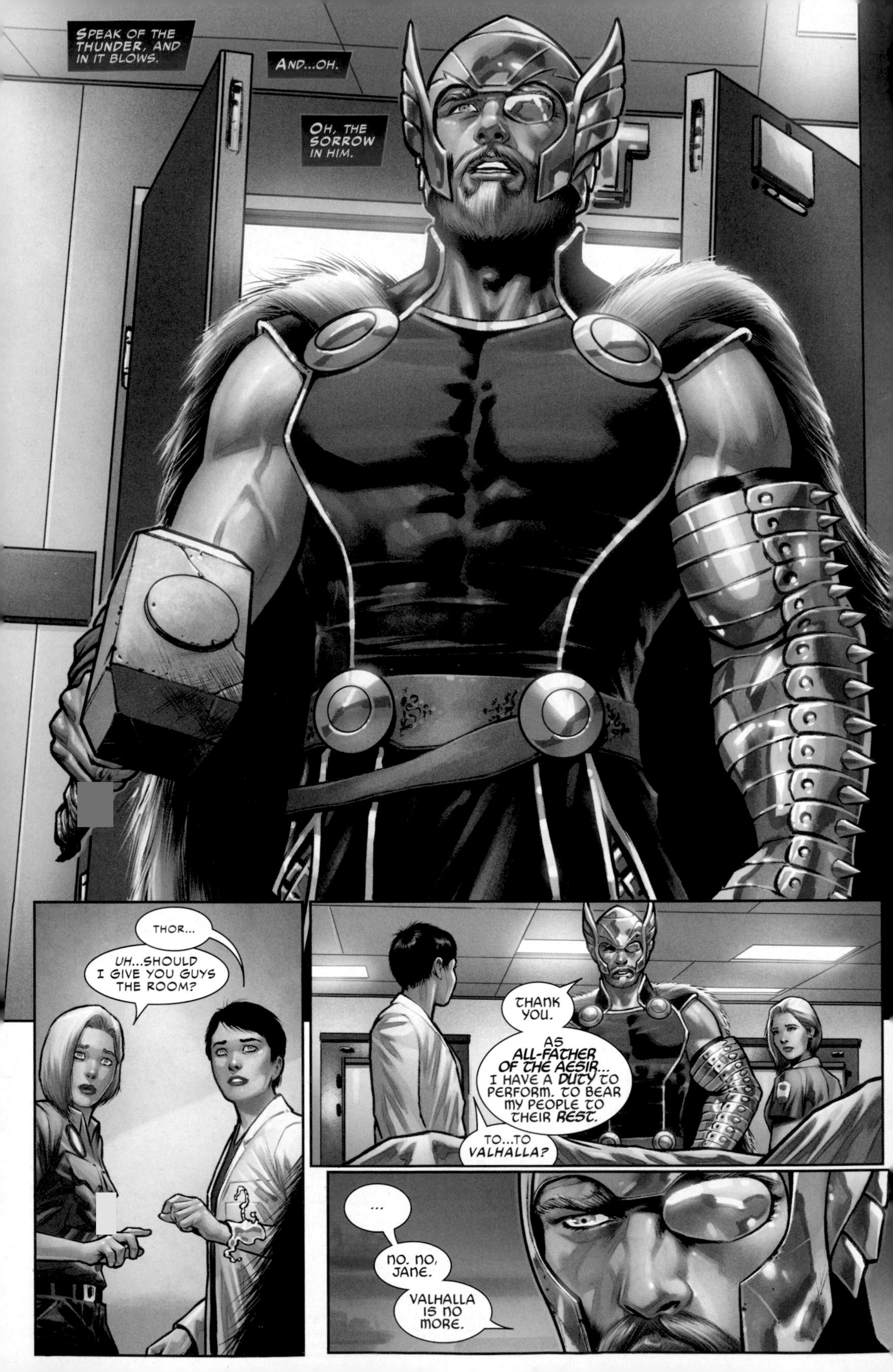
SPEAK OF THE THUNDER, AND IN IT BLOWS.
AND...OH.
OH, THE SORROW IN HIM.
THOR...
UH...SHOULD I GIVE YOU GUYS THE ROOM?
THANK YOU.
AS ALL-FATHER OF THE AESIR... I HAVE A DUTY TO PERFORM. TO BEAR MY PEOPLE TO THEIR REST.
TO...TO VALHALLA?
...
NO. NO, JANE.
VALHALLA IS NO MORE.

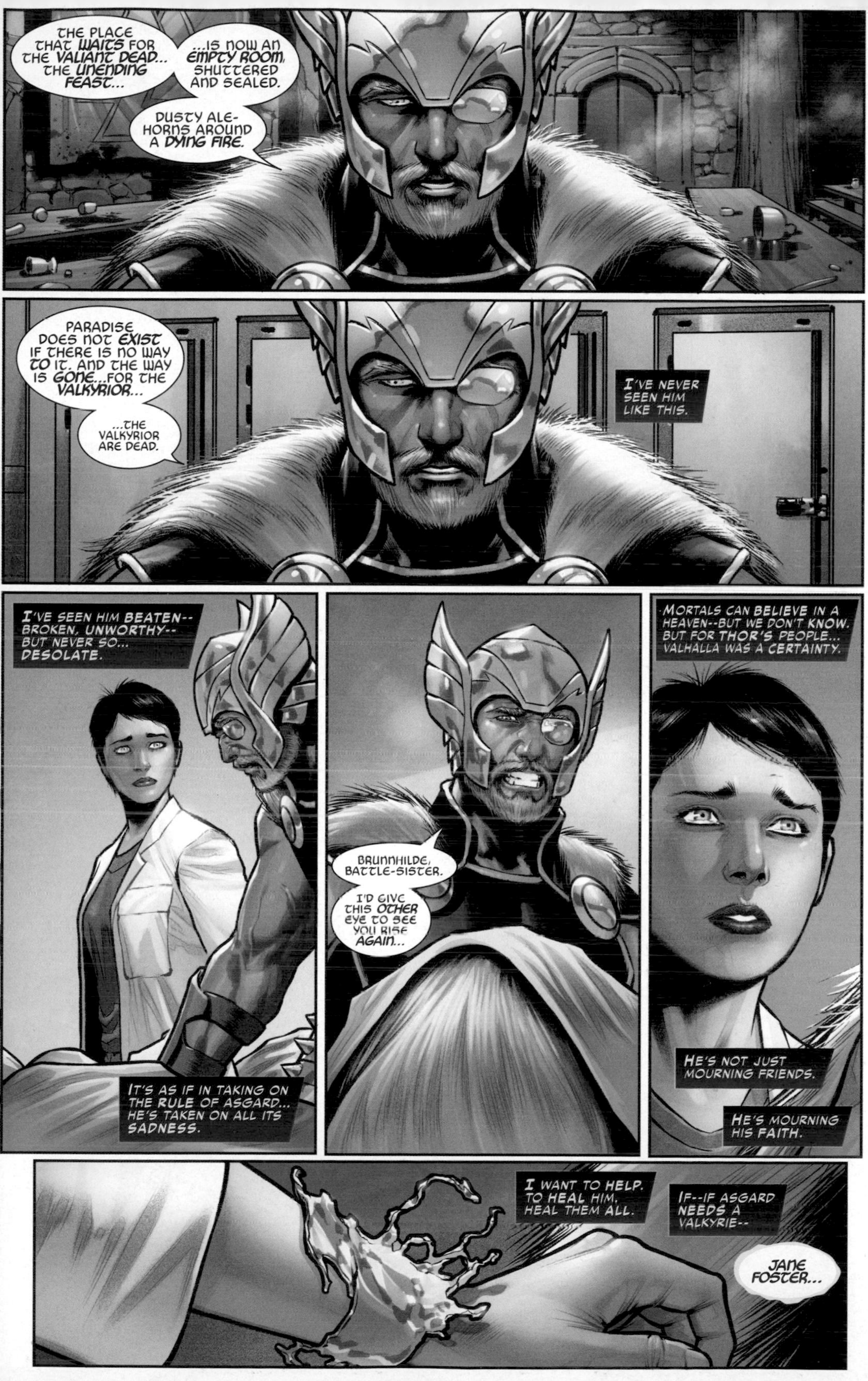

THE PLACE THAT WAITS FOR THE VALIANT DEAD... THE UNENDING FEAST...
...IS NOW AN EMPTY ROOM, SHUTTERED AND SEALED.
DUSTY ALE-HORNS AROUND A DYING FIRE.
PARADISE DOES NOT EXIST IF THERE IS NO WAY TO IT. AND THE WAY IS GONE...FOR THE VALKYRIOR...
...THE VALKYRIOR ARE DEAD.
I'VE NEVER SEEN HIM LIKE THIS.
I'VE SEEN HIM BEATEN--BROKEN, UNWORTHY--BUT NEVER SO... DESOLATE.
IT'S AS IF IN TAKING ON THE RULE OF ASGARD... HE'S TAKEN ON ALL ITS SADNESS.
BRUNNHILDE, BATTLE-SISTER.
I'D GIVE THIS OTHER EYE TO SEE YOU RISE AGAIN...
MORTALS CAN BELIEVE IN A HEAVEN--BUT WE DON'T KNOW. BUT FOR THOR'S PEOPLE... VALHALLA WAS A CERTAINTY.
HE'S NOT JUST MOURNING FRIENDS.
HE'S MOURNING HIS FAITH.
I WANT TO HELP. TO HEAL HIM, HEAL THEM ALL.
IF--IF ASGARD NEEDS A VALKYRIE--
JANE FOSTER...

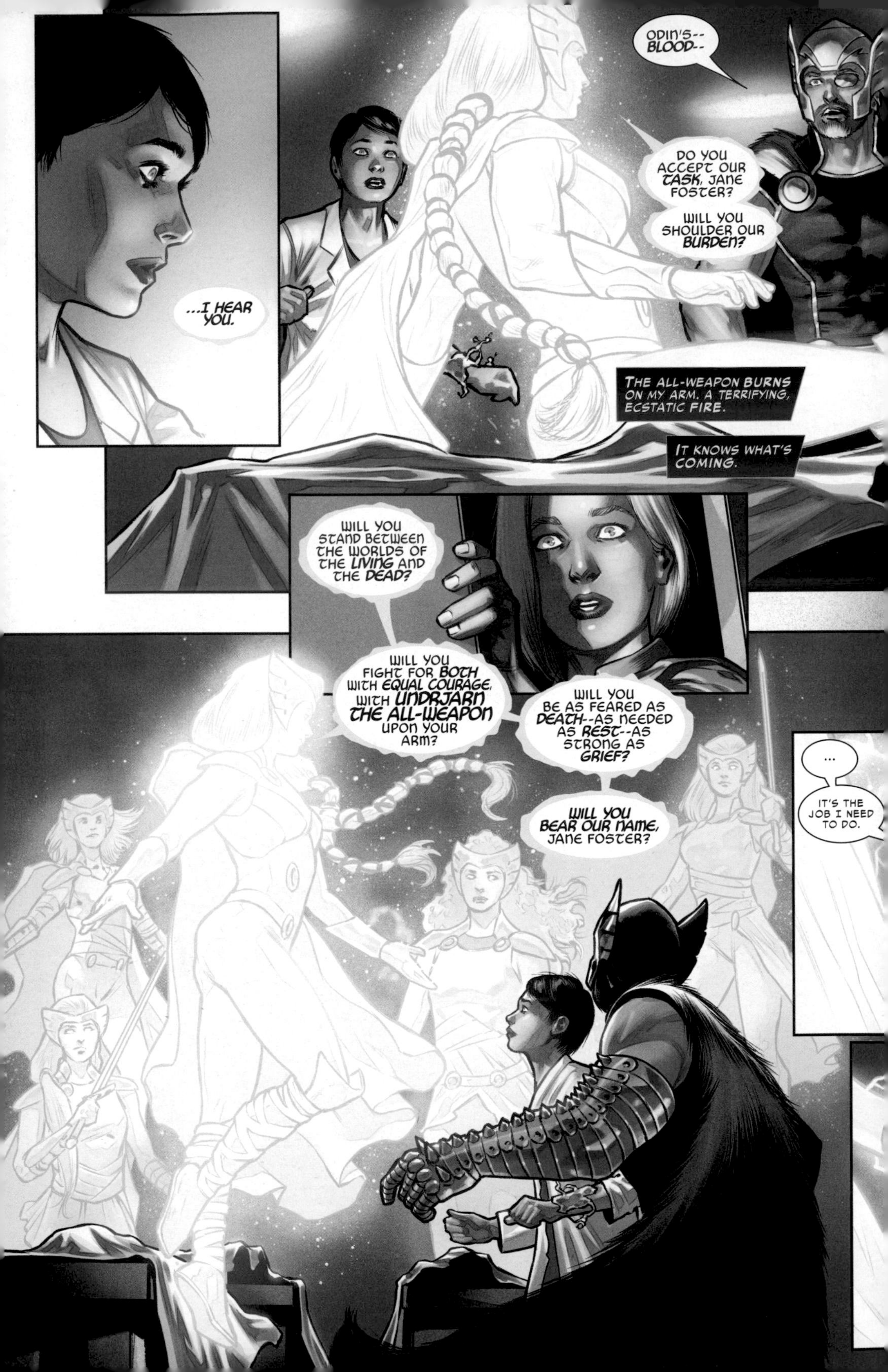
...I HEAR YOU.
ODIN'S-- BLOOD--
DO YOU ACCEPT OUR TASK, JANE FOSTER?
WILL YOU SHOULDER OUR BURDEN?
THE ALL-WEAPON BURNS ON MY ARM. A TERRIFYING, ECSTATIC FIRE.
IT KNOWS WHAT'S COMING.
WILL YOU STAND BETWEEN THE WORLDS OF THE LIVING AND THE DEAD?
WILL YOU FIGHT FOR BOTH WITH EQUAL COURAGE, WITH UNDRJARN THE ALL-WEAPON UPON YOUR ARM?
WILL YOU BE AS FEARED AS DEATH--AS NEEDED AS REST--AS STRONG AS GRIEF?
WILL YOU BEAR OUR NAME, JANE FOSTER?
...
IT'S THE JOB I NEED TO DO.

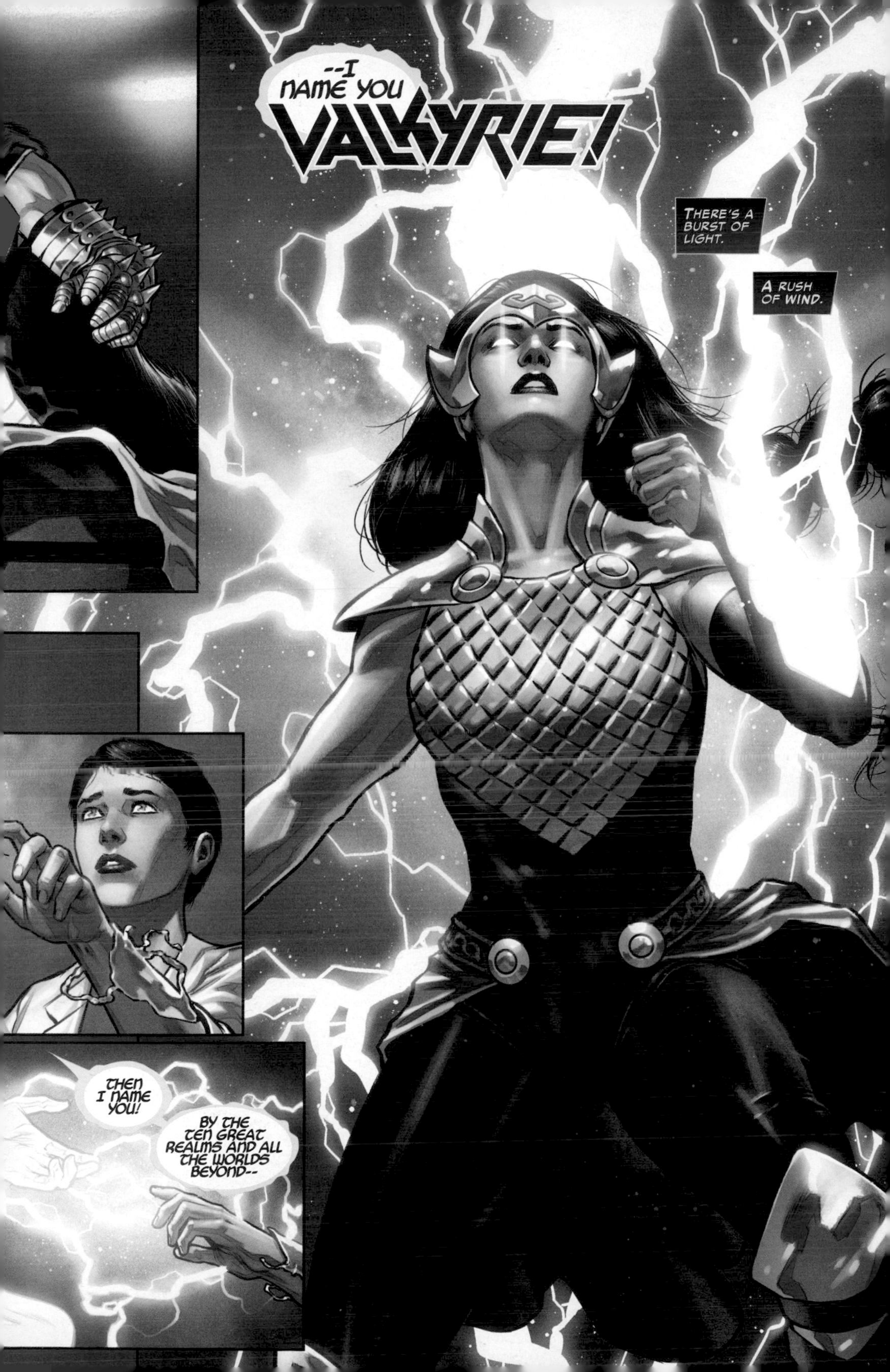
--I NAME YOU
VALKYRIE!
THERE'S A BURST OF LIGHT.
A RUSH OF WIND.
THEN I NAME YOU!
BY THE TEN GREAT REALMS AND ALL THE WORLDS BEYOND--

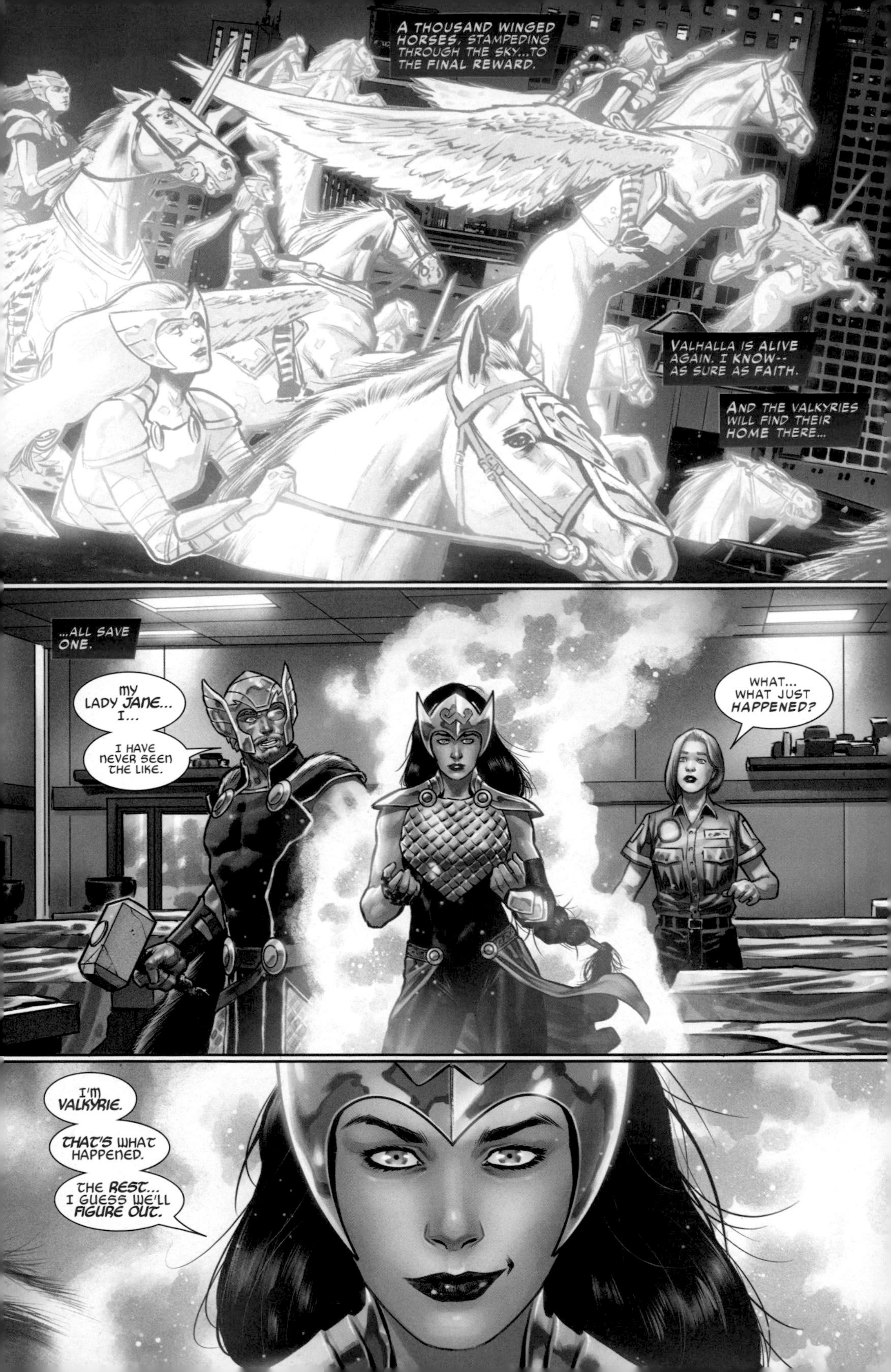
A THOUSAND WINGED HORSES, STAMPEDING THROUGH THE SKY...TO THE FINAL REWARD.
VALHALLA IS ALIVE AGAIN. I KNOW-- AS SURE AS FAITH.
AND THE VALKYRIES WILL FIND THEIR HOME THERE...
...ALL SAVE ONE.
MY LADY JANE... I...
I HAVE NEVER SEEN THE LIKE.
WHAT... WHAT JUST HAPPENED?
I'M VALKYRIE.
THAT'S WHAT HAPPENED.
THE REST... I GUESS WE'LL FIGURE OUT.

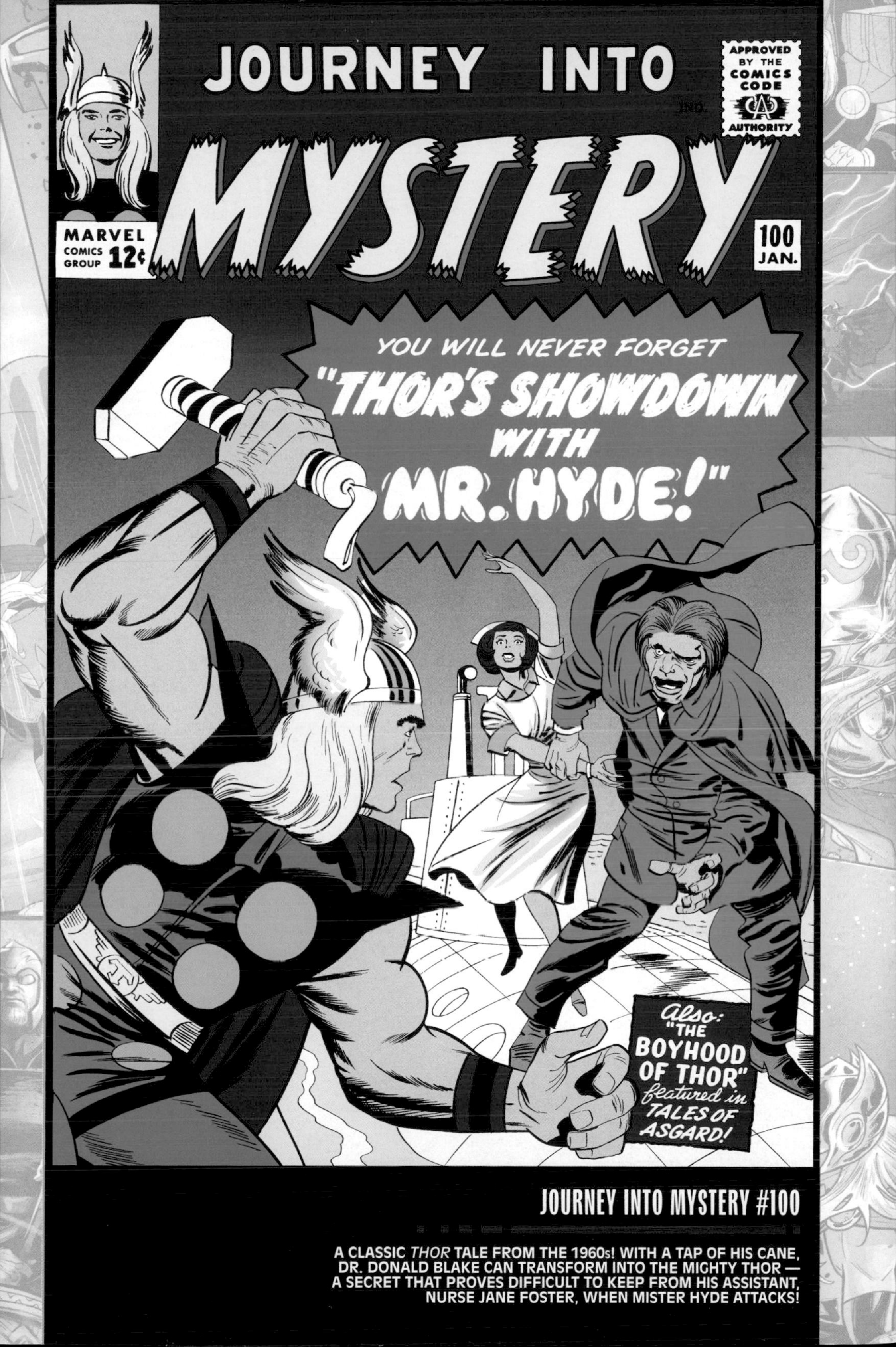
JOURNEY INTO
IND.
APPROVED BY THE COMICS CODE AUTHORITY
MYSTERY
MARVEL COMICS GROUP 12¢
100 JAN.
YOU WILL NEVER FORGET "THOR'S SHOWDOWN WITH MR. HYDE!"
also: "THE BOYHOOD OF THOR" featured in TALES OF ASGARD!

JOURNEY INTO MYSTERY #100

A CLASSIC *THOR* TALE FROM THE 1960s! WITH A TAP OF HIS CANE, DR. DONALD BLAKE CAN TRANSFORM INTO THE MIGHTY THOR — A SECRET THAT PROVES DIFFICULT TO KEEP FROM HIS ASSISTANT, NURSE JANE FOSTER, WHEN MISTER HYDE ATTACKS!

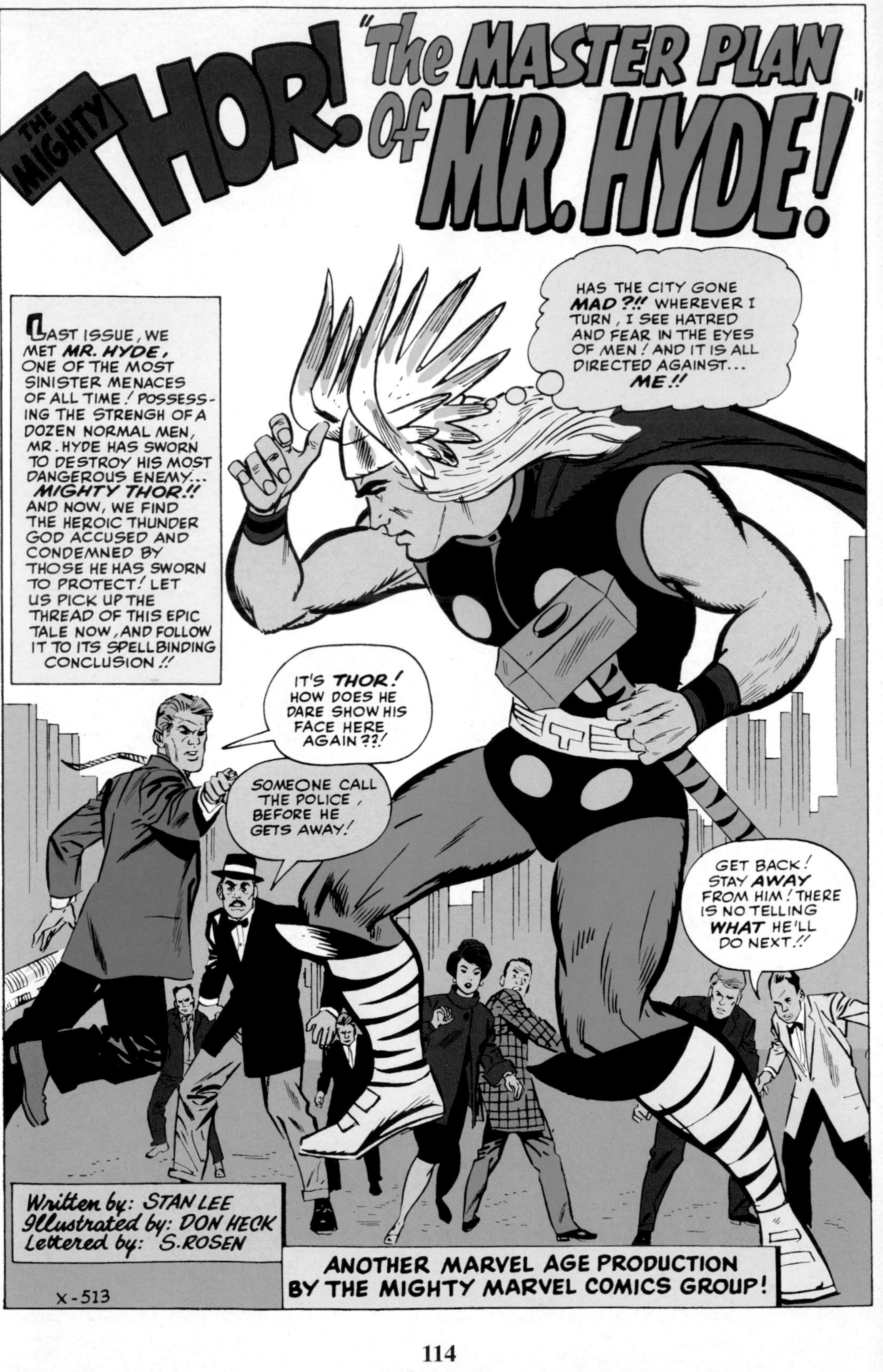
THE MIGHTY THOR! "The MASTER PLAN of MR. HYDE!"
LAST ISSUE, WE MET MR. HYDE, ONE OF THE MOST SINISTER MENACES OF ALL TIME! POSSESSING THE STRENGH OF A DOZEN NORMAL MEN, MR. HYDE HAS SWORN TO DESTROY HIS MOST DANGEROUS ENEMY... MIGHTY THOR!! AND NOW, WE FIND THE HEROIC THUNDER GOD ACCUSED AND CONDEMNED BY THOSE HE HAS SWORN TO PROTECT! LET US PICK UP THE THREAD OF THIS EPIC TALE NOW, AND FOLLOW IT TO ITS SPELLBINDING CONCLUSION!!
HAS THE CITY GONE MAD?!! WHEREVER I TURN, I SEE HATRED AND FEAR IN THE EYES OF MEN! AND IT IS ALL DIRECTED AGAINST... ME!!
IT'S THOR! HOW DOES HE DARE SHOW HIS FACE HERE AGAIN??!
SOMEONE CALL THE POLICE, BEFORE HE GETS AWAY!
GET BACK! STAY AWAY FROM HIM! THERE IS NO TELLING WHAT HE'LL DO NEXT!!
Written by: STAN LEE
Illustrated by: DON HECK
Lettered by: S. ROSEN
X-513
ANOTHER MARVEL AGE PRODUCTION BY THE MIGHTY MARVEL COMICS GROUP!

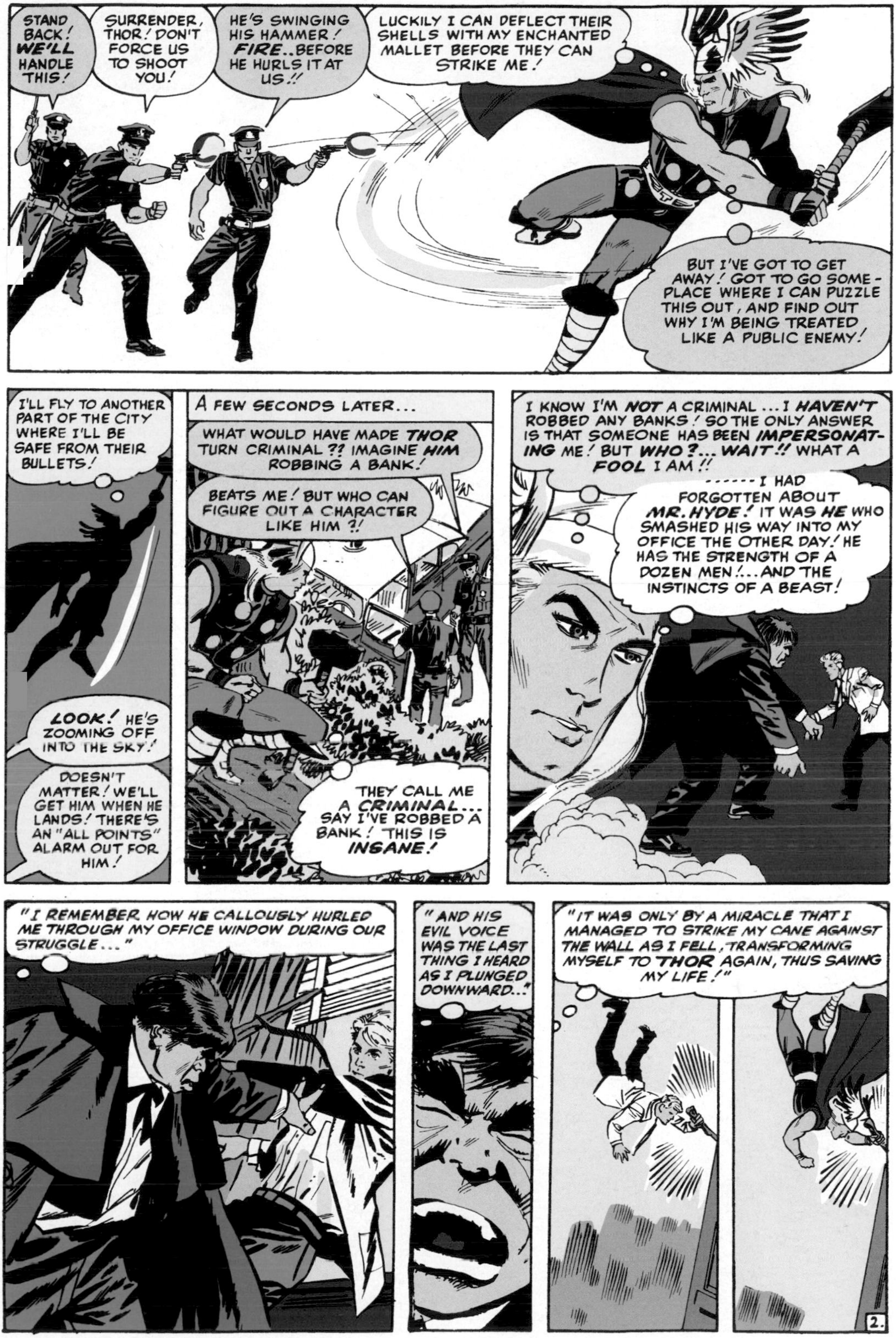

STAND BACK! WE'LL HANDLE THIS!
SURRENDER, THOR! DON'T FORCE US TO SHOOT YOU!
HE'S SWINGING HIS HAMMER! FIRE.. BEFORE HE HURLS IT AT US!!
LUCKILY I CAN DEFLECT THEIR SHELLS WITH MY ENCHANTED MALLET BEFORE THEY CAN STRIKE ME!
BUT I'VE GOT TO GET AWAY! GOT TO GO SOME-PLACE WHERE I CAN PUZZLE THIS OUT, AND FIND OUT WHY I'M BEING TREATED LIKE A PUBLIC ENEMY!
I'LL FLY TO ANOTHER PART OF THE CITY WHERE I'LL BE SAFE FROM THEIR BULLETS!
LOOK! HE'S ZOOMING OFF INTO THE SKY!
DOESN'T MATTER! WE'LL GET HIM WHEN HE LANDS! THERE'S AN "ALL POINTS" ALARM OUT FOR HIM!
A FEW SECONDS LATER...
WHAT WOULD HAVE MADE THOR TURN CRIMINAL ?? IMAGINE HIM ROBBING A BANK!
BEATS ME! BUT WHO CAN FIGURE OUT A CHARACTER LIKE HIM ?!
THEY CALL ME A CRIMINAL... SAY I'VE ROBBED A BANK! THIS IS INSANE!
I KNOW I'M NOT A CRIMINAL ... I HAVEN'T ROBBED ANY BANKS! SO THE ONLY ANSWER IS THAT SOMEONE HAS BEEN IMPERSONATING ME! BUT WHO?... WAIT!! WHAT A FOOL I AM!!
......I HAD FORGOTTEN ABOUT MR. HYDE! IT WAS HE WHO SMASHED HIS WAY INTO MY OFFICE THE OTHER DAY! HE HAS THE STRENGTH OF A DOZEN MEN!... AND THE INSTINCTS OF A BEAST!
"I REMEMBER HOW HE CALLOUSLY HURLED ME THROUGH MY OFFICE WINDOW DURING OUR STRUGGLE..."
"AND HIS EVIL VOICE WAS THE LAST THING I HEARD AS I PLUNGED DOWNWARD..."
"IT WAS ONLY BY A MIRACLE THAT I MANAGED TO STRIKE MY CANE AGAINST THE WALL AS I FELL, TRANSFORMING MYSELF TO THOR AGAIN, THUS SAVING MY LIFE!"
2.

THERE'S ONLY ONE THING TO DO!... ONLY ONE PLACE WHERE I'LL BE SAFE!

I'VE GOT TO RETURN TO MY OFFICE AND BECOME DR. BLAKE AGAIN! MUSTN'T TAKE A CHANCE OF ANYONE GETTING HURT IF THOR MUST BATTLE ANY HUMANS!

STRANGE, HOW HYDE ENTERED MY LIFE JUST WHEN I THOUGHT MY BIGGEST PROBLEM HAD BEEN SOLVED! I FINALLY FOUND A WAY TO GET ODIN'S PERMISSION TO MARRY JANE.

ALTHOUGH AN IMMORTAL MAY NOT MARRY A HUMAN, MY NOBLE FATHER MIGHT MAKE HER AN IMMORTAL, TOO, IF SHE PROVED HERSELF WORTHY!

THOSE ARE MY FINAL WORDS, THOR!

THANK YOU, FATHER! THEN I STILL MAY HOPE!

MOMENTS LATER, AT THE OFFICE OF DOCTOR DON BLAKE...THE VALIANT THUNDER GOD STAMPS HIS MIGHTY HAMMER ONCE AND...

NOW LET THOR, GOD OF THUNDER, VANISH!...

...TO BE REPLACED BY THE MORTAL DR. BLAKE..

THUMP!

OH, THERE YOU ARE, DON! FOR A MOMENT, I THOUGHT YOU HAD FORGOTTEN YOUR PROMISE TO TAKE ME TO DINNER TONIGHT, ON MY BIRTHDAY!

I...I HAD FORGOTTEN... BECAUSE OF MY PROBLEM AS THOR! BUT I CAN'T DISAPPOINT JANE...

OF COURSE, JANE DEAR! I'VE BEEN LOOKING FORWARD TO IT ALL WEEK!

I'LL PICK YOU UP AT EIGHT AND WE'LL HAVE DINNER AT THE RITZ TERRACE!

I HOPE IT WON'T BECOME NECESSARY FOR ME TO BECOME THOR AGAIN BEFORE THAT TIME!

THE RITZ TERRACE! OH, DON... IT'S THE MOST GLAMOROUS PLACE IN TOWN! I'M SO THRILLED!

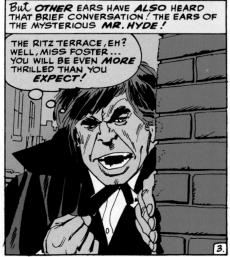

But OTHER EARS HAVE ALSO HEARD THAT BRIEF CONVERSATION! THE EARS OF THE MYSTERIOUS MR. HYDE!

THE RITZ TERRACE, EH? WELL, MISS FOSTER... YOU WILL BE EVEN MORE THRILLED THAN YOU EXPECT!

3.

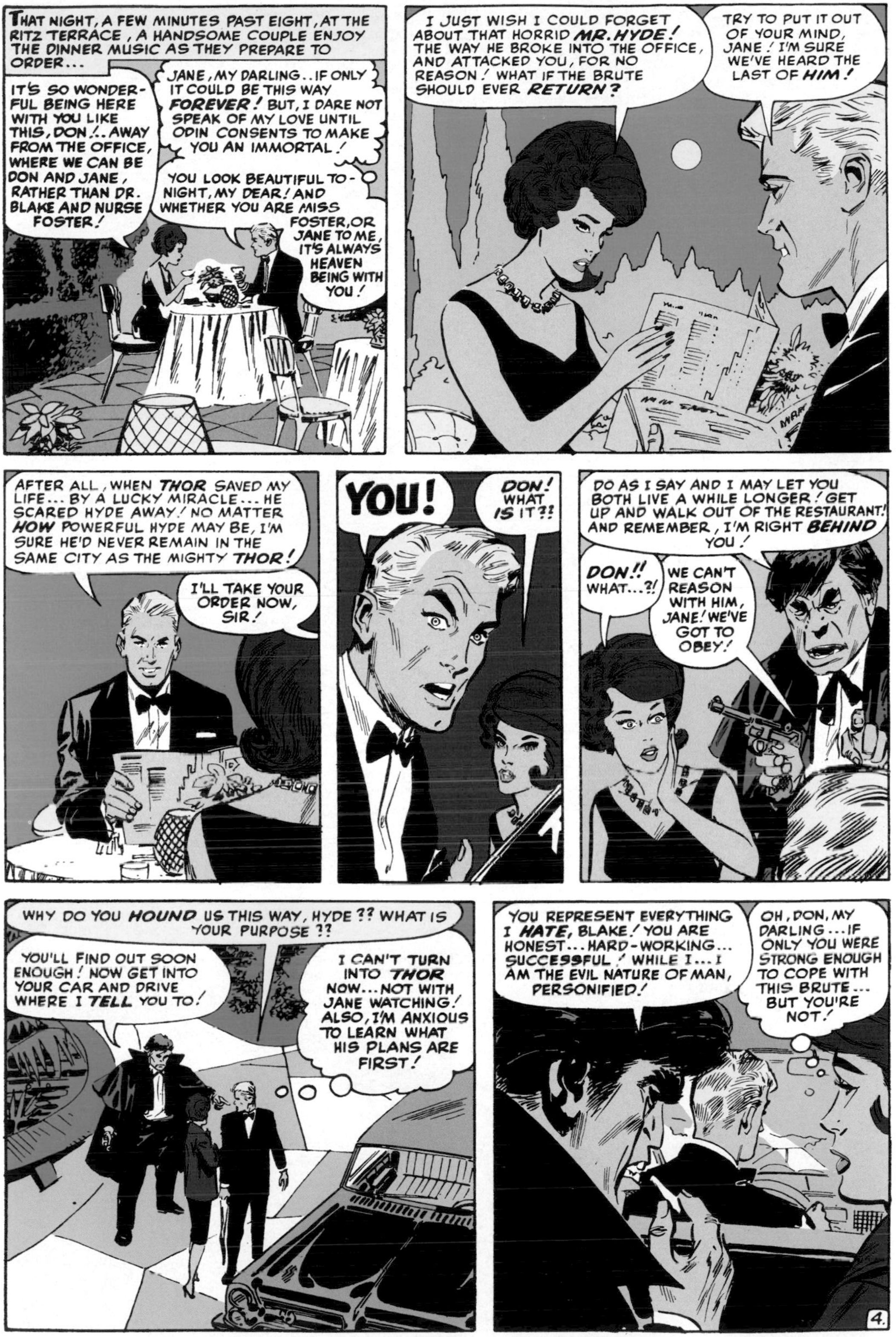
THAT NIGHT, A FEW MINUTES PAST EIGHT, AT THE RITZ TERRACE, A HANDSOME COUPLE ENJOY THE DINNER MUSIC AS THEY PREPARE TO ORDER...
IT'S SO WONDERFUL BEING HERE WITH YOU LIKE THIS, DON!.. AWAY FROM THE OFFICE, WHERE WE CAN BE DON AND JANE, RATHER THAN DR. BLAKE AND NURSE FOSTER!
JANE, MY DARLING.. IF ONLY IT COULD BE THIS WAY FOREVER! BUT, I DARE NOT SPEAK OF MY LOVE UNTIL ODIN CONSENTS TO MAKE YOU AN IMMORTAL!
YOU LOOK BEAUTIFUL TONIGHT, MY DEAR! AND WHETHER YOU ARE MISS FOSTER, OR JANE TO ME, IT'S ALWAYS HEAVEN BEING WITH YOU!
I JUST WISH I COULD FORGET ABOUT THAT HORRID MR. HYDE! THE WAY HE BROKE INTO THE OFFICE, AND ATTACKED YOU, FOR NO REASON! WHAT IF THE BRUTE SHOULD EVER RETURN?
TRY TO PUT IT OUT OF YOUR MIND, JANE! I'M SURE WE'VE HEARD THE LAST OF HIM!
AFTER ALL, WHEN THOR SAVED MY LIFE... BY A LUCKY MIRACLE... HE SCARED HYDE AWAY! NO MATTER HOW POWERFUL HYDE MAY BE, I'M SURE HE'D NEVER REMAIN IN THE SAME CITY AS THE MIGHTY THOR!
I'LL TAKE YOUR ORDER NOW, SIR!
YOU!
DON! WHAT IS IT??
DO AS I SAY AND I MAY LET YOU BOTH LIVE A WHILE LONGER! GET UP AND WALK OUT OF THE RESTAURANT! AND REMEMBER, I'M RIGHT BEHIND YOU!
DON!! WHAT...?!
WE CAN'T REASON WITH HIM, JANE! WE'VE GOT TO OBEY!
WHY DO YOU HOUND US THIS WAY, HYDE?? WHAT IS YOUR PURPOSE??
YOU'LL FIND OUT SOON ENOUGH! NOW GET INTO YOUR CAR AND DRIVE WHERE I TELL YOU TO!
I CAN'T TURN INTO THOR NOW... NOT WITH JANE WATCHING! ALSO, I'M ANXIOUS TO LEARN WHAT HIS PLANS ARE FIRST!
YOU REPRESENT EVERYTHING I HATE, BLAKE! YOU ARE HONEST... HARD-WORKING... SUCCESSFUL! WHILE I... I AM THE EVIL NATURE OF MAN, PERSONIFIED!
OH, DON, MY DARLING... IF ONLY YOU WERE STRONG ENOUGH TO COPE WITH THIS BRUTE... BUT YOU'RE NOT!
4.

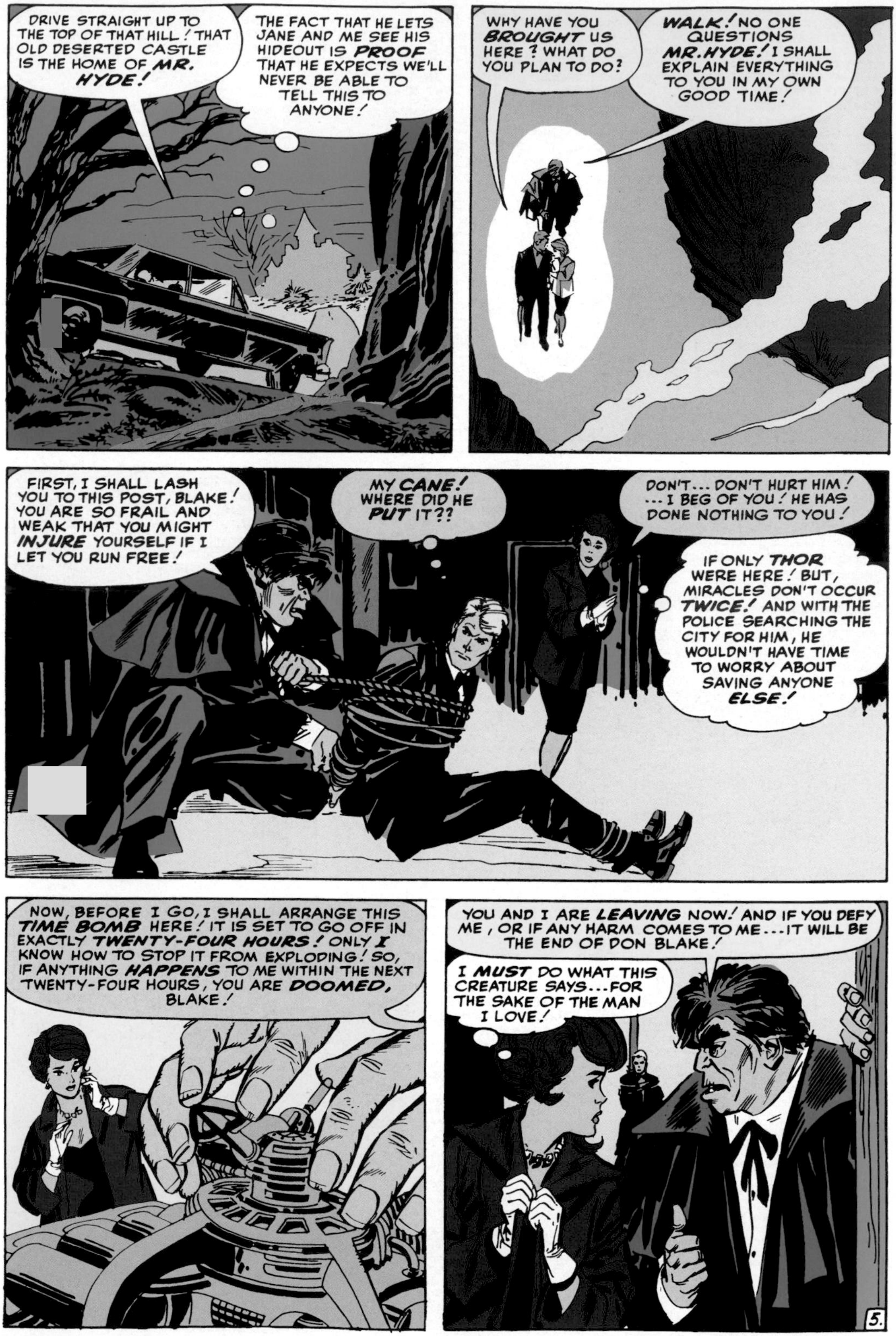
DRIVE STRAIGHT UP TO THE TOP OF THAT HILL! THAT OLD DESERTED CASTLE IS THE HOME OF MR. HYDE!
THE FACT THAT HE LETS JANE AND ME SEE HIS HIDEOUT IS PROOF THAT HE EXPECTS WE'LL NEVER BE ABLE TO TELL THIS TO ANYONE!
WHY HAVE YOU BROUGHT US HERE? WHAT DO YOU PLAN TO DO?
WALK! NO ONE QUESTIONS MR. HYDE! I SHALL EXPLAIN EVERYTHING TO YOU IN MY OWN GOOD TIME!
FIRST, I SHALL LASH YOU TO THIS POST, BLAKE! YOU ARE SO FRAIL AND WEAK THAT YOU MIGHT INJURE YOURSELF IF I LET YOU RUN FREE!
MY CANE! WHERE DID HE PUT IT??
DON'T... DON'T HURT HIM! ...I BEG OF YOU! HE HAS DONE NOTHING TO YOU!
IF ONLY THOR WERE HERE! BUT, MIRACLES DON'T OCCUR TWICE! AND WITH THE POLICE SEARCHING THE CITY FOR HIM, HE WOULDN'T HAVE TIME TO WORRY ABOUT SAVING ANYONE ELSE!
NOW, BEFORE I GO, I SHALL ARRANGE THIS TIME BOMB HERE! IT IS SET TO GO OFF IN EXACTLY TWENTY-FOUR HOURS! ONLY I KNOW HOW TO STOP IT FROM EXPLODING! SO, IF ANYTHING HAPPENS TO ME WITHIN THE NEXT TWENTY-FOUR HOURS, YOU ARE DOOMED, BLAKE!
YOU AND I ARE LEAVING NOW! AND IF YOU DEFY ME, OR IF ANY HARM COMES TO ME...IT WILL BE THE END OF DON BLAKE!
I MUST DO WHAT THIS CREATURE SAYS...FOR THE SAKE OF THE MAN I LOVE!
5.

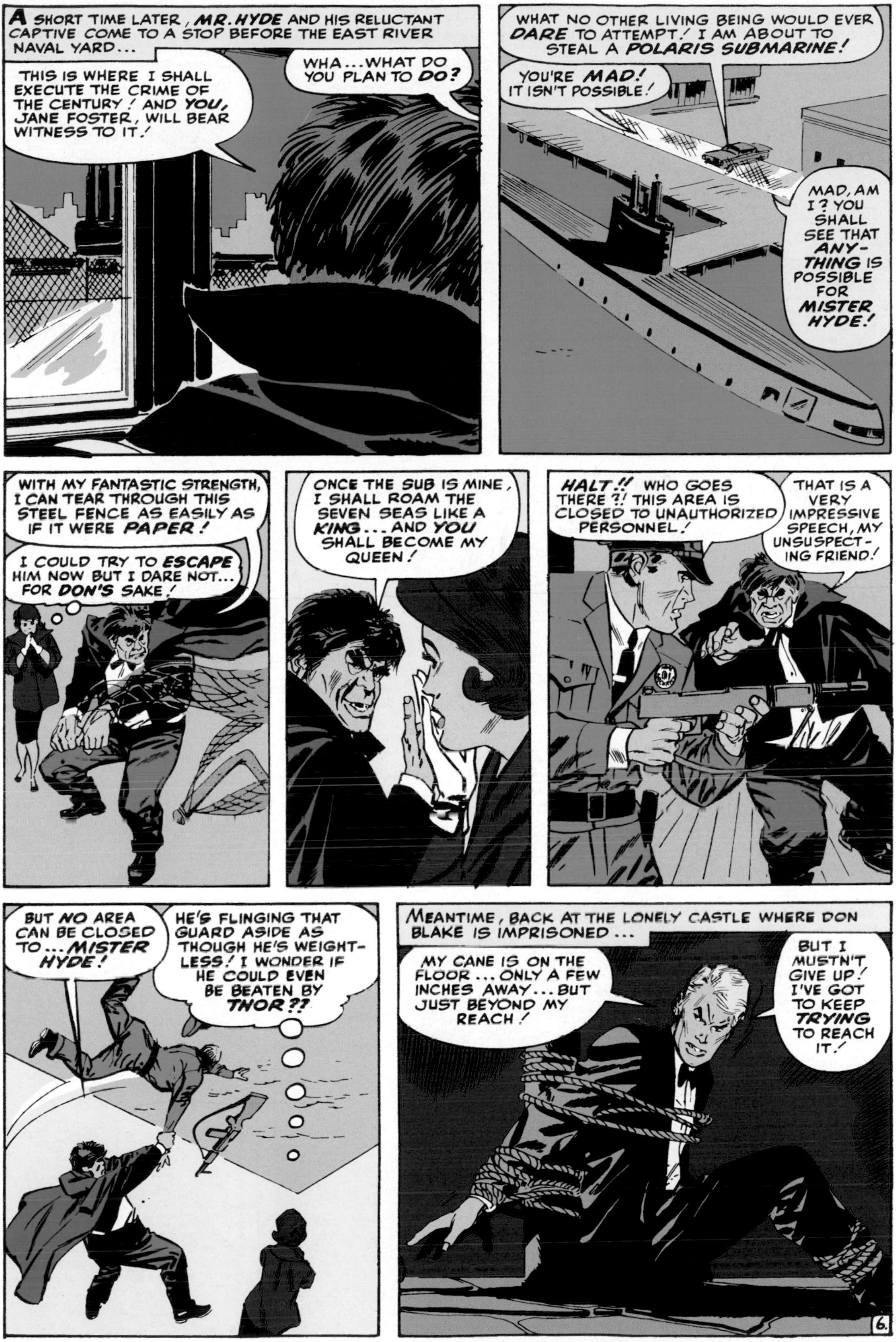
A SHORT TIME LATER, MR. HYDE AND HIS RELUCTANT CAPTIVE COME TO A STOP BEFORE THE EAST RIVER NAVAL YARD...
THIS IS WHERE I SHALL EXECUTE THE CRIME OF THE CENTURY! AND YOU, JANE FOSTER, WILL BEAR WITNESS TO IT!
WHA...WHAT DO YOU PLAN TO DO?
WHAT NO OTHER LIVING BEING WOULD EVER DARE TO ATTEMPT! I AM ABOUT TO STEAL A POLARIS SUBMARINE!
YOU'RE MAD! IT ISN'T POSSIBLE!
MAD, AM I? YOU SHALL SEE THAT ANY-THING IS POSSIBLE FOR MISTER HYDE!
WITH MY FANTASTIC STRENGTH, I CAN TEAR THROUGH THIS STEEL FENCE AS EASILY AS IF IT WERE PAPER!
I COULD TRY TO ESCAPE HIM NOW BUT I DARE NOT... FOR DON'S SAKE!
ONCE THE SUB IS MINE, I SHALL ROAM THE SEVEN SEAS LIKE A KING... AND YOU SHALL BECOME MY QUEEN!
HALT!! WHO GOES THERE?! THIS AREA IS CLOSED TO UNAUTHORIZED PERSONNEL!
THAT IS A VERY IMPRESSIVE SPEECH, MY UNSUSPECT-ING FRIEND!
BUT NO AREA CAN BE CLOSED TO... MISTER HYDE!
HE'S FLINGING THAT GUARD ASIDE AS THOUGH HE'S WEIGHT-LESS! I WONDER IF HE COULD EVEN BE BEATEN BY THOR??
MEANTIME, BACK AT THE LONELY CASTLE WHERE DON BLAKE IS IMPRISONED...
MY CANE IS ON THE FLOOR... ONLY A FEW INCHES AWAY... BUT JUST BEYOND MY REACH!
BUT I MUSTN'T GIVE UP! I'VE GOT TO KEEP TRYING TO REACH IT!
6.

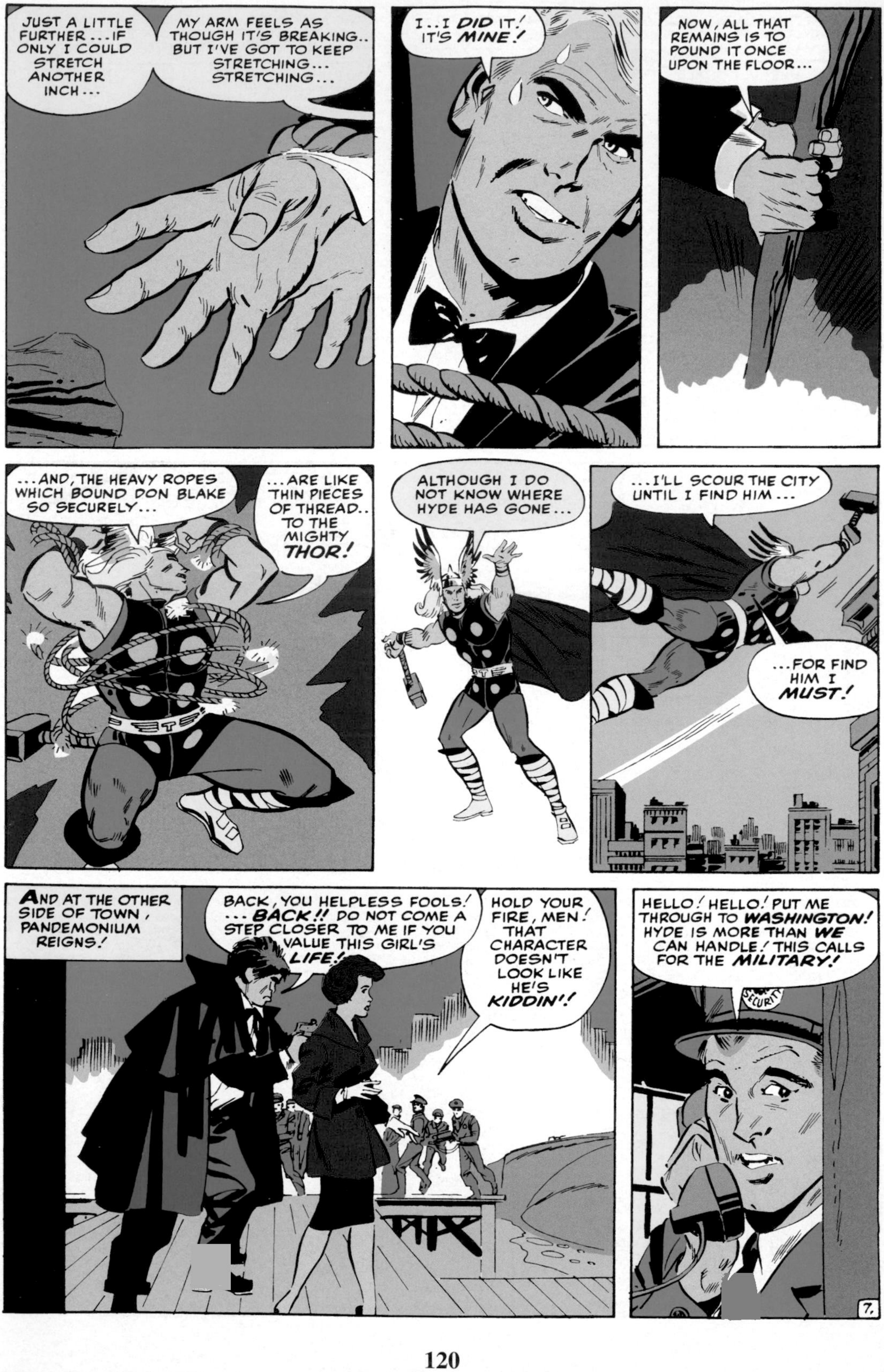

JUST A LITTLE FURTHER ...IF ONLY I COULD STRETCH ANOTHER INCH...
MY ARM FEELS AS THOUGH IT'S BREAKING.. BUT I'VE GOT TO KEEP STRETCHING... STRETCHING...
I..I DID IT! IT'S MINE!
NOW, ALL THAT REMAINS IS TO POUND IT ONCE UPON THE FLOOR...
...AND, THE HEAVY ROPES WHICH BOUND DON BLAKE SO SECURELY...
...ARE LIKE THIN PIECES OF THREAD.. TO THE MIGHTY THOR!
ALTHOUGH I DO NOT KNOW WHERE HYDE HAS GONE...
...I'LL SCOUR THE CITY UNTIL I FIND HIM...
...FOR FIND HIM I MUST!
AND AT THE OTHER SIDE OF TOWN, PANDEMONIUM REIGNS!
BACK, YOU HELPLESS FOOLS! ...BACK!! DO NOT COME A STEP CLOSER TO ME IF YOU VALUE THIS GIRL'S LIFE!
HOLD YOUR FIRE, MEN! THAT CHARACTER DOESN'T LOOK LIKE HE'S KIDDIN'!
HELLO! HELLO! PUT ME THROUGH TO WASHINGTON! HYDE IS MORE THAN WE CAN HANDLE! THIS CALLS FOR THE MILITARY!
SECURITY
7.

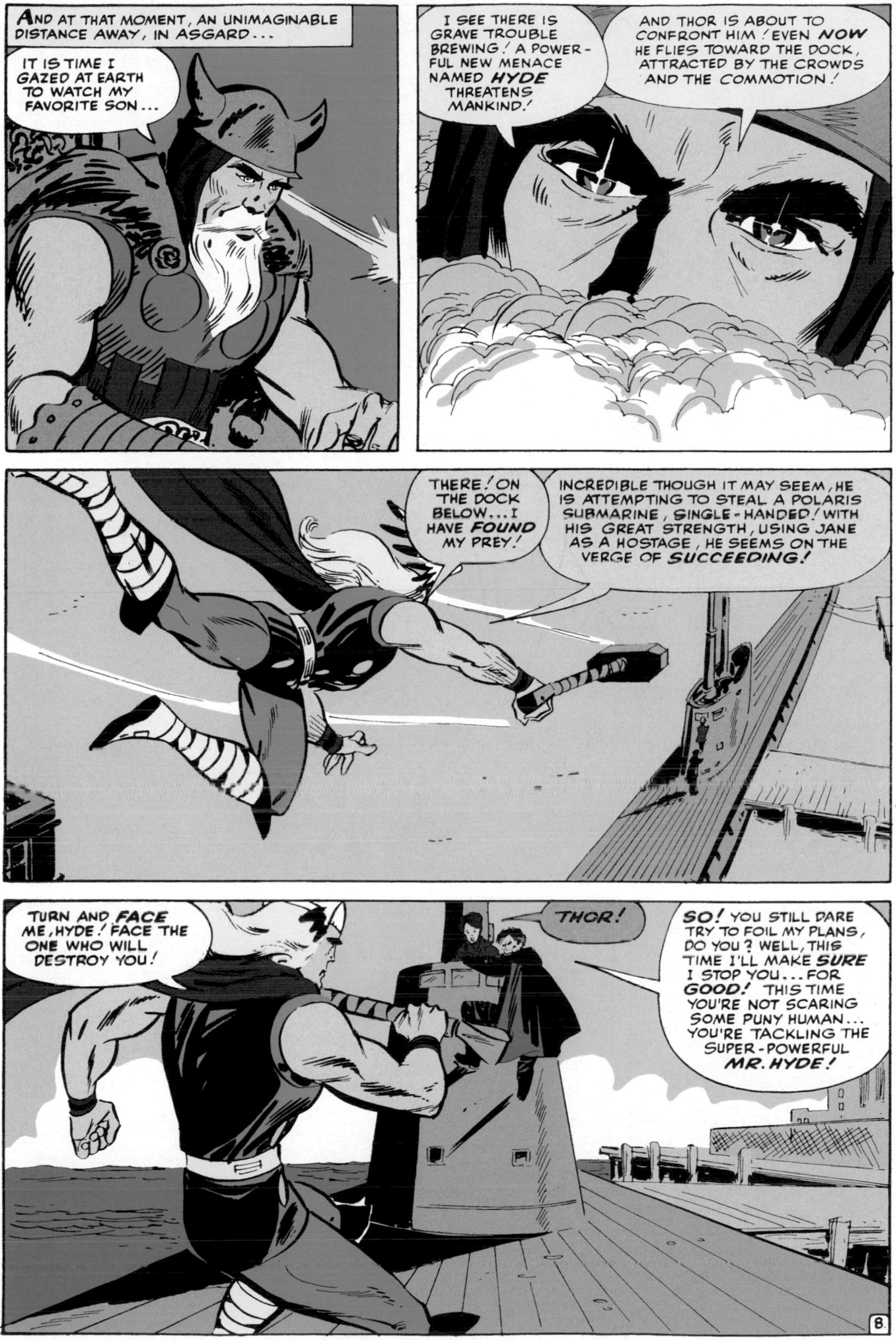
AND AT THAT MOMENT, AN UNIMAGINABLE DISTANCE AWAY, IN ASGARD...
IT IS TIME I GAZED AT EARTH TO WATCH MY FAVORITE SON...
I SEE THERE IS GRAVE TROUBLE BREWING! A POWERFUL NEW MENACE NAMED HYDE THREATENS MANKIND!
AND THOR IS ABOUT TO CONFRONT HIM! EVEN NOW HE FLIES TOWARD THE DOCK, ATTRACTED BY THE CROWDS AND THE COMMOTION!
THERE! ON THE DOCK BELOW... I HAVE FOUND MY PREY!
INCREDIBLE THOUGH IT MAY SEEM, HE IS ATTEMPTING TO STEAL A POLARIS SUBMARINE, SINGLE-HANDED! WITH HIS GREAT STRENGTH, USING JANE AS A HOSTAGE, HE SEEMS ON THE VERGE OF SUCCEEDING!
TURN AND FACE ME, HYDE! FACE THE ONE WHO WILL DESTROY YOU!
THOR!
SO! YOU STILL DARE TRY TO FOIL MY PLANS, DO YOU? WELL, THIS TIME I'LL MAKE SURE I STOP YOU... FOR GOOD! THIS TIME YOU'RE NOT SCARING SOME PUNY HUMAN... YOU'RE TACKLING THE SUPER-POWERFUL MR. HYDE!
8

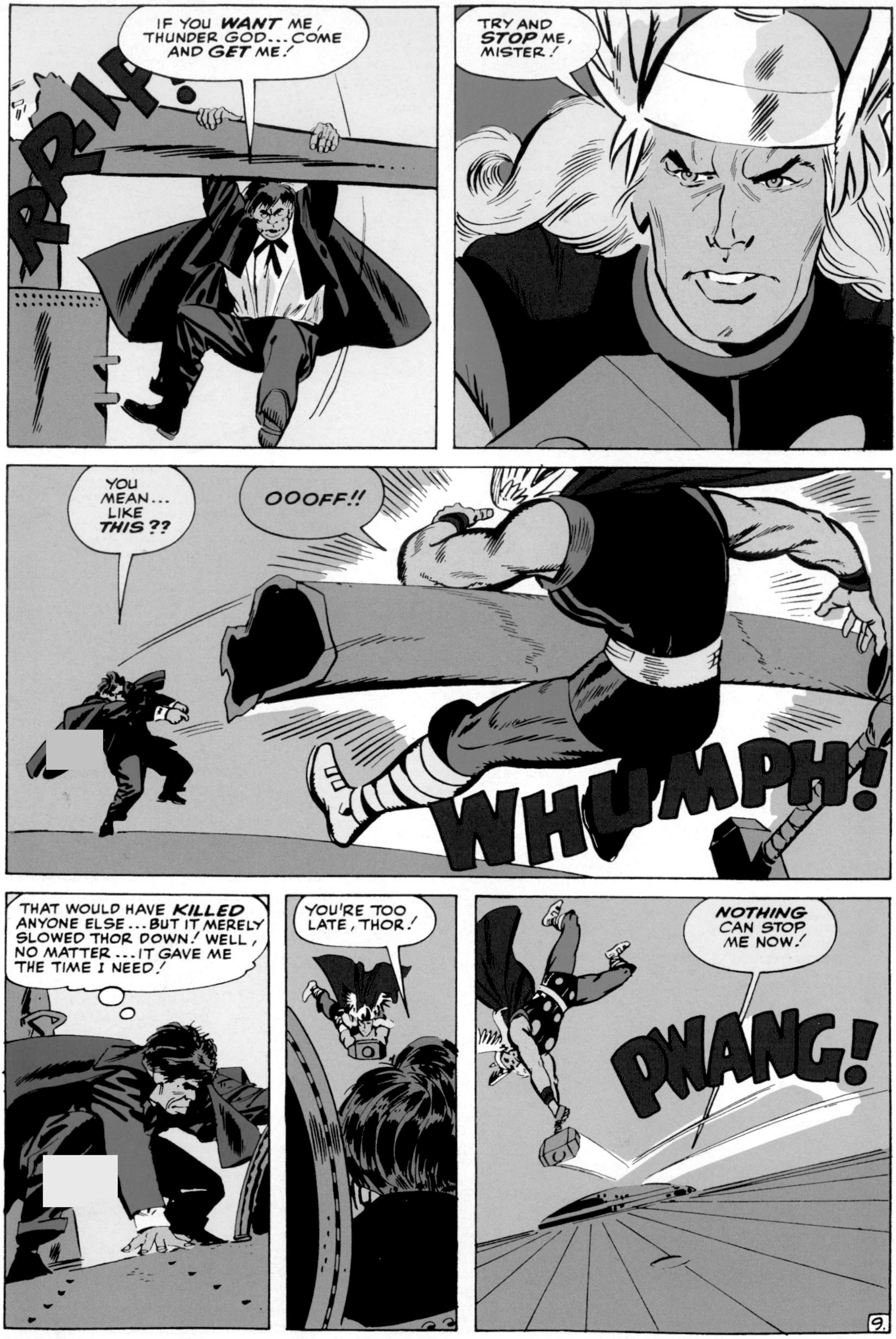
IF YOU WANT ME, THUNDER GOD... COME AND GET ME!
RRIP!
TRY AND STOP ME, MISTER!
YOU MEAN... LIKE THIS??
OOOFF!!
WHUMPH!
THAT WOULD HAVE KILLED ANYONE ELSE... BUT IT MERELY SLOWED THOR DOWN! WELL, NO MATTER... IT GAVE ME THE TIME I NEED!
YOU'RE TOO LATE, THOR!
NOTHING CAN STOP ME NOW!
PWANG!
9.

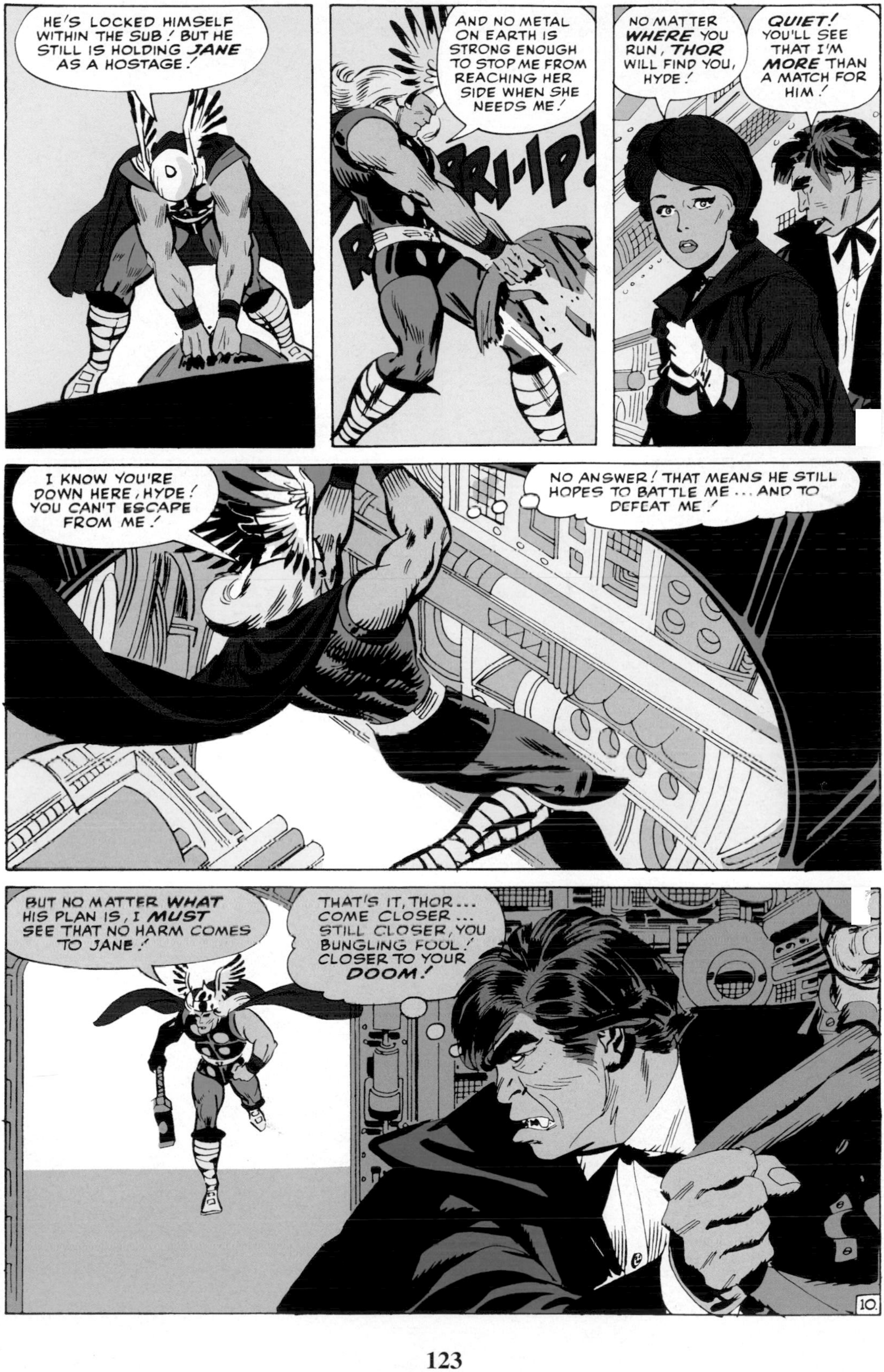
HE'S LOCKED HIMSELF WITHIN THE SUB! BUT HE STILL IS HOLDING JANE AS A HOSTAGE!
AND NO METAL ON EARTH IS STRONG ENOUGH TO STOP ME FROM REACHING HER SIDE WHEN SHE NEEDS ME!
RRRI-IP!
NO MATTER WHERE YOU RUN, THOR WILL FIND YOU, HYDE!
QUIET! YOU'LL SEE THAT I'M MORE THAN A MATCH FOR HIM!
I KNOW YOU'RE DOWN HERE, HYDE! YOU CAN'T ESCAPE FROM ME!
NO ANSWER! THAT MEANS HE STILL HOPES TO BATTLE ME... AND TO DEFEAT ME!
BUT NO MATTER WHAT HIS PLAN IS, I MUST SEE THAT NO HARM COMES TO JANE!
THAT'S IT, THOR... COME CLOSER... STILL CLOSER, YOU BUNGLING FOOL! CLOSER TO YOUR DOOM!
10.

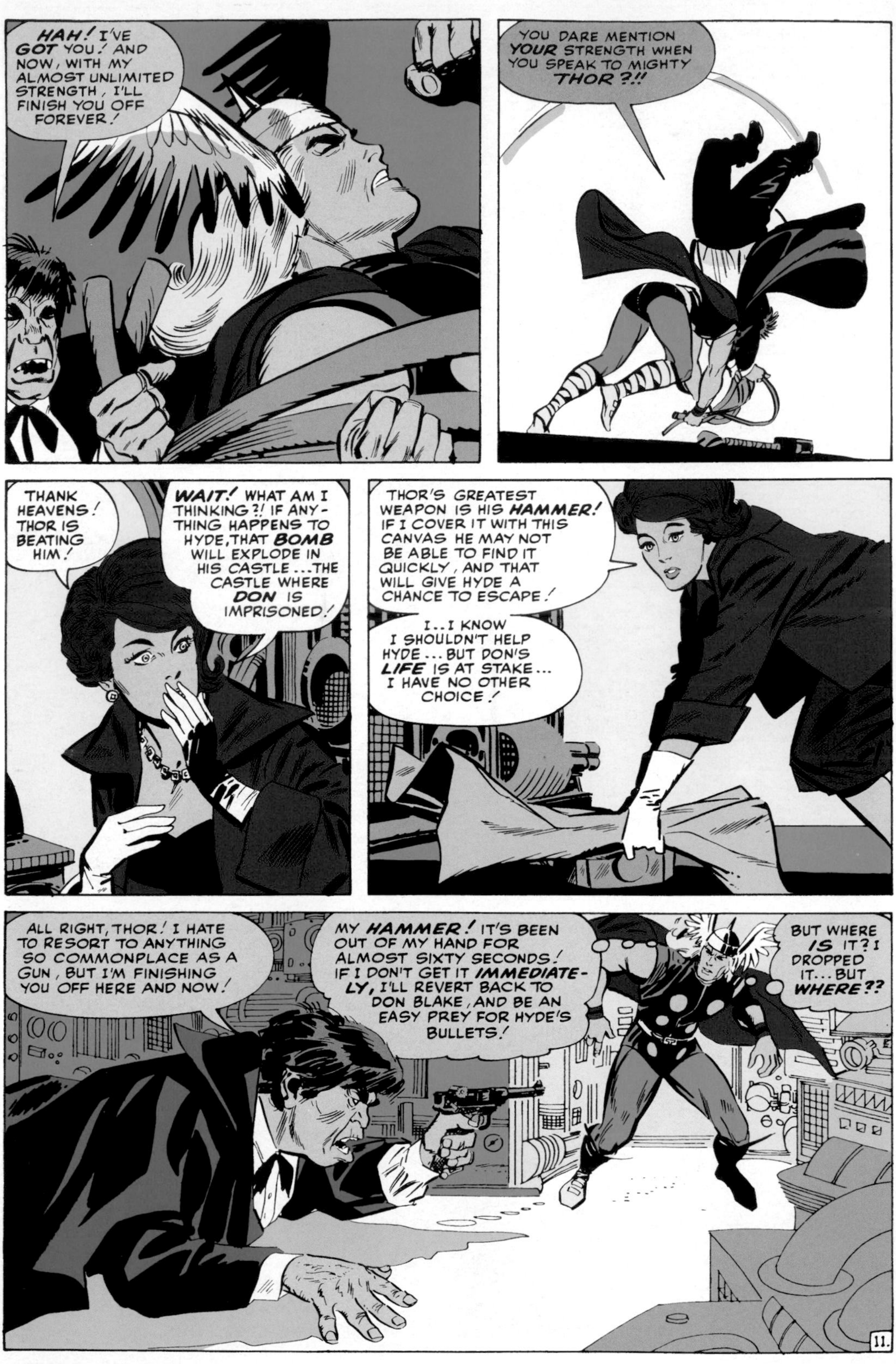
HAH! I'VE GOT YOU! AND NOW, WITH MY ALMOST UNLIMITED STRENGTH, I'LL FINISH YOU OFF FOREVER!
YOU DARE MENTION YOUR STRENGTH WHEN YOU SPEAK TO MIGHTY THOR?!!
THANK HEAVENS! THOR IS BEATING HIM!
WAIT! WHAT AM I THINKING?! IF ANYTHING HAPPENS TO HYDE, THAT BOMB WILL EXPLODE IN HIS CASTLE ...THE CASTLE WHERE DON IS IMPRISONED!
THOR'S GREATEST WEAPON IS HIS HAMMER! IF I COVER IT WITH THIS CANVAS HE MAY NOT BE ABLE TO FIND IT QUICKLY, AND THAT WILL GIVE HYDE A CHANCE TO ESCAPE!
I..I KNOW I SHOULDN'T HELP HYDE ... BUT DON'S LIFE IS AT STAKE... I HAVE NO OTHER CHOICE!
ALL RIGHT, THOR! I HATE TO RESORT TO ANYTHING SO COMMONPLACE AS A GUN, BUT I'M FINISHING YOU OFF HERE AND NOW!
MY HAMMER! IT'S BEEN OUT OF MY HAND FOR ALMOST SIXTY SECONDS! IF I DON'T GET IT IMMEDIATELY, I'LL REVERT BACK TO DON BLAKE, AND BE AN EASY PREY FOR HYDE'S BULLETS!
BUT WHERE IS IT?! I DROPPED IT... BUT WHERE??
11.

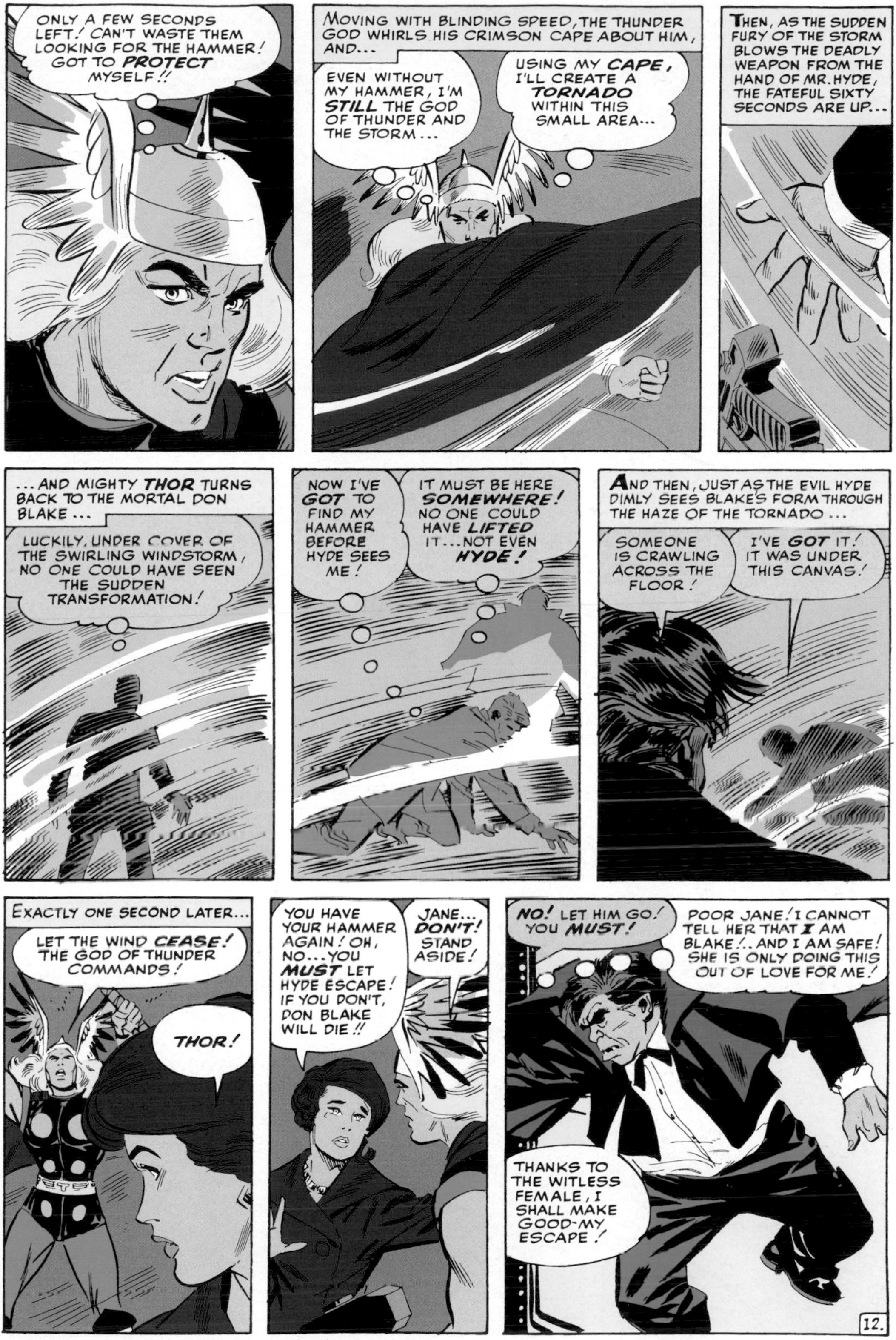
ONLY A FEW SECONDS LEFT! CAN'T WASTE THEM LOOKING FOR THE HAMMER! GOT TO PROTECT MYSELF!!
MOVING WITH BLINDING SPEED, THE THUNDER GOD WHIRLS HIS CRIMSON CAPE ABOUT HIM, AND...
EVEN WITHOUT MY HAMMER, I'M STILL THE GOD OF THUNDER AND THE STORM...
USING MY CAPE, I'LL CREATE A TORNADO WITHIN THIS SMALL AREA...
THEN, AS THE SUDDEN FURY OF THE STORM BLOWS THE DEADLY WEAPON FROM THE HAND OF MR. HYDE, THE FATEFUL SIXTY SECONDS ARE UP...
...AND MIGHTY THOR TURNS BACK TO THE MORTAL DON BLAKE...
LUCKILY, UNDER COVER OF THE SWIRLING WINDSTORM, NO ONE COULD HAVE SEEN THE SUDDEN TRANSFORMATION!
NOW I'VE GOT TO FIND MY HAMMER BEFORE HYDE SEES ME!
IT MUST BE HERE SOMEWHERE! NO ONE COULD HAVE LIFTED IT... NOT EVEN HYDE!
AND THEN, JUST AS THE EVIL HYDE DIMLY SEES BLAKE'S FORM THROUGH THE HAZE OF THE TORNADO...
SOMEONE IS CRAWLING ACROSS THE FLOOR!
I'VE GOT IT! IT WAS UNDER THIS CANVAS!
EXACTLY ONE SECOND LATER...
LET THE WIND CEASE! THE GOD OF THUNDER COMMANDS!
THOR!
YOU HAVE YOUR HAMMER AGAIN! OH, NO... YOU MUST LET HYDE ESCAPE! IF YOU DON'T, DON BLAKE WILL DIE!!
JANE... DON'T! STAND ASIDE!
NO! LET HIM GO! YOU MUST!
POOR JANE! I CANNOT TELL HER THAT I AM BLAKE!.. AND I AM SAFE! SHE IS ONLY DOING THIS OUT OF LOVE FOR ME!
THANKS TO THE WITLESS FEMALE, I SHALL MAKE GOOD-MY ESCAPE!
12.

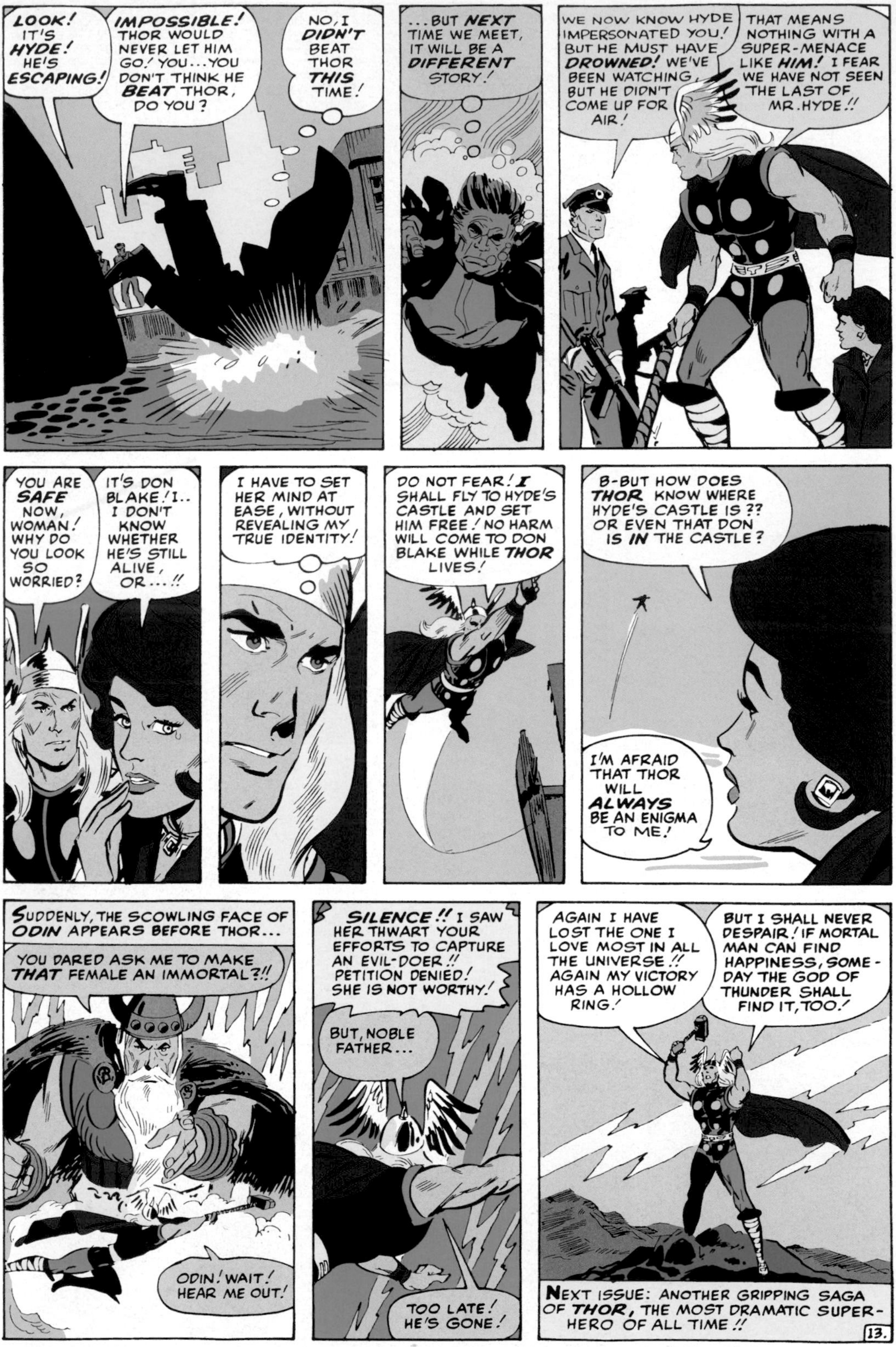
LOOK! IT'S HYDE! HE'S ESCAPING!
IMPOSSIBLE! THOR WOULD NEVER LET HIM GO! YOU...YOU DON'T THINK HE BEAT THOR, DO YOU?
NO, I DIDN'T BEAT THOR THIS TIME!
...BUT NEXT TIME WE MEET, IT WILL BE A DIFFERENT STORY!
WE NOW KNOW HYDE IMPERSONATED YOU! BUT HE MUST HAVE DROWNED! WE'VE BEEN WATCHING, BUT HE DIDN'T COME UP FOR AIR!
THAT MEANS NOTHING WITH A SUPER-MENACE LIKE HIM! I FEAR WE HAVE NOT SEEN THE LAST OF MR. HYDE!!
YOU ARE SAFE NOW, WOMAN! WHY DO YOU LOOK SO WORRIED?
IT'S DON BLAKE! I.. I DON'T KNOW WHETHER HE'S STILL ALIVE, OR...!!
I HAVE TO SET HER MIND AT EASE, WITHOUT REVEALING MY TRUE IDENTITY!
DO NOT FEAR! I SHALL FLY TO HYDE'S CASTLE AND SET HIM FREE! NO HARM WILL COME TO DON BLAKE WHILE THOR LIVES!
B-BUT HOW DOES THOR KNOW WHERE HYDE'S CASTLE IS?? OR EVEN THAT DON IS IN THE CASTLE?
I'M AFRAID THAT THOR WILL ALWAYS BE AN ENIGMA TO ME!
SUDDENLY, THE SCOWLING FACE OF ODIN APPEARS BEFORE THOR...
YOU DARED ASK ME TO MAKE THAT FEMALE AN IMMORTAL?!!
ODIN! WAIT! HEAR ME OUT!
SILENCE!! I SAW HER THWART YOUR EFFORTS TO CAPTURE AN EVIL-DOER!! PETITION DENIED! SHE IS NOT WORTHY!
BUT, NOBLE FATHER...
TOO LATE! HE'S GONE!
AGAIN I HAVE LOST THE ONE I LOVE MOST IN ALL THE UNIVERSE!! AGAIN MY VICTORY HAS A HOLLOW RING!
BUT I SHALL NEVER DESPAIR! IF MORTAL MAN CAN FIND HAPPINESS, SOME-DAY THE GOD OF THUNDER SHALL FIND IT, TOO!
NEXT ISSUE: ANOTHER GRIPPING SAGA OF THOR, THE MOST DRAMATIC SUPER-HERO OF ALL TIME!!
13.

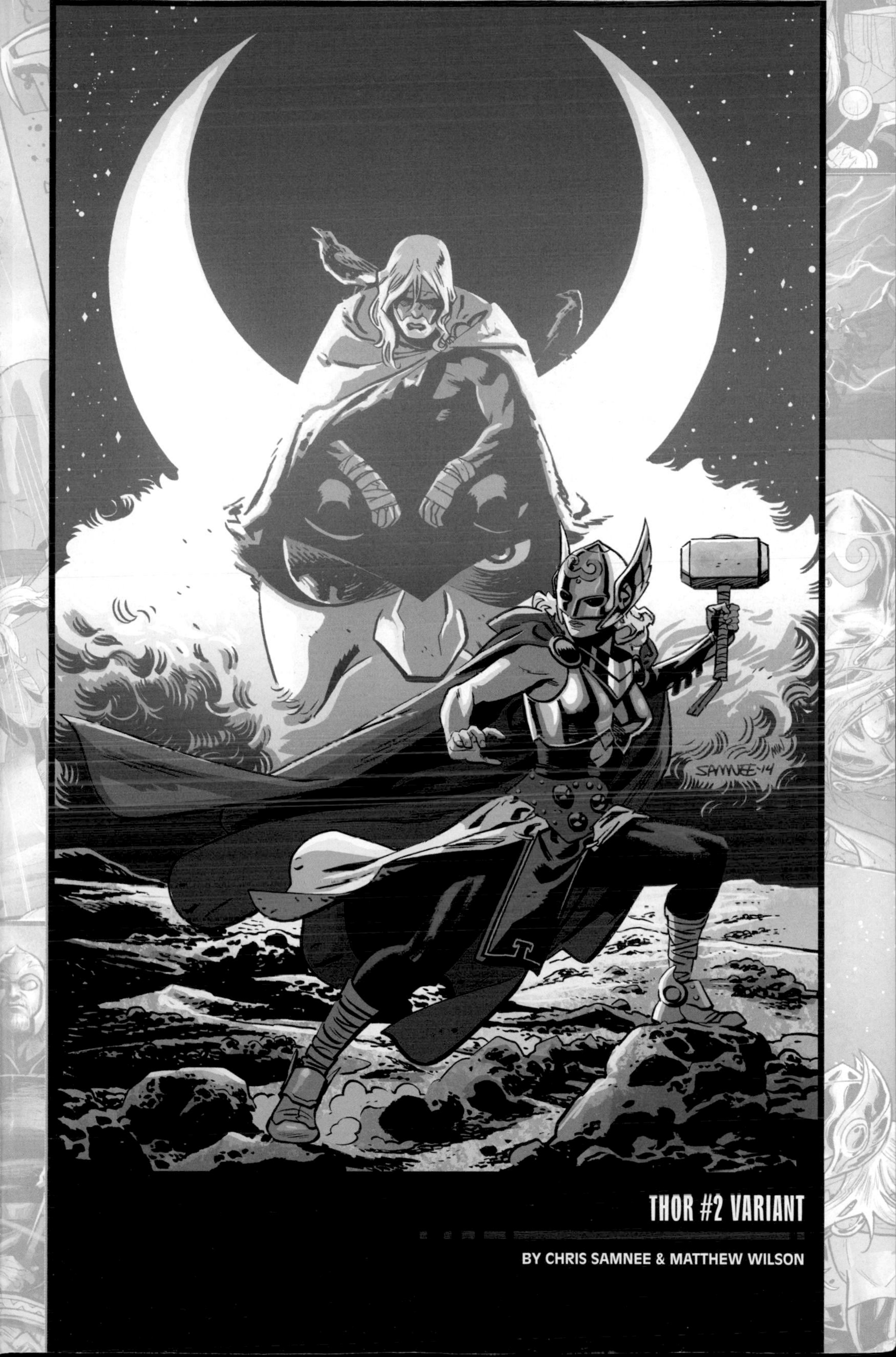

THOR #2 VARIANT

BY CHRIS SAMNEE & MATTHEW WILSON

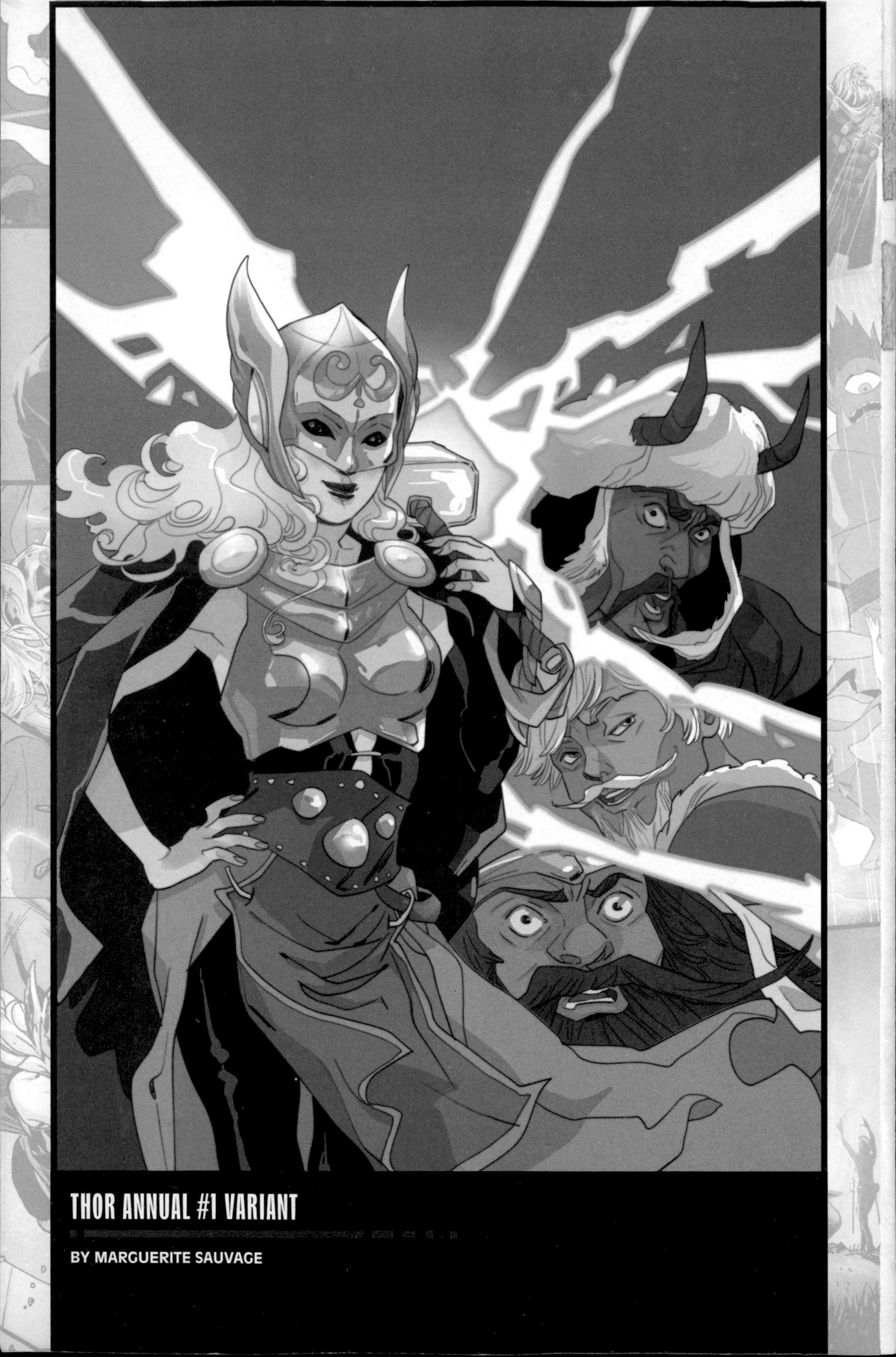

THOR ANNUAL #1 VARIANT

BY MARGUERITE SAUVAGE